Into the Wonder
Book 4

# The River of Night

Into the Wonder, Book 4:
The River of Night

Copyright © 2016 by Darrell J. Pursiful.

Published by Puggle Press

ISBN: 978-0692784471

*For Maddy,*
*Jared,*
*MaKayla,*
*and (of course)*
*Rebecca*

# Table of Contents

## Chapter 1

# Chaperones Are Useless when Monsters Crash the Party

Taylor sat on a bench outside the gym. She wished she were somewhere else.

It was the night of the Riverview High School ninth-grade dance. The late September sun hung low in the sky. A warm breeze tickled against Taylor's lavender dress.

Her best friend, Jill, who loved to dance, was inside enjoying herself. (She could be irritating that way.) Jill's twin brother, William, who could occasionally be pulled away from his video games, was inside goofing off with Jalen Harris and some of his other friends who were too scared to actually ask a girl to dance.

As usual, Shelby Crowthers was the life of the party—at least in her own eyes. The most popular girl in school held court with her retinue of cool girls as they flirted and gossiped by the refreshment table.

Taylor wondered why she'd even bothered to come. Crowds made her uncomfortable, so she had slipped outside to enjoy the evening in peace for a few minutes.

Somebody called her name, and in an instant she remembered why she'd let Jill talk her into coming to the dance.

"Hi, Jared."

"There you are."

Jared McCaughey was one of the nicest guys Taylor knew. His brains and quirky sense of humor set him apart from the usual idiot boys at Riverview. It didn't hurt that he was cute, too!

He and Taylor weren't a couple, but they had started hanging out last year, and things had pretty much stayed that way into the start of ninth grade.

Taylor liked the attention Jared gave her. She liked how he made her laugh. She especially liked that he had absolutely no clue about her weird family.

Not the Smarts, mind you. Taylor's adoptive parents were great. Her biological family? Well, they were a whole new level of strangeness. It didn't help matters that they weren't, technically speaking, human.

Jared sat down beside her. "You're quiet tonight. Is anything wrong?"

"I'm just resting," she told him. She fingered her purple hellebore flower necklace: a keepsake from her birth mother. It looked nice with the dress she'd picked out for the evening. And for some reason, wearing it gave her comfort in situations when she was unsure of herself.

"Can I bring you some punch?"

Taylor turned on the bench to look at him. "I—"

Then something seized her attention: movement in the parking lot. The sun had set, but Taylor had pretty good night vision. There was definitely something scrambling across the parking lot, darting from car to car for cover. It looked like a man: a short, bearded man with glowing red eyes and pointed ears. In other words, somebody from the Wonder.

"Yes," she said, trying to keep the panic from showing on her face. "Definitely. Some punch would be nice. Now, please."

Jared didn't know anything about Taylor's other life, and she was determined to keep it that way. Jared was the first boy who sort of liked her (other than William, but she was *not* going there!), and she didn't want to spoil that by letting things get all mythological on him.

He stood back up, confused. "I thought...maybe we could go in...together?"

"No," she said sharply. Her heart was racing, and it had nothing to do with Jared. Her eyes darted back to the parking lot. She'd lost track of Red Eyes, but something told her he was still there—for what reason, she had no idea. She only knew that these sorts of interruptions to her life were never coincidences.

She took a deep breath and gave Jared a smile. "I mean...I'll be just a minute. Why don't you go in and get me something to eat?"

Out of the corner of her eye, she spotted the fae hunkering down behind a Chevy pickup maybe twenty feet away. He peered over the hood with his blazing eyes, and then ducked back down with a muffled gasp. Taylor followed his line of sight and spied another blur of movement, a dark shape stalking forward.

Jared smiled back, oblivious. "Okay, then!"

"Some cookies, please," Taylor added. "I'm a little hungry. Do you mind?" She smiled again.

Jared grinned as he practically sprinted back inside.

Taylor stood and straightened the skirt of her dress. She took one step toward the parking lot. She realized she had already been gathering magic while she was talking to Jared. Now she just had to avoid having to use it.

*Not now!* she complained. *Not tonight!*

Red Eyes darted into view—a swarthy fae who dodged and weaved like he knew he was being chased.

The darkness parted, and the person chasing Red Eyes appeared. He wore the shadows like a cloak, which he promptly cast off to expose his frightening presence. He was barely more than five feet tall, dressed in gray work pants, a checkered shirt, and a denim jacket. But two things captured Taylor's attention.

The first thing was the sword in his hand, a gleaming silver-white blade, two feet long. He swished it once, and Taylor glimpsed the yellowed ivory pommel carved in the shape of a human skull.

The second thing Taylor noticed was his face: blotchy skin, a hooked nose, a lopsided brow ridge, and pointed ears like a sad, misshapen Christmas elf. His long, wispy hair was the colors of mud and cobwebs, and it flapped around his head in the breeze.

3

Taylor gasped with recognition. It was Captain Dingle, the right-hand man of her grandfather, Crom Cornstack. She didn't know what was going on, but she couldn't see how it would be good news for Red Eyes.

The other fae knew it, too. He kept barreling forward. Taylor realized too late he was headed right for her. She tried to duck out of the way, but too late. He crashed into her, slamming her into the wall of the gym. She saw stars and the bricks made contact with the back of her head.

Just then, a flash of light exploded over her head. Dingle had nearly hit both her and his prey with a faery blast.

Red Eyes rolled away and scrambled to his feet. With a savage look over his shoulder, he flung open the gym door and ducked inside.

Taylor's heart leaped with panic. With all those kids inside—not to mention the adult chaperones—the ninth-grade dance was the worst possible place for magical combat to break out. And yet, there came Dingle, stalking toward the door.

Maybe Red Eyes had enough sense to stay hidden inside, but Dingle? When it came to Crom Cornstack and his men, Taylor wouldn't bet on it. All she knew to do was to try to keep him from crashing the party.

She stepped forward, trying to project more authority than she had. "*You can't come in here!*" she said.

Dingle twisted his monstrous face into something like a smile. "As you wish," he said, bowing slightly. Then he blinked away. A second later, there was nothing where he had been standing but a column of quickly dispersing sparks of light.

Taylor exhaled. Projecting presence was her strongest magical talent, but she never expected it would be that easy. The fact that it was made her nervous.

And there was still a magical being loose at the dance.

Taylor rushed in. Green and blue crepe paper streamers and balloons festooned the walls and metallic blue confetti gave a splash of color to small tables along the wall where William and his friends had congregated. The decorations were fairly

4

minimal—the teachers tried to play up the idea that it was more a "social" than an honest-to-goodness dance. The distinction was lost on the ninth-graders, however.

As she took in the scene with her eyes, reaching out with her magical senses every direction. If she were a fae barging in on a bunch of Topsiders, she knew she'd mist herself before she even opened the door. The magic didn't really make you invisible, but unless you bumped into something or made a noise, you could pass without notice pretty much anywhere.

Taylor just had to find Dingle's quarry and figure out what was going on.

"Here's your food,"

Taylor nearly shrieked, catching herself as she noticed Jared with a small plate of cookies in his hand. She'd been so intent on finding Red Eyes, Jared might have been invisible himself until the moment he spoke to her.

Taylor sighed with relief. "Thanks, Jared," she said, popping a butterscotch cookie bar into her mouth. Sweet treats enhanced faery magic, and the chances were pretty good she would need all the help she could get.

She spied Jill on the dance floor and William in the corner laughing with some of his friends. It looked like neither of them had noticed anything out of the ordinary. If she had to, she'd tip them off to what was happening—but she prayed it wouldn't come to that.

"So...Taylor...," Jared began.

Taylor held up a hand. She continued to scan the room as she finished off her cookie. When her eyes scanned the refreshment table, she let out a demoralized groan. Mrs. Matthews was chatting with some of Taylor's classmates. The last thing she needed was for Jill and William's mom to get a whiff of what was going on.

Mr. Matthews had adjusted, more or less, to the fact that his kids had started developing magical powers: powers they had inherited from his wife's mom. (How many men can say that their mother-in-law is a witch and mean it literally?) And that his daughter's best friend wasn't exactly human. And that all this had led to danger for everyone involved more than once.

Mrs. Matthews? She was having a harder time. She was very religious. The whole family was super-active in their church, but Mrs. Matthews took it to a whole new level. She didn't even want her kids reading the *Harry Potter* novels. Now that they were pretty much living one.... Well, there were certain topics Taylor knew not to bring up around Jill's mom.

So it would not be a good idea for Taylor, Jill, and William to suddenly sneak off.

*Okay*, she thought. *It's up to me.*

Her magical senses drew her attention to the far wall, near a door that opened into a classroom hall. Sure enough, the door flew open seemingly of its own will. There was a shimmer, and Taylor saw the swarthy fae pulling the door closed behind him. Jalen Harris's dad, who was supposed to be guarding the door, stared blankly into the distance.

"W-would you like to dance?" Jared asked. Taylor bit her lip. She had forgotten he was even there. And he was yet another person who absolutely could not know that magical shenanigans were underfoot.

She smiled at him. "I could really use some more cookies."

He looked at the plate he was already holding and furrowed his brow. "Really?" Jared said.

"Do you mind?" Taylor said. "I'll be back in a minute."

She left Jared scratching his head and strolled as nonchalantly as possible after Red Eyes.


Outside the gym, the walls were decorated with projects from the nearby art room. The only lights were directly overhead, lighting the way to the bathrooms across the hall. To the right, the corridor ended in doors that led outside to the parking lot. To the right was the dim intersection where the corridor Taylor was in crossed another classroom hall.

There was no sign of Red Eyes. There was no sign of Dingle, but Taylor couldn't believe the spriggan had simply given up. Crom Cornstack wouldn't have sent his captain of the guard this deep into nunnehi territory just to blink away at the first sign of resistance.

*Now what?* Taylor thought.

She strained to pick up even the slightest trace of magic in the air. On a hunch, she headed to her left. When she reached the intersection, she paused to regroup.

Behind her, music from the dance was blaring, breaking her concentration.

This part of the school was laid out like an H, with two classroom hallways to the left and two more to the right. But instead of a crossbar in the middle, there was a huge open area. And in the center of that was a circular structure, the school library and the AV supply rooms, turning the open space into a traffic roundabout that could be brutal to navigate between classes.

Taylor was the only one there. She was convinced, though, that two others—the predator and his prey—had to be close by.

Something caught her attention to the left, down the math and technology hall. She spun to face it, magical energy wafting from her hands in great shimmering wisps invisible to human eyes.

She drew the magic in as soon as she saw the fae. He stood pressed as far against the wall as he could. His eyes no longer blazed, so Taylor had no trouble reading his expression of sheer terror.

"I won't hurt you," she said. "Who—?"

Before she could finish her sentence, the fae lashed out. He gestured toward the ceiling, and sparks rained down from overhead as the dim security light exploded. Red Eyes barreled past her, slamming her into a bank of lockers.

"Wait!" she called. But when she turned around, she saw Dingle approaching from the other direction.

The Red Eyes skidded to a stop. He was halfway between Taylor and Dingle and, from the look on his face, he wasn't sure whom to fear more.

She hoped another bit of presence would work on the spriggan; it was the only trick she really had.

Before she could try anything, though, Red Eyes thrust out his hands in both directions washing the entire hallway in the chaos of a miniature fireworks display. The light was blinding. The sound was deafening—for a second, she couldn't even hear the music in the gym. Taylor dropped to the floor and prayed nobody inside could hear the commotion.

Amid the smoke and confusion, she heard sounds of a struggle. Despite the other fae's best efforts, Dingle had closed in on him.

Visibility was near zero, but Taylor could make out two figures struggling in the haze. She jumped to her feet and got ready to blast as soon as she could figure out who was who.

"Best you leave while you can, jinni!" Dingle snarled as he pushed Red Eyes away.

Red Eyes answered with a savage growl. Before Taylor could blast Dingle, the other fae lunged at the spriggan. In midair, he transformed into a jackal—a lean, gray beast with a bushy tail and fierce, glowing red eyes. He chomped at Dingle's shoulder, but the spriggan spun around and flung him against the door to the school clinic.

The jackal growled and pawed the tile floor.

Dingle raised his silver sword and prepared to strike.

Taylor threw a blast and hoped for the best.

Dingle either saw or sensed the blast coming his way. He pivoted his gnarled body toward Taylor and extended his left hand, but his shield spell formed too late. The blast got through, and Dingle staggered forward.

Red Eyes saw his opportunity. He bolted around the circle toward the library entrance, resuming his two-legged form as he went. He blinked away and just as suddenly appeared on the other side of the door. Dingle stumbled after him. He had little trouble shaking off the effects of Taylor's blast, and he was once again in hot pursuit.

Her heart pounded in her chest. She took two long steps toward the library just as Dingle blinked inside behind the jinni.

There was a swirl of sparkling dust, silver and gold, picking up from somewhere in the shelves. Red Eyes had activated a ring portal.

A ring portal.

In the Riverview High School library?

A second later, with her face pressed against the window, Taylor watched as Dingle leaped after Red Eyes and vanished into the vortex as well.

Taylor stepped back, stunned. What was Dingle doing there? Who was the other fae he was chasing—and did he get away?

She lumbered to the gym in a wobbly daze. Inside, Jill was on the dance floor with klutzy Tommy Morgan of all people. He had apparently finally worked up the nerve to ask her to dance. It wasn't even close to the strangest thing that had happened that night.

Taylor found a chair along the wall and sat down.

*What just happened?* she thought. A running battle had just made its way through her school. Captain Dingle, a ranking officer of the Winter Court, was chasing another fae—a jinni, apparently.

What were they doing there?

She hadn't reached any conclusions when Jared appeared. He was still holding her punch. He also balanced not one but two paper plates stacked with half a dozen cookies, a couple of brownies, and several handfuls of mints. He looked at her and grinned stupidly.

"Cookie?" he said. There was a frantic eagerness in his voice. It reminded Taylor of a puppy that wanted to go out and play.

"Huh?"

"I...brought you some more cookies. You said you were still hungry..."

"Oh. Oh, Jared. Have you been...waiting to give me these?"

He smiled and nodded. There was something distant about his eyes. It was as if he was struggling to figure out what to do next.

Taylor felt a lump of something cold and prickly rumbling in her stomach as it dawned on her what had happened.

"I'm sorry, Jared. I...didn't mean to...." She didn't mean to sweep him up in the magic she had been gathering. She didn't mean to use that magic to compel him to bring her a snack—she just needed to get him safely out of the way. She didn't mean to mess with his mind.

He looked at her like...well, a lovesick teenager.

"Thanks," Taylor said at last. She picked a single chocolate chip cookie off the nearest plate. She tried to look like nothing was wrong, like she wasn't kicking herself with guilt. Sure, it was an accident, but that didn't make her feel any better about it.

Taylor nibbled at the cookie and accepted the cup of punch when Jared offered it to her.

"Dance?" Jared asked.

"Yes, it is," Taylor answered, scanning the scene with disinterest. When her eyes swept up to Jared's, she said, "I mean, I...I'd rather not." She tried for a reassuring smile, all the time willing herself not to overwhelm him with any more presence. "But thanks for asking."

The rejection seemed to stagger Jared. Taylor hoped the magic would wear off soon. Then they could go back to...whatever they were.

*Yeah, right*, Taylor thought.

*Chapter 2*

# Jill Blows Up a Car

Taylor and Jared still had some classes together, and they usually sat together with William, Jill, and a few other friends at lunch. But the dance pushed Jared firmly into the "just friends" category.

September passed, and so did October, with no further signs of Captain Dingle or anyone else from the spooky side of town.

By November, Taylor was finally starting to feel like she could relax her guard. Whatever Dingle had been doing, it mustn't have involved her. As hard as it was to believe, the episode at the dance must have been a coincidence.

*Who am I kidding?* she thought. *Something is up!* It took another couple of weeks before she got even a hint of what was really afoot.

It was late in the fourth quarter at one of the first football games of the season. Jill liked watching her dad coach, but Taylor had no use for football. She had pretty much zoned out until Jill shook her back to planet earth.

"Trouble," she whispered.

"Huh?"

"Over on the St. Isidore side. Bottom row."

Taylor scanned the visitors' section on the other side the Riverview High football field. There was a time out on the field, so she didn't have to worry about football players obstructing her view. Jill and Taylor sat behind the Riverview bench, and Jill's dad was waving his arms and hollering at the kid who'd just done something wrong. (Taylor had no clue what; she only went to games because Jill did.)

She relaxed her eyes, looking beneath the surface realities everyone else could see. At first, everything looked normal. The stadium was about two-thirds full. With St. Izzy fourteen points ahead with less than a minute left in the game, all but the most devoted fans had already trickled out.

Then she saw what Jill had noticed. "The girl in the red sweatshirt?"

Jill nodded. "You see it, too?"

"Now I do," Taylor said. A girl on the front row was definitely not what she seemed. When Taylor looked at her, she saw two images, one laid over the other. The first was an ordinary teenager in a red sweatshirt and blue jeans. The other was a tiny woman maybe in her thirties and no more than four feet tall, with coppery skin and black braided pigtails draped across her lap and falling to her ankles.

Taylor whispered—though there wasn't really a point with the noise of the Riverview cheering section in their ears. "What's a little person doing at a high school football game?"

"Something's up," Jill said.

Taylor nodded. The little person across the floor met her gaze, but only for a second. She was suddenly agitated, like she didn't expect Taylor to be looking at her. She reached for her purse.

Taylor sprung to her feet. "Stay here."

"No way," Jill said.

There was no time to argue; the little person was already halfway to the exit.

Taylor would give anything to keep Jill out of her ongoing family drama. Taylor's grandparents were powerful supernatural beings who had hated each other for at least a hundred years. When folks from their neighborhood came around to visit, innocent bystanders got hurt.

Taylor threaded through the bleachers as she pulled her black leather jacket close against the evening breeze. As soon as she landed on the grass, she darted right. The little person would beat her to the gate, but she wouldn't get far.

And Taylor had an advantage—or at least she hoped she did. She had been a student at Riverview since August. She knew her way around the school grounds exactly the way somebody from the Wonder wouldn't.

The wide entrance to the stadium was next to the concession stand and the restrooms. A handful of people ambled toward the parking lot or simply hung around, visiting.

On the other side of the entrance was the ticket booth, now empty with the game nearly over.

The little person was nowhere to be seen.

"Girls' bathroom?" Jill suggested.

"Maybe." Wisps of magic swirled invisibly around Taylor. Or invisibly to most people: Jill had been born with Second Sight and was sensitive to a lot of things that ordinary humans couldn't perceive. She didn't use her gift often because she could get overwhelmed by everything she saw. But she had spent her eighth-grade year practicing control with her grandmother Maymay, a kindly witch from New Orleans. Then she'd had another few months after that practicing on her own when Maymay went back home.

So it wouldn't be hard for Jill to watch Taylor's gossamer threads of magical energy waft toward the door of the girls' bathroom, sensing for anything magical on the other side. When Taylor said, "Nothing," Jill confirmed she hadn't picked up anything, either.

"Hey, what's up?" Jill's twin brother, William, approached them. He had a cup of soda in one hand and a handful of candy bars in the other.

"I don't know," Taylor said. "Jill and I saw somebody. I mean, somebody from...where I was born."

William's jaw dropped.

"There!" Jill said, looking over Taylor's shoulder.

Taylor spun around and scanned the crowd. There she was, sneaking around the back of the stands toward the parking lot, peering over her shoulder.

"Which one's mine?" Taylor said. Without waiting for the answer, she grabbed a candy bar out of William's hand and ripped off the wrapper.

"Excuse me!" William protested.

"Sorry," Taylor said. She took a quick bite. If something magical was going to happen, she wanted a quick burst of power. She took off at a lope with Jill and William following close behind.

As soon as they stepped around the corner, Taylor shouted, "Hey!"

The little person sped up. She probably hoped to escape by wrapping herself in magical mist, but this time Taylor never let her out of her sight. Instead, she trotted into the parking lot.

"*Hey!*" Taylor called again. She jammed the rest of her candy bar into her jacket.

The little person spun around to face Taylor. The pishoguery that made her look human had vanished completely. Her tiny frame heaved up and down. Her eyes were wide.

There was defiance in her eyes, but also something else. Something primitive.

Jill began to mutter to herself.

"Go away!" the little woman shouted. "We don't want you here!"

"I-I don't understand," Taylor said.

"Go away!" she repeated.

"Listen to her," a male voice called from behind them.

Taylor whipped around, nearly knocking Jill over as she did. Another little person had come up behind, a brown-skinned man in a buckskin jacket. His hand caught Taylor's attention: he was rolling something between his fingers, something small and round like a marble that gave off a slight orangey glow.

As soon as Taylor turned on him, he leaped back. He held up his left hand ready to summon a shield spell.

14

Taylor assumed a defensive crouch and did the same…but something was wrong. She'd gotten pretty good at shields, but now it was like she didn't have the juice to make a proper one—even after downing half a candy bar in one gulp.

A cold wind began to blow.

"We don't want you here," the little man said. His voice trembled; he was afraid—but why? His eyes darted between Taylor, Jill, and William.

"But this is my school," Taylor said.

The woman scoffed, and Taylor wheeled back around to face her. "Not here." She pointed to the ground. "*Here.*" She waved her arms expansively.

"Tell your friends they're not wanted here!" the little man shouted. His voice cracked.

"*Now, wait a minute—*" None of this was making sense, and that was getting on Taylor's last nerve. She took a step toward the man.

He bolted away. At the same time, the woman threw herself against William's legs, toppling him like a bowling pin and splashing his soda everywhere. He spun as he fell, slapping his arm against the pavement to absorb the shock of the fall.

"Get off me!" he screamed.

Jill hissed, "*Amou aneme!*" Answering her pushing motion, the wind picked up and blew the woman backwards. She fell to the ground and rolled underneath a pickup truck.

Taylor was already sprinting after the man as he dodged between cars. She tried to blast him, but missed. He was too fast, too agile. And she was out of breath.

"Taylor!" William called. He and Jill were jogging toward her. "Are you all right?"

Taylor shushed him. The little folk were around there somewhere, and Taylor wasn't ready to let them go. With a slow, measured breath, she extended her magical senses once more. She dropped into a crouch, ready to respond to any sudden movement.

Jill had let go of her wind spell, but the night was still brisk and breezy.

The little woman appeared out of nowhere with a blood-curdling scream.

Taylor yelped and leaped backward. William came up alongside her. The woman tripped on a crack in the pavement and went down, arms flailing. Taylor sidestepped her and watched as she plowed face-first into a cement parking block.

Taylor had barely registered what had happened when the little man bounded off the hood of an old Ford Taurus. In midair, he screamed defiantly and tossed his glowing marble toward Taylor and her friends.

Taylor tried again to raise a shield spell.

William dived over the hood of the nearest car.

Jill swatted away the marble with another wind spell. The marble changed course as it dropped, then rolled backward under the Ford and exploded in a torrent yellow and orange light and smoke.

The little man gave a defeated moan.

As the car's alarm went off, the little people vanished into the shadows.

William came up from the asphalt sputtering. He looked at his sister with eyes as big as saucers. "You blew up a car?"

"It wasn't my fault."

"YOU BLEW UP A CAR!"

"It. Wasn't. My. Fault!"

"Guys, the car's fine," Taylor said. "Fresh coat of paint... maybe have the alignment checked..."

She stopped when she heard the footsteps pounding her way.

People had apparently noticed the commotion. A campus police officer was thudding toward them. She was short and stocky, and her whole body heaved with the exertion of movement.

"Are you all right?" she wheezed. She trained her flashlight on the car. The last thin wisps of smoke gave the parking lot lights a weird, orangey haze.

"We're fine, Officer Hutchins," Jill said.

Officer Hutchins studied each of them in turn. "What happened here?"

Taylor hated direct questions. Fair Folk couldn't actually lie without sacrificing part of their magic. Sometimes, when you're a mythological being trying to lead the life of a mortal teenager, a little lying spares everybody some unnecessary headaches.

"Uh...," Jill said. Taylor winced. Jill may have been a witch, but she was perfectly human. She *could* lie—she just wasn't any good at it.

William was still standing there stupidly with his mouth open.

"There was a bright light," Taylor said. Which was absolutely true. "Then, something went off underneath the car."

"And you didn't have anything to do with it?" She sounded suspicious. Go figure.

"We never touched the car," Taylor said confidently.

Officer Hutchins frowned.

By now, a bunch of people had begun to gather around.

"Officer Hutchins," William said, "our dad will be looking for us."

She knitted her eyebrows as she took a closer look at William and Jill. "Aren't you Coach Matthews's kids?"

"That's right," William said. "We're supposed to meet him outside the locker room."

"And you're sure you don't know anything?" She looked warily at the still-smoking car.

"*Officer Hutchins*," Taylor began. She used her faery power of presence to exude a sense of self-confidence. "There's really nothing more we can tell you, and Coach Matthews *will* be looking for us."

Officer Hutchins regarded them for several seconds.

"Run along," she said.

They backtracked toward the locker rooms and were nearly bowled over when a frantic senior, apparently the old Ford's owner, pushed through them. Somebody must have told him his car had exploded. He wasn't taking it well—but Taylor and her friends had other concerns.

"Somebody want to tell me what that was about?" William said.

"I don't know," Taylor said, "but I don't like it."

"Me neither," Jill said. "Who were those guys?"

"No idea." Taylor came to a stop three feet from the school building's side door. "Cars!"

"What?"

"Something was draining me out there. Like I couldn't—" She shut up as the cheerleading squad elbowed past. The game was over, and most of the remaining fans were on their way to the parking lot.

As they entered the building, she continued. "Anyway, you know about me and iron."

"That means those little guys were smart," William said. "As soon as you spotted them, they ran for the biggest concentration of steel they could find. They didn't want to face you at full power."

"Well, they're little folk," Taylor said. Sounds of celebration echoed from behind the visitors' locker room door. Outside the home team's locker room, Mr. Matthews was talking with Mr. Benson, the athletics director. "They don't always get a fair shake from...my relatives. They probably know all the tricks."

"Yeah, they sounded kind of upset," William said.

"Who's upset?" Mr. Matthews asked. Mr. Benson had already left. "I heard there was some kind of trouble in the parking lot...."

Jill said, "It wasn't my fault!"

Taylor closed her eyes and shook her head.

Mr. Matthews put his hands on his hips and quirked an eyebrow. He had played football in college, and could look big and imposing when he wanted to.

"Jill?"

"She's telling the truth, Dad," William said.

"We'll discuss this later," Mr. Matthews said before entering the locker room. Taylor and her friends waited in the hallway for about half an hour while the team showered, dressed, and filed out. Whenever they tried to discuss what had happened, somebody came through—the team managers with the first aid kits, bottles of Gatorade, towels, and other equipment; cheerleaders heading home or (worse!) hanging around until their boyfriends came out of the locker room to meet them. The whole Saint Isidore team filed past at one point.

Finally, Mr. Matthews returned. He said goodbye to the last couple of players, locked the door behind him with one of the multitude of keys clipped to his belt, and turned to his kids.

"Now, about the parking lot..."

"Dad," Jill started.

"It's my fault," Taylor blurted. "There were some people at the game. I think they knew me."

Mr. Matthews shepherded the three toward the exit. "And by 'people' you mean...?"

"Not from around here."

Mr. Matthews froze. "You don't mean the ones with the clubs?" Mr. Matthews had had his first run-in with Taylor's world last February. An army of Native American ghost warriors with flaming war clubs will leave an impression, even if they're the good guys.

"No, the nunnehi are cool. I mean, for the most part. These were... I'm not sure."

Mr. Matthews held the door while Taylor, Jill, and William stepped outside. Once again, he locked the door behind him.

"Taylor, are you going to be all right?" That was the question he asked. Taylor was pretty sure there was another question coming right behind it.

"I'll be fine, Mr. Matthews—and so will Jill and William. There's some people I can call. They'll know what's going on."

That was all anyone said until they were halfway home. Jill and Taylor sat in the back seat of Mr. Matthews's Toyota while William rode shotgun.

Jill asked, "Are we going to tell Mom?"

Mr. Matthews didn't say anything at first.

At last, as they made the last turn onto Knottingley Drive, he sighed and said, "I don't keep secrets from your mother."

"I know," Jill said. "But if it's going to upset her...."

It was already upsetting Taylor. As close as she was to Jill, it didn't feel right to have a front-row seat for this very private conversation.

A storm had been brewing in Mrs. Matthews's soul ever since Jill had started manifesting her magical powers. Taylor tried very hard to stay clear of that subject. As long as nobody reminded her of Taylor's true identity, of the danger she'd already managed to get Jill and William into, everything went fine. Taylor just didn't believe in taking chances on that front.

So Taylor phased out, even though not much more was said. When Mr. Matthews pulled into the driveway, she thanked him for the ride and crossed the street to her own house as quickly as she could.

*Chapter 3*

# An Unwelcome Visitor

Mr. and Mrs. Smart were watching TV in the living room.

"Well, how'd they do?" Dad asked.

"They got beat," Taylor answered. Her mind was already miles away from the game, though.

"That's too bad," Dad said. "At least you got to visit with your friends."

Yeah, and fight off a couple of angry little folk. Taylor wondered how much she should tell her own parents about what had happened. But she didn't know enough to tell—at least not yet.

"Were many people there?" Mom asked.

Taylor nodded. "Saint Izzy always brings a big crowd." There was no point mentioning the people who weren't there to watch the game. What were those strangers up to, anyway? Were they just spying on her? If she hadn't gone after them, would they have left her alone?

"They always have," Mom said. "Did you have fun?"

*You mean other than the spying and the assault and battery?* She shrugged. "You know I'm not that into sports. But it was good being with Jill and William." *They're pretty good in a firefight.*

"Well, that's what matters," Dad said.

Were the intruders planning to do something to her? That glowing marble thingy meant they at least were ready for a confrontation. But why?

She'd have to see what she could find out. Then, if her folks needed to know, she would tell them everything.

Mom said something Taylor missed. "What's that, Mom?"

"I asked how pot roast sounded for supper tomorrow."

"That's fine."

Taylor retreated to her room to think things over. She lay on her bed still dressed till she heard her parents turn off the TV. The clock said it was 11:03. Was it too late to call?

She sat up and found where she had hung her purse over the arm of her desk chair. Buried under her wallet, her school ID, and a couple of breath mints was a small, smooth stone. It was the color of sand, and there was a tiny hole drilled through the middle by thousands of years of dripping water.

Sitting on the side of the bed, she breathed across the surface of the Seeing Stone and whispered, "Wasko Penholloway. Wasko Penholloway. Wasko Penholloway."

Taylor waited.

It wasn't long before the Seeing Stone shimmered in her hand. She peered into the hole and braced herself as a holographic shadow of Wasko's surroundings settled over her bedroom. Bluish, ghostly lights traced the form of a humble cottage in the background. A bluish, ghostly Wasko sat on a log in front of a bluish, ghostly fire. He was just as Taylor remembered him, in his bowler hat with its turkey feather jutting upward and wobbling in the gentle breeze.

"Miss Hellebore!" he said. His eyes widened.

"Hey there, Wasko."

He just stared at her, startled. Maybe a little bit nervous. "Uh... What d'you want?"

"Sorry for calling so late. Do you know any reason a couple of little folk would be spying on me?"

"Spying on you?" Wasko's voice cracked. His eyes darted left and right. Taylor couldn't tell who or what he might be looking at.

"That's right. What do you know?"

Another nervous pause. "Little folk, you say?"

"That's right. Yunwi tsunsdi, I think. Native American, if that tells you anything."

Wasko shook his head. "I can't say why any of us little folk would be bothering you. W-we try to stay out of other people's way, you understand? We don't want no trouble."

"Well, these two seemed pretty hostile."

"That don't sound good," Wasko said.

"That's kind of how I felt. Do you mind looking into it?"

He took off his hat to scratch his head. He might have been sweating.

Wasko's behavior screamed that something was up. That meant he had answers. And if Taylor had learned anything dealing with faery beings, it's that you had to be ready to bargain for what you wanted.

She quirked a sly smile. "Mom's making pot roast tomorrow."

Wasko perked up. He guardedly asked, "With that special sauce? What's it called?"

"Worcestershire," she said. "I could bring sandwiches."

Wasko passed word on to unseen people around him. Pete and Haggler, no doubt. Taylor had never seen one of those three little folk without the others.

He sighed. "I dunno, Miss Hellebore...."

"I'll bring cookies."

That did it. Wasko's whole body slumped in defeat. "Okay, Miss Hellebore. Me and the boys'll ask around."

"Thanks, Wasko. See you tomorrow night."


Taylor went through the motions all day on Saturday. She finished her homework. She practiced piano. She read the latest Rick Riordan book (and thought, *I don't think elves work like that*).

While her folks went out shopping, she stirred the pot roast in the slow cooker and then scooped out a tray of chocolate chip cookies from the tub of dough they kept in the freezer.

Her parents came home about 4:30. "Do I smell cookies?" her dad asked.

"Some friends are coming over later," Taylor said. "But I made extra for us."

"Friends?" her mom said. "Jill?"

"Actually," Taylor said, "they're not school friends." She let the statement hang in the air while she finished setting the table for supper. She could almost watch her dad's blood pressure rise.

"Friends from...uh...?"

"You've met them," Taylor said. "They dropped by one night last year. Wasko, Haggler, and Pete."

"I remember," Taylor's mom said as the color drained from her face. She swallowed. "The...short ones."

It wasn't easy for Taylor's folks to get used to the idea that their adopted daughter had turned out to be a mythological being. She had to give them credit, though: they tried their best.

"After supper I'm going to go out back and hang out with them for a while."

"You're just hanging out?" Mr. Smart said. "You're not going anywhere?"

"No, just...hanging out," Taylor said. He didn't know everything that had happened last year when he drove Taylor, the Matthews kids, and a couple of Fair Folk to the local shopping center—and Taylor hoped to keep it that way. But both her parents knew that sometimes her connections to the faery world got her into trouble. They were coming to terms with the fact that Taylor—with her friends to help—could usually take care of herself.

"Taylor," her mom started, "is everything all right?"

*Crud*, Taylor thought. She didn't want to lie to her folks. Something was definitely not all right, but the last thing Taylor needed was to do anything—like telling a lie—that would diminish her ability to deal with it.

"I'm still trying to understand everything about...you know. I asked Wasko and the guys to help me out."

There. What she said was completely truthful, even though she didn't really say anything.

"Well," her dad said, "as long as you're not out too late."

"I know, Dad. Oh—and I kind of promised I'd make them sandwiches. Do you mind if I take them some leftovers?"

The sun had set when Taylor headed out, but it wasn't yet fully dark. Most eldritch beings felt energized during the twilight hours, and Taylor was no exception. She hopped the back fence with her sack of roast beef sandwiches and a plastic bag of chocolate chip cookies.

She soon arrived at the ring of mushrooms that had been growing in the woods behind the Smarts' property for the last couple of years. Taylor exerted a slight effort of magic as she raised her hand, palm upward, and summoned the portal to life.

A dust devil of gold and silver sparkles spun and churned within the ring. A further impulse from Taylor, and it spread as far as the ring's boundaries.

Taylor stepped through. She released her magical hold on the ring, and the whirlwind vanished.

Looking around, everything was as it should be. Her house— and her entire neighborhood—was gone. In the Wonder, the area where her house should be was nothing but old-growth forest stretching for miles in every direction.

It was a spot Taylor had come to love.

She walked forward twenty or thirty feet to a familiar log where she liked to meditate, practicing her magic. The log was near the center of a broad clearing. As Taylor sat down, she studied a makeshift fire pit Wasko and the guys had dug over the summer. They had also left a stack of dry wood beside the log, and Taylor tried to build a fire.

Now, "building a fire" shouldn't have been too hard for someone who knew magic. Taylor could summon faery fire any time she wanted, but that kind of eerie, glowing orb didn't give off any heat. Real fire was trickier, and she hadn't yet gotten the hang of it.

After three or four attempts, she gave up.

She wished she had thought to bring matches. For now, she would just have to sit in the cold and wait for her guests to arrive.

While she waited, she figured she might as well practice her exercises. She closed her eyes and took several slow, deep breaths.

Taylor had asked Danny to teach her how to shape-shift. So far, she'd had precisely zero success, though she tried not to get discouraged. Maybe Danny was a bad teacher. Maybe she just wasn't any good at it. But she wasn't about to give up.

Her last lesson was back in the summer. She and Danny met, as usual, in this same little clearing in the woods. It was just after sunrise, but she could tell it was going to be another sweltering hot day.

"You know how you can feel magic moving around you?" Danny said, wiping his neck with a handkerchief. "How you gather it in to cover yourself with mist or push it out to sense your surroundings?"

Taylor nodded.

"Okay, this is the same thing, only different. You need to smush the magic into the shape of the animal you're trying to be."

"Come again?"

Danny scratched his curly head. Taylor got the impression he'd never really tried to explain to anybody how he shape-shifted. "Look, you been practicing faring forth, right? You know what an animal feels like—from the inside."

Faring forth was a way to project one's consciousness into another creature. If you were really good at it, you could basically take control of the animal's body and "ride" it wherever you wanted to go. For Taylor's purposes, all she had to do was insert herself within the animal's mind and soak in the sensations that came with being a deer, a lizard, a bird, or whatever.

So she knew exactly what Danny was talking about, even though her experiences with faring forth hadn't been entirely successful. "I was a raccoon once," she said. For about two seconds. "And a bird. And Mrs. Dibney's dog."

"Mrs. Dibney, your neighbor lady?" Danny said. He grimaced like he'd just swallowed school food. "She's got one of them little yip-yip dogs, don't she?"

"It's a Pomeranian—and it wasn't my first choice."

"Well, good!" Danny said. "Them things always get on my nerves. Too high strung."

Taylor sensed the pooka was getting sidetracked, so she tried to reel him in. "So I try to shape the magic into an animal form..."

"Huh? Yeah. With as much detail as you can. If you've been a raccoon, you know what its heartbeat feels like inside you, right?"

Well, sort of.

"The breeze blowing on its fur, how colors look different through its eyes. The swish of its tail, the tautness of its muscles. Heck, just seeing the world through a body that small gives you a whole new perspective. So you put all of that in your head, understand?" He tapped his temple. "Like you've got this raccoon-shaped bowl right there in front of you."

Taylor furrowed her eyebrows as she tried to imagine a raccoon-shaped bowl. "And that's how you do it?" she said.

"That's how you start," Danny said. He leaned forward, encouraging Taylor to keep up.

"So what comes next?"

Danny shrugged. "What do you think? You just...pour yourself into it."

"Into the bowl."

"Well, yeah," Danny said. He made it sound almost but not entirely like a question. Taylor realized he had been shape-shifting for the better part of 200 years. Everything he had said made perfect sense...to him.

Taylor sighed. "Yeah." She definitely didn't get it. Not really. She understood every word Danny had said, it just didn't make sense.

"Oh, and be sure you're wearing loose-fitting clothes. The first couple of times...uh...." Danny started to blush.

"What?"

Danny shuffled his feet and studied the bare ground. "See, it's just you...uh...don't want to be wearing anything...restrictive...."

Taylor's mouth fell open, and her heart pounded in her chest. "Are you telling me I don't get to take my clothes with me?" It came out like an accusation.

"It depends," Danny blurted, lifting his hands in surrender. "Everybody figures it out eventually, Taylor. There just ain't no guarantees till you've had a little practice, is all."

Taylor made a mental note to only practice alone in her bedroom with the door locked.

And that's exactly what she had been doing for the past three months. So far, she hadn't even come close to shape-shifting—with or without her clothes!

At any rate, even faring forth took a lot of practice, and Taylor gave it a try any time she could. She relaxed her body and allowed her magical senses to stretch into the night, invisible fingers of energy probing the darkness for signs of life. Finding the other creatures with which she shared her woods had become fairly easy—as long as she had time to concentrate. Taylor *thought* she had slipped into the mind of a blackbird for just a second a few weeks ago. She hadn't been able to repeat her success since.

The most interesting creature nearby was a possum somewhere in the trees over her left shoulder, and it didn't seem very cooperative. As soon as Taylor tried to touch it with her mind, it got skittish.

But that was just as well. If Taylor was seriously going to become a shape-shifter, turning into a possum wouldn't have been her first choice.

She checked her wristwatch. Her parents would start getting worried if she stayed out too much longer. Where could Wasko be?

A whippoorwill chirped in the distance.

She pulled her Seeing Stone from her jacket pocket. She blew across the stone and whispered Wasko's name three times, but he didn't answer.

"Come on, guys. I don't have all night!"

She didn't like it that Wasko was a no-show. It wasn't hard to come up with a dozen or more scenarios involving evil fae waylaying him and his friends to keep them from contacting Taylor.

If Crom Cornstack was behind Wasko and the guys' absence, it was more than Taylor wanted to think about. Whatever you could say about Wasko, Pete, and Haggler, they were harmless. It got under Taylor's skin that somebody might try to hurt them, but it was hard to conceive of any other explanation.

There was one more thing to try. And unfortunately, it was also something she was just learning to do.

Her mom—her birth mother, Shanna Hellebore—had told her she needed to learn the language of birds. As it turned out, her attempts at faring forth at least seemed to attune her to that language.

And then, over the summer, she got to spend a whole week with her mom in North Carolina. Shanna had given her a few tips, as well.

"The language of birds is pretty basic," she had said. "But there are nuances. Different birds singing at the same time produce layers of meaning. It's kind of like putting together the pieces of a puzzle. If the right kinds of birds are about, you can add all their songs together."

Taylor wasn't sure she understood. She pressed her mom to explain as they sat under the stars in the nunnehi town of

Tsuwatelda. "So just one bird isn't going to give you the whole message?"

"Not unless it's a pretty simple one," Shanna had said. "But sometimes, that's all you need."

But now, Wasko and his friends were a no-show, and Taylor was short on other options. She figured she might as well give it a try. She pursed her lips and whistled out her best imitation of a whippoorwill's call. "Whip-poor-will, whip-poor-will!" *Is anybody out there?*

The response came from a mockingbird she hadn't noticed before. *Just us birds.*

Taylor tweeted again. *No little folk?*

The whippoorwill tweeted an agitated "Quirt! Quirt! Quirt!" *No little folk! They....*

Taylor couldn't catch the last bit. She tried again. *What was that?*

This time, a killdeer answered, "Dee! Dee!"

She had no clue what it was saying, but it sounded nervous. That didn't do anything for her own nerves. Were Wasko, Pete, and Haggler in some kind of trouble? Wasko sounded pretty nervous when he talked to Taylor the night before. It was almost as if he was afraid of what might happen if he met with Taylor.

She sighed. She was determined not to get all worked up over a stupid birdcall.

She tried to reach Wasko one more time. Still no answer.

Taylor sat on her log and zipped her jacket all the way up. After fifteen minutes, she admitted to herself that he wasn't coming.

The wind picked up as she started toward home with her sandwiches and cookies.

As she walked, she pondered who else from the Wonder might know what was going on. Not Shanna: her birth mother was still holed up in Tsuwatelda, laying low lest her own parents get hold of her. Crom Cornstack and Mara Hellebore had never forgiven their daughter for running off with a boy from the "wrong" family. They had held Shanna captive for years, and abandoned Taylor to be raised in the Topside world with no knowledge of who she really was.

Taylor's biological family sucked all the "fun" out of dysfunctional.

What about Danny? The pooka was the one constant in all her dealings with the faery realm. He had saved her hide more than once, but he hadn't been around lately. The last she'd heard, he was up in Tsuwatelda as well, working as a farm hand for a family of little folk.

Then it came to her. "Silas!" she whispered. The church grim that haunted the little country church where she and her folks attended was bound to know something.

She reached for her Seeing Stone. Before she could get it out of her pocket, though, a voice rumbled, "Silas Bludgitt can't help you."

Taylor slipped her hand from her pocket and dropped into a defensive stance. Almost on instinct, she started drawing magical energy from all around.

Tree branches parted, and a man emerged: ugly as sin and sporting a gleaming silver-white sword.

*Crud*, Taylor thought.

The spriggan strolled forward, holding a blue-white orb of faery fire in his hand.

"You again," she muttered.

Captain Dingle bowed. "We didn't have a chance for pleasantries at your dance."

"What does Gramps want with me now?"

Dingle chuckled, but there wasn't any mirth in it. It sounded more like a Rottweiler choking on a tasty bite of bunny rabbit.

"Forget about your little friends," he said.

"*What did you to do Wasko?*" Taylor snarled. She threw a wave of presence with her words. It would have bowled over Danny or Silas, but Dingle barely flinched. Instead, he croaked out another malevolent laugh.

"Sweetheart, I've worked for Mr. Cornstack for 200 years. A little glamour trick like that ain't gonna—."

She didn't let him finish. She thrust her right hand forward, propelling a faery blast into Dingle's horrid face.

But Dingle was faster. His sword arced across his body, suddenly glowing with its own silver light. It deflected Taylor's blast into the woods.

Dingle lunged forward and poked the tip of his sword against the top of Taylor's sternum. She froze in place and tried not to breathe.

"Like I said, you need to forget about the little folk. Unless you *want* something bad to happen to them."

That got Taylor's attention—and not in a good way.

"I don't appreciate threats," she growled. A fine coating of frost started to form on Dingle's sword.

"No threats," he said. "Just the truth. You got the Winter Court's attention, especially after that, uh, mischief you was in the middle of earlier this year."

Yeah, news about Taylor stopping a war between the daoine sídhe and the nunnehi probably got around.

"Mr. Cornstack is curious where you stand, is all."

"Where I stand?"

"I know, I know. You're daoine sídhe. When everything is said and done, you're on your own side. I get that...but who will be your allies, huh?"

"Not Crom Cornstack!" Taylor shouted. Her body shook from head to toe.

Dingle chuckled. "See, Mr. Cornstack wonders if you might change your mind about that."

What?

There was that repulsive not-quite laugh again.

"What are you talking about?"

Dingle lowered his sword.

"Mr. Cornstack don't play around. He can be very persuasive when he wants to be."

"Well, you can tell Mr. Cornstack—"

Dingle held up a hand. He said, "You're poison, little girl. Be careful who you touch."

And then, quick as that, he was gone in a flash of yellow sparks.

Taylor wiped a trickle of sweat from her brow. She looked down and gasped to see a circle of frost had formed at her feet. She barely understood what had just happened, but she knew she didn't like it.

## Chapter 4

# Monday Morning Blues

William groaned when the alarm on his phone went off with the guitar riff from the old 90s *Spider-Man* TV show. He resisted the urge to hit the snooze button. Instead, he turned off the alarm and threw off the covers. With great effort, he sat up on the edge of his bed, yawned, and opened his eyes. In that order.

It was 5:31.

Any other day, he might have slept in. He didn't have to leave for school until 7:00, and he'd honed his morning routine until he could be dressed and out the door in under twenty-five minutes—and that was with his sister hogging the bathroom.

Any other day, he'd sleep for another hour, get up refreshed, and take his time getting ready. But his run-in with those little folk on Friday night made sleeping a luxury he couldn't afford. If anything else happened—if someone or some*thing* wanted to make trouble at school, he needed to be ready with some magic of his own. And that meant he needed time to meditate.

Sometimes being a witch sucked.

And yes, it's "witch," not "wizard." As his grandmother explained it, only high-level practitioners had earned the right to call themselves wizards. Merlin, Gandalf, Dr. Strange: those guys were wizards. The kind of magic Maymay taught—potions and powders and amulets and such—made you a witch, and it didn't matter if you were a guy or a girl.

There were other terms, of course. "Practitioner" was kind of generic. "Cunning man" had a certain ring to it, but William was still a couple weeks short of his fifteenth birthday, and he was not setting himself up for somebody to call him a cunning *boy*. "Root doctor" sounded like some kind of supernatural tree surgeon. For now, he would just try to get used to being a witch.

Whatever he was, he was still sleepy. He set the alarm for 6:30, just in case he fell back to sleep. He slid down the side of his bed onto the floor and crossed his legs. He didn't bother to turn on the light; the dark made for fewer distractions. He focused on his breathing—in through the nose, out through the mouth—while mentally repeating the simple mantra his grandmother had taught him.

Mostly, he tried not to think about his progress—or lack thereof.

"Folks think magic is all about the flashy stuff," Maymay had told him more than once. "They don't realize it's mostly about the right frame of mind. Learn to see from a new point of view. Puzzle things out. Think outside the box." William could still see her sitting with him and Jill in the basement, teaching them the basics of the gift they had inherited from her.

"Get your head in the right place," she said, "and the flashy stuff will come soon enough."

That was easy for her to say. Even though she had mostly quit using magic years ago, it must have come back awfully fast. And Jill! She could do all kinds of stuff, like summoning that wind Friday night, and hardly break a sweat.

William guessed that was because of something Taylor's grandmother had done to her two summers ago. Mara Helle-bore had "awakened" Jill's gift. It had thrown her Second Sight into overdrive, and William suspected it ramped up her other abilities as well.

What Mara did came with a price, though. For the longest time, Jill was barely keeping it together. Whenever she tried to use her Second Sight, she couldn't shut it down. Everything she saw started to get to her. That's when Maymay came to visit, to try to keep her from going over the edge.

And that's why William tried not to say anything whenever he felt jealous that magic came so easily to Jill.

*Okay, enough distractions*, he told himself. He went back to his breathing exercises. In through the nose, out through the mouth. "*Eulamo*," he hissed.

Maybe the tingling he sensed running up and down his spine was magic seeping up from the Wonder and settling on him. Then again, maybe it was just sitting still for so long. As soon as he became aware of the sensation, he put it out of his mind and went back to his breathing.

At 6:09, voices from the next room over—his parents' bedroom—interrupted his concentration.

He couldn't make out what they were saying at first, but he could hear the emotion.

Eventually, he tuned into his mom's voice. "I can't believe you're okay with all this," she said. William felt a stone drop into his gut. He'd heard this argument before.

"Sophie, I don't see as we have a choice," his dad said. He said some more things, but William didn't catch them. They were trying to keep their voices down, but William had discovered that deep meditation tended to sharpen his senses, hearing included. He wasn't sure it was magic or simply learning to pay closer attention to the world around him. Maybe at some deep level, the two were the same thing.

William took one last deep breath and got up. He was stiff and sleepy, but something tempted him to keep listening. He sat down on the side of the bed.

"I still say we should tell Reverend Johnson," his mom said.

"Tell him what? That William and Jill have magical powers?"

There was a long silence. Then William's mom said, "Maybe he can do something. Talk some sense into them."

"Listen, Sophie," his dad said. He added something more, and once again William couldn't make it out. He raised his voice again when he said, "You weren't there last winter. Those... *things* out there? Prayers and clean living are not going to keep them away from our kids."

Mom scoffed and said something back.

Dad shot back, "It's *exactly* like gangs. Only worse. They're gangs like nothing we can understand." A brief pause. "Your mother knew what they're up against."

"You leave Momma out of this!"

"I'm just saying, William and Jill have to be able to take care of themselves. That doesn't mean I like it. I just know that's the way it is. Your mother can't protect them—certainly not all the way from New Orleans."

The next bit was too muffled to understand. As William came fully out of his meditative state, his senses tapered off to their normal level. Whatever his parents told each other after that was their secret.

William sighed. He got up, did a few stretches, and started getting ready for school. At least he'd beat Jill to the bathroom.

As soon as he was dressed, with his teeth brushed and his hair combed, he opened his closet and pulled out an old blue and white gym bag with a picture of the Riverview Raiders mascot on the side. He set it on the bed and opened it up.

Dad was right about one thing: he and Jill had to be able to take care of themselves. That meant knowing enough magic to at least make the Good Neighbors (what Maymay called the psychotic side of Taylor's family) think twice about messing with them.

Magic and high school didn't exactly go together, though. Most magic had a physical component—at least at William's level. Jill was pretty good at raw magic, what Maymay called evocation. William grasped the principles behind magic better than his sister, but he couldn't come close to her when it came to actually casting spells.

Anyway, school security put some pretty hard limits on how many magical goodies William could bring to class. A blasting rod was out of the question—they'd probably confiscate it as a weapon. (Which it was, but still.)

On his first magical excursion last year—the one where his dad saw the Good Neighbors in action for the first time—he had brought some little plastic bags filled with magical herbs and powders. Right, like he wanted campus security to think he was a drug dealer!

No, he'd have to stick to the basics. A grease pencil and a couple pieces of chalk for drawing magic circles were always a good start. A circle of power could sharpen and focus a person's magic or shield him from outside magical assaults. He tossed the drawing implements on his bed beside the gym bag: the beginning of a small pile of tools he could reasonably bring to school without any difficulties.

He added a gold ring. It was his Pawpaw's class ring from before his mom was even born. It didn't have a gemstone, just an engraved crest and the inscriptions "Grambling College" and "1963." Maymay had left it for the twins to share when she went back to New Orleans at the end of summer. The gold was good for light and healing spells, even if it wasn't twenty-four carat.

He tossed a small compact on the bed—he'd found a brown plastic one at Walgreens that didn't look girly at all. The mirror was good for spells of protection or clairvoyance. He'd taken out the powder and the powder puff. There was bound to be a way to replace them with a single dose of some kind of useful spell. He just hadn't figured it out yet.

Then there was a handful of salt packets he'd collected from fast-food places. With a little advance preparation, you could actually make a pretty good defensive spell from salt. He dropped seven or eight of the packets into a zip-top bag, and then loaded all of his tools into the front pocket of his backpack.

Of course, he always carried his jet amulet in his pocket, a small black stone etched with a maze of jagged lines. Maymay had given him and Jill matching amulets. They were the best tools they had for counteracting faery glamour or other assaults on the mind.

His last tool was hanging downstairs in the coat closet. Months before, he'd opened the seams of his denim jacket enough to slip two iron nails into the fabric near the waist-line. Iron put the whammy on fae magic. Even though a couple of nails wouldn't do diddly, after three weeks studying his grandmother's notebooks until his eyes crossed, William had figured out how to imbue his jacket with a few defensive charms. He'd done the same thing to Jill's school jacket, and sewed up the seams on both garments as best he could.

If it worked, he'd have a layer of armor against attacks both magical and mundane. He'd never put it to the test, and he hoped he'd never have to. Even so, it made him feel better to know that both he and his sister at least had a last-ditch line of defense if things got serious.

William skipped breakfast. He'd taken too much time packing his backpack. It was just as well, though. Maymay said witches needed to fast every now and then to sharpen their powers.

He came down the stairs with minutes to spare. He stuck the energy bar Mom offered him into his backpack and headed to school.

## Chapter 5

# A Food Fight for the Ages

Taylor tried to answer Jill's questions as they hunched over a table in the cafeteria waiting for the first bell. William sat a couple tables over helping Jalen Harris factor trinomials. It was just as well, because Jill was still freaking out over their little adventure Friday night. Getting grilled by one Matthews at a time was plenty for Taylor to deal with.

"You honestly have no idea what those little guys were talking about?" Jill asked.

"No clue. I've barely visited the Wonder since this summer—and even when I do, I just go to the woods behind my house." Taylor contemplated saying something about the firefight at the ninth-grade dance, but decided not to. Jill was freaking out enough as it was.

"Well, they were pretty insistent for you to leave them alone," Jill said.

Taylor clenched her fists. "They were the ones following me," she said. "I don't even know who they were. And Wasko knows something, too. He and Haggler and Pete were supposed to come by Saturday night."

"Were supposed to? You mean they didn't show up?"

"No," Taylor said. "And by oak, ash, and thorn, I'm going to find out why." She hung her head. Before she could say anything else, she heard footsteps approaching from behind her.

"Hey, Taylor. Jill."

Taylor sighed. When did Jared McCaughey get so good at appearing out of nowhere? And why did he always pick the most inconvenient times possible?

Jill covered her mouth to hide her grin.

"What's up, Jared?" Taylor said. She tried to sound perky but probably didn't.

"Did you understand the math homework? I got lost."

"Pretty much. Didn't Mrs. Kowsky said she'd go over it again today?"

"I guess. It's just..." He sighed. "I guess I'll see you third period."

"Yeah," Taylor said. She smiled. "Well, have a good morning."

Jared smiled back. "You too!" He walked away.

Other kids were gathering up their things. The bell was about to ring. It was time to get to their first-period classes.

But apparently Jill thought there was still enough time for a little good-natured teasing.

"Isn't that sweet," she said, grinning. "He wants to get back together with you."

Taylor shouldered her backpack. As she stood, she said, "We can't get 'back together' because we were never 'together' in the first place."

"Are you sure about that? 'Cause the way I remember it, you two were pretty chummy up until the dance." Jill stood up, and the girls joined the crowd filing into the hallway. "And you still don't want to tell me what happened between you?"

"Jill..."

"I know, I know," her friend said. "None of my business. Even though I'm your best friend and you never shared any of the juicy details about you and Jared..."

"There aren't any juicy details to share," Taylor said flatly. "He's a nice guy. That's all."

"And cute."

"*Jill, just let it go, okay?*" She let a little presence seep into her words. Her magical powers of persuasion didn't work on Jill, but Taylor winced anyway. Now that she had gained more control of her powers, she didn't like the idea of using them on mortals. And now that she realized she could use presence to win people over instead of scaring them off...

"Look, he's...really nice." She noticed Shelby Crowthers a few feet away. In other words: within gossiping range. She decided to avoid using names. "We just don't have much in common."

"Hmm. You're both smart, you've both got a snarky sense of humor..."

"You know what I mean," Taylor said. She didn't give Jill the death-glare, but she made herself understood with an arched eyebrow. She leaned over and lowered her voice to a whisper. "How am I supposed to explain to Jared about...where I'm from?"

They came to an intersection in the hallway. Jill had to hang a left to math class; Taylor had to turn go straight to get to social studies.

Jill gave Taylor a sympathetic look. "I understand," she said. "Really. I'm sorry for playing with you."

"It's okay," Taylor said.

"Though you realize," Jill said, a twinkle in her eye, "now that you and Jared aren't together, William might start getting his hopes up again."

"Go to class, Jill," Taylor growled.

"Okay. See you at lunch.

As far as Taylor was concerned, the best thing about Riverview High School was no Mrs. Markowitz. Her middle school English teacher retired last spring, but Taylor worried it was all some terrible joke, that some day the red-haired, beach-ball shaped teacher would come back to haunt her, maybe subbing for her regular ninth-grade teacher, Mr. Moore. So far, that particular nightmare hadn't come true.

Otherwise, things were mostly a wash. The teachers were awful to so-so in about the same proportion. (Mr. Matthews was actually pretty good. If Taylor hadn't spent her eighth-grade year getting in shape running for her life from homicidal Fair Folk, though, she would probably have a different opinion.)

The worst thing about Riverview? Lunch, hands down. They served the same greasy, overly salted (ahem) cuisine that they did at Bulloch Middle School. And for the last week or so, they did it with an even surlier attitude. The old lunch crew had gotten fired—or retired, or paroled or something. The new lunch ladies gave off a vibe that said they'd rather be doing something fun like burning down orphanages or strangling small woodland creatures.

A tall, gaunt woman slid a plate toward Taylor. She looked like she hadn't eaten in about a month.

Lucky for her.

Taylor looked at the brown mass on the plate. Her best guess: it must have been some kind of meat. She set it on her tray, shook her head knowingly at Jill, who was in line behind her, and scooted forward.

At the next station, Taylor got a scoop of macaroni and cheese. She was proud of herself for not saying anything sarcastic, but her expression must have given her away.

"All kids like mac and cheese," the towering lunch lady said to Taylor's unspoken complaint. According to her nametag, she was called Olga. Olga wasn't fat. By definition, a brick wall can't be fat. Tall and thick, maybe, but not technically fat. Nor does a brick wall have much personality.

"Maybe some day we'll have some," Taylor quipped. She eyed her plate. "Bound to be tastier than plaster of Paris."

Olga glared at her and motioned her on.

Taylor announced her name at the end of the line. The third lunch lady, Loretta according to her nametag, couldn't have been more than five feet tall. She had already checked Taylor's name on her clipboard. "Yes," she said. Taylor took her disdainful expression as an invitation to move on.

William had saved seats for Taylor and Jill. As soon as Jill sat down beside him, he glowered at Loretta and whispered, "Man, I miss the old lunch crew!"

"Me too," Jill said.

"You remember how Miss Hazel used to give us extra fries?"

"Well, she's gone to a better place," Jill said.

"Some place in Florida," Taylor said. "Wasn't it?"

"That doesn't mean I can't miss her," William said. "Or the others."

"Why'd she have to retire?" Jill added.

"At least she was friendly," William said. "Not like Loretta. That woman gives me the creeps!"

"Guys?" Taylor said. "Are we really going to spend our lunch talking about the cafeteria ladies?"

"You got something to report?" William said.

Taylor frowned. "No." She rearranged her macaroni with her fork. "I haven't heard from Wasko since Friday night."

"What about that other one Jill told me about," William said. He dropped his voice to a whisper. "You know: the one that lives at your church."

"I haven't talked to Silas," Taylor said. She studied her food, unwilling to make eye contact. Saturday night, Dingle had made it sound like her Wonderling friends would be in danger if she had any further contact with them. She hadn't dared contact the church grim after that.

"I'm not sure it's a good idea," she added.

"I wish I knew what those two little people were talking about," Jill said. "What have they got against you, anyway?"

"I wish I knew," Taylor said. "Last year, Wasko and his buddies acted like I was the next Mother Teresa. A symbol of hope or something." She rolled her eyes. "But those guys last Friday..."

"Maybe they don't want people to have any hope," William said.

"Huh." Taylor hadn't thought of that. "What if—?"

Before she could ask her question, voices on the other side of the lunchroom caught her attention.

Mrs. Woodhouse, one of the other gym teachers, had stopped a couple of kids Taylor didn't recognize at the entrance to the lunchroom. Mrs. Woodhouse didn't seem to recognize them, either.

"Either show me your ID, or we're going to the office," she said. She kept her voice low, but Taylor had pretty good hearing.

"Who are they?" Taylor asked.

"Who?" William said.

"Those kids talking to Mrs. Woodhouse."

"The guy is...." He frowned. "I'm not sure. A senior, maybe?"

"Woodhouse would know all the seniors," Taylor said. She suddenly got a queasy feeling in her stomach—and she hadn't eaten a bite.

She relaxed her eyes and tried to see traces of glamour.

Jill beat her to it. "Trouble!" she whispered.

"Story of my life," Taylor sighed. But Jill was right: those two teenagers trying to get into the lunchroom weren't what they seemed.

"Those kids look short to you?" William said.

"They're the little folk from the other night," Taylor said.

"And they're looking at us," Jill added, scooting away from the table.

"We'd better get out of here," Taylor said. She stood up and turned toward the end of the table in a single, easy motion.

The little folk were moving, too. The woman had put some kind of charm on Mrs. Woodhouse. She stood in a daze with her mouth open. Now both of the little folk were skirting the edge of the lunchroom.

Escape was no longer an option. The best Taylor could hope for was to defuse the situation before it got any worse. She slipped down the row of tables to intercept them. William and Jill followed close behind.

The little folk skidded to a stop. There was no way they could get around Taylor and her friends; they'd have to get out another way. They looked at each other, and the man nodded.

"Can't we talk this over?" Taylor said. Even as she spoke, she steeled herself against an attack.

The man lunged at the nearest table and tipped Tommy Morgan's plate into his lap. The woman gestured. Taylor sensed more than saw the waves of magical mist swirling around her.

"Hey!" Tommy yelled. He was on his feet in a heartbeat, shaking the macaroni and cheese off his shirt. The woman gestured again, and Tommy glared at the kid across the table from him. He splashed his tea in the kid's face.

The little woman grinned as she backed away.

William and Jill mumbled something under their breath, probably some kind of spell against faery glamour. Their eyes never left the action along the wall of the cafeteria.

The commotion was spreading. Some kids laughed at the uproar while others decided to get in on it. It took just a few seconds for the entire lunchroom to descend into chaos.

"Follow them!" Taylor shouted. She plowed ahead, using a shield spell to deflect incoming globs of macaroni, peas, and banana pudding.

As the little folk passed Mrs. Woodhouse, they shoved her into the oncoming teenagers.

"They're getting away!" Jill said.

Just then, energy crackled across the room. Something exploded against the wall where the little folk would have been a half-second later.

"What the—?" Taylor gasped. "Who's—?"

Loretta the lunch lady had edged around the far side of the cafeteria. Magical energy swirled in her hands. Taylor groaned. *I knew there was something wrong with those lunch ladies!*

Beside her, her tall, gaunt partner swatted away flying bits of food with her spatula.

"Keep me covered, Desirée!" Loretta hissed. "Olga, secure the girl!"

Olga grunted as she bounded toward Taylor.

"Secure the girl" didn't sound pleasant.

Now that the lunch ladies weren't hiding their true forms under glamour, Loretta was even shorter—no bigger than a nine-year-old. Olga, on the other hand, towered over the cafeteria at over seven feet. She took a plate of banana pudding to the side of the head, but it didn't slow her down.

Taylor stopped. Food flew in every direction. Only her shield spell kept her and the twins from getting plastered with it. Straight ahead, the little folk were trading blasts with Loretta. To the left, Olga barged across the lunchroom, ignoring the food flying by as she pushed teenagers willy-nilly out of her way.

The little folk were retreating toward Taylor. The man provided cover as the woman charged toward her, a glowing yellow marble in her hand. It was a race to see whether she or Olga would get to Taylor first.

Suddenly William stepped in front of Olga. He had something in his hand—a *compact*? It was open, with the mirror facing Olga like he was holding a vampire at bay with a cross.

He hissed, "Protect us in the present hour! *Bientôt, bientôt! Vite, vite!*"

On the last syllable, Olga lurched forward and slammed headfirst into the gravy-splattered floor.

The female little person wound up and hurled her glowing marble toward Taylor.

It bounced against Taylor's magical shield and slammed into the ceiling, where it exploded with a thunderous BANG!

No one seemed to notice. The food kept flying. Teenagers kept cursing and screaming. It was like everybody was bewitched or something.

*Well, duh. That's exactly what's happening*, Taylor thought.

At least Mrs. Woodhouse had finally come out of it. Shaking macaroni and cheese from her hair, she blew her whistle and pulled kids out of the melee left and right.

Other teachers had apparently started to clue in to the food fight as well. Mr. Pennywise huffed and puffed down the hall from the direction of the office. Behind him, Dr. Krueger, Riverview's principal, screamed into a walkie-talkie for campus security.

Taylor had a feeling the office was about to run out of detention slips.

Olga lurched to her feet—not an easy feat on a disgustingly slippery floor.

Both little folk stalked toward Taylor. She summoned all her magic and willed them to mess up—to forget where they were going or what they were doing, to generally do something stupid that would let Taylor and her friends get away. Addlement was something Taylor had learned to do a year ago, and she was getting pretty good at it. Sure enough, the little folk stopped and stared at her, like they had completely forgotten what they were supposed to do.

Their confusion gave Taylor, Jill, and William time to maneuver. "This way!" Jill yelled. She yanked Taylor backward by her sleeve.

Off from the lunchroom was a hallway the led to the band room and an exit into the parking lot. That was apparently Jill's goal.

Halfway to the band room, though, something invisible lunged into them, slamming them against the wall.

Suddenly, there was someone else in the hall with them: a four-foot-tall, bat-eared little person with a round belly and an expression of wide-eyed terror.

"P-pete?" Taylor said.

"Inside!" he gasped, pointing.

A windowless door opened behind them. Inside, two other little folk bid them enter.


It was the door to a janitor's closet. The room was cramped, but fortunately, little folk didn't take up much room.

In addition to Pete was Haggler, an albino with wooly white hair, and Wasko. Wasko was the leader, for lack of a better word. He wore a bowler hat with a long, tapering turkey feather in its band. All three wore simple clothes a little worse for wear.

Haggler traced a design on the back of the door with a grease pencil and whispered an incantation. "That'll give us some privacy," he announced. "But not for long. Wasko?"

"Yeah," Wasko said. He stood on an overturned plastic tub that put him at eye level with Taylor. "We better say our peace and get out of here."

"W-Wasko...?" Taylor stuttered. "Where did you all come from?"

"The library," Haggler said.

All three teenagers stared at him. "The library?" Jill said.

"It ain't as good as a mushroom ring or a circle of standing stones," Pete said, "but it'll do in a pinch."

"Plenty of wonder and mystery in some of those books," Haggler agreed. "It adds up."

"Look," Wasko interrupted, "like Haggler said, we gotta talk fast before they find us."

"Who? Those other little folk?" Jill said.

Wasko shook his head and motioned toward the door. "Naw, it's those cafeteria ladies!"

"They've been a royal pain in the.... They been a big bother," Pete added. He sat on an empty shelf near the floor and leaned forward so he wouldn't bump his head on the shelf above him. "Every time we try to get close: boom!"

Haggler agreed. "If it ain't them, it's some of their friends."

The screams of students and Mrs. Woodhouse's frantic whistling continued outside the door.

"Wait a minute," Taylor said. This wasn't making sense. "You couldn't come see me Saturday because people have been keeping you away?"

All three nodded.

"Then...those others, the little folk who attacked me at the football game—"

"And just now," William added.

"We don't think they meant to attack you," Haggler said. "Just keep an eye on you. Make sure..." He trailed off. Nobody seemed eager to explain any further.

"Guys?" Taylor said.

"You gotta understand," Wasko said. He looked down like he was ashamed to say more. "We don't believe a word of it."

"A word of what?" Taylor said.

"You see," Haggler started, "people been saying nobody's to mess with Selena Hellebore."

"People? What people?"

The sounds of the food fight were dying down. It wouldn't be long until order was restored, and then it wouldn't be long until someone started looking for them.

"Well, they say...," Haggler said. There was pain and fear in his eyes. "They say they're following orders straight from—" He stopped. Taylor could tell he didn't want to say the rest.

"Yes?"

"Well, straight from Crom Cornstack."

Taylor cursed.

"Wait, you mean your grandfather?" William said.

"That's the one," Taylor muttered. But it still didn't make any sense. With a start, she remembered what had happened at the ninth-grade dance. Her grandfather's agent was chasing another fae, a jinni. Was he trying to scare away somebody who had wanted to contact Taylor? Somebody who wanted to help her?

"That doesn't make any sense!" she said. "None of this does. Last I knew, Crom disowned me when he disowned my mom."

"I guess things change," Wasko said.

"Not this much," Taylor said. Then she realized something that made her shake all over. "Wait, those little folk...they think I'm on Cornstack's side?"

Wasko shrugged. "Nobody wants to say it that plain," he said. "Mostly, Miss Hellebore... Well, folks don't rightly know what to think."

"But I hate the Winter Court!" she said.

"We know that," Haggler said. "The thing is, word's gotten around Winter's trying to win you over...and..."

"*And what?*"

Haggler flinched. "It's just... People don't know what to believe."

"And *that's* why those little folk have been spying on me? In case I might turn evil or something?

"Like Wasko said," Pete piped up, "we don't believe it for a minute!"

Taylor clenched her fists. Magic swirled around her unbidden. "All right. This is officially insane. Crom Cornstack hates me! And... and he can't just send his people into the Nunnehi Lands. He almost started a war doing that last year."

"See, that's the thing," Wasko said. "Those cafeteria ladies? The others that have been running interference against us? Technically speaking, they ain't his people."

"They're locals," Haggler explained, "and they don't exactly cotton to how the nunnehi run things."

"Unseelie," Taylor said. To William's confused expression, she added, "The nunnehi take up for Topsiders, for people like you and Jill. They protect them. So the lunch ladies—and whoever else is out there working with them—are going to be the opposite."

"That doesn't sound good," William said.

"It isn't," Taylor said. She rubbed her eyes and tried to put the pieces of the puzzle together. "So these lunch ladies and their friends, they're wanting to get in good with Crom. And they think—" Taylor shook her head and fought back a wave of nausea. "They think protecting me is the way to do it?"

"That's about the size of it," Wasko said.

"But why?" Taylor wished she could pace, but there wasn't room.

"The Winter Court's looking strong," Pete said with a shrug. "I bet they figure it's a good time to try for an alliance."

"But...but the Summer Court is united again, isn't it?"

"United," Haggler agreed, "but they got their hands full, what with the mess at Tobarty and all."

"What's that?" Jill asked.

"A rath—or a castle, you might say," Wasko explained. "It's on the border of the Nunnehi Lands. Summer's run it for going on two years now, but they're having problems. Ever since they installed the new Teyrnus—what's his name? Lovejoy?"

"Lovejoy was three months ago," Haggler said.

"Right," Wasko agreed. "The new guy is..." He scrunched his face up, trying to remember. "Well, it'll come to me. The point is, the Summer Court's not looking so good these days.

"I don't see how that gets me a bodyguard from Crom freaking Cornstack!"

"Us neither," Wasko said. "But it makes folks nervous, that's for sure."

"It makes *me* nervous!" Taylor said.

Everyone stood or sat in silence. Outside, teachers were barking orders. The bell rang. Fifth period started in five minutes. At last Jill said, "So what are we going to do?"

Taylor looked at Wasko and his friends. "If you find out anything else," she said. "Well...try to get through to me. Okay?"

"You got it, Miss Hellebore!"

"But don't do anything stupid!"

"Don't you worry about us, Miss Hellebore," Pete said. "We'll stay out of trouble."

"Good," Taylor said. "And thanks."

Outside the closet, it sounded like the chaos had died down. She looked at William and Jill. "We better go. We're late for class."

## Chapter 6

# Trouble in Tobarty

The spriggan held Danny's hands behind him in a viselike grip. His shoulders were sore, and gobs of tomato purée matted down his curly black hair, but other than that, he was in pretty good shape, all things considered.

He and his spriggan guard stood in the outer office of the Teyrnus of Tobarty. Outside in the corridor, a dozen or more fae clamored for the Teyrnus's attention.

Danny hung his head. *Next time*, he thought, *I ain't using that much tomato.*

A second guard rapped on the Teyrnus's door.

"What?" the Teyrnus barked from inside. He had a hair-trigger temper, Danny knew, and he was at his wit's end trying to keep the peace at Tobarty.

"We caught him, sir."

"Who?"

"The uh...." The second guard looked to his partner for help. His partner shrugged, pinching Danny's wrists in the process. The second guard started again. "Well, you know about the disturbance in the lower city."

"Of course, I know about it! They're going to be cleaning up that mess for a week!" The Teyrnus flung open his door. He was a tall sídhe with sandy hair and blazing blue eyes. He turned those eyes toward Danny.

The crowd outside screamed things liked "We demand restitution!" and "Satisfaction!" and "Kill the pooka!"

The Teyrnus blew a weary breath. "Inside. And Cubie"—he eyed the second guard—"do something about the mob."

Danny's guard shoved him into the inner office. The Teyrnus collapsed into his plush leather chair behind a great mahogany desk. He threw back his head, closed his eyes, and took a deep breath.

At last, he leaned forward, crossed his arms on the desk, and looked up at the guard. "Well?"

"Says his name's Underhill, sir."

"Underhill? *Danny* Underhill?"

"You've heard of him?" the guard asked.

*Here it comes*, Danny thought. It didn't matter how much you did for the Summer Court, how many changelings you switched out, you launch one Gentryman into a pumpkin patch and you never live it down.

"You helped rescue my wife from the nunnehi last February," the Teyrnus said.

Danny's eyes widened. He hadn't put it together—Tobarty had been through four or five Teyrnuses in the last couple years. He'd forgotten that the latest one, Aemeron Wakefire, was married to Gwenllian Birdsong. Maybe he'd get out of this with all his limbs intact after all!

"That's right, sir," he said, and he puffed out his chest.

"I should be grateful," the Teyrnus said.

"I was just doing what anybody'd do, sir. You—"

The Teyrnus pounded his fist on the desk. "I should be grateful, pooka, but this morning's escapade... *What were you even thinking?*"

Danny shrunk beneath the Teyrnus's withering gaze.

"I have a rath to rule! A rath full of foul, ungovernable lowlifes. By Danu, they'd just as soon have my head on a platter as listen to a single word I have to say. The ungrateful—"

He broke off as he opened and closed the drawers of his desk. "Arrgh! Where is my seal? I can't sign the order for your execution without my official seal!"

"Execution?" Danny gasped. "But Mr. Wakefire, I didn't mean no harm!"

The lowest desk drawer was stuck. The Teyrnus yanked at it, cursing, until it finally gave way. He pulled out his seal. "I would have sworn I'd put this in the top drawer. Well, no matter." As he continued to speak, he fumbled with a stack of papers on top of the desk.

"My cousin the Primus trusted me to put things in order at Tobarty, pooka. I do not intend to let him down. And if that means you must serve as an example for others... Gah!" He slammed his fist on the table and glared at the bewildered guard. "Where are my execution orders! I swear, it's like someone keeps rearranging everything in this blasted office!"

There was a knock at the door. Before the Teyrnus could roar at the interruption, a tall black woman showed herself in. She was dressed impeccably in a green business suit, and she held a writing tablet in her hand.

Danny breathed a sigh of relief. If anybody could get him out of this mess, it was Claudia Fountain!

"And what do *you* want, Miss Fountain?" the Teyrnus grumbled. "Has Dubessa sent you to spy on me? I'll bet she hopes I turn out like Seaborn—or Dewberry. Oh, she'd love that, wouldn't she?"

"Mr. Wakefire," Claudia said, her voice calm and even, "I am indeed the assistant to the Chief Matron, but I'm not here because of you."

"Then wait your turn in my outer office," the Teyrnus said. "I've got a pooka to kill, *and somebody has stolen my seal!*"

"*Mr. Wakefire,*" Claudia said again. This time, there was a rumble in her voice. Danny could feel it, like a storm about to break. "*I'm here for Mr. Underhill.*"

"Mr. Underhill is a menace."

"As much to himself as to anyone else, I'm afraid," Claudia said. "Even so, he is necessary for my purposes, and I've come to collect him."

"Your purposes?" the Teyrnus said. "Dubessa's got a job for him?"

Danny nearly swooned. Taking a job from Dubessa Fairchild was better than getting the death penalty, but not by much.

"Mr. Wakefire, I won't beat around the bush. It is vital that you release Mr. Underhill."

"You're asking a lot." The Teyrnus's eyes flashed. Danny recognized the look. The Teyrnus was putting two and two together and imagining how much Danny's freedom would be worth to the Chief Matron.

"You have requested additional men for your garrison," Claudia said. "They are already on their way. They'll be here tomorrow at the latest."

Aemeron Wakefire stopped fidgeting.

Danny wondered what kind of negotiator the Teyrnus of Tobarty was. He didn't have to wait long to find out.

"If they're already on their way, that means I'd have gotten them no matter what I do with the pooka."

Danny's legs wobbled. The Teyrnus was high-strung, but apparently he was no fool.

"I'll be honest with you, Teyrnus," Claudia said. "I intend to leave here with Mr. Underhill. But I'm willing to make it worth your while to part with him." She reached into her pocket. She brought out a small glass flask of crimson liquid and set it on the corner of the Teyrnus's desk.

His eyes grew big as saucers. "That's not...?"

"Dragon's blood," Claudia said. "Horned serpent, to be precise, and one hundred percent pure."

The Teyrnus licked his lips. "But...that's got to be..."

"Six and a half ounces. More than enough for any use you'd care to put it to."

The Teyrnus sat transfixed. Danny couldn't blame him; he'd never seen that much dragon's blood in one place before. Somebody who knew what he was doing could turn it into magical ink, or incense, or an alchemical solvent. Danny could think of at least half a dozen potions he could make with the stuff—if he were brave enough to handle it.

"Mr. Wakefire, I'm going to leave this flask on your desk," Claudia said. "And Mr. Underhill and I will be on our way."

The Teyrnus looked at Claudia, Danny, and the flask. He gestured for the spriggan to let Danny go.

Claudia clutched Danny's arm and led him from the office.

"I really, really owe you for this," Danny whispered.

"Keep that in mind," Claudia said. "There's somewhere we need to go."


It must have been twenty or thirty years since the last time Danny was in Tobarty. Back then, the Winter Court ran things, but they pretty much kept out of people's business. The Fair Folk weren't too big on rules and such, and a smart Teyrnus knew better than to rock the boat.

He didn't figure much would have changed now that the Summer Court was in charge. Walking through the lower city with Claudia, he was forced to reconsider. He'd seen it when he'd first arrived in town a couple of days ago, and the longer he stayed in town, the more he was sure about it. Something was wrong.

Tobarty had always been a neat little town in the mountains. Even this close to the Nunnehi Lands border, things were peaceful most of the time. Folks took pride in their homes and businesses. They kept things clean and orderly and mostly kept to themselves. Sure, the water folk around the hot springs could be a pain, but Danny had no use for a mineral bath, anyway.

No, it wasn't anything Danny saw that worried him as much as what he felt. People didn't always appreciate his pranks, but he hadn't been hauled in by the city watch since that unfortunate misunderstanding with Ambicatus Bright forty years ago. Everybody in Tobarty seemed on edge, from the Primus on down.

He worried that was why Claudia had scried him three days ago to meet her here.

"You really should be more careful," Claudia said. Her tone was distant, professional. When she looked at him, though, he could see her concern.

"I try, Claudia. I really do."

"Given the circumstances, would it kill you to try harder?" She sniffled and turned her head away.

"Maybe," Danny said. "But don't you think a little good, clean fun could...you know, lighten the mood a little?"

Claudia laughed in spite of herself. "I'm not sure the Teyrnus thought your little prank was good, clean fun."

"Yeah, I figured that out. Some folks have no sense of humor."

"This is serious, Danny!" Claudia said. She stopped in the middle of the narrow street and set her hands on Danny's shoulders. "You've got to think before you act."

"I'm sorry," he said. He hung his head. "I never meant no harm."

"I know." She started walking again. Soon, she picked up the pace. As they walked through town, Danny couldn't shake the feeling of being watched. More than once, he saw locals cast furtive glances toward the rath proper—the ring fort at the top of the highest hill where the Teyrnus kept his headquarters.

Danny and Claudia were on the far end of town, so even the folks that had heard about his little prank earlier weren't likely to recognize him. Even so, a lot of people gave Danny and Claudia a wide berth. Strangers almost always attracted attention in a rath. Townsfolk pretty much knew one another, had known one another for centuries. A new face in town might be the subject of conversation.

That didn't make Danny feel any better about coming here. He'd just as soon have stayed in Tsuwatelda to help his boss butcher hogs.

The way Claudia had talked, that wasn't going to happen.

"You said Mrs. Fairchild had a job for me?"

"Actually, I said you were necessary for *my* purposes," Claudia said. She held at bay the grin that threatened to spread across her face. "The Teyrnus assumed these purposes had to do with the Chief Matron."

Claudia was a lot better at keeping a straight face than Danny was. The pooka's eyes widened as he worked out what Claudia had told him. "You mean the two things ain't related?"

"If the Teyrnus believes they are.... Well, I was speaking plainly enough."

"You're beautiful, Claudia. You know that?"

Claudia studied the cobblestone street. "It's nearly suppertime. Are you hungry?"

"Starving," Danny said.

"Then let's get something to eat. We need to talk."

They wound through the twisting lanes, following sounds of laughter and the yeasty smell of homebrew. If somebody had recently brewed up a batch of ale, their house would be the place to be.

They came to a good-sized house with one main room that opened onto the street. Ten or twenty Fair Folk of the lower classes—ellylls, pisgies, and the like, plus at least half a dozen little folk—milled about or sat at long tables enjoying cups of ale or cider and simple fare: bread, cheese, cold meats. A fire in the hearth kept everyone warm. Some sang and danced while others in a far corner rolled dice.

"My treat," Danny announced. These were his people, and he could usually get a meal for himself in exchange for his stories and maybe a few trinkets. (He always traveled with a pouch of faery dust and a few magic beans when he could get some. It made no sense that Topsiders bartered for pieces of paper that didn't even do anything!)

"Always the gentleman," Claudia said, smiling.

Danny ushered Claudia inside. They eased into empty seats near the door and listened as a trio of pale-skinned elves regaled the crowd with a song. They were probably nightwalkers, but Danny didn't judge them. As long as they weren't blighting *his* crops or bothering any of *his* Topsider friends, they were somebody else's problem.

Before long, the fae next to him passed a pitcher of cider his way along with two earthenware cups.

"Thanks," Danny said. His tablemate was a suave, dark-haired fae with a winsome smile. Attached to his arm was a sultry Native American woman with big, brown eyes. A deer woman, Danny guessed—though he knew better than to peek at her feet to make sure.

He pulled his knife from his belt sheath, shaved off a hunk of cheese from the nearest round, and passed it to Claudia on his left. Then he shaved off another morsel for himself.

"You got a job for me?" he said.

"You might say that." Claudia nibbled at her cheese. She listened as the elves sang and joined the applause when they finished.

"Well?"

She leaned toward Danny. "How long have you been in Tobarty?"

"A couple days. I came as soon as you called. Well, as soon as I could arrange it with the little folk I work for back in Tsuwatelda, anyways."

"I see," Claudia said. She sipped her cider.

The crowd called for Lewie to sing something. A stunted, foul-looking fae stood up and bowed, grinning. He opened his mouth, and proceeded to croon a slow, rambling song.

"And what do you think of the rath?" Claudia continued.

Danny waited for the crowd to get into Lewie's singing. He had a fantastic tenor voice—probably a bendith y mamau, by the looks of him.

"I dunno, Claudia. It's...it's like the place is living under a cloud." A loaf of bread passed their way. Danny and Claudia both broke off pieces for themselves. Danny called for someone to pass the meat tray.

Claudia nodded. "Go on."

"Well, like when those shopkeepers…uh…took offense at me trying to put a little humor in their lives. By oak, ash, and thorn, you'd think I'd let loose a brood of tie snakes!"

"Is that all?"

He slapped a slice of meat on his bread and took a bite. As soon as he swallowed, he said, "The whole town's like that. Everybody's looking over their shoulders, like they know something bad is about to happen but they don't know what."

"Everybody, you say?"

Danny nodded. "The Teyrnus is the worst, from what I hear. Folks don't trust him. They say he's…" He spun a finger at the side of his head.

"Is that so?"

"You saw him for yourself. He was about to string me up— and for what? Okay, so my prank got a little out of hand. But still, there weren't no call for him to try to kill me over it!"

"It's hard work to be a Teyrnus," Claudia observed.

"Seems like it's twice as hard in Tobarty," Danny said. "I mean, how many have they been through the past couple years?"

"Five, I believe."

"Let's see." Danny counted them out on his fingers. "First was Seaborn. Then Dewberry, and after him was the tylwyth teg. Whitehorse?"

"That's right," Claudia said.

"That's when things really went downhill," Danny said. "And then it was Owen Lovejoy, and now it's Aemeron Wakefire. Five Teyrnuses less than two years!"

"That does seem excessive, doesn't it?" Claudia said.

"You ask me, the place is jinxed—and I ain't the only one that thinks so."

"Is that so?"

Lewie finished one song and the crowd urged him to sing another. He apparently didn't take too much convincing. He belted out an old Welsh ballad. Another fae strummed along on a guitar.

"Look, I was there—" He stopped himself and looked around. The place was crawling with nightwalkers, bendith y mamau, deer women, and plenty of other unseelie folk. He lowered his voice and leaned into Claudia's shoulder. "I was there when Crom Cornstack got snookered into giving up Tobarty to the Summer Court. And I tell you, something wasn't right."

"What do you mean?"

"It was too easy, is what I mean," Danny said. "He barely put up a fight. It was almost like he wanted Summer to take Tobarty."

Claudia's eyes flashed, but she quickly turned her attention to her cup. "That seems hard to believe," she said.

"Maybe. But the longer Tobarty's in Summer hands, the bigger a problem it is. I mean, five Teyrnuses, Claudia? Five?"

"And that strikes you as improbable."

"It don't you?" Danny sputtered. "I heard you say the Primus was sending his cousin some more troops. How much you bet it won't be enough? He'll be asking for even more before long." Danny shuddered. "Folks are on edge. It's only getting worse."

"I see," Claudia said.

Danny helped himself to another hunk of cheese. He emptied his cup of cider and called for another. "You still ain't told me what you want me to do."

"No," Claudia said. "I didn't give you any instructions whatsoever, wouldn't you agree?"

Danny knitted his brow. "I reckon not."

Claudia sighed. "It's been good visiting with you, Danny. But given the circumstances, I imagine it would be best for you to head home soon."

Danny scratched his head. Why had Claudia brought him this far? What did she even want him to do? "I was planning on leaving tonight, but..."

"And be sure to give my regards to our mutual friends there."

Then it clicked. "Oh! You mean.... Yeah. You bet." *Don't worry, Claudia. I'll make sure Chief Tewa knows all about what's happening in Tobarty.*

Claudia smiled.

"You be safe, too," Danny said. "Don't be getting into no trouble."

Claudia smile became a chuckle as she said, "No, that's your department. It has been for the last—what? A hundred and fifty years?"

"Longer than that," Danny said. A sly grin crossed his face. "Though I didn't rightly reach my stride till after you came around."

She set her hand on top of Danny's. "You're not blaming me for your foolishness, are you?"

"Naw, nothing like that," Danny said. He didn't feel disposed to pull his hand away. "But I gotta admit: having you around makes things a lot more interesting."

Lewie had finished singing and the guitar-player was halfway through a tune of his own.

"You probably need to get back to Bisgarra Verry," Danny said.

"True," Claudia said. She slumped her shoulders. Then she looked at Danny and flashed a smile. "But I'd rather have some more of that cider."

## Chapter 7

# An Unplanned Vanishing Act

Thanksgiving break started well enough. Jill came over to Taylor's house Friday after school while William and his friends went to a movie for his fifteenth birthday bash. Jill had something planned with her friends for the following week—she and William were twins but, to hear Jill tell it, separate birthday parties were less volatile.

That was fine with Taylor. It meant that Jill ended up over at the Smarts' house again Saturday afternoon. The girls were hanging out in Taylor's room when Taylor felt a shiver course through her body. Someone was trying to reach her on her Seeing Stone. She reached behind her for her purse, slung over the chair at the desk in her bedroom.

"What's up?" Jill said.

"Don't know." Taylor breathed on the smooth, reddish-brown teardrop. Immediately a purple-red hologram erupted from the stone, overlaying her room with another scene painted in purplish red lights. It was a woodland scene, and in the middle, looking Taylor in the eye, was a familiar face.

"Ayoka?"

Ayoka seemed grim, determined. She spoke in a rapid spurt: "The park near your house. Ten minutes." Her eyes darted toward something out of the picture over Taylor's shoulder. "Gotta go!"

"Wait a minute! What—?" Too late. Ayoka broke the connection.

Taylor stood up.

"Change of plans," she said. "I've got to be somewhere."

"What's going on?" Jill said. "Who was that?"

"Ayoka. Something's up. I'm supposed to meet her in the park."

"Then I'm coming too."

"No. With everything that's been going on...."

"That's *why* I'm coming too." Jill already had her cell out. She punched out a text as she said, "Let's go."

They stopped long enough to tell Taylor's mom they were going to the park. Then Taylor burst into the front yard with Jill on her heels.

"Jill, seriously: Ayoka meant business. This might not be the best time for you to come along."

Jill kept up no matter how fast Taylor walked. "Too bad," she said.

They hadn't made it to the end of the block before William jogged up beside them. He was wearing khaki cargo pants with lots of zippered pockets, a UGA tee shirt, and his denim jacket. "Jill, what do you think you're doing?"

"Oh, for crying out loud!" Taylor steamed. "What do you think *you're* doing?"

Over his shoulder, William had slung his gym bag, the one Taylor knew he kept stocked with magical equipment. The walking stick poking up through the opening was new, though.

"Jill, what's going on? All of a sudden you and Taylor decide to go to the park?"

"We go to the park all the time."

"Yeah, but you never text *me* about it instead of just calling Mom or Dad. Something's up."

They turned the corner.

"It has to do with those little guys, doesn't it?" William said.

"William...," Jill started.

"And you didn't even bring supplies?"

"I've got my amulet and a couple other things in my purse," Jill said. She eyed William's gear. "And don't you have things to do? Homework or something?"

"Listen, if something is up—"

Taylor deliberately cleared her throat. Jill and William settled down. The three walked on silently.

The park was too chilly for anyone to be playing on the swings or eating at the picnic tables—which was fine with Taylor. Whatever Ayoka wanted, it was good they had the place to themselves.

Taylor checked the time on her phone. They were a minute or two ahead of schedule. She looked around, but of course nothing seemed unusual. Like all nunnehi, Ayoka was an expert at invisibility. She could be standing right beside them and they'd never know it.

Taylor took a breath and pushed out with her magical senses.

Jill pulled a small mirror from her purse and gazed into it, putting her Second Sight to work.

William raised his stick in what might have been a defensive stance.

"Expecting ninjas?" Taylor quipped.

"Shh!" William said.

He was trying to concentrate. As Taylor focused on the stick, she perceived patterns of magical energy swirling around it. Only then did Taylor notice the ring of geometric symbols carved around each end.

She couldn't believe it. "Is that some kind of magic wand?"

"It's just a hanbo," Williams whispered. "A fighting staff. I've been practicing in tae kwan do class. But I tricked this one out. You know, just in case."

"You know how to do stuff like that?" Taylor was impressed.

"It's all in Maymay's notes," he said. "If it works, I'll make one for Jill and—"

He spun around and gazed over Jill's shoulder. The two girls turned to see what had caught his attention.

Ayoka stood behind a tree near the picnic tables. She wore jeans, a red tee shirt, and a fringed buckskin jacket. She might have looked like an ordinary teenager except for the club in her hand and the stripes of red and black paint across her face. She nodded when they saw her, then vanished into thin air.

"Well, what are we waiting for?" Taylor said. She marched toward the spot where Ayoka had vanished with William and Jill close behind.

When she got to the tree, she asked, "You still here?"

"Over here," Ayoka said. And just as suddenly, she was visible again.

"I'm never gonna get used to that," William said.

Taylor ignored him. Ayoka looked serious. "I thought you were back in Tsuwatelda," Taylor said.

Ayoka cut her off. "We don't have much time." She set her hands on Taylor's shoulder. "You've got to tell me what's going on. I promise I'll believe you."

"What?"

"Seriously?" Jill said. "You think Taylor's siding with her grandpa?"

"No!" Ayoka protested. Her eyes never left Taylor's. "Not for a minute. That's why we've got to get you to Ichisi. Give you a chance to explain yourself."

Taylor clenched her fists, immediately defensive. Her face flushed. "The Chiefs think I've turned evil?" Why should she have to prove herself to anyone? Didn't the Chiefs of Ichisi remember her help last winter?

Ayoka sighed. "You've proved yourself before..."

"You're darned right!"

"Look, I know," Ayoka said. "But these last few weeks have been rough. Ogres have been getting unruly. Well, more unruly than usual. Deer women, tie snakes." She threw up her hands. "The Chiefs don't know what to think, but if you're somehow involved—"

In the distance, somebody shouted in anger—or maybe in pain.

Ayoka backed away. She leveled her war club, and it burst into flame.

"They're coming," she warned.

"Who?" Jill said, her eyes wide.

"You'd better leave," Ayoka told Jill and William. "I can get Taylor to safety."

"Wait," Taylor said. "What's going on?"

"Your 'bodyguard,' I suppose you'd say" Ayoka said. "Tsisgwa's been running interference. It was the only way I could get through."

Something exploded, not too far away.

"But this so-called 'bodyguard' finally wised up," Taylor guessed.

Ayoka nodded. "Sounds that way. Does that ring behind your house still work?"

Taylor nodded. She turned to Jill and William. The first order of business was to get some distance between her and her Topsider friends. "You two stay put. Give us about five minutes and then—"

Before Taylor could finish, Ayoka shoved her to the ground and threw out her left arm. A flash of purple light exploded against her shield spell.

Jill helped Taylor up. They both gasped at the trio stalking toward them.

The tallest was a woman. Well, a female anyway. Between her clawed hands, pointed ears, and fangs, it was obvious the eight-foot tall creature was not human. Her size 5XL yoga pants and her bright yellow "World's Best Mom" tee shirt did nothing to put Taylor at ease.

Whatever she was, she stood slightly in back of the others: a skinny older man dressed in black with a ball of fire in his hand and a shorter, broad-shouldered guy that Taylor had seen before. His name was Mr. Hook. Most recently, he had been hanging around with Mara Hellebore when she paid Taylor a visit two Halloweens ago. Then, he'd been dressed in jeans and a tee shirt. Now, he sported black and gray camo and a black beret.

It was he who spoke. "Are these miscreants bothering you, Miss Hellebore?"

Jill started to mutter a spell. Ayoka swung her club to Taylor's right. William took up a position to her left. He also whispered something. To Taylor's magical senses, his staff radiated subtle energy.

"*Leave us alone*," Taylor said, firmly but calmly.

The world's best mom took a step backwards.

Fire-guy gave Mr. Hook a concerned glance. Mr. Hook nodded reassuringly.

The fire-guy spoke up. "That won't be possible, I'm afraid."

"*Try harder.*"

All three came to a halt fifteen feet in front of Taylor. Mr. Hook raised a hand to steady his flunkies.

"Dustu?" he said.

Fire-guy smiled. He whipped his ball of fire toward William. William shrieked and dodged it, hitting the ground. At the same time, Jill extended her hand and hissed, "*Sharba pesharba!*"

The fireball flashed and then sputtered out five feet short of its target.

At the same time, Ayoka charged toward Mr. Hook. He leaped into the air, and his body contracted. His arms sprouted dusky gray feathers, and he took to the sky in the form of an owl.

Ayoka changed direction, but it wasn't fast enough. The world's greatest mom snagged her with an enormous outstretched arm.

"Let her go!" William snarled. He had regained his feet and was stalking toward the giantess. His staff now crackled with magical energy.

She laughed at him and tossed Ayoka aside like a rag doll.

Dustu the fire-guy summoned another fireball. He lobbed it at Jill at the same time Taylor blasted him. He fell backward, stunned, while his fireball careened toward Jill. But she had kept up her incantation. She deflected the attack, slamming the fireball into the ground.

A spot in the grass smoked, but only for a second.

In that time, the giantess slammed into Jill. She groaned as she sprawled on her back.

"Best you come with us, dearie," she told Taylor. Her voice was deeper and harsher than it had any right to be. "We'll take you someplace safe."

"*I don't want your stinking help!*" Taylor blurted. "*When are you going to get it through those thick, misshapen heads of yours that I'm not on your side!*"

The ogress shook her head and then reached out for Taylor. Just as quickly, she recoiled, yelping in pain. An arrow had sprouted from her arm above the elbow. She staggered backwards.

Tsisgwa appeared out of nowhere, standing atop the nearest picnic table. He had another arrow nocked in his bow and two more at the ready in his draw arm.

Three more nunnehi warriors became visible behind him.

Mr. Hook took a step toward them and growled, "Miss Hellebore is with us!"

"That's not what I heard," Tsisgwa said.

Dustu growled and flung a fireball at Tsisgwa.

Ayoka's cousin leaped from the table, firing in mid-air and nocking his next arrow before he hit the ground. Three more arrows sped toward Dustu from Tsisgwa's men.

The fire-guy threw up a shield spell; the arrows vanished as they made contact.

Just then, a dusky shape plowed into one of the other nunnehi. He wailed in pain as Mr. Hook dive-bombed him, resuming his normal shape in the process. He slammed this warrior into the one next to him and then caught the third one's flaming war club as it whipped toward his head.

Mr. Hook snarled as the flames licked his hand, but he yanked the weapon away and flung it into the trees. He came up blasting Tsisgwa from behind. Ayoka's cousin had spun around to face him, but his shield wasn't fast enough. He fell limp to the ground.

Dustu threw out his hands. A ring of fire appeared, encircling the nunnehi.

Mr. Hook strode toward Taylor, grinning. "I didn't realize you lived in such a rough neighborhood. Shall I remove these... annoyances?"

"That's not going to happen," Jill said. She staggered forward, her left hand extended. A few feet away, Ayoka squared off against the giantess.

Mr. Hook rolled his eyes. "Give me a break," he said. "You think I'm gonna turn and run because of some Jack kid?"

Taylor stepped forward. "*I asked you nicely to leave us alone,*" she said.

Mr. Hook gestured. A distortion erupted from the ground, a crease in the fabric of the universe ten feet tall and razor-thin. He gestured again, and it drifted toward Taylor and her friends.

She took a step back. She'd seen this trick before from Mara. The distortion worked like a ring portal. If it got too close, she'd be sucked in—and there was no telling where she'd end up.

"As soon as I throw away the trash, we'll escort you home, Miss Hellebore."

Taylor gasped. The portal wasn't for her, she realized. It was for Jill and William.

"Guys, you'd better get out of here," she whispered.

Then everything happened at once.

One of the nunnehi uttered a sharp command and dispelled their fiery prison.

Ayoka hammered the giantess with her club.

Jill let loose the same wind spell she'd used the other night, slamming Dustu to the ground.

William charged toward Mr. Hook and shouted "*Bazagra!*" A pulse of magical energy jetted from the tip of his staff, but Taylor could sense it didn't have the kind of kick William was hoping for.

Mr. Hook knew it, too. He didn't bother to conjure a shield. Instead, he directed his portal toward William. It picked up speed.

Taylor screamed, "No!" and dove toward William to push him out of the portal's path.

Suddenly she felt her entire body shriveling away to nothing. She whipped through a kaleidoscope of hills and forests, deep caves and bare, sun-bleached rocks.

It was completely disorienting—even worse than her first-ever trip through the rings when she was thirteen.

She could barely catch her breath. She was fairly sure she was screaming.

No, that wasn't her. It was William—she was still holding on to the collar of his jacket.

*Oh, crud!* she thought.

"Hang on!" she yelled, but she wasn't sure William could hear her over his shrieks of terror, to say nothing of the hurricane winds whipping around them.

She looked for a place to land. Anywhere would do, but she had to find it soon.

She focused on a riverbank in the distance. If she could just concentrate...

The ground came up faster than Taylor expected. Now, she did scream—and accidentally let go of William's collar. He hollered like a baby as they descended through the trees.

Taylor hit the ground with a thud.

Everything went dark.

## Chapter 8

# Jill Gets to Work

Jill's heart jumped into her throat when William and Taylor vanished. She rounded on the guy in the black and gray camouflage. It suddenly struck her that she had seen him before. The last time was on the back lawn of a burning mansion deep in the Louisiana bayou.

He worked for Mara Hellebore, and that told her everything she needed to know. "What did you do with my brother?" she yelled. She trained her mirror at him like it was a weapon.

He furrowed his brow. His eyes darted left and right.

Jill began to chant a binding spell, but in an instant her target was an owl again and jetting into the sky.

Tsisgwa's arrow missed him by an inch. When Jill turned around, she saw the huge woman monster had barreled into the nunnehi, knocking him against the picnic table.

"Time to go!" the fire-guy called. He held a ball of crackling flame in each hand. He launched them both at Tsisgwa's men, who dived for cover. One of them got off an arrow before he hit the grass. It pierced the fire-guy's shoulder, and his knees buckled beneath him.

The woman bellowed and plowed through the dazed and wounded warriors like bowling pins. Having knocked them to the ground, she kept on running until she vanished into the trees.

Jill turned on the fire-guy. He moaned, barely conscious. There was a stray arrow on the ground. She picked it up and used it to trace a circle in the grass, enclosing the one remaining attacker. He was slowly coming to when she finished her circuit around him. She pulled a long, iron nail from her purse and jammed it into the perimeter of the circle with her thumb.

The fire-guy shook himself awake.

Jill had no time to lose. She took three more nails from her purse and hurried around the circle, planting the others so they marked the four cardinal directions.

Fire-guy finally noticed she was there. He muttered, "Wait, wait—"

Jill touched her finger to the last nail and hissed, "*Eulamo!*" Then she grinned. She'd cast the circle in time.

Fire-guy slumped, defeated, as Tsisgwa, his men, and Ayoka converged on Jill. she stood up straight.

A fog began to roll in. She'd seen that before, too. Jill figured the fight was bound to have attracted attention. She guessed nunnehi summoned the fog to keep the publicity to a minimum.

Jill turned her attention back to fire-guy. "Where's my brother?" she demanded. "And Taylor. What did you do with them?"

Fire-guy still looked dazed, but he twisted his mouth into a derisive sneer. "It was Hook's portal, not mine. How should I know?"

He tried to back away on all fours, but came up short at the boundary of Jill's circle of power.

"You think your puny magic can hold me for long?"

"It seems to be working so far," Jill said. She planted her hands on her hips. "If you want, I can reverse the spell and you can take your chances with these guys."

Tsisgwa pulled his war club from the strap on his belt and said, "That would be fine with me, Miss Matthews."

Fire-guy sighed and slumped his shoulders. He knew he was beaten.

"She asked you a question," Tsisgwa said. "Where did Hook send the other two?"

"I have no idea," he said. "Nobody knows what Hook's going to do. He just...improvises."

"Looks like he's improvised his way to freedom," Tsisgwa continued. "He didn't seem very interested in helping you and the ogress get away."

"Yeah, well..."

"You don't have any idea where he's sent them?" Ayoka said. "You swear it?"

"By my own true name," fire-guy said. Then he grinned and turned toward Tsisgwa. "But even if I did know, I'd never tell the likes of *you*."

"He's lying," Jill said. "He knows something."

"No, he doesn't," Ayoka said, and cursed in Cherokee.

Jill hung her head. Now it was her turn to feel defeated. "Right. You guys can't lie."

"Not without effort," Tsisgwa said. "And never with our true names at stake."

"Looks like you got nothing," fire-guy said.

"We've got you," Tsisgwa said. He tapped his war club against his palm. "You may not know where Hook sent the others, but I'll bet there are plenty of things you do know."

Fire-guy's face fell.

"But what about William and Taylor?" Jill said.

Tsisgwa addressed the tallest of his men. "Homatah, you and the others take charge of the prisoner." Homatah bowed curtly. Tsisgwa pulled a Seeing Stone from a pouch on his belt. He turned toward Jill. In a softer, more compassionate voice he said, "I'll request Ichisi send out search parties."

"You'll find them?"

"Of course they will," Ayoka said.

"We'll try." Tsisgwa bit his lip. "A portal like that is a tricky piece of magic—and Hook is more powerful than most."

Jill felt herself beginning to shake. "You're saying they could be anywhere."

"We'll find them," Tsisgwa said.

"Tsisgwa Imathla?" Homatah said. He and the others had taken up positions around Jill's circle, war clubs at the ready.

"What? Oh, yes." He turned to Jill. "If you'd be so kind..."

Jill returned to the circle and pulled up a nail. The magic popped like a soap bubble, and Tsisgwa's men rushed in. They grabbed fire-guy, bound his hands behind his back, and dragged him away.

"We should go, too," Tsisgwa told Ayoka. "We've been too long on human earth as it is."

"You're just leaving?" Jill's face flushed.

"They have to," Ayoka said. "Like Tsisgwa said, they have to arrange search parties. And they have a fire carrier to deal with."

As if on cue, the nunnehi and their captive blinked away.

"I want to go, too," Jill said.

"That wouldn't be smart," Ayoka said. "Our world is too dangerous for you."

"Don't you think I know that?" Jill said. She was shaking again. Memories of her time in the Wonder two years ago spun around in her head. It had been almost too much to bear. But her brother...

"That's where William is," she said. "He's never been in the Wonder before. He could be hurt. He could be trapped."

"They'll find him," Ayoka said.

"And I'm going to help."

"I told you: I don't think you ought to travel to the Wonder."

"Then I'll do the next best thing." Jill stormed off.

Jill could tell Ayoka was following her, but she couldn't think of a reason to tell her not to. She just wasn't sure what her mom would think when she got home.


"What do you mean, 'gone'?" Mrs. Matthews said through clenched teeth. Her tone was accusatory. She stood with her hands on her hips while Jill and Ayoka stood at the front door. They could have easily gone past her, but it wouldn't have been wise. Her face was a mixture of fear and anger. Even suppressing her Second Sight, Jill could tell her mom was about to lose it.

Mr. Matthews stood by stoically, but there was no mistaking the look of distress on his own face.

"I don't know anything more than I've told you," Jill said. She had explained about the park, but in a few words. Sparing her mom the gory details seemed the way to go. She tried to keep her voice calm even though she was terrified, too. One second William was there in the park, and then he was gone. He could be anywhere. He could be hurt. "I'm going to the basement to try to look for him."

"And she—?" She glared at Ayoka.

"Ayoka's a friend. She wants to help."

"I have never liked this...this...foolishness!"

"I know."

"It was bad enough when you disappeared. Now William, too?"

"I came back, Mom. So will he."

"You don't know that!" Mrs. Matthews yelled. Tears rolled down her cheeks. "Don't you dare promise me that! Do you hear me?"

Jill sniffled and wiped tears from her own cheeks, but she stood her ground. She had to keep calm. No, she didn't know that William would come back. But she couldn't let herself think about that, not right now. She had work to do.

"Mrs. Matthews," Ayoka said. "My cousin can be very determined. He'll find them."

Jill's mom just stared at Ayoka and seethed.

"Mom, let me go to the basement. Let me try to find William, okay?"

Her mom fell into Mr. Matthews's arms and sobbed.

Jill backed away with Ayoka close behind.

Even though Maymay went back to New Orleans in July, Jill and William had convinced their dad to let them keep their workroom set up in the basement. All Jill had to do was scoot some stray boxes of Christmas decorations to the corner and she was ready to get started.

"What can I do?" Ayoka said as she reached the bottom of the stairs.

Jill pulled a wooden bowl from the workbench along the side wall. "The laundry room is back there," she said, indicating a door next to the stairs going up. "There's a sink. Fill this with water. I'll be right back."

She fished through an old cigar box and grabbed a lump of beeswax about the size of a grape. She bounded up the stairs, then up to the second floor, to William's bedroom, blocking out the sound of her mom yelling at her dad in the living room.. She needed something to build a tracking spell. Something that could form a strong link to her brother—wherever he was.

She rummaged through his dresser. She picked some tight coils of hair from his comb and pushed them into the wax.

"Please, God, let this work," she whispered.

Back in the basement, she took her scrying bowl from Ayoka and set in on the tile floor. Then she grabbed a grease pencil from the workbench and traced a large, nearly perfect circle to sit in.

She kneaded the wax until it was soft, pacing as she did. Then she added it to another good-sized hunk. She flipped through her Maymay's notebook. She thought she knew what to do, but she had to get it right.

"What are you doing?" Ayoka asked.

"Magic." Jill kept working the wax as she read, flattening it out in her hands, then smashing it back into a ball.

Ayoka arched an eyebrow. "Not any magic I know."

"Well, it's what *I* know." She left the workbench and sat cross-legged inside her circle, the scrying bowl in front of her. "The part is the whole."

Ayoka gave her a quizzical look.

"Look, my grandmother says things that used to be connected are always together on a deeper level. William—" she sucked in a breath when she thought about him. "William says scientists call it quantum...something. I don't remember. Anyway, I found some of William's hairs in his room."

"Oh!" Ayoka said, suddenly understanding. "I do know this! You can use hairs or blood or some other relic to target a spell."

"Exactly," Jill said. By this time she had shaped the beeswax into a crude humanoid figure. She clenched her teeth. She'd almost forgotten something. "There's a wooden stylus on the table over there."

Ayoka handed it to her and stepped back out of the circle.

Jill took a breath and willed the circle to close.

She wrote William's name down the side of the effigy she had made, all the while forming a mental image of her brother. It had to be perfect—or as close to perfect as she could manage.

Inside the circle, she was shielded from any magical turbulence. As she called up her own magic, the circle acted like an amplifier, shifting and redirecting the energies she controlled.

She set the effigy beside the scrying bowl. She imagined William sitting across from her in the circle, practicing Maymay's energy-flow exercises with her. In through the left hand, out through the right.

Ayoka stepped back.

Jill closed her eyes for several long, shallow breaths.

When she opened them again, she gazed into the bowl.

The water was still and clear...and empty.

She bore into it with her eyes.

It was almost impossible to concentrate. The yelling continued upstairs. She couldn't make out the words, but she knew what it was about.

Magic was threatening her family again, and her mom felt helpless to stop it.

*Where are you, William?* Jill thought.

She wiped tears from her eyes. The water in the bowl wasn't revealing its secrets.

*Just send me some kind of sign, okay?*

"Jill?" Ayoka whispered.

"Nothing yet," Jill said. "Maybe...just a little longer."

*Come on, bro*, she thought. *Where are you?*

## Chapter 9

# William Meets the Welcome Wagon

William remembered getting sucked into the owl-man's vortex. He remembered screaming like a banshee as he and Taylor careened through space and a kaleidoscope of discordant images flashed in front of him. (He hoped Taylor hadn't noticed the screaming part. Hopefully she was too busy fearing for her own life.)

The next thing he knew, Taylor had let go of him, and he was rolling to a stop on a wet, cold patch of ground.

That was probably when he threw up.

His heart pounded. Laying on his back, he bent his knees and forced himself to take slow, deep breaths from his diaphragm or else he'd hyperventilate. In through the nose, out through the mouth.

The air had a weird, spicy aroma.

He opened his eyes and looked around. His staff was a few yards away. He could get it when he worked up the nerve to try walking. The sky had a weird almost greenish tint, like he was looking through colored sunglasses.

He ached all over. It had been a rough landing. There were grass stains on the knees of his pants and the elbows of his jacket. His left shoulder throbbed. It didn't feel dislocated, but it hurt—bad! He took another deep breath and whispered an incantation against pain: "*Argidam, margidam, sturgidam.*"

That helped a little. He repeated the chant while he took stock of his surroundings. He was in a forest. That was about it: there were no landmarks, no people, no majestic mountains in the distance. Just him, his bag, his staff, and his throbbing shoulder.

When he was mostly sure he wouldn't pass out, he sat up. With a little effort, he scooted backward so he could rest against the trunk of a tree.

It finally registered that there was no sign of Taylor. He got out his phone, but he didn't have any bars.

"Okay," he told himself, "I'm alone in the wilderness. I can't do anything about the monsters attacking my sister, so I'm gonna just hope Ayoka and her buddies can handle it."

He tried to stretch—and wished he hadn't. His shoulder really ached.

"Only have minor injuries," he continued. "That's good. But I've lost Taylor. That's bad. Very bad."

He called Taylor's name. There was no answer.

Maybe if he looked around with his Second Sight.

He took another slow breath. He shut his eyes, counted to three, and then opened them again, allowing his Second Sight to open with them.

Shadows uncoiled across the ground in ways that didn't entirely correspond to the trees that surrounded him. And the trees themselves were different: they twisted upward into the turquoise sky at odd, impossible angles that made William dizzy. Everywhere he looked, there were faintly glowing bits of...something. Like the specks of light you see when you shut your eyes tight and then open them.

It was disorienting, unsettling—like the entire universe was somehow wrong.

William started to feel woozy. Even though he was still sitting safely on the grass, the blood rushed from his head and made him giddy.

"Whoa!" he sighed. If he hadn't emptied his stomach shortly after impact, he'd have probably thrown up again. His mind started to wander.

He shut his eyes hard and shook his head to shut down the flood of lights and colors and textures.

"Okay," he said. "I don't know what that means, but it looks like no Second Sight for a while."

He pulled his gym bag onto his lap. With the right ingredients, he could whip up a tracking spell, but without a relic from Taylor—a strand of her hair or a fingernail clipping—there was no point trying. But he had to do something. Taylor might be hurt. Jill might still be in danger. Sitting beneath his tree, he rummaged through the bag. It was hard to concentrate on anything besides his aching shoulder. The dizziness and confusion from opening his Second Sight didn't help any.

Someone approached him from behind. He heard footsteps, and twisted his body around to see. Grimacing through the pain in his shoulder, he saw girl about his age. She knelt beside him, a look of concern on her face. She asked, "Are you hurt?"

He nodded. The next thing he knew, he was lumbering through the woods, leaning on the girl's shoulder. His legs didn't collapse, but they were leaden and uncooperative on the rough ground. He stumbled over exposed tree roots as he ducked under branches or knocked away cobwebs that seemed to jump out to ambush him.

It was frustrating work. Disorienting. It was hard to stay focused on anything but the path.

At last he stumbled into a clearing and the girl eased him to the ground.

"You poor thing!" she said.

William lay on the ground, using his gym bag for a pillow, as the girl built a small fire.

He winced as he tried to sit up.

"Let me give you something for that," the girl said.

Wait, who was she again? He shook the cobwebs from his mind and looked at her clearly for the first time.

She was pretty, that's for sure. She wasn't wearing makeup, and she didn't need to. She had perfect brown skin, luscious lips, long dark hair, and deep, brown eyes—bigger and brighter than any William had ever seen. On further thought, she didn't look William's age. She was old enough to be a senior, seventeen or eighteen.

She knelt beside the fire in a pair of cutoffs and a bright green tank top.

William grit his teeth and sat up straight. It didn't do anything for his shoulder, but at least he could get a better look at her.

He realized he was staring, and his face grew warm. Sweat trickled down his forehead as he looked at the ground and said, "I'm all right." He massaged his shoulder.

"I've got something that will help," she said. She took a clay jar from a leather bag that had been lying near the fire. "Take off your jacket."

"It's okay," he said, "I'm good."

She had already scooted around behind him. "You're not one of those macho guys that can't handle a little mothering, are you?"

"It's not that," William said, "it's just—"

"Some ointment will help. Please?" There was something musical about her voice as she whispered in his ear. Her hair smelled like wildflowers and honey.

And his shoulder really did ache.

A bird lit on a branch above him. It shook its body and then flitted away with a harsh creak, like the sound of rusty hinges.

"I'm looking for a girl," he said as he slipped out of his jacket.

"You're in luck," she answered. William could almost hear the smile spreading across her lips.

"What? No. I mean, a particular girl. Her name is—WAAAA!"

Her hand slipped up his shirtsleeve all the way to his shoulder.

She giggled. "That's an interesting name." She kneaded William's shoulder, applying just enough pressure to work in the salve. It tingled as the warmth spread through his sore muscles.

William was getting lightheaded again. For some reason, it felt a lot nicer than the first time.

The fire was warm and inviting, and the pain in his shoulder was starting to subside. He found himself leaning backward.


William stretched awake. He must have dozed off, because now the sun was low in the sky.

He was resting his head in the girl's lap, and she was caressing his forehead.

He bolted upright.

"What's the matter?" she said.

"Nothing." His heart pounded. Who was this girl? What was she up to? Why was being so...forward? "Look, thanks for fixing my shoulder and all, but—"

"What?"

"I mean, I don't even know your name!"

"Imaiyah," she said, smiling.

"William."

She came around to his side, walking on her knees. She smiled and said, "Pleased to meet you, William." She extended her hand. He took it automatically. It was warm and soft.

"Do you feel better?"

Surprisingly, he felt great. No pain at all. He thought about the ointment she had rubbed on his shoulder. "Yes, actually. Thanks. What's in that stuff you put on me?"

"A little of this, a little of that. Are you hungry?"

He hadn't thought about it, but his stomach rumbled at the suggestion. Then he remembered where he was. Or where he was pretty sure he was, anyway. Any food she offered him was off limits.

And he still needed to find Taylor and get home. How long had he dozed off? The nunnehi were bound to have taken care of owl-man and his buddies. He'd give anything for a text from Jill that she was okay.

"No thanks," he said. "I need to get back to Macon," he said. "Is that far from here?"

"I've never heard of it," she said.

He must have teleported (or whatever you called it) farther than he thought. "Okay.... Then...where are we?"

"The Bubbling River is not too far that way," Imaiyah gestured over her right shoulder. "We're a few miles upstream of the Forks."

*Ah, that clears everything up,* William thought.

"So that would be...Alabama?"

Imaiyah giggled. "I've never heard of that, either."

"Don't worry about it. I just need to get home."

"Well, you can't travel at night," she said. The sun had ducked below the trees. He realized Imaiyah hadn't let go of his hand. Now William's heart was really pounding. It was a miracle she didn't hear it herself.

"Is she your girlfriend?"

"Who?"

"The girl you're looking for, silly!"

"No. Nothing like that, just...uh..."

"Hmm," she said, like the answer pleased her. She sniffed the hairs on the back of his neck. It was very distracting. And when did his hands get so sweaty?

William had never had a pretty girl pay him this much attention before—or any girl, for that matter. But somebody like this? Dang!

It was kind of nice, but scary, too. He was shaking with nerves. And there was still a corner of his brain where he could hear his dad hammering into him how a gentleman was supposed to behave....

"Who? Oh. No, Taylor's...uh..." He wasn't sure, actually. Definitely not his girlfriend. Not that that would be a bad thing...

Imaiyah looked him in the eyes. "Then what about Jill or Ayoka?"

"How do you know about them?"

"You talk in your sleep."

"Jill's my sister. Ayoka..." Okay, technically Ayoka was just a friend of Taylor's that he met once almost a year ago. And even though she had kissed him on the cheek, he didn't know what she meant by it. They hadn't seen each other since, so probably nothing. "Ayoka's just a friend. Sort of."

She stretched toward her leather bag and brought it to her side.

"Trail mix?"

"I'd rather not." He edged away.

"Don't be shy," Imaiyah said as she handed him a paper sack. "I've got plenty to share." William had never seen eyes so deep and big and brown. Looking into them, he felt like he was being drawn into another world.

"You really don't have to...."

"It's my pleasure," Imaiyah said. Then, before William knew what was happening, she leaned forward and kissed him.

The warmth of her lips made William's whole body tingle. If he were a cartoon character, two or three bluebirds would be circling over his head, and his heart would be pounding so hard you could see it throbbing under his shirt.

She brushed her hand across his chest, and never broke eye contact with him.

Weren't you supposed to close your eyes when you kissed?

He figured it didn't matter. Imaiyah obviously knew what she was doing, and she was gorgeous. Kissing her was amazing. It was breathtaking. It was...

It was wrong.

He turned his head away and said, "Wait."

"What?" Imaiyah whispered. Boy, was she pretty!

"This isn't..." He scooted backward, away from Imaiyah's embrace. "I'm sorry. It's just..."

"What's the matter?" Imaiyah said.

William got to his feet, and so did Imaiyah. She was almost as tall as he was.

"I-I don't think this is a good idea," William said. He was suddenly cold in just his tee shirt.

Imaiyah pouted. "You don't like me."

"That's not the point," William said. "It's just—"

He stopped in mid-sentence when he noticed her hooves.

Below her knees, Imaiyah's legs were covered with fine, tawny fur and ended in cloven hooves like a deer's.

William's jaw dropped. He jerked his eyes upward to her face as it contorted in anger, like he had walked in on her getting dressed or something. In the second it took William's brain to process what he was seeing, Imaiyah sprung into the air and planted one of those hooves in the middle of his chest with a flying kick.

He fell on his back, breathless, and raised his arms defensively as she began to stomp at his head.


Taylor couldn't see how things could get any worse. She was lost in the Wonder, and William was nowhere in sight.

She was in a thick pine forest. It seemed warmer than it had been in Macon. Gnats buzzed around her head. Did that mean she'd come south? She'd have to find a faery ring to get home. Hopefully, that wouldn't be too hard.

But first things first. William was out there somewhere, too. Taylor had held onto him as long as she could on their wild trip through the owl-man's portal, but her grip hadn't been strong enough.

It would be great if he had ended up Topside, but Taylor wasn't going to bet on that. She had to assume he was alone in the Wonder, which meant he was either already in mortal danger or would be soon enough.

At least she wasn't injured. She was sore. A little dizzy maybe, but that would pass. She wasn't going to die before she could try to fix things.

She called William's name once, twice. Nobody answered.

"Should have known it wouldn't be that easy," she grumped.

She wasn't in any immediate danger. But William? Taylor had to find him—and fast.

"Okay, Danny," she said to herself. "Let me show you how it's done."

She settled on the ground with her back against a tree. Danny had been trying to teach her to fare forth for over a year. It was now or never.

She took several long, slow breaths, clearing her mind and focusing on her true name. She allowed her magical senses to unfurl, to reach into the woods, searching for signs of life.

There were some rabbits holed up in a burrow a few yards to her right. A couple of lizards in a nearby tree. Nothing that would make a good scout.

Ah! A blackbird on the wing. Well, by species it was a blackbird. It was a female, so it was actually more of a dark gray bird with a reddish-brown head. Taylor gave it her full attention, shadowing it in her mind's eye and calling upon her true name.

*I am Neunhirri*, she thought. *I am Laughter in Winter*.

She let herself descend into the bird's consciousness—but slowly, gingerly. Danny said she always tried to rush things, and that would only scare creatures off.

As much as she wished she could get on with it, there was no hurrying the process. If she wanted to see with the bird's eyes and hear with its ears, she would have to take her time.

She hated taking her time.

She intoned her true name over and over, all the while simply taking note of the bird's movements: the flutter of its wings, the way it darted its head around, looking for predators.

It took forever, but Taylor finally decided it was time to push further. She had managed to ride an animal a couple of times before, but only for a second or two. Now she'd need it a lot longer.

*Slowly*, she told herself. *Slowly…*

And then, there was just the blackbird. Taylor could see in nearly every direction. Her peripheral vision was incredible—and she realized it was because she had eyes on the sides of her head. It made her dizzy, but she buttoned down her feelings. She had to keep going slow if she was going to find William.

At first, she let the creature continue its flight. She had no idea where to start looking for William, anyway, and she didn't want to lose her connection by going too fast.

For at least an hour, she soared above the trees in the blackbird's body. Faring forth had never been this easy for her. The fact that it was made her nervous, though. How deep in the Wonder was she? And what did that mean about her chances of getting home?

There was no sign of William, but a beetle inching along a branch suddenly captured her attention. The bird dived and snapped it up in a heartbeat.

*Nasty!* Taylor thought, but she kept her composure. Even blackbirds deserved a snack.

Then she saw him.

At least, she thought it was him. Her ride still had beetles on its mind and veered away before Taylor could get a good look.

*Okay, let's do this*, she thought. With an exertion of will, she slid even deeper into the bird's consciousness, edging out the bird's will and replacing it temporarily with her own.

She landed on a branch above William's head. If any other birds were paying attention, they'd probably think she'd flunked her flying lessons, but she hit her target and didn't fall off, so there was that.

He was sitting underneath a tree, a lot like she was. And he was sitting with a girl—a knockout in a green tank top and a pair of Daisy Dukes. She had her feet tucked under her legs, and she leaned in like she was sharing a secret with William.

*Uh... What?*

Taylor couldn't imagine how this could be good news. But she kept it together. It was now or never.

William looked up at her—or at the blackbird, rather.

She didn't dare stick around. She wouldn't be able to fare forth for too much longer, and she had to figure out the quickest way to get back to William in her own body.

*Hang in there!* she cried. *And please don't do anything stupid!* But it came out as a harsh creaking sound.

She flitted off. High in the sky, she took her bearings and found her way to where she was sitting under a tree, several miles away from William and the girl. She tried to pay attention to every landmark along the way: the fire ant colony she'd have to avoid, the tree stump where she'd need to turn a hard left, the deer path that led straight to William's location.

Then she found herself, sitting under a tree with her eyes closed. Looking at herself like that was about the wrongest thing she'd ever experienced. She shivered, and the blackbird slipped away from her.

Taylor opened her eyes.

She knew where to go, but it would take a while to get there. The going was rough through untamed woods. Plus, faring forth had worn her out. She pressed on, though, woozy and slightly disoriented, as fast as she could. The sun had almost set when she nearly tripped over a three-foot long staff with geometric patterns at each end.

*Why doesn't William have his staff?*

*Crap!*

She looked around. His bag was there, too. This was the point where Aragorn would examine the spot and announce, "No signs of a struggle." But Rangers of the North were a little thin on the ground, and Taylor wouldn't know a sign of a struggle if one tap-danced across her nose.

William was close, though. She picked up his staff and gym bag and looked for the deer path she had seen earlier.

Taylor trudged forward, opening all her senses.

She sniffed the air. Wildflowers? Honey?

She heard voices and picked up her pace. It was definitely William. He was saying, "I-I just don't think this is a good idea."

A girl's voice said, "You don't like me."

"That's not the point," William said. "It's just—"

When William stopped in mid-sentence, Taylor got nervous.

When she heard his startled grunt a half-second later, she picked up her pace.

The path opened into a small campfire-lit clearing.

William was still there, and so was the girl—and he was lying on top of her with her wrists pinned over her head.

"*WILLIAM MATTHEWS!*" Taylor shrieked.

"Taylor! Thank God!" he shouted.

Only then did Taylor notice the girl didn't have feet: her legs ended in hooves. Taylor's mouth fell open.

"Hey, a little help here?" William called.

Other than the hooves, the girl was...well, she wouldn't have looked out of place draped over a Porsche in a car magazine. "Uh...William?"

The girl pulled her right hand free and clawed at William's eyes. When he flinched away, she pushed him away and sprung to her feet. He flailed his hands to grasp hers, but she was too fast. As she bounded into the woods, her body shimmered and she fell forward, landing on all fours as she took the shape of a white-tailed deer.

Just that quickly, she was gone.

Taylor rounded on William. She tossed him his bag.

"Do you think you may have forgotten something?" she said.

"I must have—"

"*Like maybe your freaking MIND?*"

## Chapter 10

# A Night in the Wonder

"*Are you nuts?*" Taylor paced back and forth, shooting William icy daggers with her eyes.

"Taylor, I—"

"*Have you gone completely insane?*"

"Let me explain—"

"*I mean, seriously!*" Wave after wave of presence flowed off of her like water over Niagara Falls. Somehow, William held up under the pressure. He knew he was in trouble. What was he thinking, anyway? It wasn't like him to...well...

He tried to come up with a defense that didn't sound completely lame while Taylor kept talking. "*You fall into the Wonder and just start making out with the first girl you meet?*"

"It wasn't like that!" he yelled. His ears were warm even though the temperature had been dropping steadily ever since Taylor showed up. His heart raced. He felt stupid enough as it was. Why did Taylor have to keep piling it on? "She tried to kill me, you know!"

"Yeah, I guess you two were locked in mortal combat by the fire earlier."

William's heart beat even faster, and he suddenly felt even more stupid. "Wait, you know about that?"

"A little bird told me."

William's neck tightened with stress. This was a disaster, and it was only getting worse. "Look, I can explain. I didn't ask her to kiss me—"

"*SHE KISSED YOU?*"

William's whole face warmed. *Stupid, stupid, stupid.* He wished he could hit "rewind" on the last couple hours, undo everything he'd done since he ran into Imaiyah. He realized she must have been some kind of monster—a vampire or something who got into his brain and flipped all the wrong switches. If Taylor hadn't shown up, there's no telling what might have happened.

Facing Taylor was the worst part. She must have thought he was just another guy with too much on his mind. Maybe he deserved her tongue-lashing, but it still hurt. "I made a mistake, okay? I was hurt. I wasn't thinking straight. Come to think of it, I think she might have done something—some kind of glamour trick. Look I wish I could take it back, but I can't. And just so you know, she tried to kill me!"

"What?" Taylor narrowed her eyes. For the first time, she seemed to settle down enough to listen.

"You must have missed that part," William said. It sounded more like an accusation than he would have wanted. "Just look." He stretched his hands, showing the angry welts on his forearms where Imaiyah's hooves had dug into him.

"She attacked me," he said. "I've got another one in the middle of my chest, and it hurts. A lot." He pulled at his shirt. There was, indeed, a tear in the fabric and a dirty hoof-shaped smudge. "Can we just agree I was an idiot and work on finding a way home?

Taylor said nothing, but her expression softened. The temperature began to rise again.

William noticed Imaiyah's jar of ointment still laying by the fire. "That's some kind of healing salve," he said. "D-do you think it's safe? I mean, it won't put me under a spell or anything, will it?"

"How should I know?" Taylor said. She stood with her arms folded, but it looked like the storm had passed.

William felt sore all over. The rush of adrenaline at Imaiyah's attack was quickly wearing off. He felt a headache coming on. He stooped down. "Well, I'm going to try it." He pulled off the top of the jar and dipped two fingers into the warm goo. He rubbed some on his chest under his shirt. It felt warm and soothing, but somehow not as energizing as before.

"Come on, Taylor. You know me. You don't seriously think I'd...you know...." He gestured in the direction Imaiyah fled after she'd turned into a deer.

Taylor looked down. "I guess not," she said. Was that a suppressed giggle William heard?

"I mean...maybe if I'd gotten to know her and, you know, she wasn't a homicidal maniac and—What? Why are you laughing?"

Taylor didn't even try to keep a straight face. "William Matthews, are you expecting me to believe you know the first thing about girls?"

"I know enough."

"Okay, first of all: No, you don't," she said. "If you did, you wouldn't melt into a puddle of goo every time a girl showed you any attention."

"Hey, I don't—"

"I saw you at River Crossing after Ayoka kissed you, you know," Taylor said. "It was pretty embarrassing, if you ask me."

"Well, I didn't—"

"And second: By oak, ash, and thorn, William! What were you thinking? The Wonder is no place to be picking up strange girls!"

"Hey, assault victim here." He showed her his forearms again. "A little sympathy?" He applied more ointment—gingerly. His arms were definitely going to bruise.

Taylor looked at the red welts on William's forearms, then up to his eyes. She took a breath and seemed to settle down again. "I'm sorry," she said. She took a step toward him. "You've just got to be careful in the Wonder. Things aren't always what they seem, and neither are the people."

"Yeah, I figured that much out by myself."

"She had hooves, for crying out loud!" Taylor yelled. "How did you miss that?"

William shook his head. "She must have used some kind of glamour. I guess I should have checked her out—"

Taylor coughed pointedly.

"You know what I mean! But I had some trouble with my Second Sight earlier. It freaked me out a little. I was afraid to try it again."

Imaiyah's fire was going down. William backed away. He glanced around for some more dry wood to throw on it. It was pretty dark now, and the air was turning cold—from the sun setting this time, not from Taylor's out-of-control anger. He found his denim jacket and put it back on.

"That makes sense," Taylor said.

"What?"

"It makes sense your Second Sight would be ramped up. I used magic to find you here. The same thing happened to me: way more power than I was used to."

"What do you think is happening?" William asked. He stooped to pick up a dry tree branch. He moved on to another one a few feet away.

"Best I can tell, we're pretty deep in the Wonder," Taylor said. "There's a lot of magic in the air. It's bound to mess with a Topsider."

That did make sense. Mortals and fae alike drew their magic from the Wonder—though it came a lot more naturally to somebody like Taylor. If they were closer to where the magical energy actually came from, accessing it would be that much easier.

"Do you know where we are?" William said.

"No clue." Taylor looked around like she had lost something. "But if there's a portal around—a ring of mushrooms or some old ruins, something like that—I can get us home quick enough."

"I haven't seen anything like that." He came back to the fire with his dry branches. It looked like there were more nearby—maybe enough to keep a small fire going through the night.

Taylor sighed.

William started a little wood stack far enough away they wouldn't catch a spark, but close enough they could reach it when they needed it. By the fire sat the bag of trail mix Imaiyah had offered him. One bite, and he might be stuck in the Wonder forever, or at least have major problems trying to return to the mortal world. It really needed a warning label: "May contain evil."

"If we're in the Wonder," he said, eyeing the bag, "then I guess I shouldn't eat that."

Dread descended over Taylor's face. "Oh no. Oh, William." She raked her hair away from her face. "We've got to get you home. You can't eat faery food. You just can't. There's' no telling what might happen."

"It's okay, I figured as much," William said. He reached for his gym bag. "I've got some energy bars. Want one?"

"Save them for yourself." She snatched up Imaiyah's trail mix. "I'll try this."

They sat close to the fire as they each ate a barely satisfying supper. They didn't speak for the longest time.

William still felt like an idiot for the way he acted with Imaiyah. He feared Taylor was never going to let him live it down. (Because that's the kind of awesome friend she was.)

He searched his heart for any kind of connection with Jill. If she were still in trouble, he'd know, right?

And he feared what tomorrow might bring. They were stuck in the Wonder with no obvious way out. His energy bars wouldn't last forever—they'd probably be gone by tomorrow night. He and Taylor had to find their way home, with no one to help them, and soon.

William was mad at himself. He let himself get sucked into that vortex. He let himself get bamboozled by a deer woman. He'd let Taylor down.

Did Jill mess up this bad on her trip to the Wonder?

Thinking about his sister only made it worse. He was worried about her. What had happened back in the park after he vanished? And what were his parents doing? They must have been freaking out big time.

He was afraid.

He sighed. He knew he needed to be strong. He was *not* going to let Taylor worry about him. But he didn't know if he could hold it together.

Taylor sat down next to him. They both stared at the fire. William put another log on, but it somehow didn't keep the chill from creeping in.

"Taylor," he whispered. "Are we gonna make it?"

She leaned into his shoulder. She was already fast asleep.


Taylor dreamed of a laundromat. She was alone with her grandmother Anya Redmane, the disgraced former Chief Matron of the Summer Court of Arradherry. They were in the back row of washing machines at the coin laundry near Taylor's house.

Sometimes, Taylor dreamed Mrs. Redmane was pale and frumpy like she remembered her that November night last year. Sometimes, she imagined her as she was when she had first met her two years ago: fiery and beautiful in her green gossamer gown.

This time, the dream featured frumpy Mrs. Redmane. But it didn't matter. Whatever her appearance, the scene always played out the same. She was about to tell Taylor which of her loved ones would be the next to die.

Taylor hated this dream.

"Whatever I once was, Selena Hellebore," Mrs. Redmane was saying, "I am now a portent of death." She spread her arms. "It's what I do."

*No,* Taylor thought.

"But whose death? That is an interesting question, isn't it?" She pulled a white sheet from her laundry basket. Only Taylor knew it wasn't a sheet at all. It was a shroud, like they used to wrap dead people in for burial. It was meant for someone she knew, someone she cared about.

At first, the shroud was pure white, but bloodstains began to spread across the fabric like crimson serpents, writhing and growing and melting into one another.

"Y-you're trying to scare me," Taylor said. The room spun. Sinister shadows twisted across the walls, across the floor.

"I'm trying to prepare you," Mrs. Redmane continued, unfazed. "Watching a loved one die is hard, but I'm afraid it's on your horizon. Within the year, I'd say. Two at most."

"I don't want to know!" Taylor shouted.

"Forewarned is forearmed," her grandmother said with a chuckle. "Isn't that what the deathlings say? Let me tell you and you'll be ready—"

"*I don't want to know!*" Taylor screamed herself awake.

William hovered over her. "Taylor, it's okay!"

"*Don't tell me!*"

"Taylor, it's okay! It was just a dream!"

She lurched up, her chest heaving, her breath coming in cold, harsh gulps like she was suffocating.

She threw her arms around William.

"T-Taylor?"

"Don't go," she said.

"I'm not going anywhere."

"Don't go!"

"I'm right here."

Taylor squeezed him tighter. "I couldn't hold on. I let go of you...." She sniffled. "You don't have any food. That...deer tramp could have killed you.... I'd never forgive myself..." But she couldn't keep talking. She'd lose it for sure if she tried. She just hung on as tight as she could. *Not William*, she prayed. *Not now.*

She refused to let go, even when William shifted his weight.

"Uh...Taylor? Needing to breathe here."

She loosened her grasp, though she wasn't quite ready to let go. "Right. Sorry."

"S'okay. It's not your fault. We've just got to...make a plan. Figure things out."

It was still dark, but there was gray in the eastern sky and the slightest hint of pink. It wasn't quite morning, but it wouldn't be long.

Taylor shivered. The fire had gone out.

"What now?" she said. She summoned a ball of faery fire. It had no warmth, but it helped both of them see.

"I don't know. I guess figure out where we are?"

Taylor studied the sky. "Sun's rising over that way." She pointed out the cardinal directions. "So that's east, then north, west, south."

"But which way is home?" William said.

Taylor frowned. They both sat in silence for a minute.

"Okay," William said. "Let's start with something more basic. Breakfast."

Taylor realized her stomach was rumbling.

"Then we need to get moving," William said. "Moving will keep us warm till the sun comes all the way up." He rubbed his arms against the cold.

"Another energy bar?" Taylor said.

"Unless you've got some bacon and eggs in your purse." William smiled. He had a goofy smile. Safe. Unassuming.

Taylor returned the smile in spite of herself. "Just a couple of candy bars," she said. Then she bit her lip as an idea came to her. She'd never tried anything like this before, but this deep in the Wonder, she might risk it. If it had any chance in the world of working...

"You don't suppose there's any way to use magic to whip up some more food, do you?"

William sighed. "I'm not sure. Hang on." He reached for his gym bag and brought out a stack of index cards wrapped with a rubber band. They looked for all the world like...

"Flashcards?" Taylor said.

"Magic is hard, okay?" He rolled the rubber band onto his wrist and flipped through the cards.

"If you say so."

He found the card he wanted. "Here it is. Ectoplasm."

"O-o-okay?"

William squinted as he tried to read his sloppy handwriting by the light of Taylor's fire orb. "Ectoplasm. Maymay defines it as 'transient matter.'"

"Transient? Meaning temporary?"

William nodded. "It responds to magical energies. You can draw it up from the Wonder and shape it however you want. When your friend Danny turns into a horse, I bet the extra mass is ectoplasm."

"Then he turns back into a person, and the extra mass goes away."

"And, in the process, he upholds the law of conservation of matter."

"I'm sure that's a great relief to pookas everywhere," Taylor quipped. It felt good to tease William a little bit. She was still shaky after her nightmare, and some lighthearted banter took the edge off.

"No, I'm serious. There's a whole branch of magic that deals with shaping ectoplasmic forms." He flipped to the next card. "Conjuration."

"Are you saying it's possible to conjure food out of thin air?"

"Maybe," William said, skimming the card. "It would be easier if you had some seed material to get the process started."

"Like an energy bar?"

"Yeah, like an energy bar. If you've got one, you ought to be able to stretch it into two." Then his face fell. "But it won't work on food."

"Why not?"

"It's too complex," he said, gesturing with the card. "It only works on simple substances like water or salt. And even then... Well, like I said: it's not permanent."

Taylor looked into his eyes. "I still say it's worth a try. Your grandma knows her stuff, but she never tried to do magic this deep in the Wonder. And don't take this the wrong way, but she probably doesn't know much about my kind of magic. Give it a chance. It might work."

William shook his head. "I don't know."

"But if Danny can turn ectoplasm into horse flesh…"

"That's different," William protested. "It's…" He flipped through his cards. "It's bound to be…."

"Will you at least let me try?" she snapped.

William looked at Taylor. She could hear his stomach rumble.

"Sure," he said. "What have we got to lose?"

He passed her an energy bar.

*All right*, Taylor said to herself. *Here goes the most ridiculous plan ever.*


"No Second Sight," Taylor said. "I don't need you passing out on me."

"You got it."

William watched as Taylor carefully unwrapped his energy bar without dismissing her fire orb. The bar and both her hands were bathed in blue-white light. She held the bar as she sat cross-legged on the ground. She took a couple of deep breaths and knitted her brow.

He'd never seen anyone concentrate so deeply on an energy bar.

He wanted to ask if it was working, but he didn't dare break her concentration. As much as he put on a brave front for her, he didn't relish the idea of starving to death if they couldn't get home right away.

Then something started to happen. The bar twitched in Taylor's hand. William held his breath.

The bar began to vibrate. The blue-white glow intensified.

Then the bar began to grow before William's eyes. He felt his face stretching into a bewildered grin.

Taylor spread her hands apart slowly, deliberately. Each hand held one end of an elongating hunk of granola, chocolate, and dried cranberries.

And then the halves separated, and she held two identical energy bars.

She offered one to William as she let out a sigh. She looked exhausted.

"Try it," she said. Her icy blue eyes fixed on him like lasers.

William's eyes darted between the two bars. He reached for the one Taylor was offering. She slipped the other one back into its wrapper.

"Well?"

He nibbled one corner. It didn't taste exactly right—too bland, not enough salt. Come to think of it, it didn't taste like much at all. But it was food. It kept its mass as it landed in his stomach—not quite satisfying, but maybe enough.

"Taylor, that's...amazing."

"Well, I'm just like that, I guess." She bumped his shoulder. "So which way do we—?" She suddenly tensed.

"What's the matter?"

"Listen," she whispered.

Then William heard it, too. It was a kind of plaintive yodel echoing through the trees. They were not alone in the woods! He and Taylor kept quiet, listening.

It was an eerie sound. It made William want to just sit and listen. He instinctively reached for the carved amulet of jet in his pocket, a ward against faery trickery—if he could remember to use it! His hand brushed the outside of his pocket. It was still there if he needed it.

The call kept bouncing around the forest. As soon as it stopped, another call as unearthly as the first started up somewhere else.

"Uh...," William said, "what's that?"

"Somebody hollering."

"Somebody friendly?"

"I wouldn't count on it," Taylor said. "But I bet they could tell us where we are, maybe point us the way home."

William stood up. He stared away toward the east. "Imaiyah—that was the girl's name from yesterday—she said there was a river that way."

"That's where the sound is coming from," Taylor said. She got to her feet as well.

"You think we should risk it?"

Taylor brushed grass off her jeans. "Not if you have a better plan."

William sighed. "I wish I did."

*Chapter 11*

# The *Misery*

William and Taylor found the caller on the bank of a river about a mile from where they'd spent the night. In fact, they found him and two dozen of his friends breaking camp and loading their things onto a sixty-foot long poleboat.

William pulled Taylor behind a tree, out of sight, as they watched them work. They looked like a faery United Nations: black, Hispanic, Native American, and white, and lots that William couldn't place. Who has green hair, anyway? There were both human-sized and little folk crew members, all dressed in shabby work clothes. Some had animalistic features that gave William the creeps: pointed ears, tails, or big slit-pupil eyes. Others looked perfectly human, but just as menacing.

The boatmen took orders from a short black man—maybe five feet tall—with a pointed beard and glowing yellow eyes. He swaggered across the deck in tan woolen trousers and an over-sized white cotton shirt opened halfway down his chest. William noticed the funnel-shaped barrel of the blunderbuss he carried at his side.

The boat itself was something from another century. Except for a small cabin at the stern, the wooden deck was exposed and loaded down with crates and bales of cotton covered with tarps.

The caller was a splotchy-skinned fae with pointed ears and a mouth that drooped on one side. He raised his hands to his mouth and let out another mournful wail that echoed up and down the river. It was a haunting sound, one that sent a shudder through William's whole body. He found his jet amulet and brought it out of his pocket. He started stroking it with his thumb. Under his breath, he intoned, "No fairy takes, nor witch hath power to charm."

"You okay?" Taylor whispered.

William nodded, but there was definitely something magical about that holler. It was disorienting. It left him feeling unsettled, like it was breaking down his inhibitions, goading him to express his deepest, darkest emotions. Without his amulet, he wondered what listening too long would do to him.

"Maybe this wasn't a good idea," he said. "Those guys look pretty shady."

Taylor agreed. "It looks like they're leaving. Once they're gone, we'll—"

She stopped mid-sentence when she sensed a presence behind them. William felt it, too. They both turned around at the same time.

William stared into a wall of black fur. His mouth dropped open and his eyes gazed upward, past an enormous barrel chest into a hairy face with beady black eyes, flared nostrils, a wide frown, and a crest across the top of the skull like a gorilla's.

William had dealt with kolowas once before—and that was one time too many. The man-eating ogres didn't seem to have much magic, but they made up for it with brute strength and general nastiness.

Taylor flexed her fingers.

The creature grunted. It sounded like a question.

William remembered to breathe. He looked behind him. He thought he might be able to stun the creature. He knew the spell from Maymay's notebook although he'd never tried it in real life.

He shifted a step to Taylor's right and fell into a defensive stance. He held his staff by one end like it was a sword and rehearsed in his mind the incantation for a simple stunning spell. If he was lucky, he could give the creature one good lick—but then what? They couldn't run toward the boat, and William's stunner would bring the boat hands running toward them anyway. But there was no way past the kolowa without risking it.

A sidewise glance told him Taylor was making the same calculation. The way she cupped her right hand said she had gathered a ball of magic. Without using his Second Sight, William couldn't see the telltale subtle distortion that meant she was ready to blast the creature, but he could guess that was her plan—although she didn't look enthusiastic about it. Her eyes darted in William's direction, looking for a signal.

The creature filled its lungs and bellowed like a bull elephant.

Work at the poleboat halted. Somebody shouted, "Roger, is that you?"

There was no more time for planning; they'd just have to make a run for it. Taylor blasted the kolowa in the gut. It staggered backward, its massive arms flailing, and brought down a young pine tree as it hit the ground.

"Run!" William cried. But Taylor was already heading back up the path they had come.

"Roger!" somebody called again. The boatmen's camp was in chaos as a dozen or more workers charged into the woods after them.

William caught up to Taylor. "Faster!" he shouted. He grabbed her by the arm.

A shot rang out.

Taylor fell headlong into the dirt.

William skidded to a stop. "Taylor, come on!" he cried. He knelt down and tried to get Taylor to her feet. He didn't see any blood, no evidence she had been shot, but she grimaced in pain.

"My leg!" she gasped.

"I-I don't see a wound!"

"It's elf-shot," Taylor said. "And it hurts like—" She sucked in a breath.

"Okay, let's get off the path." William hauled Taylor upright, but her right leg wouldn't cooperate. She said a few choice words as she tried to put her weight on it. William was just going to have to drag her off the path and try to set up some kind of masking spell....

"Hold it right there!" someone called. It was the leader, the black man with the old-fashioned muzzle-loader. He didn't have time to reload, so he held the weapon in his left hand and extended his right hand ready to blast. Two other polemen flanked him, and they didn't look any happier than their leader.

One had a goat's horns, and his eyes had weird rectangular pupils. The rest of his face was a nightmare: a hawkish nose, fangs, and a shaggy salt-and-pepper mane that ringed his face and made him look vaguely like a lion.

The other was a tall Native American, bare-chested despite the chilly morning air. A fierce scar ran from the center of his forehead to a spot beneath his left ear. He held a bronze-bladed machete in his hands.

"Take them to the boat," the leader said. He had an exotic accent William couldn't quite place. French maybe?

The goat-man surged forward. William dragged Taylor backward. If he'd had another second, he could have set her safely on the ground and then tried to fight the creatures off. Before he could do any of that, the goat-man slammed into him, and all three hit the ground hard.

"That's for Roger!" he said.

The kolowa rumbled a low growl that William felt in his bones as much as he heard.

"Gently, Mr. Glut!" the leader warned. "Until we decide what to do with them."

Mr. Glut the goat-man growled, but obeyed. He hauled William to his feet. Meanwhile, the Native American stalked forward and lifted Taylor with one hand by the collar of her jacket. Her kicking and screaming had no effect whatsoever. The goat-man shoved William back down the path while the Native American hoisted Taylor onto his shoulder.

At the riverbank, the rest of the crew gathered around them. The Native American dropped Taylor on the ground. She was still wincing from the pain in her leg. The goat-man kept hold of William, though.

The leader sauntered up to him. He planted his hands on his hips and said, "Perhaps you'd like to explain why you two were bothering my crewman?"

"C-crewman?" William said.

The kolowa growled at the back of the crowd. Its wide mouth curled into a mirthless smile. It held its giant-sized gut like it had eaten something that disagreed with it.

"You got something against ape-men?" Glut snarled.

"No!" William sputtered.

"Good!"

The kolowa grunted and hooted.

"Roger's right," Glut said. "He should have 'em."

The leader frowned. "They'd take too long to butcher," he said. "We're behind schedule as it is."

"That ain't no problem for Roger," the goat-man argued.

"Please, sir," Taylor said. She gritted her teeth, forcing back the pain. She took a deep breath to settle herself. "We meant no harm," she said.

"Is that so?" the leader said.

Taylor nodded. *"We're lost...and Roger surprised us,"* she continued. *"That's all. It was a simple misunderstanding."*

William felt the hairs wriggling on the back of his neck. She was doing something, and William hoped it worked.

"Seems legit," the Native American said.

The goat-man shook his head and glared at the leader. "Don't trust her, Cap'n." He turned up his hooked nose at her. "She looks tricky."

The Native American hauled Taylor up and wrapped a giant arm around her waist, which made her yelp. He cast an inquisitive glance toward the captain.

The rest of the crew started to chatter and elbow each other. William heard somebody say "We ain't seen a good fight in weeks."

*Great*, William thought. *I haven't been in the Wonder twenty-four hours, and I've already been in two fights!*

"She don't look like much of a threat to me," another fae said. He stepped forward in no particular hurry. He was only a little taller than the captain, a man dressed in green with a young freckled face and fiery orange hair. (Thankfully, that was only a metaphor.)

"I don't see as Nat gets a vote," Glut said. "Roger's the one they attacked."

Roger growled again. Then he eyed William and licked his lips, which was even more frightening.

"I'm the patroon of this boat," the captain said. "Mine's the only vote that counts."

"Mr. Jackalberry, you can't possibly—"

"Just give me a minute to think—and take off that gosh-awful face!"

Glut glared at Dennis as his features softened and morphed into something more human. His horns retracted into his forehead and his fangs shortened into ordinary teeth. His eyes took on a human shape, and his hair even shortened until he looked for the most part like an ordinary long-haired, bearded man. Only his pointed ears gave away his true nature.

"That's better," the captain said. "Now, what am I supposed to do with you two?"

The kolowa grinned.

"*Let us go?*" Taylor suggested.

The polemen laughed out loud.

"It doesn't seem right to deprive Mr. Roger of satisfaction," the captain said. "After all, you did blast him."

"It was an accident!" Taylor said. William could tell she was having a hard time concentrating. Her magical whammy wasn't doing anything.

William considered his options, which took about half a second. Glut had taken his staff and his gym bag. Without his tools, there wasn't anything he could do magically. He might be able to fight his way free—but how could he take on two dozen polemen and rescue Taylor in the process?

"If you asked me...," the redheaded fae started.

"Nobody asked you, Bundlestraw!" the goat-man spat.

"Well, I'm afraid you've got me there, Tobias," he continued. "And I'd never question Roger's right to satisfaction in this matter."

"That's better," Glut said, crossing his arms.

"It's just that, it seems we may be overlooking something."

Did William imagine it, or did the redhead just wink at him?

"Go on," the captain said.

"Like I said, Cap'n, far be it from me to cast scurrilous aspersions upon our hirsute comrade." He regarded Roger and smiled.

The goat-man nodded and grumbled agreement. Roger folded his arms across his massive, hairy chest.

"Roger is a paragon of simian fortitude, an ape-man whose laconism is matched only by his pilosity."

The captain knitted his brow, but gestured for the redhead to continue. "Y-yeah?"

"Now, it seems there are two sides to every story, right?" He held his two hands parallel to each other, like he was showing Dennis the size of a fish he'd caught. "And to ascertain whether those sides are coplanar, we must simplify the equation by eliminating the variables."

"Uh...right," the captain said. He tried to look like he was following all this, but to William, it sounded like a bizarre mixture of a geometry lecture and gobbledygook.

"Now, young man"—the redhead turned to William—"may I ask what brings you and your associate to these parts?"

William shook himself alert. "Nothing. I mean...we're lost. That's all."

"We're just trying to get home," Taylor added.

"Well, there you are!" the redhead exulted.

"There we are, what?" Glut said. "What are you talking about, Nat?" He scowled, but he didn't seem as hell-bent on violence as he was a minute ago.

"It's quite simple," Nat said. "It's purely fortuitous that these two wayfarers have been inserted into our side of the equation. And it seems to me they'd be agreeable to a modicum of consideration for their predicament."

"A...modicum?" the captain said.

"A smidge, Mr. Jackalberry," Nat continued. "A trifle. A minim, if you will. As magnanimous as you've always been, to which every member of your crew would attest, I don't see how you could forswear the perspicacity of the borific plastitude adhering to the abundance of our circumscription. Wouldn't you?"

The captain blinked. "But..."

"Exactly!" Nat said. "But...and also if. And if not, then who?" He patted the captain on the back and laughed. The captain joined in, but his expression told William he didn't get the joke.

"Cap'n, are you taking Nat's side?" Mr. Glut said with a scowl.

William wasn't sure what Nat's side was, but it was bound to be preferable to the goat-man's.

"He makes a good point," the captain said.

"Captain!" Tobias said. The captain silenced him by raising his hand.

"If you ask me," Nat said, "it's a stroke of genius. That's what I'd say: Dennis Jackalberry is an absolute genius, d'you hear? And you've got my support, that's for sure."

The captain scratched his head. "Mr. Bundlestraw, what... uh...what was it I agreed to do?"

"And a wise decision it was," Nat said, beaming. "Make no mistake about it. That's why you're the patroon and I'm just the mate."

He strolled over to William. "As it turns out, we're a man short," he said. "Which way are you two headed?"

"We...don't rightly know," William admitted.

"North maybe," Taylor said.

The captain frowned. "Wrong answer. The *Misery* is headed south."

Nat interrupted, "But, of course, the quickest way anywhere is down the River of Night. Anybody could tell you that, am I right?"

"Uh...," William said.

"So it looks like you're in luck. Captain Jackalberry says if you'll carry your weight, we'll take you as far as Osaa's domain. From there, it's just a hop, skip, and a jump to...well, anywhere, really."

"If it's all the same to you," Taylor said, "I think we'd rather..."

"It's a fair offer," The captain said. "Two, maybe three day's work, and we'll drop you off with Osaa."

Nat looked William in the eye. This time, William was sure Nat winked at him.

"We really appreciate it," Taylor said, "but we could never repay you..."

"I've made my decision," The captain said. "Mr. Glut, Mr. Itchu: let's get these two on the boat. If we're going to deliver this cargo on schedule, we've got to make the Forks by nightfall."


Taylor wasn't sure exactly what happened, but it wasn't long until she and William were taken aboard the *Misery*. The splotchy-faced fae whose hollering first drew them to the boat escorted William to the foredeck, where Taylor saw him hand William a pole and give him his first lesson in poleboating.

Taylor's own guard took her to the aft cabin. He set a stool in front of her and gestured for her to sit. She hobbled over and plopped down. Her leg was still sore, but the muscle was finally loosening up.

The place hardly counted as a cabin, Taylor judged. It was more of a rickety shack strewn with makeshift furniture made from wooden crates. In the back, an assortment of copper pans and kettles hung from nails on the wall next to a huge closet or pantry. There stood a pointy-eared little person in a greasy apron and a yellow neckerchief.

"Who are you?" He wore a sour expression. Apart from Nat, it seemed to be standard issue on this boat.

"Your new assistant," Nat said as he came in. He turned to the Native American. "Thanks, Itchu. Now get to your place."

Itchu nodded and left.

Nat was dressed all in green. Forest green trousers. A pale green shirt with a green paisley patch on one elbow. His work boots were green from grass stains. Even his eyes seemed to glow with green fire.

He bowed to Taylor. "I didn't get your name."

"I didn't give it."

Nat smiled. "Your name is safe with me."

Taylor bit her lip.

"What about my friend?"

"Well, aren't we the stickler for the Eldritch Law?" The little person jibed.

"Don't mind Squint," Nat said. "He doesn't like people. Never has." He sat down on a wooden barrel. "But he makes a fantastic Brunswick stew."

"And I don't need an assistant who's never washed a pot in her life."

"You don't have to be that way," Nat said. "It's just for a few days." He turned back to Taylor. "For the time being, you and your friend are members of the crew. It would make things easier if I knew what to call you."

Names could be a touchy subject among the Fair Folk. Someone knowing your name could give them magical leverage they could use against you. But Nat wasn't asking for her true name, just her everyday name. From what she'd been told, sharing it was still a risk, but not a very big one.

"Taylor," she said at last.

Nat smiled. "You'll help Squint here with the cooking, Taylor. You can cook, can't you?"

"Of course," Taylor said. Peanut butter sandwiches counted, right?

Squint scoffed. "She ain't no cook. Just look at her ears. I bet she ain't worked a day in her life."

Taylor's hand went instinctively to her ear.

"Now, Squint!" Nat scolded. "Everyone is equal on the *Misery*. There's no call to calumniate the girl just because she's a neophyte."

Taylor sensed the subtlest wave of magic. It wasn't exactly presence, but it seemed familiar.

Squint started to say something. He'd already raised his hand to jab an accusatory finger, but then he stopped with his mouth open and just stared at Nat.

"Your kindred doesn't matter to me, Taylor," Nat said.

"Well...good," Taylor said, though she still didn't know what her ears had to do with anything.

"If she starts singing, I'm out of here," Squint said, not quite as testily as before. "Tobias is right: she looks tricky."

There was a sigh. It didn't come from either Nat or Squint.

"W-what was that?" Taylor said.

"Do you have something to say, Cora?" Nat said. He looked past Taylor to the wall behind her.

Taylor looked for evidence of glamour, but there was none. The room was just as it appeared: a jumble of crates and home-made furniture, a stack of blankets on a simple cot, a beat-up dressing table with a mirror, an old cigar-box banjo, a kerosene lantern, and a powder horn—no doubt for the captain's blunderbuss. If Cora was invisible in the room, she was as good at it as a nunnehi.

"Nat, our ship's cook is a complete and utter Philistine," a woman's voice said. Taylor still couldn't find the source.

"I'm a kobold!" Squint protested. He was looking at the same spot on the wall. He snapped his fingers, and a blue flame shot up. He held it out like he was holding a match.

The banjo shuddered.

"Absolutely no appreciation for the finer things in life. If the girl wants to sing, let her sing!" It was definitely a woman's voice: a matronly voice with a trace of a Gullah accent.

That was it: the voice was coming from the banjo. Taylor stared wide-eyed as the cook continued his argument.

"And let her glamour us into oblivion?" Squint said.

"Bless your heart," the banjo laughed, "that wouldn't happen to you if you weren't so stupid."

"Don't mind Squint, child," the voice said. "You and me'll make all the music we want come nightfall."

"Uh...thanks," Taylor said.

Squint gave Taylor a sidewise glance. "Tricky," he mumbled. Then he stalked from the room.

Nat watched him leave. He stood up and found a banjo case propped against the wall. "Cora, I'm going to put you away while Taylor and I speak in private."

"Oh, Nat. I hate that box."

"It'll just be a minute. Promise."

He put the banjo in the case. Taylor watched as he gently set it back against the wall.

"Is that banjo...alive?" Taylor said.

Nat shrugged. "It's not as unusual as you might think. Anything made with love can become quickened if people use it long enough."

"But...a banjo?"

"Banjos, harps, swords, end tables. You'd be surprised." He leaned forward and rested his elbows on his knees. "I hope you don't judge the crew of the *Misery* by Squint," he said. "Or Tobias."

"Or Roger?"

"Definitely not Roger!" Nat said. "Most of the crew is good folk. A little rough around the edges, I suppose, but they grow on you."

"With all due respect," Taylor said, "we're not planning to be here long."

"Of course not," Nat said. "You're trying to go home. I aim to help you get there."

That's what worried Taylor. The Fair Folk almost never did anything out of the goodness of their hearts. Nat wanted something, she just didn't know what.

"We didn't ask for your help."

"Now that you mention it, I don't believe you did."

"What I mean is, I can't repay you. Neither can William."

Nat gave her a good, long look. "I know."

"So, why—?"

"May I ask you a question, Taylor?" Nat said. "I think I know the answer, and that's why I want to help you. But if I've made a mistake, I need to know that before we go any further."

"W-what do you want to know?"

"By any chance, is your last name Hellebore?"

## Chapter 12

# Introductions Are Made

Taylor jumped off her stool and backed away. Nat knew who she was—or at least strongly suspected it. But what did that mean? Was he suspicious of her, too. Or worse: would he try to get in Crom Cornstack's good graces by trying to "protect" her. She and William were still in a mess from the last time an unseelie fae tried to do that!

"*What do you want?*" she snarled. Her eyes shot beams of presence in Nat's direction. He shivered a little, but brushed it off.

He threw up his hands. "Don't worry, I don't mean to tell anybody unless you want me to."

"*I don't!*" She eyed the door. To get out, she'd have to muscle past Nat and then fight through a mob of boatmen.

"You look like your mom," Nat said. "Except around the nose. That's definitely Aulberic. That and the hair."

Taylor brushed her hair back from her ear. It took her a second to remember to breathe. "Y-you knew my parents? I mean, my birth parents?"

He nodded and flashed her a smile.

"But...," she looked around the shabby room. "How? What are you doing *here*?"

He shrugged. "Folks up north got a little too curious about me once your folks ran off, if you know what I mean."

Taylor knitted her eyebrows. "You're a sídhe, too?"

Nat laughed out loud. "Oh, I can just see Aulberic's mom's expression if she ever heard that!" He stood and bowed at the waist. "I'm a pisgy, Miss Hellebore. We're cousins, I suppose you could say—distant cousins as far as the daoine sídhe are concerned."

She sat back down on the edge of her stool. "But...you knew my mom and dad..."

"Your dad, mostly," Nat said. "I still owed him a favor when he...you know." Nat lowered his gaze to the deck.

Taylor shuddered. She knew her mom's dad, Crom Cornstack, killed Aulberic Redmane before she was born. Apparently it was pretty gruesome, but she'd never heard the details—and didn't really want to know.

"Bundlestraw!" the captain called.

"I'll be needed on deck soon," Nat said. "Listen, Taylor. Your dad meant the world to me. I couldn't help him, but it looks like the universe has given me a chance to help his kid."

Taylor sighed.

"I heard Shanna had a kid. Every time I make it to Ichisi, I think about looking you up. It just...never seemed like the right time."

"You may not want to be seen with me," Taylor said. "It's kind of bad for your health these days."

Nat chuckled. "I heard that, too. You brought down Anya Redmane. Some folks would call that a big favor for the Winter Court."

"But I didn't know that was what I was doing! It was all Mara's doing." She leaned forward. "I'm not like them."

"You don't have to prove it to me," Nat said. He gazed at her with his eerie green eyes. "I take it you're looking for a way Topside?"

She nodded.

"I don't know of any ring portals in these parts," Nat said, "and I can't say I'd feel comfortable sending you to one if I did. Likely as not, Osaa's boys will be watching them."

"I heard that name before, outside," Taylor said. "Who's Osaa?"

"You might say he's the law in these parts. And he gets pretty touchy about folks passing up and down the river without his permission."

"Bundlestraw!" Mr. Jackalberry called again. Nat glanced toward the door.

"Anyways, the fastest way home's going to be through his domain."

"I see," Taylor said.

Nat put the banjo case on the table and unlatched it.

"About time!" Cora said. The banjo shuddered. Taylor wondered how it could move at all—let alone speak.

"Sorry, Cora. It had to be done."

To that, the banjo harrumphed indignantly.

"Nat," Taylor said. "This Osaa...he's one of the good guys..., right?"

Nat waited before answering, and Taylor wished she were better at reading people's emotions. At last he simply said, "He can be dealt with."


The splotchy-faced fae—whose name, it turned out, was Mr. Eels—gave William a thirty-foot long pole and placed him in a row of boatmen lined up along the right side of the *Misery*. William reminded himself that right was starboard and left was port. "Left" and "port" both have the same number of letters, so they go together. And "right" and "starboard".... Well, they were just the opposite. The front was the bow, the rear was aft or the stern. The rest, William hoped he could pick up along the way.

The boat was about sixty feet long and eighteen feet wide, and most of it was piled ten feet or higher with goods: enormous bales of cotton, stacks of lumber, wooden crates and barrels, and an assortment of metal implements—whether these last were cargo or intended for use on the boat, William had no idea.

Elevated above the deck was a narrow, cleated walkway. That's where he was told to stand. The others had dropped their poles into the river while grasping them near the top. William followed suit. Then, when Mr. Jackalberry gave the order to shove off, they all faced aft, dug their poles into the river bottom, and pushed with all their strength.

The boat eased away from the bank and started to head downriver. William wasn't sure what to do, but the yelling and cursing from his new crewmates were all the training he got. It didn't take long to figure out he was supposed to dig in with his pole and push toward the stern. That, as Isaac Newton could have told him, pushed the boat itself forward. Once he got a little traction, William kept pushing so that he eventually walked the length of the boat, stepping in time with the work song the members of the crew intoned as they put their shoulders to the poles. When William got to the stern, he drew his pole from the water, stepped onto the deck, marched up to the bow, and started over the whole process over again.

The *Misery* was steered by a rudder at the stern, where Dennis stood at his post. Near the stern was the cabin house—little more than a shack, really. It was the only part of the *Misery* underneath a roof. It's where Taylor was first taken when they boarded the boat, though now she'd hobbled to the bow and was standing next to Mr. Bundlestraw, the mate.

Poling mostly involved walking and pushing for hours on end. Directly in front of him, meaning to the stern of him, was a swarthy fae with long, dark hair tied up in a ponytail that fell halfway down his back. He had a broad nose and a horsey sort of face to go with his haircut. The others called him Luther.

Behind William was Mr. Eels of the splotchy face. All told, the crew numbered twenty-four polemen, Mr. Jackalberry the captain (the polemen called him the "patroon"), and Mr. Bundlestraw. He only caught the names of a few others: Itchu, the huge Native American fae who had taken charge of Taylor. Mr. Hackjaw was a short black guy, darker skinned than the captain, who wore a golden amulet around his neck on a chain.

William was surprised to see some little folk in the crew. They were taller than the few little folk he'd met before. The shortest was as big as Pete, who was the tallest of his trio of friends. The rest ranged up to a foot taller than that, maybe four and a half feet. He couldn't imagine they'd be tall and heavy enough for this kind of work, but they kept at it just as hard as the tall folk.

Then, of course, there were Tobias Glut and his furry best friend, Roger, who thankfully were stationed on the port side of the boat. Roger was the only ape-man in the crew. He pushed his pole through the water with hardly any effort at all. His only friend—or at least the only one who seemed able to understand him—was Tobias. For his part, Tobias settled into a nearly constant death-glare aimed right at William whenever the two caught sight of each other across the deck.

Other than Tobias and Roger, nobody seemed outright hostile. Surly, maybe, especially when he got out of rhythm, but not looking for trouble.

Poling a boat was hard, sweaty work, but it gave William time to think.

He wondered about Taylor. She'd toned up a lot over the past couple of years, and he couldn't even remember the last time she'd had an asthma attack. He still wasn't sure her lungs would hold out if she tried poling, though. At the same time, he doubted she'd take too kindly to anyone telling her that. His head told him that Taylor could take care of herself—she had more, and more powerful, magic than he did. Not to mention, she'd been dealing with the Fair Folk for a couple of years now. Without his staff and his gym bag, now tucked away with the rest of the crew's personal belongings (Lord, please don't let them touch anything!), he was pretty much helpless.

His ears burned as he thought about how Taylor found him with Imaiyah. Of all the times to forget about his jet amulet! He felt like an idiot. Worse than that, Taylor must have thought he was an idiot, too.

In a way he couldn't put into words, that mattered to him.

And what did it mean, anyway, when she'd hugged him so tight and told him not to go?

"Put your back to it, boys!" Dennis called from his perch at the stern of the *Misery*. "We've got to make fifty miles today to get back on schedule!"

Hackjaw struck up a fresh work song, livelier than the one they'd been singing. The polemen really put their heart into this one, and many grinned and chuckled as they sang. William wondered if the lyrics were supposed to be dirty or something. They didn't make any sense to him, though. Whatever the case, he put his back into it as the *Misery* sped farther and farther down the river.

It wasn't long before his stomach began to rumble. Taylor's energy bar filled him up a lot more than he thought it would, but breakfast was a long time ago. He knew they would eventually stop for lunch, but he didn't dare eat any of their faery rations. He'd have to rely on Taylor to conjure him something to eat. And he'd have to keep doing that until they got home.

Not only could he do nothing for Taylor, he needed her even to survive in this place. If they got separated, if anything happened to her....

He grunted and pressed on. Maybe all this time to think wasn't exactly a blessing.

From his station at the bow, Nat spied ahead and alerted the crew to obstacles to avoid—a downed tree trunk to port, a giant gator to starboard.

William wished he knew what Nat had done to convince Mr. Jackalberry to take them on. It didn't seem quite the same as Taylor's power of presence. He didn't project power or confidence. He just double-talked his way into getting what he wanted.

That, Tobias's weird demon face, and Mr. Eels's hollering were the only displays of magic he'd observed among the crew. He figured Jackalberry would have some talent or he'd have never made patroon. Roger could probably get by with brute force. And, of course, Tobias was buddies with Roger.

So, mostly different kinds of mind-control magic as far as William could tell. With his jet amulet in his pocket, he might actually come out okay.

William leaned forward and called to Luther, "Where are we going again?"

"Headin' down to the Forks," Luther called back. Of course, that didn't tell William anything.

"Then where?"

"Straight on to Osaa's domain."

"Most of our cargo's for him," Eels said from behind. "The rest'll go down to the mouth of the river. There's a village there: Hasossa. Plenty of folks looking to trade."

William tried to remember what the redhead had said earlier. "So this is the River of Night?"

Mr. Eels chuckled. "This is the Bubbling River. That and the Waterfolk River come together at the Forks. That's when we enter the River of Night."

"W-why do they call it that?"

"Less talking, more poling," Luther said.

"Sorry. It's just...I've never been in these parts before."

"Yeah," Eels said, holding back a chuckle. "Osaa's gonna love you."

William reached the stern for what seemed like the thousandth time. He'd long since lost count of how many trips he'd actually made. He pulled up his pole, hurried back to the bow, and plunged it once more into the river.

Once Mr. Eels rejoined him, William said, "The redheaded guy, Nat? He said something about Osaa getting us home?"

"Uh huh," Eels said. He dug his pole into the river bottom with a grunt. "If the mood hits him."

"Okay," William said. He trudged forward three paces before he spoke again. "Is he likely to be in a good mood?"

Mr. Eels just chuckled and shook his head.

*Chapter 13*

# A Call for Help

Jill stood beside her parents at St. Michael's African Methodist Episcopal Church. They were in their usual spot, halfway down the sanctuary along the outside aisle. Above and to the left was a stained-glass representation of the parable of the Good Samaritan. Ahead, Sister Watson led the congregation in the closing hymn.

> Pass me not, O gentle Savior,
> Hear my humble cry;
> While on others Thou art calling,
> Do not pass me by.

Everything seemed so ordinary. Some folks read the words from their hymnals; others looked upward in prayer, or stood with their eyes closed and their hands uplifted. The organist found the perfect blend of reverence and earnest soulfulness, leading the congregation to consider the state of their souls.

If it weren't for the empty spot on the pew where William should have been, Jill might have believed this was just another Sunday. She glanced to the left, where her mom slumped into her dad's shoulder. With his arm around her, they swayed gently with the music.

Jill took deep breaths. The emotion in the room would have been nearly overwhelming for anybody. For somebody blessed with Second Sight, it was the next best thing to a minefield.

Sister Blyden ambled down the center aisle, fighting back tears. She paused to speak to Reverend Johnson. He laid his hand on her frail shoulder, exposing his white dress shirt beneath the wide sleeve of his robe. Sister Blyden nodded at whatever the Reverend told her and then knelt at the altar to pray. Everybody had heard that Eunice's oldest grandson had gotten mixed up with the wrong crowd. She'd taken that burden to the altar every Sunday for two months, but so far the Lord hadn't seen fit to do anything about it.

A young man whose name Jill didn't know also made his way forward. Reverend Johnson prayed with him for a good, long time.

The congregation swayed as they sang.

Let me at Thy throne of mercy
Find a sweet relief;
Kneeling there in deep contrition,
Help my unbelief.

Distracted as she was by William's disappearance, and by her mom's fragile state, it was harder than usual for Jill to keep her Second Sight under control. The swirl of emotions—the grief, the fear, and even the hope and the sense of release the invitation hymn inspired among the faithful nearly overwhelmed her. They sometimes sang, "Take your burden to the Lord and leave it there." She never realized how literal that line could be. Before Maymay had taught her to control her gift, church was a challenge. Everybody came with their own story, their own anxiety, their own burden—and Jill could see it all. Sure, it was almost always symbolic—a color, a shadow, a superimposed image—but it was all there if she looked for it. She could see the bad as well as the good, even when people thought they were hiding behind a smokescreen of religiosity. But especially she could see the broken parts: everything they brought with them when they came to the altar.

Given her own mental state, she wasn't about to take any chances. Whenever she was afraid she might slip, she shut her eyes—tight—and breathed a prayer for more control.

Her mom and dad stood with heads bowed, barely paying attention to the hymn. They were doing their best to keep their own emotions in check. As far as anyone at church was concerned, William was just home sick today. They didn't like lying, but telling the truth—he'd been assaulted by faeries and whisked away to parts unknown—was out of the question.

*Lord, please bring William back*, she prayed.

She knew he was still alive. Call it a twin thing, but she was convinced she'd have known if...if something had happened to him. She choked back a tear as she remembered how he just vanished from in front of her eyes.

At least he had Taylor with him. Together, they'd figure out a way home. They had to, because Jill wasn't coming up with any clues, no matter how much she scried.

Savior, Savior,
Hear my humble cry,
While on others Thou art calling,
Do not pass me by.

The final refrain ended, and the organist improvised on the tune of the refrain as Sister Blyden, the young man, and a handful of others made their way back to their places. A few kept singing or moaning, hands waving gently, taking their time coming down from the mountaintop.

Mom, thankfully, was one of them. She looked better than when they had arrived. More composed. At least, Jill hoped that wasn't wishful thinking. And she hoped the feeling would last, because there was no telling how long it would take for William to get home.

At least there was one more thing Jill could try. The idea came to her late last night as she pored over Maymay's notebook, looking for any lead, anything she hadn't thought to try. She found it near the back, in a section she and William had never explored before. A midnight call to New Orleans confirmed she was on the right track

The service would soon be over. As soon as they got home, she would go to work.


Jill took the longest, coldest shower she'd ever had. She had to wash away every last trace of magical residue, every particle (or whatever it was) of the aura that naturally built up around her whenever she used magic.

Ceremonial magic required absolute purity. The instructions in Maymay's notebook looked tricky, and Maymay confirmed over the phone that there was little room for error. This was subtle magic, more William's department than hers. But it was the only option left, and she wasn't taking any chances of messing it up.

*Witches used to do this all the time*, she told herself. Maybe they still did, though Maymay insisted Jill proceed with great caution.

Jill scrubbed down the tile floor of the basement on her hands and knees, then took her time drawing as large and as perfect a circle of power as she could. Inside the circle, she inscribed an equilateral triangle, and inside that, a smaller circle, maybe three feet across.

Then she purified her tools as well. She lit a cone of sandalwood incense in a brass burner and passed most of the implements through the smoke: three brand-new white votive candles, a small hand mirror, a horseshoe, a salt shaker, Maymay's blasting rod, even the spell book itself with her notes in the margin of the page in question. (It was just a loose-leaf binder with photocopies of Maymay's original pages, but that didn't matter: a spell book is a spell book.)

At each point of the triangle, Jill set a candle. It burned clear and yellow-white—she had no aura to make it turn any other color. Beyond the circle, past the eastern point of the triangle, she set the mirror. Just inside the triangle, she placed the horse-shoe. She sprinkled salt all along the perimeter.

At last, it was time. Jill stood in the inner circle with her spell book in one hand and her blasting rod in the other. She wondered if the defensive precautions were really necessary. But she didn't want to mess up the spell by leaving anything out. And then again, she had no way to guess how her soon-to-be guest would react to what she was doing. Better safe than sorry!

With an effort of will, Jill cast the circle. She felt a snap as the magic closed around her. She settled her mind until she could detect the magical field wrapping around her, focusing and intensifying her power. If things did go badly, the same circle would be her first and best line of defense.

Several slow, cleansing breaths put her in the right frame of mind. She had everything she needed. She even had his name. After one more breath, she began to read aloud from the spell book, noting the personalized additions she'd scribbled in the margin:

"I summon the pooka, the trickster, the shape-shifter.
Leave your abode and render me the service I require of thee.
Come away, servant, come. I am ready now.
Approach, Danny Underhill, come.

"I adjure thee, conjure, and straightly charge and command thee,
by earth and air and fire and water,
by all the powers of this world and the next.
Come away, servant, come. I am ready now.
Approach, Danny Underhill, come.

"I adjure and command thee, that thou appear
presently, meekly, and mildly in this glass
without doing hurt or danger unto me or any other living creature.
Come away, servant, come. I am ready now.

Approach, Danny Underhill, come.

"To this I bind thee by salt and iron and mountain ash. *Anakalo, ekkalo, elicio, accio.*"

Nothing happened.

Jill held her breath. She'd done everything right. Now she just had to have confidence it would work.

She dared to open her Second Sight. The room was awash in a torrent of magical energy. It had no effect on the physical environment. The candles didn't even flicker, but Jill braced herself against a growing pressure in her body.

*Come on*, she urged. *I just want to talk.*

The shimmer in the room folded in on itself, manifesting as a single magical presence directly above the mirror on the floor. The shimmer darkened, solidified.

In seconds, the presence resolved itself into the shape of a man—or a pooka, to be more precise—floating above the mirror. It wasn't exactly a physical presence; it was more like a holographic projection. Danny's colors were muted and almost transparent at the extremities. His entire form exuded amber light. That was to be expected, as Jill was looking at a construct made of light and not a flesh-and-blood being.

"W-what?" Danny said. His eyes widened, and he dropped into a defensive stance. He brandished a bronze-bladed meat cleaver, looking for somebody to strike. His bib apron was streaked with blood. Even in the best circumstances, Danny looked a little scary with his tapered, devilish ears, his bushy black eyebrows, and his enormous nose. Armed and bloody and with his eyes glowing with fear and anger, Jill took a half-step back in spite of herself.

Disoriented, the pooka tried to back away, but he couldn't. His right leg moved around just fine, but his left foot was stuck to the surface of Jill's mirror. He jerked at it like he had stepped in glue, cursing under his breath.

"Danny, it's okay. It's me, Jill."

The pooka finally spun in her direction. His eye tracked to the blasting rod in her hand, the horseshoe in front of him on the floor.

"By oak, ash, and thorn, Jill!" He gestured with his cleaver—which did nothing for Jill's nerves! His tone was accusing. "What's with all this?"

"I'm not going to use it," Jill quickly assured him. "It's just…a formality, I guess. I had to contact you, and this was the only summoning spell in Maymay's book."

Danny's body relaxed, but only a little. "I got things to do!" he yelled. "I'm only half finished with this hog." He gestured toward the hog that he apparently could still see, even though Jill could not. "If I don't get the butchering done, my boss is gonna—"

"Danny!" Jill interrupted. "William and Taylor are missing."

His eyebrows danced as he processed that. Even in holographic form, his eyes flashed. "No!" he gasped. "Who…?"

"Crom Cornstack's people attacked us. I don't know why. And then there was a flash of magic and…they were just gone."

"Aw, this is bad!" Danny said. "By oak, ash, and thorn, this is real bad!" He tried to pace, but once again found himself bound to the mirror. He looked at Jill. "Do the nunnehi know?"

"They're looking," Jill said. "So far, they're coming up empty." To hear Taylor tell it, there wasn't much the nunnehi couldn't do. They should have had them back in time for last night's supper. Unless…. She bit her lip, she was doing everything she could to keep it together.

Danny rocked from side to side. "Okay, let me think…" He settled down. The fire in his eyes diminished without going completely out.

"Danny, I'm sorry about summoning you this way. That… wasn't the nicest spell."

Danny waved off her apology. "It ain't the worst thing a Topsider's ever done to me. Shoot, I might have tried something this desperate if I was in your shoes. But what are we gonna do about Taylor and William?"

"We've got to find them," Jill said. Her whole body was shaking. "We just have to! Is there anything you can do?"

The pooka pulled against the mirror, but it still wouldn't budge. "I don't know," he said.

"Anything at all?"

"Just let me think." He scratched his curly head for several silent seconds. At last, a light of realization dawned upon his face. "Maybe," he said.

"I'll do whatever I have to," Jill said. "I'm not letting my brother and my best friend just disappear."

Danny looked her straight in the eye. "Listen, I've absolutely got to finish butchering this hog, okay?"

"But William and Taylor—"

"I know!" Danny blurted. He tried yet again to unstick his foot. "But you gotta understand. Winter's coming. We gotta get meat in the smokehouse now if we want to eat come January."

"But—"

"And I'm already mostly done, okay? And as soon as I'm finished, I'm gonna make a scry. Tonight. And then I may have to take a side trip to Bisgarra Verry. But I can be at your place by tomorrow afternoon."

Jill sighed. "Okay. I don't like it, but I guess that's fair. Just hurry."

"You bet, Jill. Just...don't give up. Tomorrow, I promise."

*Chapter 14*

# The Forks

It shaped up to be a warm day on the river. Squint kept Taylor busy in the cabin house doing some housekeeping chores he'd apparently put off for years. After dusting, cleaning, sorting the pantry, and throwing out wilted vegetables, the kobold grudgingly dismissed her. She spent the afternoon sitting on a barrel near the bow of the Misery, keeping an eye on William while Nat watched for predators.

It wasn't the most comfortable seat, but it gave Taylor more time with Nat, and she had about a thousand questions for the pisgy. He had known her father! He'd known him well enough to be in his debt. Taylor was determined to find out more.

"You...You knew my dad," she said. When Nat didn't answer, she went on. "What was he like?"

Nat smiled. "He was—" He abruptly cut himself off and turned his full attention forward. Taylor leaned over to look around him, trying to catch a glimpse of what was so interesting. She couldn't see anything but the river, and yet something had definitely changed aboard the boat. The crew was agitated. She saw concern on everyone's faces as they poled onward.

"Coming to the Forks!" Nat called.

Dennis started barking orders. The work song picked up in pace—everyone was suddenly in a hurry.

"Something's up?" Taylor said. She looked at Nat, inviting a response.

The pisgy kept gazing forward. "What I just said. We're coming up to the Forks." He gestured forward. "See there?"

Taylor looked ahead. Another river was feeding into the one the *Misery* was traveling. Usually, two rivers formed a Y when they came together, but at the Forks, they came together in a perfect T: the Bubbling River and its counterpart flowed into each other at such an angle that they created a churning whirlpool.

Taylor slipped off her makeshift seat and stood squarely on the deck. She spread out her hands to brace herself—and wished she were a better swimmer.

"We'll be all right," Nat said. He must have sensed her nervousness.

The boat rocked as it approached the whirlpool. Taylor looked around for a handhold. They were picking up speed.

"Are you sure?"

Taylor slipped her hand around a rope that held a stack of barrels in place. All around, polemen traded wary glances.

"I've run this river for fifteen years," Nat said, "It's just a matter of—"

The *Misery* listed suddenly to starboard on the crest of a powerful wave. Taylor yelped, but Nat had seen it coming. He yelled at the crew to pole harder as he jogged to the stern to help Dennis at the tiller.

Taylor followed behind. She passed William, straining at his pole. The blotchy-faced fae behind him shouted, "Put your back to it, you poxy oaf!"

Taylor tensed. *He's doing his best!* she thought—but she didn't have time to come to her friend's defense. The boat rocked from side to side, and it was all she could do to keep her footing.

Dennis and Nat pulled at the tiller. The boat leaned to port as it kissed the edge of the whirlpool and spun clockwise around it. The timbers of the old boat creaked and strained. Taylor was sure the massive towers of cotton would lean too far and come crashing down, but they never did.

It wasn't long before the *Misery* was pointed back the way it came.

Taylor searched in vain for handholds. The best she could do was push herself up against the rear wall of the cabin house. "We're turning around!" she said.

Nat nodded. He dug into the deck with his feet and, with a grunt, threw all his strength into the tiller. "We're borrowing a little power from the whirlpool. Watch."

The *Misery* completed its circuit of the vortex and started a second lap. This time, though, as soon as the boat was pointed downstream, Dennis howled for his crew to pole even harder.

The boat broke free of the whirlpool and coasted away. They had left the upper section of the "T" and entered the tall central staff.

Nat sighed with relief. The polemen cheered and whooped in triumph.

"Is it over?" Taylor asked.

"Not even close," Nat said. "We've made it to the River of Night is all. We're in Osaa's domain now. Best we all keep our eyes open."

"For what?"

He frowned and gazed out over the river. "Know it when I see it."

"Mr. Bundlestraw, take the tiller," Dennis commanded. Nat obliged as Dennis strode to the bow, his blunderbuss in hand.

Taylor remained at the stern. She tried to settle herself, to extend her magical senses. As hard as she tried, though, she couldn't sense anything past the side of the boat. The river was grounding out her magic.

She peered ahead. The trees weren't too different from what she knew from Macon—both from her Topside home and from the faery woods around Ichisi.

"Where are we, exactly? I mean, relative to the Topside world?"

"I'm not rightly sure," Nat said. "I reckon technically the nunnehi claim this river." He chuckled. "I doubt they come by to visit all that often."

"I see."

Something caught Taylor's attention: a dark shape in the water, moving against the flow. She strained to get a better look.

"What's that?"

Nat leaned forward. He'd seen it, too. "Water master to starboard, Dennis!" he called. He pulled the tiller, steering the *Misery* to port.

Dennis leveled his firearm at the swiftly moving shape. He pulled back the hammer and trained the weapon on the swimming creature.

"Easy does it," Nat said, as much to himself as to anybody else.

They poled past the shape. As it came up on the right side of the boat, Taylor finally got a good look. At first she thought it was a panther swimming in the river. She furrowed her brow. Do panthers swim?

Then she peered into the water. It was bigger than any panther she'd ever seen in a zoo. It was more the size of a lion or a tiger, and it looked squarely at her with ghostly green eyes.

She held her breath until the *Misery* was safely past. Dennis uncocked his blunderbuss and relaxed his firing stance.

"He must've already had lunch," Nat commented.

*That's a relief.*

"So, that was a water master," Taylor said.

"The River of Night is hopping with monsters," Nat said. "You just have to expect that, as deep as we are in the Wonder."

Taylor took in her surroundings. It was nearly noon, but somehow the sun looked dimmer than it should have been. The air was warm for the season, but the shadows seemed to gather along the riverbanks.

"Steer clear of water masters," Taylor said. "Good to know."

"Water masters, tie snakes, man-eaters, water cannibals...," Nat said.

It took a second for all of that to process. When it did, Taylor said, "You're kidding, right? I mean, that's an awful lot of monsters."

142

"Like I said, the River of Night's just hopping with 'em. Of course, they aren't all bad, precisely. The ghosts will give you a hard time, but they're mostly harmless."

"Ghosts?"

Nat nodded. "It's the living creatures you need to watch out for."

"The water masters and such," Taylor said.

"And the horned serpents. They're the worst of the bunch. You see a horned serpent coming, you run the other way. You hear?"

"Right." Taylor glanced at William as he drew his pole from the water and began to trudge back toward the bow.

Nat acted like he wanted to help Taylor. At first she wasn't entirely sure she could trust him—why shanghai them onto a poleboat that was headed the wrong way?—but if there were monsters about, she didn't like the odds on two teenagers alone in the woods.

Maybe at least there would be strength in numbers if anything came their way that *hadn't* already had lunch. And Nat seemed like he knew what he was doing.

"Have you ever run into a horned serpent?" she asked.

Nat shook his head. "I'm alive, aren't I?"

Taylor furrowed her brow. Nat could see she was lost.

"Look, you know what a dragon is, right? Everybody knows what a dragon is."

"Sure," Taylor said. "Big lizard. Breathes fire."

"Some of them, anyways," Nat said. "That's the thing: there's a whole bunch of different breeds of dragon all over the world. They're all different, but they're all bad news."

Weren't most things in the Wonder bad news?

Nat traced a finger across the handle of Dennis's blunderbuss. "The dragons in these parts are called *chitto yapthlakko*, 'the Great Horned Serpent.' And they're some of the worst there is."

"Ah." This was just getting better and better. "And you say they're serpents? Just...great big snakes?" Taylor knew the

143

dragons in Greek mythology were usually depicted as snakes: no wings, no claws, just a whole lot of slithery, venomous death.

"Great big snakes with hypnotic eyes. Venomous fangs. A leathery hide like bands of steel and more magic resistance than a slant-eyed giant." He put his shoulder to the tiller as they rounded a bend in the river. "They're bad news, I tell you."

"Obviously," Taylor said.

"The folks that hunt 'em are just plain crazy if you ask me."

"Yeah." Taylor's head reeled. The River of Night suddenly sounded like the worst possible place to be—and with a Topsider to take care of! She gazed at the riverbank. Her ears perked up for the slightest sound of anything slithering through the trees.

"You okay, Taylor?"

"I'm fine," she said with a sigh. "Dragons. Giant aquatic panthers. Man-eaters. This is going to be awesome."


Taylor didn't see any more water masters the rest of the day. Around noon, Squint had her take lunch to the crew. They drifted downstream as Dennis and Nat took turns at the tiller while a couple of polemen guided the *Misery* around shoals or fallen branches. Meanwhile, the rest of the crew sat on the walkway and gnawed on hunks of hardtack biscuit and dried jerky that looked, felt, and tasted like shoe leather.

Taylor brought William an energy bar. It wasn't much to eat after a hard morning's workout, but she didn't see any other options. He took it gratefully and nibbled it in four or five bites to make it last.

Tobias watched the exchange and sneered.

Shortly after they got back underway, Taylor noticed movement in the brush on the left bank of the river. It looked like a man in a torn gray jacket, but it moved so silently that Taylor never got a second look.

Nat followed her gaze. "Probably just a ghost," he said as he wiped sweat from his brow with his sleeve.

Dennis and Nat continued to take turns at the tiller. Whoever wasn't steering the boat stood at the prow with Dennis's blunderbuss and watched for dangers up ahead.

The sun was beginning to set when they stopped for the night. The crew poled the *Misery* up to the left bank, moored the boat to a gigantic live oak, and began to make camp.

They had barely come to a stop when Squint started working on supper. Of course, this involved a good bit of ordering Taylor around: haul pots and pans, mind the fire, chop the carrots and onions—and leave the pantry in better shape than you found it. Before long, a stew of salted meats and a few pathetic vegetables was simmering in a huge copper kettle.

Supper was almost ready when the ghosts arrived.

Some of the polemen noticed them first while setting out their bedrolls. A green-haired, black-skinned fae perked up his pointed ears, looked toward the woods, then nudged the little person next to him. The splotchy-faced fae named Mr. Eels stood up and called for the captain.

At first, Taylor only heard voices—two men, apparently arguing about something. Soon, however, she saw a moving shadow in the woods. Less than a minute later, a pair of strangers emerged, gesturing heatedly as they continued bickering.

They were dressed in Civil War uniforms—one Union blue, one Confederate gray, and both wearing corporal's stripes. The Union soldier had apparently taken a massive gunshot to his belly. His shirt was streaked with blood and powder burns. The Confederate's right shoulder had been hacked clean through to the bone.

Neither of them seemed bothered in the least by their injuries, which is what tipped Taylor off they were probably no longer among the living. As soon as she made the connection, she noticed they weren't entirely solid. She could see how the light played against the fabric of their clothes and even their skin, revealing the shapes of objects behind them. As they strolled through camp, though, Taylor noted that the cooking fire burned brilliant green in their presence.

"All I'm saying," the Confederate snarled, "is if we'd a' had more cannon, we'd a' held Griswoldville."

"You don't know what you're talking about, Mike!" the Unionist said. "You guys had three brigades. Three! And General Walcutt cleaned your clock with just one!"

"I'm a' gonna clean *your* clock if you ain't careful, Archie!"

"Gentlemen!" Dennis shouted. The belligerents stopped in their tracks as they noticed the polemen's camp for the first time. They looked around, stunned, for only a second, then kept walking and arguing.

"It ain't just a matter of equipment," Archie the Union soldier said. "It's tactics. Smarts." He tapped the side of his head. Polemen scooted out of their way as the soldiers drifted through. In another minute, they had disappeared around a bend. The echo of their voices was the only proof they had been there.

"Stupid ghosts," one of the polemen muttered. He went back to straightening up his patch of ground, rummaging in his knapsack for a deck of cards.

In another minute, the interruption had been forgotten. Apparently ghosts were an acceptable nuisance on the River of Night.

Taylor went back to her chores. It wasn't long until she had been left alone by the fire. Everybody else had drifted to the edge of camp, where Tobias and Luther had squared off for some kind of contest. They faced each other about five feet apart, arms up and palms outward. Then they began to grimace and dig in their heels as if they were struggling to subdue a giant invisible wildcat.

The onlookers cheered and made bets. There was a flash of light, and Luther fell on his back. Seven or eight crewmen ran forward to pat Tobias on the back as he lifted his fist in triumph.

Taylor went back to stirring the pot, Nat approached her. "Don't mind about those ghosts earlier" he said. "Like I told you, they're mostly harmless."

"I'm fine," Taylor said. "What was that all about?" She nodded toward where Tobias and Luther had their contest.

"Yeah, that," Nat said. Now Tobias was squaring off with a different fae, one whose name Taylor hadn't learned.

"Some of these fellas get antsy if they go too long without a good fight," Nat said. "Hexenkreis lets them blow off a little steam."

"Hexenkreis, huh?"

Nat nodded. Then he leaned in and whispered, "You know, at first I assumed your friend was a changeling."

Her eyes met Nat's. Her heart started to thump.

"He's never bought in, has he?" Nat said.

Taylor sighed and shook her head. "We've got to get home soon or..."

"I saw that little trick you pulled at lunch with the granola bar."

Her face warmed. "I had to do something," she protested.

"I know," Nat said. "I reckon I'd do the same." He glanced back to where Tobias had thrown his next challenger to the ground. "You know Tobias saw it, too, right?"

"I was afraid he might have," Taylor said. "He...doesn't like William. If he wants to make trouble for him—"

"I'll do what I can," Nat said. "But you've got to understand. These fellas have learned the hard way that they've got to take care of themselves. Your friend had best stay out of Tobias's way. Hear?"

"Yeah."

Nat sighed. "Listen. Another day or two and we'll be at Osaa's place. Can he hold out that long?"

She watched as William spread out a tattered, borrowed bedroll beside his gym bag and staff. He looked pretty wobbly.

"I...think so. If I could make my own magic stronger...."

"You'll do fine. Strong magic's in your blood." Nat allowed a sly smile to cross his face.

"You mean my dad?" Taylor said.

"Your mom, too, as I remember. Kids mostly get their magic from their moms, you know. Then again," he chuckled, "Aulberic Redmane never did anything by the rules."

Taylor wiped sweat from her brow. She gave the kettle another stir. "We got interrupted before. I was wondering...if you could tell me about my dad."

Nat smiled, and his posture relaxed. He scratched his head and looked around. Nobody was close enough to listen in. "We met at Bisgarra Verry. That's the capital of the Summer Court. He stuck up for me once when I'd gotten into some trouble. I don't think his folks were too pleased."

"Why not?"

He shrugged. "Just wouldn't do for a sídhe kid to rub elbows with a lowly pisgy, now would it?"

Taylor scrunched her nose. "How should I know?"

"Sorry, I forget you're still pretty new to life in the Wonder—yeah, I've heard a little bit of your story. Anyway, let's just say we pisgies haven't always gotten respect from our cousins."

"Why not?"

"Well, they say we're too chummy with the lesser kindreds—and they're probably right. Most of us have some elfish or ellyll or even spriggan blood in us." He brushed his red hair back, exposing the slightly tapered shape of his ear. "You see these? Your grandparents would say these ears are a sign of poor breeding."

"Mr. Bundlestraw!" Dennis called.

"Coming, Cap'n!" he answered. He leaned in toward Taylor and said, "Actually, they'd probably have some other things to say that I'd rather not repeat to a lady."

Dennis was marching toward them. Nat turned to the patroon. "Yes, Cap'n?"

"Is that all the firewood we've got? Take Hackjaw and Itchu and find us more."

"I'll get right on it, sir."

The patroon walked up the gangplank onto the deck of the *Misery*.

After Dennis stalked away, Taylor looked back at Nat. "That's what the daoine sídhe say, but what do you say?"

Nat straightened up. "I say you'd better take care of your friend." He nodded toward William sitting on his bedroll with his head in his hands.

Taylor's stomach churned to see him like that. Take care of William? That's all she wanted to do, but how?

"Right," she said with a sigh.

# Chapter 15

# Hexenkreis

William shivered as Mr. Eels stood by the riverbank and began to holler. It was the same mournful howl he'd heard that morning, rolling over the camp and up and down the river.

Everyone stopped to listen.

When the echoes faded away to nothingness, he hollered again. And once again, the echoes bounced up and down the river and eventually trailed off into silence.

This time, though, an answer came back: a different call, a high-pitched wail that William could hear only faintly from somewhere else on the river.

"Is that Dick Pugmire?" Luther said.

Eels nodded. "It's the *Slippery Sylph*, all right. But they're farther away than last night. I can barely hear 'em."

"They're falling behind," Luther said. "Might be a full day behind us by the time we get to Osaa's place."

William sat down on his bedroll and opened his bag. His muscles throbbed and protested his every movement. Poling a boat was definitely worse than any yard work he'd ever done.

What was worse, the smell of Taylor's stew made his stomach rumble. He forced the thought of a decent supper out of his mind. It was going to be energy bars for the foreseeable future.

There was something he could do, though. He'd already refilled his sports bottle from the river. Now he set it in front of him and pulled a stoppered plastic vial and an eyedropper from his bag.

The vial was labeled "Gumption" in Maymay's spidery handwriting. He shook it a few times, opened it, and dripped a single drop of golden liquid into his water. If he understood correctly, it would keep up his energy and focus, at least for a while. It wasn't as good as a bowl of stew, but it was better than nothing.

Suddenly, Taylor was beside him. He hadn't even noticed her coming. She knelt at his side.

"How are you doing?" she asked.

William thought about it. "Not too bad," he said. It was mostly the truth. Anyway, he didn't want Taylor to worry about him. He'd come to terms with the fact that she was eventually going to be the one to get them both out of the Wonder because seriously, what could he do? But he didn't want her distracted by worrying about him. "I was getting a little lightheaded on the boat, but I'm better now."

"Good."

William wished he knew what Taylor was really thinking. He didn't dare open his Second Sight. But even if he did, it wouldn't tell him anything about Taylor—or anybody else in the camp. The Good Neighbors simply didn't register in Second Sight. Maymay said it was because they didn't have souls. William really didn't want her to be right about that. But whatever the reason, Second Sight could see through faery illusions, but they couldn't tell him anything about what was going on in somebody like Taylor's heart and mind.

Maybe that's what made Taylor so interesting.

"How about some supper?" Taylor said. She looked around. Everybody else was staking out their place for the night—Mr. Jackalberry, Squint, and the other higher-ranking crew closer to the fire, those further down the pecking order at a distance. William, of course, was near the edge of the camp.

Taylor pulled William's energy bar from her purse, concentrated, and duplicated it like she had done that morning and that afternoon.

She offered the newly-conjured bar to William. As he took it, something came to him. "I bet the river was grounding out my magic."

Taylor nodded. "Mine, too. It was all I could do to...make you lunch earlier." She winced like the thought made her uncomfortable.

"I couldn't do anything." He took a bite. It tasted better than Taylor's previous attempts. She must have been getting the hang of it—or he was just getting hungrier. Chewing the snack made him feel warm inside. "I think my kind of magic is easier to shut down that way than yours..."—he looked around at his fellow crewmen—"...or theirs."

"Could be," Taylor said. "I've never really thought about how what you do is different from what I do."

Someone grumbled behind him. He didn't have to turn around to recognize Tobias's derisive tone.

"*Can I help you?*" Taylor said. She made it sound like a threat.

William shook his head. *Don't do it, Taylor.*

"Yeah," Tobias snarled. "You can walk back into the woods—and take your lapdog with you!"

William's ears burned.

Taylor was on her feet in half a second. "*Lapdog?*" The hairs on William's neck stood on end.

*Please, Taylor. Just let it go!*

Tobias backed up a step. William stood up, if for no other reason to be within reach if he suddenly had to keep Taylor from doing anything stupid. Tobias was just a big bully, but that didn't mean he wasn't dangerous.

"Bundlestraw should have given you both to Roger," Tobias said. His black, beady eyes narrowed.

"And yet, here we are," Taylor said. She planted her hands on her hips.

William put an arm on her shoulder, but she lurched away.

"Taylor...," he said.

153

Three or four crewmen had gathered. Roger lurked in the background, a evil grin on his apelike face. Luther and Eels stood closer to the action. A couple of the little folk jostled for a better view.

Tobias jabbed his finger at Taylor. "You're tricky," he said.

"And you're—"

"Taylor, come on," William said. "He's not worth it."

"What was that?" Tobias said. "Does the lapdog have something to say?"

"Look, we don't want trouble—"

"I don't care what you want," Tobias snarled. He stalked toward William.

William looked around. His staff was beside his gym bag, well out of reach. He tried to assume a defensive stance without making it too obvious that was what he was doing.

At the same time, Taylor stepped in front of him. William sighed. He was getting tired of having her rescue him.

"Out of the way, Taylor," he whispered. "Please."

"Yes," Tobias said. "Move aside. I don't fight girls."

"Smart decision," Taylor said. She flexed her fingers.

"Taylor, no," William said, more firmly this time. "I can handle this." He gently pushed her to one side.

"Cap'n says no fighting" someone called. He was a short, pale-skinned fae with a scar across his tattooed face.

"Fergus is right," Mr. Jackalberry said. He stormed through the crowd to where Tobias and William were circling.

"But Captain!" Tobias spat.

"No buts," the captain barked. "You got a problem, you settle it peaceably."

"Fine," Tobias said. He glared at William. He stretched out his arms and held his palms forward.

The crowd began to howl with approval. Luther clapped his hands. Roger growled like the Hulk did when Captain America told him to smash, gleefully.

"Well?" Tobias said. He flexed his fingers much as Taylor had done. William still didn't trust himself to use Second Sight, but it was pretty obvious Tobias was gathering magic.

"Are you ready?" he taunted. "Or would you rather have another bite of air first?"

"What?"

Tobias looked past William to scowl at Taylor. "Nobody can conjure food, boy! Not even a sídhe."

William's stomach suddenly churned.

"Don't listen to him!" Taylor said.

Tobias laughed and spun his arms in tiny circles. William couldn't see the magic, but he could feel the waves pulsing from Tobias's hands.

"T-Taylor?"

"She's been feeding you illusions," Tobias continued. He stalked to William's left, trying to flank him.

Was that true? Had Taylor been using glamour to make him *think* he'd been eating? Sweat trickled down his face, and his legs tried to give out beneath him.

"That's not true!" William shouted.

Tobias merely grinned. He raised his hands and turned them palms-out toward William. "After I put you in your place, boy, I'll be happy to feed you a proper meal."

"Don't call me boy," William snarled.

He was mad. He was sick and tired of taking grief from Tobias. He realized with a start that part of him was stunned at the idea that Taylor would have tricked him. Would she really do that? He didn't know what to think, but he was tired of feeling helpless.

"I'm going to drag you over to that kettle and force some of that stew down your tupping throat," Tobias said.

"No!" Taylor cried. "He's going home! He can't buy in and get stranded here!"

Tobias's mouth stretched into a mirthless grin. "Ask me if I care."

"It's okay, Taylor," William said. He raised his hands to mirror Tobias's stance. He'd watched Tobias and Luther earlier and realized he was being challenged to some kind of contest. He just didn't know the rules.

He glanced toward Taylor for guidance. She looked just as lost as he was.

"Just let the magic flow," the scar-faced fae, Fergus, said. "Whatever he sends you, you shove it back at him."

That actually made sense. Maymay had taught him and Jill to do something similar to practice moving magical energies around. Sometimes his sister pushed a little too hard, and it was all he could do to keep his balance.

It figured somebody like Tobias would love turning that into an exercise in macho posturing.

Pretty much everybody had gathered around by now. The captain stood by with his arms crossed. Luther and Eels elbowed each other. There was fire in their eyes.

"All right," William said. He braced himself. "When do we—"

He was on his back before he knew what happened. A jolt of magical energy drilled into his left hand, up his arm, and through his entire body in the blink of an eye, and he crumpled to the ground.

All around him, fae and little folk hissed and guffawed.

"William!" Taylor called.

He got back up and brushed grass from his knees. He glared at Tobias.

"Where I come from, sucker punches are against the rules."

"There are no rules in Hexenkreis."

William exhaled. He should have let it go. He wanted to walk away. But everybody was laughing at him, and Tobias was a bully.

"Fair enough," he said. "Then we'll just call that a practice round. Are you ready to do this for real now?"

"For real," Tobias growled. He resumed his stance.

William did likewise, but this time he was ready. As soon as he extended his hands, he pushed his own magical energy toward Tobias. At the same time, he braced himself to receive the charge he knew was coming.

The two competitors formed a circuit. Magic flowed into William's left hand, raced across his arms, and jetted back toward Tobias from his right hand.

By the time one pulse left his body, another had already begun to flow through him. But he was keeping up.

Tobias gritted his teeth.

The onlookers stomped their feet and cheered—almost all of them for Tobias.

William braced himself. He felt like he was chest-deep in the ocean, standing his ground against wave after crashing wave. He might have levitated a quarter of an inch off the ground; he couldn't be sure.

But he held on.

Tobias's eyes flashed. Then he scrunched his face and let out a fierce animal growl. At the same time, his face changed. Horns sprouted from his forehead, his hair grew long, his nose and mouth contorted into a wolflike muzzle.

"Ah!" William shrieked. He lost his concentration for just a second, but that was long enough. Before he knew it, he was lying on his back with a throbbing headache.

"Oooh!" the crowd shouted. They descended upon Tobias to congratulate him.

William picked himself up from the ground once more. He glared and took a step toward Tobias.

"William, you don't have to—"

"It's all right, Taylor," he said. "I think I understand how this game works now. What do you say, Tobias? Best two out of three?"

"I've proven my point," Tobias said. His face returned to normal.

"That's cool," William said. "I'm just a lapdog, right? I ain't got game. If you don't want to take a chance on losing to somebody like me, I can understand that."

The crowd tittered and jabbed at each other.

Taylor looked at the sky, exasperated.

Tobias rounded on William. He'd gotten the fae's attention.

"But if you think this gives you the right to force me to eat some of that nasty stew—no offense, Taylor—then you are sadly mistaken."

"Do you want me to humiliate you even further?"

"Hey, *I'm* not the one backing down from a challenge."

"Oh!" Luther called, laughing and slapping his thighs. A little person gasped, his mouth hanging open in wonder—and amusement.

"Suit yourself, deathling," Tobias said.

"Just let me grab my jacket." William didn't turn his back on Tobias, but he reached behind him for his jacket. Taylor brought it and put it in his hand.

The crew started making side bets. Almost everybody seemed to think William was a goner. Maybe he was, but at least now he had a plan.

"Are you cold?" Tobias said, sneering.

"Not especially," William said. He reached his hand into a sleeve and pulled it inside-out. Then he did the same with the other sleeve.

Tobias suddenly looked confused, even nervous.

William smiled. He put on his jacket inside-out.

The crowd gasped and swayed nervously. Everyone looked suddenly agitated. A couple even turned away or held their hands over their eyes.

The Good Neighbors could be pretty obsessive. Things always had to be in their proper place. There was a right way and a wrong way to do everything. William had learned a year ago that wearing your clothes inside-out was a pretty easy way to mess with their heads.

And Tobias needed messing with.

William assumed his stance. He didn't wait for his opponent to begin. He just rammed the biggest jolt of magic he could muster out his right hand and toward Tobias's left.

The fae caught it, but it took him by surprise.

When the energy circled back around to William, it wasn't nearly as strong. The iron nails and the protective charms he'd sewn into his jacket worked after all.

Now he and Tobias were more equally matched. From the fae's expression, that didn't happen often.

Tobias reverted to his ugly face again, but this time William just smiled. He concentrated on the jet amulet in his pocket, his last-ditch defense against faery glamour. With an effort of will, he threw everything he had into his next pulse of magic.

Tobias broke off the circuit. He didn't fall back, he just stepped away, nursing his left arm like it had been yanked out of joint.

"Take your jacket off!" Luther cried. Half a dozen fae echoed the sentiment.

William looked around. The whole crowd was nervous, rocking back and forth, biting their nails, averting their eyes.

Taylor shivered, wide-eyed.

"Best two out of three, Tobias. Come on."

He snarled. "Not while you're wearing...that!"

"There are no rules in Hexen...whatever you call it." He gestured for Taylor to bring him his water bottle. He took a swig and braced himself as warm, golden gumption oozed into every cell of his body.

"Your call, Tobes." He handed the bottle back to Taylor. "I'm ready when you are."

"Make him take it off!" a different fae shouted.

Tobias assumed his stance. William did the same.

The magic flowed furiously between them, but this time William wasn't worried at all. Tobias was still stunned to have been beaten the first time, and with every passing moment he was more and more distracted by William's inside-out jacket.

It took less than thirty seconds for William to send him flying. Tobias pounded his fist on the ground and let out an angry, anguished growl.

*That went better than I'd expected*, William thought. He planted his hands on his hips with a satisfied swagger. He grinned as Taylor ran to him.

She pulled his jacket off of him. "It's all in the wrist," William joked.

Taylor slapped him in the face. "That was stupid," she hissed. She straightened out the jacket, slammed it down on the bedroll. William stared open-mouthed as she stormed away.

## Chapter 16

# A Journey Down the River

Taylor didn't like blowing up at William, but he deserved it. Who picks a fight with a creep like Tobias, anyway?

She could maybe understand him playing one round of that stupid game. Tobias had challenged him, after all. Guys had a thing about proving they were tough when other guys got in their faces like that.

But why couldn't he let it go? Tobias might have unleashed bloody fury on William. Didn't he know that?

She put her muscle into stirring the stew and then dishing it out to the polemen. They didn't seem appreciative. William was her friend, after all, which did nothing for her own popularity.

He'd worn his jacket inside-out. Didn't he know you just don't do that? Taylor shuddered to even think about it.

This whole excursion had been a nightmare from the beginning. And why did Tobias have to notice Taylor's glamour trick with the energy bar? She was just trying to keep his spirits up, give him a little bit of stamina until they could get out of the Wonder. But the way he said her name, like she had betrayed him. She feared something had changed between them.

*Stupid!* she told herself. William had never been anything but great to her since they first met in the fourth grade. Sure, he was a great big dork, but darn it, at least he was....

"Whatever," she muttered. He didn't deserve all the grief she'd put him through. If Anya Redmane was right, if one of Taylor's loved ones was slated to die soon...

This was why she'd put the brakes on her and Jared, she realized. The thought of Jared stuck in the Wonder was too much to handle. He would have never lasted the first night—he'd probably have been trampled to death by that deer woman.

At least William had skills. He was smart—usually. And if he overreacted to Tobias, it was at least partly to take up for Taylor. That had to count for something—if it wasn't such an unnecessary risk!

*Why do boys have to be so...frustrating?*

After supper, Taylor cleaned the bowls, spoons, and cooking utensils, wiped down the kettle, hauled everything back aboard the *Misery*, and stayed as far away from William as she could. She wanted to forgive him, but at that moment it was all she could do to keep from blasting William herself.

Under the stars, Nat brought out Cora the banjo and plucked out a few tunes. She'd heard better playing, but she wasn't really listening.

*He knew my dad.*

Her birth mother had told her a little about her dad, but not much. Not as much as Taylor would have liked. It was a sensitive subject. Taylor figured it was hard for Shanna to talk about Aulberic without remembering how her own father had murdered him in cold blood.

*But Nat knew him*, she thought. *They were friends. He'd probably known him even longer than Shanna had.*

Nat handed the banjo to Mr. Hackjaw. The black-skinned fae was a real virtuoso. He played all kinds of strange melodies and got sounds out of Cora that Taylor would have never believed possible.

Cora never spoke, though. At least, not that Taylor could hear.

William also sat and listened to the music—from a safe distance. He hadn't made any friends with that inside-out jacket stunt. Maybe there weren't any rules in Hexenkreis, but that didn't mean the Fair Folk didn't have a strong sense of right and wrong. Sure, it was about as twisted a concept of right and wrong as Taylor could imagine, but there were still things you just didn't do.

She got the feeling even the polemen who were happy to see Tobias taken down a notch didn't appreciate how William did it. Tobias and Roger sat opposite William and shot him evil looks all night long.

People began settling down for bed. The ground was hard and cold, but at least tonight Taylor had a borrowed bed roll and enough other people nearby to scare off any predators. Well, Roger probably qualified as a predator, but she didn't think he'd try anything with Nat and Dennis around.

Taylor laid her bedroll next to Nat's. He nodded and smiled at her unspoken request. There were only two welcoming faces in the camp, and she was currently infuriated with the guy attached to one of them. She pulled her covers tight and tried to get some sleep. She promised herself she'd bring up the subject of her dad with Nat again in the morning.

Long before sunrise, Squint kicked Taylor awake to help start breakfast. It wasn't much: hardtack biscuits fried in bacon grease, peach preserves, and bitter coffee the consistency of maple syrup.

Taylor spent as little time with William as possible. She could tell he was anxious, though, when he came by to help her haul the cooking supplies back onboard.

"Are you okay?" Taylor said. She didn't make eye contact.

"A little hungry," he said. "Good thing I still have a few *real* energy bars."

Taylor bit her lip at that. That comment probably came out more bitterly than William had intended. Maybe. She hoped it had.

"I was trying to keep you going," she said.

William shook his head. "I know. I should have known you can't conjure food. If I'd have been listening, my jet amulet would have tipped me off."

She quirked an eyebrow. "Yeah, you really need to pay more attention to that thing."

William sighed. "Are we bringing *her* up again?"

"I didn't say a word!" Taylor said. "I'm just trying to get both of us out of here. Maybe you could try not to die." She went back to scraping the last of the bacon grease into a little tin tub. She didn't make eye contact with him; her comment definitely came out more bitterly than she had intended.

"Taylor, what was I supposed to do?" William said. "I couldn't back down."

"I'm not saying you could."

"Then what's the matter?"

She shook her head. "You just can't be taking chances like that. It's dangerous."

"Did I hear right?" William said. "Did *Taylor Smart* just tell me I shouldn't take chances?"

Taylor scowled. "I'm serious, William. I can't let you—" She stopped herself from saying more. Yesterday's dream of Anya Redmane and her bloody shroud was still too fresh in her mind.

"Listen, Taylor," William said, "I don't need you holding my hand."

At a distance, Luther chuckled at that. Taylor blushed and stared him down. The fae looked down at his plate, but not before flashing William a mischievous grin.

"You don't need to worry," Taylor said, glowering. "I won't be holding your hand anytime in the near future."

"What's that supposed to mean?" William said.

Taylor went back to scouring a skillet. She said, "Nothing," and immediately felt a sharp twinge in her stomach.

"Are you sure about that?"

She sighed. "I just don't want you to...get hurt. Okay?"

"Well...fine," William said. He started to walk away.

"William, wait."

He stood with his back to Taylor.

"I'm sorry," she said. "It's just...."

William turned. Taylor brushed a strand of hair from her face.

Nat strolled up beside William. "I hear you made quite an impression last night, young man," he said.

Taylor glanced in Nat's direction and put on a smile. "You could say that."

"I was gathering firewood when you and Tobias went at it," Nat continued. He smiled and patted him on the back. "I figure the old percht deserved it."

"Percht," Taylor said. "That's what Tobias is?"

Nat nodded. "Think of him as sort of a satyr with a mean streak. But don't let him get to you, son. He's mostly bluster."

"Mostly," William repeated.

Nat's face darkened. "He's not the main thing you two have to worry about."

"Osaa," Taylor guessed.

"If you want to get home, you're going to have to go through him."

"Everybody acts like he's trouble," William said.

"That's because he is," Nat said. "And he's been flexing his muscles lately." He gestured toward the *Misery*. "That cargo back there? Most of it is for him. Raw materials, supplies to stock his garrisons, muskets and elf-shot, every kind of useful magical trinket from here to Dunhoughkey."

"It sounds like he's preparing for war," Taylor said.

"That it does," Nat agreed. "Osaa controls the river, but others wish he didn't. The men of the swamp mostly keep to themselves, but other than them, pretty much everybody on the river is riled up. Water folk, ogres, deer people, tie snakes.... You name 'em, they're looking to grab themselves a bigger piece of the pie."

"And Osaa has the advantage," Taylor said.

"He's been stomping everybody else like June bugs," Nat said. "At least, he has been the last few months. Those that are smart are coming around to his side."

"But the nunnehi—" Taylor said.

"Keep their distance," Nat said. "Making a stink over Osaa would bring on a bigger headache than they're ready to handle, I expect."

Which meant Tsisgwa and his warriors probably wouldn't be launching any rescue missions. Taylor sighed. Things just kept getting worse.

"This is the guy who can get us home?" William asked. He arched an anxious eyebrow. "And we trust him...why?"

"I don't trust him any farther than I can throw him," Nat said. "He's bad news. Dennis likes doing business with him—don't ask me why. But if you want to get home, he's about your only chance."

"I don't understand," William said.

"He's got the whole river buttoned up tight," Nat explained. "He's not letting anybody else get a toehold in his territory, and that means no ring travel. Period."

Taylor remembered how the nunnehi had shut down the ring network around Macon last spring to keep a fugitive from escaping. And before that, her grandfather did something similar and forced her and Claudia Fountain to make an unplanned stop at Judaculla Rock.

"Sure, he could open a portal long enough to send you two home," Nat continued, "but that's not likely to happen."

Taylor started to say something, but Nat cut her off. "The good news is his power doesn't reach any farther than the Narrows. That's what the river men call a stretch about a day's journey upriver from the mouth. Once you get past the Narrows, you come around closer to the Topside world again. Hit the right spot at sunrise, and you should pop out on human earth with hardly any effort at all."

"And...he's just going to let us pass?" Taylor said. "He's not going to want anything from us?"

Nat waved dismissively. "He and Dennis have an arrangement. As far as he knows, you two are just part of the crew. And even if he did decide to get testy, I'll be there." He grinned. "I can pretty much talk anybody into anything."

Dennis called for everybody to load up. Polemen started carrying their rucksacks and bedrolls back to the boat. William excused himself and gathered up his own stuff.

Squint didn't seem interested in helping Taylor load up the cooking supplies. She said a few choice words about that under her breath and finished packing up.

Just as she was about to haul the kettle back aboard, Nat reappeared.

"Let me help," he said.

"You don't have to."

"I want to." He smiled and grabbed the kettle by its handle. Taylor lugged a box of cooking utensils behind him.

On their second load, they had to stop behind Tobias and William, who had arrived at the gangplank at the same time. They glared at each other, but William made a show of letting Tobias pass in front of him. Tobias muttered something in German. William gritted his teeth, let another couple of polemen pass, and then shouldered his bag and trudged aboard.

Taylor shook her head and sighed.

Nat chuckled to himself.

"Is something funny?" Taylor asked.

Nat held the cabin door open and let Taylor in with her box of cooking utensils. He followed her in and set the morning's unused firewood in a box near the door.

"You might say that," he said.

"What?"

"That annoyed look you gave William." He looked at her, and his smile faltered a little. "You reminded me of your mom. She gave Aulberic that look. A lot."

Taylor's heart pounded. *This is it*, she thought. She cleared her throat. "So...my dad."

"Yeah?"

"He was your friend."

Nat held the door open for Taylor. They left the cabin to make one more load. "We both fostered at Mullandy."

"I beg your pardon?"

Nat explained as the plodded back down the gangplank. "It's customary for boys to spend a few decades with their mom's brother. He's supposed to be sort of a second father, make sure a guy learns all the things it takes to be a man."

"Your moms both had brothers at...Mullandy, did you say?"

Nat nodded. He collected the last of the kitchen supplies. Taylor hefted her bedroll and Nat's. They headed back aboard. "Aulberic's uncle was an advisor to the Teyrnus. Mine was in the palace guard."

"You said..." Taylor wanted to be diplomatic, but she didn't really understand enough to know what landmines to avoid. "That is...earlier it sounded like a sídhe and a pisgy being friends..."

"Yeah," Nat said. "The Gentry aren't warm to the idea of getting too close to folks who are beneath their station. Your dad, though...he didn't have much patience for that."

Taylor's heart fluttered. They entered the cabin. Nat set his box on the floor and finished his story. "We spent...must have been twenty years...giving our uncles grief. Aulberic was bored with palace life. He was on track to be the Teyrnus of his own rath some day—being the son of the Chief Matron and all—and to tell you the truth, I think the whole idea gave him the shivers."

"My dad—my adoptive dad—is an accountant," Taylor said. "He sometimes complains about being cooped up in his office."

"Being a Teyrnus was more than Aulberic could take," Nat said. "I don't think there was a single thing he liked about helping his uncle run the rath, until..." The pisgy smiled.

"Until what?"

"Well, there was this big to-do over in Dulauny. That's the capital of the Spring Court. Luey Heath was being installed as the new Primus, and, of course, all the fae nobility were invited. And I mean *all* the nobility. Every Court sent representatives."

Taylor gasped. "That's where he met Shanna."

"You guessed it," Nat said.

"And they fell in love."

"*Aulberic* fell in love," Nat said with a wink. "Shanna took a little convincing. That annoyed look I told you about?" He shook his head. "If I was Aulberic, I think I'd have given up then and there."

If he had, Taylor thought, then he'd still be alive. Of course, Taylor would have never been born.

"But they got together, though. I mean, obviously."

"You have to understand, this was a week-long event. Processions, magical contests, banquets, parties every night, the whole thing. The second or third night, Aulberic had me run interference for him. Shanna had come with some bonehead named Mold. But I...uh...I'm pretty good at leading people on wild goose chases."

"So you took care of Mold, and Aulberic got to spend time with Shanna."

"That's about the size of it," Nat said. "And eventually, I guess he kind of grew on her."

"Bundlestraw!" Dennis yelled.

"It's time to get underway," Nat said.

"Thank you...for telling me all this."

"I'd hoped I'd get the chance," Nat said. "And one more thing—if I'm not being too forward?"

"Uh..."

"Your friend William seems like a nice enough guy," Nat said. "I wouldn't ride him too hard about last night if I were you."

Taylor knitted her brow.

"He was defending his honor, and that's not a bad thing. And on top of that, if I might be so bold, I wonder if he wasn't hoping to impress you."

"Impress me?"

Nat smiled. "Guys can do some awfully stupid things when there's a pretty girl around to watch them."

Taylor's face warmed, and the deck beneath her tilted a little. Surely William was past that phase! "He's just my best friend's brother," she protested. "That's it."

169

"If you say so," Nat said. He chuckled and turned toward the door.

*Chapter 17*

# Mothers and Daughters

Jill peered into her scrying bowl. She tried to concentrate on William, but her thoughts kept drifting to her mom.

Mrs. Matthews had spent all of Monday morning curled up on the couch, seemingly in a daze. Jill was afraid to even go near her. She made her own lunch and worked in her room on the little bit of homework she'd been given for Thanksgiving break.

Jill couldn't imagine what it would be like for one's child to disappear, and she realized this was the second time in as many years her mom had had to deal with that. Jill herself had gotten caught up in Taylor's family drama a couple summers ago, and now William was gone.

But as bad as that had to be for a parent, what happened to William was even worse. Jill's mom had never gotten used to the idea of magic. As far as she was concerned, it was something evil she barely tolerated in her house. It didn't matter that her own mom was a witch, or that Maymay had taught Jill ways to keep her Second Sight in check so she didn't go nuts from constantly seeing the deepest parts of people's souls.

Jill sighed and stretched.

She was once again seated inside a circle of power in the basement, her scrying bowl in front of her.

"Come on, William," she whispered. "Where are you?"

Maybe if she could use magic to bring William back....

She took a long, shallow breath.

What was keeping Danny? Shouldn't he have been there by now?

"Jill," her mom called from the top of the stairs. Her tone was flat, but Jill could hear the weariness in it. She'd been crying.

"Yes, Mom?"

"Are you going to spend the whole day down there?"

The candles she'd set at the four cardinal directions had burned down to half the size of when she'd started. "Just a few more minutes."

The door to the basement closed with no further comment. Jill didn't think that was good news.

*Can't worry about that now*, she thought. Her mom didn't like it, but Jill had to do something.

*Focus!* she told herself. William was alive, he had to be. But where?

She peered into the water. It rippled, almost imperceptibly.

The colors of the room began to shift, to brighten. Shadows twisted at odd angles. Jill recognized the sensation. Rather than resist it, she allowed her Second Sight to open wide.

The candles started to burn green.

The next instant, Jill was no longer in the basement. She was in a small room with cinder-block walls.

She'd experienced something similar that first summer on the run with Taylor. She was having a vision.

Jill panned the room, looking for William. He wasn't there.

The four people in the room were all white men, all redheads with hair ranging from gingerbread to carrot top. They were all dressed in shabby clothes in ten or twenty different shades of green. They had pointed ears and impish, upturned eyebrows.

It was summer, or at least they all looked hot and sweaty. That surprised Jill, since she'd only ever had visions of things in the present. She'd figure out what it meant later. For now, she just took in the rest of the scene.

The place looked like some kind of cheap dormitory. Maybe the kind of place migrant workers would camp out. Two of the men played cards around a beat-up table. The third hung out on a couch that might have been rescued from the dump while the fourth kicked back reading a magazine on the single bare bed in the corner. Somebody unseen was rattling pots and pans in the next room.

Disco music played on a transistor radio.

"How much longer, Meryasek?" One of the card-players said. He had an easygoing Creole drawl.

And then she heard crying.

Her eyes locked on the doorway to the back room—the kitchen, apparently.

A fifth man appeared in dark green bellbottoms and a lighter green striped shirt with the sleeves rolled up. Meryasek, apparently. In his arms was a little black girl. She couldn't have been more than three years old. She was barefooted and wearing a pink sundress stained with ketchup. Her hair was a mess. Her little hand clutched the handle of a sippy cup with Big Bird's face on it.

"Can't be much longer," Meryasek said. He bounced the little girl on his hip. "We left enough breadcrumbs."

The rest of the men laughed at that.

"Teach that Jack lady to mess with the boss!" a guy on the couch said to general agreement.

Meryasek ambled toward the window and pulled back the blinds. "You see your momma, little girl?" he said. His mouth stretched into a smile that had nothing to do with friendliness.

"Momma!" the girl cried. Jill's pulse began to race. She did not like the way this was going.

Outside, a black cat stalked toward the building. The little girl squirmed to get out of Meryasek's arms.

Everyone else laughed at a joke that nobody said out loud.

"What's it been? Three hours?" the card-player asked.

"Something like that," Meryasek answered. "I don't think it'll—"

There was an explosion at the back of the building. The little girl shrieked while the men sprung to their feet. The one nearest the doorway to the kitchen lunged forward.

A woman's voice thundered, *"Shari enechthron!"* There was an undignified grunt, followed by a flash of light. Someone—or something—flung the green-clad man back into the main room, unconscious.

The woman emerged.

Jill gasped.

She was short and curvy, about twenty-five or thirty years old, with a big, proud Afro held in check by a yellow headband that matched the stripes in her red dashiki. In her right hand was a wooden staff with an ornate carved knob at the top.

It was Jill's grandmother, only younger. It had to be—she'd used that staff as a walking stick as long as Jill could remember.

So this was definitely a vision of the past. But that meant the little girl...

"Give me back my daughter!" Maymay demanded.

Jill gulped. "Mom?" she whimpered.

One of the men thrust forward his hand and a bolt of magical energy arced toward Jill's grandmother. It glanced off an invisible barrier emanating from Maymay's staff.

At the same time, she flicked her blasting rod toward the attacker with another angry incantation. He crumpled to the ground.

The black cat appeared at Maymay's feet. It yowled and raised its hackles.

Maymay held her staff horizontally with both hands. It crackled with golden light.

The remaining men eased backwards.

"Momma!" the little girl squealed, now with joy. She squirmed even harder in Meryasek's arms.

"I said," she spat through gritted teeth, "Give me back my daughter, you filthy pixie."

Meryasek handed little Sophie to one of his henchmen. He let his arms hang loose at his side, but Jill could tell he was summoning magic. He'd try to blast her grandmother before long.

"I'm afraid you're too late, Mrs. Blay," Meryasek said with a shrug and a wink. If Jill weren't for all intents and purposes an invisible ghost, she'd have slapped that mirthless smile off his face.

"Now," Maymay said, her voice barely above a whisper.

Meryasek said. "She took the faery food from my own hand," Meryasek said. He could barely contain his glee. "She's mine!"

*Oh no*, Jill thought. Her head swam.

Her mother had bought in? She had become bound to the Wonder? That couldn't be! Her mom was as unmagical as you could get!

Jill watched as fear and desperation tightened her grandmother's expression. She clenched her fists on her staff.

"So let's cut to the chase," the leader said. "You may surmise that we're mired in a predicament from which neither of us is poised to actualize an auspicious causatum. You are in error. In fact, your position is patently unamelioratable. That's why mark riffle throbe within the parambuments of—"

The cat squalled and slashed at the pixie's ankle. He kicked at the creature, but missed as it darted behind Maymay's legs.

"I'm not as easily addled as *that*, Meryasek," Maymay said.

"All right," he said. "Then let me tell it to you straight. Here's what's going to happen, Mrs. Blay." He took a step forward, but stopped when the cat took a swing at him with its claw. He raised his hands when Maymay trained her staff on him. "My boss has decided to let you live, but you're going to keep your ugly nose out of his business. Understand?"

A tear snaked down Maymay's cheek, but her voice was hard as steel. "You can tell your boss—"

"Unfortunately," Meryasek interrupted, "Mr. du Lac says you need to be taught a lesson." He looked pitifully toward little Sophie. "Say goodbye to your mommy, sweetheart."

Maymay switched her staff to her left hand and pulled a tiny square mirror from the bag slung across her body. She held it in front of her like a cross holding a vampire at bay. "Lay one finger on Sophie, *Carscoddrog*, and I promise you'll regret it."

Meryasek's eyes widened and his jaw dropped.

"That's right, Meryasek, I know your true name. And don't think I won't use it."

The other pixies quaked and scrambled for cover.

"H-how did you...?" The dynamic in the room had suddenly changed. Meryasek's face flushed. "You wouldn't dare!"

"*I command thee, Carscoddrog!*" Maymay thundered. "*I bind thee, Carscoddrog! I adjure thee, Carscoddrog! Baphenem! Ithonyome!*"

With each utterance of the pixie's true name, he flinched as if his insides were being tied into literal knots. She tossed the mirror to the ground in front of Meryasek as she shouted, "*Eseshopi!*"

There was a pop, a sudden change in air pressure, and Meryasek vanished.

The other pixies wailed in terror. One of them took a tentative step in Maymay's direction, but she leveled her staff at him and he backed off.

Maymay looked down at the mirror on the ground. Jill followed her gaze. When she saw Meryasek's terrified face staring out of the glass, his fists pounding against it, her heart nearly leaped into her throat.

Maymay slammed the butt of her staff against the mirror, smashing it into a thousand pieces. She rounded on the pixie who'd been given charge of Sophie.

"Anybody else want to make a claim on my daughter?"

The pixie set the girl gently on the ground.

"It d-don't make no difference, lady," he said. "She done bought in, remember? Sh-she won't never be at home on human earth no more."

Sophie flew to her mother. Maymay hoisted her up onto her hip while keeping her staff extended in her right hand.

"We'll have to see about that, won't we?"

"What you gonna do?" a different pixie said. Maymay spun to face him, and he flinched backward. He braced himself, though, and continued. "You gonna suck the magic out of her?"

She bit her lip. There was fire in her eyes, but also deep, deep sadness. "That's exactly what I'm going to do." Her eyes flashed. "Now get!"

The remaining pixies disappeared in a flash of light.

Maymay held her little girl tight and sobbed quietly. She stood there for at least a minute.

The cat leaped up onto the bed and watched the scene play out.

"Come on, Circe," Maymay told the cat. "We've got some magic to do."

The phone rang upstairs, jolting Jill out of her vision. She was back in the basement. Her breaths came hard and fast. She stopped herself from shaking and tried to make sense of what she'd seen.

Faeries had kidnapped her mom, years ago. Worse than that, her mom had bought in: she'd eaten faery food and bound herself to the Wonder.

Jill had been tricked into doing the same thing two summers ago. It had thrown her natural Second Sight into overdrive and nearly driven her insane until her grandmother had taught her how to control it.

But the vision didn't make sense. Her mom didn't have any magic. She hated the idea of doing magic. If her mom had bought in, how was she able to have a normal life in the mortal world?

"Jill," her mom called from the top of the stairs.

"Yes, ma'am?"

"That was Mrs. Smart on the phone. She says there's someone over there who's hoping to see you."

Danny.

"I'll be right up." Maybe that meant he had an idea how to find William and Taylor.

She met her mother at the top of the stairs. She'd worn the same haggard look for days now. Jill could barely make eye contact with her.

Her dad was there, too, with his hand on her mom's shoulder.

"I don't know why you have to go over there," her mom said. "Why couldn't this person just come here?"

"The wards," Jill said. She'd just figured it out herself. "Maymay put wards around the house. William and I've been keeping them up. I don't think Danny could even reach the doorbell without our permission."

"Charles, are you hearing this?" her mom said. Her voice was brittle, ready to break. "Are you telling me you still approve of this?"

"Honey—" her dad started, but cut himself off when Mrs. Matthews glared at him.

"Mom." Jill found the courage to look her mom in the eye. Then she opened her Second Sight.

She'd Seen her mom before, of course. To her supernatural senses, Mrs. Matthews was a mass of contradictions. She gave off a golden aura, light and kind and generous, but it was often overshadowed with reddish-gray mist: anger and frustration about her own mother hiding her magical nature from her, about her children being born with the gift, about her inability to make sense of what this could mean for her life, both now and in the future.

Jill peered deeper. Beneath the anger were doubts and fears—which seemed perfectly reasonable, given everything she'd been through the past year or so.

Normally, this would have been where Jill looked away. It was hard to see her mom as a frail, fallible human being. Almost as hard as knowing there was a big part of her life that her mom didn't understand and didn't even want to.

But she looked deeper still, and that's when she saw it.

Second Sight was usually more symbolic than literal, at least for Jill. She was used to seeing people bathed in different colored auras, or surrounded by clouds, or somehow dressed to represent different personality traits.

It was usually all she could handle to See the clouds of fury swirling around her mom when she was upset about something magic-related.

Now, though, she found the courage to look even deeper. Or maybe it wasn't courage. Maybe her vision in the basement made it more obvious.

As Jill kept looking, she Saw a hole in her mother's heart. It wasn't angry or gory. It wasn't even a wound, just an empty spot as big as a softball in the middle of her chest that Jill could look through and see her dad's shirt as he stood behind her.

"Oh, Mom," she said, and threw her arms around her. She let out a great, gasping wail as tears filled her eyes and spilled onto her mom's shirt.

It had only taken a second, but that was enough. She understood. The pixie in her vision had said something about Maymay sucking the magic out. That had to be it. It was the only way Maymay could save her mom, the only way she could keep her tied to this world.

Jill shuddered. She remembered a moment of utter despair she'd faced two summers ago. Mara Hellebore started to do something like that to her, but it nearly drove her over the edge, and Taylor made Mara stop.

"Oh, God." She squeezed her eyes shut and tried to calm herself.

Mara hadn't even tried to be gentle, like her grandmother would have. But even so....

"It must have been terrible," she said. "I'm so, so sorry."

"Baby, what are you talking about?" Mrs. Matthews said.

"Y-you probably don't even remember, do you?"

"Jill," her dad said, "what's going on?"

With her Second Sight safely turned off, she looked at her dad. "You remember Danny Underhill, right, Dad?"

Mr. Matthews nodded.

"He and I are going to...." She glanced at her mom and winced against the firestorm that was about to erupt. "...We're going to go find William and Taylor."

"You're *what*?" her mom said.

"Mom, just listen. I know you don't like... I mean, I know it's hard for you to understand...but I can find them, Mom. With Danny's help, I know I can."

Mrs. Matthews looked to her husband, asking a hundred questions with her eyes.

Dad turned to Jill. "Tell me the truth," he said. "Do you really think you can do this?"

"Charles, you can't seriously—"

"Not by myself," Jill interrupted. "But Danny's...pretty impressive. He knows lots more magic than I do."

"Magic." Jill's mom said it like a curse word.

"Yes, magic," Jill said. She planted her feet. "Mom, if calling the police would have helped, you and Dad would have done it right away. But you didn't. You know the police can't help."

Her mom started to say something, but Jill cut her off.

"I can." She took a breath. "I know I can."

There was a long silence. At last, Jill's dad said, "What can we do?"

"Pray. Hard."

# Chapter 18

# Going South

Danny watched as Jill used a knife to trace a small circle of power next to the log where Taylor liked to sit and meditate. Sitting cross-legged on the grass, she worked the relic Claudia had given Danny into a little lump of wax, which she then shaped into a crude human shape. She etched Taylor's name on the left thigh with a stylus.

"Are you sure this tooth is Taylor's?" Jill said.

"Claudia says Mrs. Redmane slapped it right out of her mouth the first time they met," Danny answered. He hung his head as if remembering a bad time. "She used it to find you and Taylor the time you two ended up in New Cephalonia. Or Louisiana, I guess you Topsiders call it."

"I'm not sure I like the idea of somebody just holding on to something like this."

"Claudia believes in being prepared. She's almost like a Winter that way."

Jill scowled at that. Then she got back to work. She waved the effigy three times over her scrying bowl, filled with water she'd poured with trembling hands from a plastic bottle in her backpack. She meditated, peering into the bowl.

"Oh!" she groaned. Something was wrong.

"Jill?"

She leaned back and seemed to gaze into the sky, but her eyes were distant, unfocused.

"Jill, what's the matter?" Danny said.

She gulped down a couple of deep breaths. Fearing she might hyperventilate, Danny reached out his hand. She stopped him before he could break her circle.

Staring at the ground, she said, "I'll be all right."

"Are you sure?"

She nodded. "It's been a while. Something about the Wonder...."

Danny didn't say anything, but he was worried. Jill had bought in two summers ago. Even though she'd learned some tricks that let her get along fine Topside, the pooka realized she was still bound to the Wonder.

"M-maybe this wasn't such a good idea," he said. "How about you just...let me go by myself?"

"No!" Jill protested. She took another deep breath. "I'll be fine. Just give me a minute."

"Jill, there ain't no shame in backing out. I can find Taylor and William and—"

"Just give me a minute, okay?"

Danny backed off. "If you say so, but I really think..." He stopped when Jill shot him an icy stare.

"It's just a matter of control," Jill said. Was she talking to Danny or to herself? She took another breath, not deep and desperate this time but measured, disciplined. Then she took another. In through the nose, out through the mouth. Slow and steady.

She extended her hand toward the circle. As she expelled her next breath, she hissed, "*Eulamo.*"

Danny felt a surge of magic that made his neck-hairs tingle. Jill was strengthening her circle of power, using it to shut out as much of the Wonder as she could. The pooka hadn't realized how strong Jill was. If she ever learned how to harness all that raw talent....

He crouched to one side of her, trying not to distract her but eager to see if her tracking spell would work. His amber eyes glowed with expectation.

Jill passed the wax fgure over the bowl one more time. Then she settled into an eerie stillness.

A minute passed.

Jill started. She looked up at Danny and announced, "I see her! She's on a boat."

"A boat?"

"On a river somewhere," she added.

"The nearest river is the Bubbling—what you Topsiders call the Ocmulgee. Could that be it?"

"Maybe," Jill said. "But I'm pretty sure she's south of here."

"How do you know that?"

"No idea. Just a feeling, I guess. And William is with her, except...."

"What?"

She shook her head. "Something is up. I don't know what, but their emotions are...on edge, I guess you'd say."

"That don't surprise me none!" Danny said. "How big is the boat?"

She chewed on the question for a second and then said, "Maybe twenty yards long. Men were pushing it down the river with poles."

"All right, then," Danny said. "That gives us a plan. We'll follow the river south. We'll go twenty or thirty miles, then stop and let you scry again. What do you think?"

"That'll work," Jill said. She took another long, shallow breath before gathering her things and breaking the circle.

Danny walked with her to the edge of the mushroom ring where they'd first entered the Wonder. "You've done this before," he said.

"That's right," she said coolly. "And in case you forgot, I *don't* like it."

"Yeah, most Topsiders have that reaction. I don't see as we have a choice, though." Danny gestured, and the ring came alive with a whirlwind of gold and silver lights.

"I can handle it," Jill said. She grabbed Danny's arm so tight it throbbed. "Let's go."

Danny and Jill stepped into the ring. This time, instead of going straight through—and ending up behind the Smarts' back yard again—Danny guided them in at an angle that spun them deeper into the Wonder. Fierce winds howled all around them as images of forests and springs, graveyards and standing stones, flashed through the pooka's consciousness.

It only took a second before they emerged from the vortex. They were standing in a different mushroom ring, this one overlooking a wide, muddy river. Jill started to topple over, but Danny grabbed her. He watched her carefully. She looked like she might throw up. More than that, she looked out of it, distracted. She closed her eyes and leaned forward, resting her hands on her knees.

Danny swallowed. He knew this was a bad idea!

"Hey, Jill," he said. He tried to keep his voice even. "Is everything okay?"

"I'm fine." She stood up straight again and fished her scrying bowl out of her backpack. "Let's just keep going."

"Are you sure? 'Cause if you need to rest a minute—"

"No!" she snapped. "We've got to keep going!"

Danny backed off. Jill started to mark out another circle.

"Let me do that," he offered.

"I'll do it."

She gouged a circle into the grass, all the while muttering and sighing. The first time, she'd been more deliberate in her actions. Now, she just looked agitated. Finally, Danny couldn't take it anymore.

"Jill, it ain't gonna help nobody to rush through this.... You want to tell me what's wrong?"

She sat in the circle and poured water into her scrying bowl. Then she looked up at the pooka with tears in her eyes.

"My mom," she said.

"Y-yeah?"

Jill sighed. "I'm afraid she's about to snap. She can't take much more of...this." She gestured to the circle, the scrying bowl.

"It must be tough to find out your kid's got magic."

"And what would you know about it?" Jill said. There was an edge to her voice.

"Nothing, I guess."

"Exactly."

"This isn't my world, Danny."

"No, it ain't."

"I've got to find William. I've got to get him home. If anything happens to him...." She sniffled and turned to her scrying bowl.

"You're doing fine," Danny said. "We'll find him. We'll find them both."

"And then...maybe it's time for William and me to give this up."

"You mean magic?" Danny furrowed his bushy brow.

Jill nodded. "It might be the only way to save Momma. If we could just put all this behind us...."

How could anybody give up magic? For Danny, that would be like giving up his right arm. "Are you sure, Jill? I mean...ain't it part of you?"

"Maymay gave it up for forty years—and for the same reason. She saw how it complicated things. How it threatened the people she loved."

Danny pondered that. What would he be willing to give up for somebody he loved? "If you say so, Jill. It's your decision. Just...don't do nothing rash, okay?"

Danny fidgeted with his hands in his pockets while she collected herself.

Finally, Jill said, "We should get started."

Danny made sure he was outside the circle. "Just take your time."

She bit her lip. Then she closed her eyes and brought her breathing under control. This time, she meditated for a solid three minutes before she even tried to cast the circle. She took her time with her tracking spell, too. Even so, it looked to Danny like she was struggling not to pass out.

"You're doing great," he offered.

She acknowledged him with a nod. A minute later, she said, "They're still on the river. And they're south of us. Don't ask me how I know."

"It's probably best to go with your gut," Danny said.

"And something else: wherever they are, there's a lot of magic flowing around. Waves of it." She shuddered and wiped sweat from her brow. "It was a little distracting."

"It can get that way the deeper you go," Danny said. "We'll have to be careful." He stretched out his hand to help Jill up. They turned back to the mushroom ring, and Danny brought it to life with a gesture and a pulse of magical energy.

"I really, really hate this part," Jill muttered.

"I know," Danny said. He offered his arm, and Jill wrapped both of her arms around it. He slowly but firmly guided her into the whirlwind.

They bounced through swamps and woodlands, past mushroom rings, sparkling springs, and ancient burial mounds, farther south and deeper into the Wonder. The sound of rushing wind and the frenzied kaleidoscope of lights and colors freaked Jill out, but she managed to hang on. She didn't scream this time, but she nearly cut off circulation to Danny's arm, and he could feel her starting to shake. He extended his magical senses, looking for a good, safe place to land and give her a breather.

A vision of a gentle spring crept into his consciousness. The pooka directed his will to it. They'd land, regroup, and see how much farther—

Something jerked Danny's whole body backward. He reached his other arm around to wrap around Jill's waist.

As the two tumbled in a forward barrel roll, the girl did start to scream. Danny gritted his teeth and tried to keep his focus on the spring, but now he couldn't find it anywhere.

Something was wrong. He'd been yanked off course, and now he and Jill were hurtling through the Wonder, accelerating to the point Danny wasn't sure he could land them safely. He had to break off their flight before they got any faster.

With a savage yell, Danny struggled to break free.

In a heartbeat, the vortex disappeared, and Danny and Jill stumbled to their knees. Jill fell face-forward on the top of the burial mound where they had landed. Danny rolled halfway down the slope. His head pounded.

He opened his eyes and wished he hadn't.

Crouching before him was a giant panther, its fangs bared.

A gigantic figure appeared from behind it—at least eight feet tall, dressed in a loincloth and streaked with war paint. He held a club at the ready. When he opened his mouth, Danny could see the ogre's sharpened teeth.

"Up," the ogre grumbled. He swung his club in a lazy arc. "Now."

*Chapter 19*

# Everyone Is
# Strongly Encouraged to
# Abandon Ship

The sun didn't rise on Tuesday. Taylor could guess at the spot on the horizon where it might have risen, it just never did. Even by lunchtime, it was no lighter than dusk. A dim, orange-pink light was coming from somewhere, bathing the woods and the river in eerie hues, as if Taylor were wearing tinted sunglasses. The temperature wasn't any colder than the day before. There were even thin clouds in the sky. Just...no visible sun.

That was the kind of weird day in the Wonder it was shaping up to be.

Even the crew members, who had surely been this way before, seemed nervous. They shared wary glances. They hung lanterns on poles at the bow and stern of the *Misery* and kept on working as hard as the day before. Captain Jackalberry and Nat both spent more time pacing the deck, encouraging the crew and double-checking that the cargo and supplies were firmly secured. Most of it, Nat explained, were in waterproof containers as per Osaa's specifications.

Sometime after lunch, the *Misery* was strafed by a flock of giant birds. They were as big as condors, but were shaped more like crows or pigeons. They sported big patches of white on their otherwise black feathers, which gave them a look not entirely

189

unlike Holstein cows with wings. There were seven of them, all flying single file and screaming bloody murder.

"Mr. Bundlestraw!" the patroon called as he spied them approaching. Nat had been at the bow while Mr. Jackalberry steered the boat. But Nat had already heard them. He had the patroon's blunderbuss in his hand with the hammer cocked.

The birds' wailing set Taylor on edge—and everyone else, too. A couple of polemen flinched and ducked. Roger bellowed an ape-like warning while swatting at the air.

Nat raised his hand and summoned a blazing yellow light. It scared the birds off—all but the last two in line. Those dived straight for Jim Bob, one of the little folk polemen, grabbing him by the arms in mid-flight and pulling him off the deck.

Nat fired the blunderbuss. A spray of elf-shot erupted from the muzzle, clipping two of the birds on the wing. They dropped Jim Bob, and he fell into the river. In seconds, his buddies were reaching a pole to him and dragging him back aboard.

"What the heck were those?" Taylor said as she uncurled from ducking behind a barrel.

"Wakomos," Nat said. He kept his eyes on the place where they disappeared into the trees. "They like to hunt about this time of day."

"Hunt? You mean...for people?"

"They usually prefer wolf meat," Nat said. "But they'll eat anything if they're hungry."

That was not at all comforting to Taylor. "All right," she said. "Good to know." She peered over the water, following Nat's gaze and waiting for her heartbeat to settle back to normal.

"Taylor!" Squint yelled. He stood at the door to the cabin house.

"Yes?"

"Quit your jawing! We've got work to do!"

Squint made Taylor tie down every piece of equipment in the cabin. Even Cora consented to being put in her case and stored in the patroon's footlocker. Maybe she could tell something was up. Maybe Taylor was still jumpy after the run-in with the wakomos, but it seemed like the whole crew was getting antsy. Either way, her intuition told her to expect the worst.

As soon as she finished packing things up, she stepped back out onto the deck. Nat was hollering at the men, urging them to keep at it. Their work song set a quicker rhythm than they'd used yesterday.

Before long, Nat relieved Mr. Jackalberry at the tiller. He gave the patroon his blunderbuss as they traded positions.

The pisgy flexed his fingers just like Taylor did when she summoned magic. Aboard the *Misery*, magic was harder to come by, surrounded by running water as they were. It wasn't impossible, it just took a lot more effort.

William and the others kept poling. Even to Taylor's untrained eye, it seemed like they were going a lot faster than they were the day before, even faster than their hurried work song and faster poling should have accounted for. Taylor wondered if some unseen force was drawing them onward—toward what, she couldn't guess.

Nat stood at the tiller, peering back the way they had come. The patroon watched forward and paced nervously.

"Is this normal?" Taylor whispered to Nat as she joined him at the stern.

He grunted. "Osaa must be getting antsy. He wants his cargo, and he wants it now."

"He's making the boat go faster?" Taylor could only imagine how much magic that would take, even for something traveling on dry land. But something in the water...?

"Looks that way," Nat said. "And he's sent us a welcoming party." He gestured with his chin toward the water. Taylor followed his cue. Something dark, sleek, and fast rippled just below the surface.

"Do I want to know what that was?" she asked.

"Nope."

"Well, okay then." Taylor decided to let the matter drop, but as she glanced out at the river, she saw another ripple that might have been larger than the first.

191

William reached the stern and pulled his pole out of the water. As he stepped off the walkway and began to trudge toward the bow, she matched his pace.

"Keep your eyes open," she whispered.

"I'm kinda busy here," he said. He looked nervous, disoriented. He was wobbly and short of breath from lack of food.

"Let him do his job!" Tobias snarled from the port-side line. Roger growled in agreement.

"I'm doing fine!" William called back defiantly.

Taylor glared at William. "We really don't have time for this," she said.

"You'll listen to the wench if you know what's good for you, deathling," Tobias snapped.

"Wench?" Taylor whipped around. She trained her death-glare on Tobias. "Oh, no. You did *not*—"

"Taylor, we don't have time for this," William called, his eyebrow arched. "Remember?"

"Jackalberry never should have taken you aboard," Tobias said. "Then we wouldn't have to put up with your constant yammering!"

"Hey!" William called.

Tobias threw his pole down on the deck and marched across the empty space between the cabin door and the mountain of cotton that made up part of the *Misery*'s cargo. Taylor could see he was gathering magic.

She stepped in front of him. "*Let it go*," she said. It took extra effort to project the level of presence she wanted to. Tobias stopped inches away from Taylor, but he kept his fists clenched.

She felt a hand on her shoulder. William was gently pushing her out of the way.

"William, no."

"I don't need you fighting my battles, Taylor."

"Actually, I sort of think you do," Taylor said.

"Listen to the girl, deathling," Tobias sneered. "You'll thank her later."

"Back to work!" the patroon thundered from the bow. But it was too late. Tobias lunged forward. William sidestepped Taylor and brought his arm up to block the fae's attack. He was holding his compact—Taylor would never get used to that!—and the spell glanced off it into the cotton.

The color suddenly drained from Tobias's face. A second later, Taylor understood why: Tobias hadn't thrown a simple faery blast. Rather, he'd used some kind of fire spell, and now a tiny patch of cotton was starting to burn. A wisp of black smoke wafted toward the sunless sky.

"What's going on!" the patroon called.

William reached up to pat the fire out, but it was too high to reach.

"Fire!" Luther yelled.

"Fire?" Squint said. "Oh, Brother Mike!" He grabbed a tin bucket and pushed through the polemen to the walkway to lower it over the edge.

At the same time, Tobias had jumped on William. The two of them wrestled on the deck. Half the polemen tried to deal with the fire while the other half gathered around the fight. Even with no one poling the boat, it raced forward at startling speed.

Taylor took a half-step forward. She tried to gather magic to hurl against Tobias, but came up empty.

Some of the senior crewmen pushed their way through to stop the fight. Nat held William back while Mr. Hackjaw and Mr. Eels teamed up to restrain Tobias.

The smoke grew thick and black, and sparks wafted into the air. Some of them blew back onto the deck...or onto other patches of cotton. In a matter of seconds, Taylor counted three or four separate fires.

Squint passed his water bucket to Luther, who splashed it on the burning cotton. By now, though, it was too late.

Mr. Jackalberry was beside himself. "Get more water on those fires!" he hollered. "And man the poles before we run aground!"

Squint ran to dip his bucket in the river again, but the situation was starting to look hopeless.

The river churned all around them.

Then the *Misery* lurched to port. Itchu fell overboard, shrieking.

William turned away from the fight. He and Nat grabbed a pole and extended it to their crewmate. "Hang on!" Nat called. Tobias, still restrained, kept spitting threats and profanities.

They drew the pole in, but not fast enough. Something wrapped around Itchu's waist and pulled him under, yanking the pole from William's and Nat's hands and pulling it overboard.

The boat hurtled on. If anything, it was gaining speed even with no one poling it. Everybody was trying to put out fires in both the cotton bale and on a nearby crate where a spark had landed.

Whatever had pulled Itchu underwater had brought friends. They had to be the "welcoming party" that Nat had spied earlier. The river churned with sleek, black shapes that buffeted the boat from every side.

Some of the crew reached for crowbars or other tools to use as weapons.

"Stay calm!" Mr. Jackalberry called. No one listened.

Taylor found William's staff and bag among the supplies and hurried to bring them to him.

"What are those things?" she called to no one in particular.

"Tie snakes," Mr. Eels said, shivering. "Look sharp."

One of them slithered onto the deck. William trained the mirror at the approaching beast and hissed, "Protect us in the present hour! *Bientôt, bientôt! Vite, vite!*"

The snake pulled itself up to waist height. It chuckled and said, "Cute." Then it lunged at William. He was too stunned to defend himself—and Taylor wasn't far behind him. All she could do was call his name.

No sooner had the tie snake wrapped itself around William's ankles, another poleman dove into the fray. It was Mr. Hackjaw. He held his golden amulet in his hand, pressing it against the tie snake's flesh. The monster's leathery hide sizzled and smoked where the amulet touched it, and it flung itself away.

Another black snake leaped onto the deck. "What do you think you're doing, you dimwits?" the tie snake hissed. It wrapped itself around Mr. Eels's ankle. "You're burning Osaa's cargo!"

The splotchy-faced fae shrieked while three or four polemen grabbed him by the arms to keep the creature from pulling him overboard.

Tie snakes began yanking the waterproof crates and barrels into the river with distressing ease. One of them, whose hide was bluer than it was black, hissed, "The cotton's ruined! Leave it!"

So they were claiming Osaa's property, apparently. Which made sense if the boat that carried it was going up in flames. Taylor blasted frantically at the nearest tie snake. It rolled over on its back, and Taylor dared to smile. *At least blasting works on them*, she thought.

But now that she'd used her blast, what could she do? Even under the best of circumstances, it took a while to recharge after a blast, and it took Taylor longer than most. And needless to say, these were not the best of circumstances. She backed toward the cabin, hoping to find a place of safety.

Tie snakes were all over the deck now. About half the crew was either wrapped in their coils or fending them off with whatever weapons they had. Mr. Jackalberry got off a shot with his blunderbuss. Tobias flung stunning spells, miniature pyrotechnics that erupted in a confusion of lights and sounds.

*That's all we need*, Taylor thought, *more fire!*

As if things couldn't get any worse, a tie snake yanked the captain off the deck and into the river. Taylor frantically looked around for Nat, hoping the pisgy realized he was now in command. She couldn't see him anywhere.

Roger danced across the deck, stomping on every tie snake that came close to him. Soon, though, he was swarmed by four or five of the creatures at once.

The *Misery* drifted out of control. Taylor eyed the quickly approaching riverbank. They would run aground in no time if they couldn't get the boat back under control.

William scrambled to his feet. He slammed his staff against the deck, swatting at a different reptile as it slithered toward Mr. Hackjaw. The short, black fae grabbed William's wrist to keep from being pulled overboard.

The *Misery* spun about, buffeted in the churning river. Soon, they were heading downriver sideways as even more tie snakes circled the boat. Taylor couldn't shake the feeling that they were acting a lot like hungry sharks.

Then the whole boat lurched to port and half the crew emptied into the water, screaming and thrashing. Taylor braced herself in the doorway to the cabin house.

William and Tobias were braced against one of the *Misery*'s massive, burning cargo crates.

From within the cabin, Taylor heard Cora's muffled screams. She darted inside and pulled at the footlocker's latches.

"What's going on?" the banjo asked. Her tone was frantic.

"Tie snakes," Taylor said.

"Well, get me out of here!"

Taylor wasn't getting anywhere with the latches. She rummaged through the kitchen supplies for the biggest knife she could find. Seconds later, she was hacking away at the lock.

Just then, someone yelled "Sandbar!"

There was a terrible crack. The cabin lurched backward, slamming Taylor and the footlocker hard against the back wall. The cabin door was now directly above them, looking out onto the dusky orange-pink sky.

Fortunately, the impact finished Taylor's work on the lid of the footlocker. Taylor pondered whether a banjo case would serve as a flotation device.

"Come on," she said, and grabbed the case.

The cabin was filling with water. Even worse, the walls were under assault from what sounded like a dozen massive hammers pounding on every surface.

It wasn't long until a tie snake's head splintered the wood and the creature itself dropped into the cabin followed by a jet of water.

Taylor was already thigh-deep, but she blasted the creature. It had absolutely no effect on the tie snake, but it threw her off balance. She tipped backward and held on to Cora's banjo case with both arms.

When she managed to stand up again, the water was chest-deep. She knew what was coming, so she took a deep breath.

As her head went under, she heard two more thunderous cracks. Then something wrapped itself around her legs. It yanked her upward toward the cabin door.

She held onto Cora's case with all her strength as the tie snake pulled her away.

The rope securing the cargo crate made a decent handhold. William grabbed it first, but Tobias was at his side in a second. The fae glared at him and kicked him hard in the shin.

William gasped but didn't let go. "What are you doing?" he yelled. Didn't that idiot know they were sinking?

Tobias gestured, and William's consciousness was suddenly filled with flashing lights and the sounds of explosions. He scrunched his eyes shut, but didn't dare release his grip.

He concentrated on his jet amulet, but he didn't trust it to work. Even if he wasn't about to faint from hunger, his magic was pretty much depleted as long as he was on the river.

"Seriously?" William exclaimed. "We're both about to go down with the ship!"

"Are you afraid, deathling?"

"There's more important things going on right now, you know?" he said. *And it's no fair you've still got so much magic!*

Tie snakes slithered across the deck. They chomped through the ropes securing the cargo, and when a poleman got in their way, they tossed him effortlessly into the river.

Then somebody yelled "Sandbar!" A second later, the *Misery* lurched and snapped in two. The aft section broke away and began to sink. William's vision was still blurry from Tobias's stunning spell.

Taylor was back there!

He sensed motion through the rope. He swung his staff upward just as Tobias took a swipe at him. It found the back of the fae's hand.

Tobias snarled with agony and rage.

The next thing William knew, something had wrapped itself around his arm—something alive, wriggly, and impossibly strong.

The tie snake had yanked William away from his handhold. It might have yanked his arm away from his body if he hadn't let go. The thing had a grip like iron, and it flung William into the water as easily as he might toss one of Jill's old dolls.

All he could do was take a deep breath and hope for the best.

## Chapter 20

# Bad Times with Osaa

As William sank into the water, more tie snakes wrapped around him, entwining his arms and legs and dragging him deeper.

He opened his eyes, but the water was black all around him—and cold as ice. Struggle as he might, he wasn't strong enough to break free from the tie snakes. He felt their bodies undulating, pulling him along.

He was completely disoriented. He couldn't tell which way was up. Then, when his lungs had nearly given out, his head broke above the water. He gasped for air and tried to stop his teeth from chattering. He felt himself being dragged onto land—a slimy, hard-packed mud that gave only slightly against his weight.

The tie snakes slithered over his body and then away. He heard labored breathing in the darkness, which told him he wasn't the only survivor. He tried to call out, but crumpled in a coughing fit as soon as he tried. The echoes told him he was in some kind of vast chamber, probably a cave. It was ventilated, though. He could hear a faint whistling sound, wind passing through unseen openings in the rock.

The cold was nearly unbearable. William reached for his bag—and then cursed. He'd lost both his bag and his staff in the confusion, which meant they were currently at the bottom of the river. All he had to work with were the few items he kept in his pockets. His denim jacket was as soaked as the rest of him, and it would keep him soaked as long as he wore it. He shrugged it off until it could dry; he didn't need a case of hypothermia on top of everything else.

His head throbbed with cold, hunger, and lack of oxygen. He was running on pure Gumption. But he wasn't alone. There were definitely others around him: he could hear them breathing in the darkness, groaning from their injuries.

He got his breath under control and tried again to call out. "Taylor?" No answer.

He needed light and heat, but his options for conjuring any were limited. He rummaged through his pockets. He came across an energy bar—his last one. Part of him wanted to unwrap it and wolf it down, but he didn't dare, not until he knew more about his surroundings. He rifled through the rest of his pockets and took inventory: he still had his jet amulet, a couple packages of salt, a small vial of myrrh...

Then he found it, and breathed a prayer of thanks.

William drew his Pawpaw's gold class ring from a zipped pocket on the thigh of his cargo pants. Gold had magical associations with light, fire, and healing. He rehearsed in his mind what he would have to do to call forth those powers.

He took a long, slow breath. He tried to convince himself his bath in the river would work to his advantage, cleansing his body and mind of any residual magic that might get in the way of effective spell-casting. At least, he hoped that would be the case.

In the darkness, William traced a circle around himself with his finger. He couldn't see it, and it was likely far from perfect, but he'd practiced drawing circles of power for so long in his basement, maybe he could at least get it partly right. A circle wasn't technically necessary for what he had in mind, but he needed every advantage.

He closed the circle with another expelled breath and the incantation "*Eulamo.*" As soon as the final syllable left his lips, he felt the subtle snap of magical energies coming to bear. He grinned. He sat cross-legged inside the circle.

William held the ring loosely in his right hand and tried to relax. He practiced the incantation in his head before he said it out loud. Some of the more powerful spells Maymay had taught him were in a mixture of foreign languages. But what he had in mind was pretty basic. It pretty much had to be. Most of the basic spells were in English. A lot of those, for reasons William still couldn't fathom, were lines from Shakespeare.

"Give me the light," he intoned, gentle as a whisper, "upon thy life, I charge thee."

The ring began to glow with a soft, golden gleam. It was enough to reveal William's surroundings. He stood up.

As he'd guessed, he was in a cave. The ceiling was so high it was still shrouded in darkness, but William could see the lapping water to one side and a large dry patch higher up the muddy slope. Other shapes moved and scratched against the ground: Squint, the cook; Taylor (thank God!) clutching a banjo case to her chest...and Tobias and Roger. William's temples pounded even harder when he saw them.

Tie snakes were dragging survivors onto the beach, most of them unconscious. Others hauled charred barrels from the wreckage, and teams of two or three tackled the crates.

"Is everybody all right?" Squint groaned. An orb of faery fire burst into existence in his hand. As soon as the little person gained his own feet, he helped Taylor up.

William took a step. As he left his circle, the ring's light dimmed, but it didn't go completely out. He ran to Taylor, who was clutching the handle of Cora's banjo case. He wanted to throw his arms around her, but before he could, a voice echoed throughout the cave.

"Which one of you is in charge?"

It was a low, gravelly voice, almost a whisper—but a loud one, like a stage whisper meant for everyone to hear. The speaker also sounded impatient. He had the same tone William's parents would take when he or Jill had done something stupid.

William slipped the gold ring onto his finger and aimed it at the source of the sound. With another effort of will, he cranked the light back up. The high ground in the cave looked like a rounded mound of ropy blackness. William had seen pictures of lava flows in Hawaii and wondered if that's what he was looking at.

At the edge of the mound, near the mud-caked shore, a tie snake reared.

William sucked in a breath. The monsters that had attacked the *Misery* were six or seven feet long at most, but this one was twice that size and bigger around than his thigh. It swayed back and forth hypnotically with half of its length trailing behind it.

Its head curved downward at the snout, giving it a mouth that reminded William of a hawk's beak. Above its eyes were horned ridges that formed a spiky crown. It was all black except for a patch of white under its jaw and down the length of its throat.

Lanterns hung from bronze wall sconces suddenly lit of their own accord all around the cavern. It was bigger than William had guessed. The dim light threw weird shadows that seemed to writhe with impatience.

"Well?" the tie snake said. William remembered the tie snakes talking onboard the *Misery*. He wondered how they actually did it with no lips or anything. Then he reminded himself there were more pressing issues to deal with.

Squint stepped forward. "Squint Crunkle at your service, sir."

"Where is Dennis Jackalberry?" the tie snake asked. It twisted and swayed as it spoke.

Roger began to stir. He thrashed his enormous arms to and fro and struggled to his feet. As soon as he saw the tie snake, he hooted an agitated comment to Tobias.

A tie snake dragged another crewman out of the water: Itchu, the Native American fae who hung around with Tobias and Roger. He coughed up water and moaned.

"I...uh...don't rightly know where the patroon got to, sir," Squint said. "It got a little crazy there at the end."

"Then you are the mate?" the tie snake said.

"The cook, actually...sir."

The tie snake sighed, but it turned into a hiss as it trailed off. "Then I suppose you'll have to do." With that, its form changed. It melted and contracted. Arms and legs sprouted. In a second, it had taken on the form of a man: a six-foot tall handsome Native American with close-cropped, spiky hair. He was now dressed in a black suit of the finest material, black alligator shoes, and a black silk shirt. The only splash of color was a white silk necktie that corresponded to the white patch on the tie snake's throat. It gleamed against the blackness of his ensemble.

"I'm told at least a third of my cargo is damaged beyond repair," the human-shaped tie snake said. His voice was just as low and breathy as before he transformed.

William felt a ball of lead land in the pit of his stomach.

"*Y-your* cargo?" Squint said. He didn't look any happier than William felt. "Then I take it I have the honor of addressing Osaa?"

"As you say."

The tie snake stepped onto the mound and seemed to glide five feet upward to a raised chair William hadn't noticed before. It reminded William of a throne, but there was something odd about it.

It didn't take long for William to figure it out, and when he did he nearly fainted. The chair itself was made of tie snakes—a dozen or more of them wrapping around each other, holding each other in place in the form of a high-backed throne. And then it hit him: it wasn't just the chair. The mound wasn't made of lava as William had first assumed: the whole thing was a heap of tie snakes. What he had first thought was the sound of wind was actually the hissing of hundreds, maybe thousands, of the creatures.

"Now," Osaa said, "who is the idiot who set fire to my property?"

"He did it!" Tobias shouted, jabbing a finger at William.

Taylor blurted, *"That's not true!"* Her voice echoed around the cavern, where it was joined with the sounds of a thousand hissing tie snakes.

Her head was still swimming, and she was freezing in her waterlogged clothes. Her eyes darted between William and Tobias. They both looked angry, like they were itching to finish what they'd started on the boat.

"You threw the fireball!" William said.

"And you let it land in the cotton!" Tobias countered. "If you had any sense in your head, you'd have sent it into the air."

They rounded on each other. Tobias gathered magic. William was wearing a ring that blazed with golden light. His hands were clenched into fists, and he was angling his body to give the percht a smaller target to aim for.

"I'm getting tired of your lip!" William yelled.

"And I'm already quite tired of both of you!" Osaa roared.

Tobias and William both flinched at the sound of the tie snake's voice. They turned toward him without quite taking their eyes off each other.

"You," Osaa called. He pointed to Itchu. "Who set fire to my property?"

Itchu glared at William. Roger took a step in William's direction and growled.

"Now, wait a minute—" Taylor interrupted.

Osaa addressed Taylor. "I take it you dispute this?"

"You're darn right! William was defending himself. If Tobias hadn't picked a fight, none of this would have happened." She projected as much confidence and power as she could. If presence worked on tie snakes, she hoped it would work on this one.

"Don't trust her!" Tobias yelled. "She's tricky!"

"I'm telling the truth!" Taylor said.

"Of course you are," Osaa said. "The Fair Folk can hardly do otherwise. And yet...." He gestured toward Tobias. "There seems to be a difference of opinion as to where the blame for this disaster truly lies."

"But William—"

"All I know is that someone owes me for my lost property." Osaa's eyes glowed in the dim light of the cavern as they tracked from Tobias to William. All around, tie snakes hissed and writhed. "One of you is going to pay. I don't particularly care who."

William kept his arms up defensively toward Tobias, but he kept a wary eye on Osaa as well.

"Then let us fight!" Tobias growled. There were about a dozen survivors in the cavern now, more than half of them conscious. Led by Itchu and Roger, most of those murmured in agreement. Tie snakes hissed. Osaa leaned forward in his slithery throne.

"Let us fight," Tobias repeated. "Let the loser serve you as repayment for your losses."

Osaa leaned back and crossed his legs. "We haven't had any proper entertainment around here for years," he mused. He glared at William. "You've been challenged. Do you accept?"

"No!" Taylor said.

"I wasn't asking you," Osaa said. "The boy has a tongue. Let him use it."

William glanced from Taylor to Tobias to Osaa. He rocked on his heels, not sure which direction to turn.

"Promise you'll let Taylor go," he said, "no matter who wins."

"William—"

"Taylor," William said, "I've got this."

Taylor ignored him. "Mr. Osaa," she said. She took a second to settle herself. *"Isn't there another way?"*

Osaa sat dazed—but only for a second. He shook off the effects of Taylor's glamour as easily as anybody ever had. Then he leaned to his right and spoke to empty space. "She's not bad... for one so young."

"No," a voice said in agreement, and suddenly a second serpentine throne appeared to Osaa's right. That single word pierced the silence and collapsed the speaker's glamour. Taylor shivered with recognition as she saw who had been secretly observing them this entire time.

On the second throne sat a brooding figure in a crimson cloak lined with white fur. He addressed the tie snake, but his icy blue eyes never left Taylor. "She's apparently an early bloomer, like her mother."

Crom Cornstack rested his massive hands on a pair of wriggling armrests.

"We seem to keep running into each other," he said dryly. "Though we have Mr. Hook to thank—this time." He gestured almost imperceptibly toward William. "For the record, his portal was only meant for your deathling friend. It was foolish of you to dive in front of it."

"T-Taylor?" William whispered.

It took Taylor another second or two to remember to breathe. She squared her shoulders and faced her grandfather, hoping she looked more confident than she was. Actually, she hoped he couldn't tell she was scared out of her wits.

This whole situation was getting worse by the second.

"We're related," she told William. "I'll explain later."

William's jaw dropped as he studied Crom's tattooed and bearded face.

Taylor gazed up at her grandfather. "What are you—?" She figured it out before she could finish the question. "You're helping Osaa. You're the reason he's been growing in power."

"You make it sound like my esteemed host would be helpless without me," Crom said. "I assure you, that is not the case." He nodded deferentially toward the tie snake.

"Lord Cornstack and I run in similar circles," Osaa said. "And, of course, we have been allies before the Deep Council. We share similar goals."

Taylor gulped. Overthrowing the Summer Court, weakening the nunnehi, inflicting terror on everybody. And apparently, she realized with a start, making her own life miserable.

"The cafeteria ladies," Taylor said, glaring at Osaa. "The others at the park. They were your people, weren't they?"

"I'm honored to offer my assistance to Lord Cornstack," Osaa said.

Taylor didn't know what to think. "You set me up! Half the Wonder thinks I've joined the Winter Court!"

"Do they?" Crom said.

"Of course they do!" Taylor shouted. "You've got people scared to death of me! They don't know what I'm going to do next!"

"I really can't claim responsibility for *that*," Crom said. "One summer, you help depose the Chief Matron of the Summer Court. The following winter, you build up the Summer Court by ensuring the election of Gwenllian Birdsong to their Triad."

He sat on his reptilian throne in perfect ease—which just made him that much more infuriating. Technically he was right, but it didn't matter. Taylor had been manipulated. She had acted without having all the facts—twice—and it ended up costing people who were close to her. Her face reddened as Crom continued.

"It seems to me the only faction you've never lifted a finger to help...is the nunnehi—"

"Now wait a minute—"

"—and if they harbor doubts about your loyalties...." Crom shrugged.

Taylor clenched her fist, holding back the blast she so passionately wanted to thrust toward her grandfather's face.

"Lord Cornstack," Osaa said, "as enjoyable as this little family reunion has been, it doesn't solve my immediate problem."

"My apologies, Lord Osaa," Crom said with a bow. "Do continue."

Osaa rounded on William and Tobias. "Your little escapade has inconvenienced both me and my esteemed guest. It is a minor setback, to be sure—but I *will* have satisfaction."

"So shall I," Tobias hissed.

Taylor gazed at her grandfather. "Your wife isn't going to like it if anything happens to me," she said. "I still owe her a favor, remember?"

"True," Crom allowed, "but I hardly see how I can whisk you to safety. I doubt you'd leave without your deathling friend, and his life is currently...under dispute."

"But—"

"And at any rate, Mara still wants to see you tested. She needs to know if you're up to what she has in mind for you."

Taylor's heart pounded. She had played the I-owe-Mara-a-favor card the last time she'd had a run-in with her grandfather. She might have suspected the same trick wouldn't work twice.

"You think facing Osaa is a test?"

"Without question," Crom said. "And Mara has...uh... strongly suggested I not interfere. Personally, I'm quite curious to see what happens next." He gestured toward Osaa.

"Otulga! Neha!" Osaa called. A dark, skeletally thin man emerged from the shadows. Taylor guessed he was some kind of bogeyman. He was joined by one of the tie snakes, this one more navy blue than black, and a good ten feet long. "Escort the combatants and their seconds to appropriate quarters."

Tobias tapped Roger on the chest.

William turned to Osaa. "Even if I lose, you'll let Taylor go?"

Osaa glanced at Crom, who merely gestured for the tie snake to proceed. "Of course."

William held out his hand to Taylor. *Seconds?* she thought. *As in, dueling?* They glanced at each other, William asking the favor with his eyes. He looked determined to go through with it, with her or without her. Taylor realized she was the only person in that cave that he could count on.

She sighed with resignation as she firmly clasped his hand. She thought, *This is stupid.*

Osaa gazed down at William. "Since you have been challenged," he explained, "it is your right to choose the contest. That is how it's done, isn't it, Crom?"

Crom nodded.

"I beg your pardon?" William said.

"The contest, boy. What shall it be?"

"Combat," Tobias whispered. There was an unearthly gleam in his eyes, a bloodthirsty expression on his face. "Let us fight."

"C-can we get back to you on that?" Taylor interjected.

Tobias sniffed dismissively. Tie snakes hissed.

"As you wish," Osaa said. "You shall have—oh, let's say an hour to prepare. Then, you shall be escorted to the surface, and we'll see who is to repay what I am owed." He gestured, and the blue tie snake led Taylor and William away while the bogeyman guided Tobias and Roger in the other direction.

"I still say it was Tobias's fault," William said as they threaded their way through a maze of underground tunnels.

"You act as if anyone cares," their tie snake guard said.

"But Osaa will keep his word, right" William pressed on. "He'll let Taylor go, no matter what?"

"William," Taylor said, "there are more important things to worry about right now than—"

"No," William said through clenched teeth. "I'm going to get you out."

When, Taylor thought, did her safety become William's job? After all, it was her fault he was in this mess. And if he thought he could take Tobias in a fight.... She could almost hear Anya Redmane taunting her, she could almost see her waving that stupid bloody shroud in her face. "You may not have heard," she said, "but it's the twenty-first century. Knights in shining armor aren't really a thing any more."

William sighed. "I guess I'm just an old-fashioned kind of guy."

She just shook her head. The whole thing would probably be sweet if it wasn't suicidal. How do you keep somebody alive when they absolutely refuse to cooperate?

Soon they arrived at a rough-hewn wooden door. The tie snake flipped its tail into the air. Only then did Taylor notice the brass ring near its tip. It waved the ring in front of the keyhole, and the door swung inward.

"Inside!" the tie snake hissed.

Taylor took one step toward the door and stopped in shock.

Inside, a curly black head tilted upward to see her. "Danny?" she gasped. "What are you doing here?"

## Chapter 21

# Taylor Gets an Idea

Danny knew they were in trouble when things went haywire on their second ring-jump. They landed—roughly—in front of a grim welcoming party. The panther wasn't any ordinary beast. It was a water master: big and well-muscled, with green tinted fur. Its long tail ended in sleek reptilian hide.

Danny immediately marked the brutish humanoid beside it as an ogre. The pooka scrambled to his feet while Jill backed down the other side of the ancient burial mound, but the water master had already circled around to cut her off.

He started to gather magic. His best bet was to stun both monsters and get away with Jill as fast as he could.

Then the water master began to shimmer. Danny recognized what was happening almost before it did. The creature wasn't a water master at all, but some kind of shape-shifter. Its whole body folded into itself until all that was left was a tail and a reptilian head with a curved hawk-like beak of a mouth.

"Don't move," the creature said. It reared two feet off the ground and turned its head upward to glare at Danny.

"Tie snakes," he muttered. "Why did it have to be tie snakes?" He looked over his shoulder. Jill was eight feet away. Danny could get to her in a second when it was time to move.

"The River of Night is Osaa's territory," the tie snake said. Its partner paced back and forth, hefting his tomahawk.

"We got no fight with him...or her," Danny said. "Or...it."

Jill took a step toward Danny. "Please...um...sir," she said, "we don't mean to bother you. Just let us go and—"

"Quiet!" the tie snake hissed. "My orders are clear. Anyone trespassing on the river goes straight to Osaa." He swished his tail impatiently. "No exceptions."

*We ain't got time for this!* Danny thought. He cast a glance toward Jill, willing her to understand he was getting ready to make a move.

"I'll take the bag," the ogre said, extending a huge clawed hand toward Jill. She pulled her backpack close.

Danny threw up his hand and unleashed a conflagration of sparks and explosions. At the same time, he grabbed Jill's arm and dragged her away.

The ogre stumbled backward, and the tie snake hissed in defiance.

"Grab my neck!" Danny said.

"What?" Jill yelped.

He yanked Jill's arm across his shoulders, slamming her into his back. A second later, he had taken on the form of a horse. He nickered and blinked away.

They reappeared a few yards from the mound. Jill gasped and wrapped her fingers in Danny's shaggy mane. The ogre bellowed in the distance. Danny spied the closest thing he could find to a path and bolted forward. When he reached a dead end, he blinked again. When he got to the end of that path, he blinked a third time.

At the third landing, Danny found himself at the edge of the river itself. He resumed his everyday shape and looked around, breathing hard.

"Sorry if I scared you," he said. "I had to be bigger to blink and carry you."

"But now what—?"

Danny put a finger to his lips. The sound of hissing all around was unmistakable. He yanked Jill's arm again and started off downriver.

Before he could go three steps, a different tie snake slithered in front of him. This one was even bigger than the one they'd escaped. With lightning speed, it flipped Jill's bag off her shoulder and chomped the strap between its jaws.

Behind him came the thud-thud-thud of massive footsteps and the sounds of snapping twigs.

"We told you we don't have a fight with your boss!" Jill hollered.

Another tie snake joined the first.

"Then you won't object to coming with us to explain to him what business you've got in his territory," the second tie snake said.

When they've got you outnumbered, Danny knew that sometimes the best thing you can do is throw yourself on their mercy. So that's what he did. Jill didn't resist, either. It was pretty obvious there was no point to it.

The ogre and the first tie snake caught up to them a few minutes later. They exchanged some words with the other two creatures, then disappeared back into the forest.

The remaining tie snakes marched Danny and Jill half a mile or so downriver, then demanded they enter the water. When they'd gotten in knee-deep, reptilian coils wrapped around their legs and pulled them under.

They were deposited in a great cavern, where a trio of water cannibals collected Danny and Jill and escorted them to a holding cell. Along the way, Danny took note of his surroundings.

Osaa's domain was a network of natural caverns. Lamps in wall sconces, wooden support beams, or an occasional door-frame were the only evidence of intelligent inhabitants. The passageways were empty except for the occasional tie snake, ogre, water cannibal, or other loathsome creature.

The water cannibals shoved Jill and Danny into a cell. Immediately, Danny felt the weird, chilly sensation of magic being leeched away. As he feared, the walls were set with iron braces.

Soon after their arrival, another sprite paid them a visit. He was shorter than Danny, bandy-legged and grotesquely ugly.

He tossed Jill's confiscated bag onto the floor at her feet. Jill looked at the guard with a puzzled expression.

"Nice of you to bring your own food," he said. "Keeps Osaa from having to feed you."

Jill had brought a bunch of sandwiches and energy bars to avoid having to eat any faery food. She was already bound to the Wonder, but she figured keeping from eating any more could only be a good idea. Plus, if everything worked out all right, she would need to share most of it with William.

"You could just let us go," Jill said. She furrowed her brow as if trying to piece something together.

"Not my call," the stranger said. He chuckled when he looked at Jill. "I sure never thought I'd see you again."

At last, Jill gasped with recognition.

Danny studied the stranger and realized he knew him, too. Danny had led him on a wild goose chase around Judaculla Rock two years ago. "You're one of Cornstack's men!" he said. "Tingle, Pringle...?"

"Dingle!" he said. "And it's *Captain* Dingle, if you please."

"The Winter Court is doing business with this Osaa character?" Danny said.

"Mr. Cornstack is Osaa's new best friend," Dingle said with a scowl. "Once he finishes off Belas Wakefire, things are gonna get really interesting in these parts."

"By oak, ash, and thorn," Danny said, "he ain't gonna move against the nunnehi..."

"The Primus will do as he pleases," Dingle said.

"But...he can't just overthrow the Primus of the Summer Court!" Danny's eyes glowed with amber fire.

"He ain't overthrowing nobody," Dingle said. He crossed his arms. "He don't have to."

"What do you mean?" Jill said.

"Tobarty's about to come apart at the seams," Dingle said.

Danny remembered how edgy things were in Tobarty. He'd passed the information on to Chief Tewa like Claudia asked him to, but he still didn't understand it.

Now, however, the pieces were starting to fall in place.

"I knew that place was jinxed!"

Dingle shook his head. "Close, pooka, but that ain't quite it. More like, Mr. Cornstack's got a friend on the scene. Working right under the Teyrnus's nose, you might say." He chuckled. "But I've said too much." Dingle reached for the door. "Enjoy your supper. You can make your case to Osaa tomorrow." He slammed the door on his way out.

There was something strange, though. When Jill dug into her bag for a sandwich, she found that all of her magical supplies were still there, too. Danny had assumed they'd confiscate anything that might be useful to hatch an escape, but it was all there. Either they didn't think very highly of their magical talents or they knew it would be stupid to even try to get away.

When Dingle slammed the door behind him, that was the last either of them had seen of their captors until Taylor and William were thrown into their cell the next day.

Danny nearly jumped out of his skin when Taylor stepped into the cell, and then William right behind her. Jill had been napping on the cell's single cot. Danny nudged her awake. She needed to know about this, even though she needed her rest.

He didn't know if he should be happy or sad at the reunion. The last twenty-four hours had been a complete disaster. Would Taylor and William help them get out of this mess, or were they just two more helpless kids he needed to protect?

Danny and Jill took turns explaining his and Jill's adventures to Taylor and William as soon as the heartfelt reunions were over. William used a gold ring to make some welcome light and heat. (It wasn't fair how Topsiders could still do magic wrapped in an iron box!). The whole time, Jill's eyes never quite focused—the Wonder had a grip on her for sure, but there was nothing Danny could do about it.

Then they listened with growing unease as Taylor and William told their own story of their time aboard the poleboat *Misery*, Tobias's rivalry with William, their capture by the tie snakes, and the contest that awaited William.

"You WHAT?" Jill shrieked. Taylor's story shook her awake with a jolt.

William's ears burned. He looked at his shoes and said it again. "I'm gonna face off against Tobias."

"You're fighting an evil monster," Jill muttered. "Someone with literally hundreds of years of experience? Someone—and I think this is important—who is not going to hold back from killing you?"

"He won't kill me," William said, defensive. "If he does, he's the one who'll have to pay back Osaa for all that stuff we burned."

"Oh, well thank you for clearing that up. He'll just beat you to a pulp and leave you enslaved to a magical talking reptile. That's *so* much better." Jill sat on the edge of her cot, fuming.

"What was I supposed to do?" William said. "Osaa and his snake posse could have swallowed us all whole! This way, we at least have a shot."

"Of all the lame-brained..."

"Tobias started it, all right?"

"William Toussaint Matthews, you know as well as I do what Mom and Dad would say about that!"

"I know, but...." He turned to face the cell door. He'd been on edge ever since he landed in the Wonder. Magical energy was literally in the air, pulsing through him, overwhelming him. It was making him reckless—first with Imaiyah and now (and not nearly as enjoyably) with Tobias.

*Is this how Taylor feels all the time?* he wondered. *Is that why she's always so fearless?*

"Does anybody have a plan?" Jill asked. She glared at her brother. "I mean, a good one?"

"Yeah," William said. "Step one: I beat Tobias."

"Oh, please!" Jill said.

"I think he can do it," Taylor said.

William's heart raced. He felt a grin crossing his face. "Thank you," he said triumphantly. "Wait. What?"

"I'm sorry," Jill said. "I thought you said this Tobias guy was bigger, meaner, and stronger than him."

"But William gets to choose the contest," Taylor said. "That's what they said, right?"

"Right!" Danny chimed in. His amber eyes began to glow with excitement. "All we gotta do is figure out something Tobias ain't no good at. Something where William has all the advantages."

"That's what I was thinking," Taylor said. "Get Tobias out of his element, and William has a real chance."

"I beat him before at Hexenkreis," William offered.

"He's not going to let you get away with that inside-out jacket thing again," Taylor said.

"You turned your jacket inside-out?" Danny said. He shivered. "I hate that!"

William turned to Danny. "Okay, no Hexenkreis. What else is there?"

"Could be anything," Danny said. "If it was me, I'd pick shape-shifting." He chuckled. "Folks always want to see how good a pooka can shape-shift. I tell you, if I had a magic bean for every time—"

"Danny, William knows less about shape-shifting than I do," Taylor reminded him.

"Oh. Right." The pooka started to pace. "Well, conjuration is always a real crowd-pleaser. Controlling the elements. Transmutation. You can't go wrong with transmutation."

"Uh...I can't do any of that, either," William said.

Danny frowned. "You mean not even a little?" he said. "Well, okay then, what are you good at?"

"Rule-keeping," Taylor said.

"Yard work," Jill added.

Danny frowned. "I don't see how that helps us much."

"He has excellent study skills," Taylor said with conviction.

"Come on," William said, "am I really that lame?"

"William, you're great," Taylor said. "It's just…you've got to pick the right contest. Something that'll give you an easy win, or at least something where you can hold your own until we can find a way all of us can escape. I'm not leaving you behind." There was something sad in Taylor's eyes. It reminded William of how she woke up crying on Monday morning, saying, "Don't go." He didn't know what that was about, but he got the feeling Taylor knew something she wasn't telling him.

"*We're* not leaving you behind," Jill said. "So, let's put our heads together, people! How can William beat this guy?"

Jill leaned back on the cot, apparently fighting off a headache. The others all paced the floor—which was hard to do in a prison cell.

Taylor stopped mid-stride. William bumped into her and apologized.

"Anything?" she said. "The contest can be anything at all?"

"That's right," Danny said.

"So…if William just wanted a straight-up duel with ninja sticks…"

"Which I no longer have," William interjected. "But even if I did…I mean, I've been practicing and all, but—"

Taylor gestured for him to be quiet. "What about it, Danny?"

"Sure, I guess," Danny said. "Of course, that wouldn't keep nobody from using whatever magic they wanted. In a contest like this, you do whatever you can to gain an advantage."

Taylor smiled. "Then I think I've got an idea. But we'll need a diversion." She arched an eyebrow toward Danny.

The pooka grinned. "How big d'you want it?"

## Chapter 22

# William Talks Smack

After scarfing down a couple of Jill's sandwiches, William took the rest of his preparation time to draw a few more protective sigils on his denim jacket with a grease pencil. He didn't see how he could buff his own magical stats without a lot more meditation than he had time for. But maybe his enchanted coat could nerf Tobias's stats like it did before.

Then everyone got ready. Jill had brought Maymay's blasting rod. William was relieved his sister had thought to bring it. He took it when she offered and hid it underneath his jacket. For her part, Jill sat on the cot and started working with a fresh block of beeswax. Danny rummaged through the rest of the equipment in her bag, picking out ingredients he thought would be useful for his diversion.

Taylor paced and stared at the door.

William did one more thing, though. From Jill's bag, he borrowed a white votive candle and a small magnet. He worked the magnet into the base of the candle, then etched some geometric designs he'd learned from his grandmother's notebook. Sitting cross-legged on the floor, he lit the candle and intoned, "*Revenez à moi. Accio. Revenez à moi. Amou. Revenez à moi. Chiii.*" He held out the final syllable as long as he could, like air escaping from a flat tire.

"What was that?" Taylor asked.

"I'm trying to get my staff back."

"You can do that?"

William looked around the cell. "Apparently not. When I made it, I put a charm on it so it would always return to my hand." He sighed. "I guess I did it wrong."

"That does sound like pretty powerful magic."

William slumped his shoulders. "I thought I had it figured out." He turned away and focused on the candle, repeating the incantation twice more.

Taylor sat on the floor next to where Cora's banjo case rested. She leaned her back against the wall. Jill was on the other side of the room, trying to help Danny find the things he needed.

William stretched but didn't stand up. He took a breath and looked Taylor in the eye. "Have I done something wrong?"

"What?"

"It's just that you've been...kind of snippy toward me lately."

Taylor's face fell. "I shouldn't have slapped you."

"It's not that," William said. "I mean, that was part of it.... But it's more than that. I get the feeling there's something you're not telling me—"

"William—"

"If you don't think I've been pulling my own weight on this road trip—"

"*William,*" Taylor hissed. Jill and Danny looked over, but Taylor death-glared them back to their own conversation.

She took a long breath. "You're doing fine. I meant what I said before. You're great. That's why...."

"What?"

She stared at the floor. "It's my fault you're in this mess. You don't deserve any of this."

"You're right about that second part. I'm not so sure about the first part." He didn't *have* to invite himself along with Taylor and Jill to the park, after all. "Maymay once told me the secret of strong magic is sacrifice. Struggle. You've got to see what you're made of. So maybe this is all some kind of cosmic midterm exam."

"Yeah." She didn't seem convinced.

"We'll get out of this. We've got help now."

She nodded but didn't say anything at first. She swiped her hand beneath her nose. "And no dying!"

"You either," he said. He offered his hand in a loose fist with his pinky finger extended. "Pinky swear?"

Taylor laughed, which made William feel a hundred times better. "You're such a dork." She hooked her pinky around his.

"That's why the chicks dig me."

From inside the banjo case, Cora said, "Well, ain't that sweet?"

It wasn't long before a pair of tie snakes arrived to escort William and his cellmates. The contest took place above ground, as Osaa had promised—and for which William was grateful. A flotilla of small rafts transported William, Taylor, Tobias, Roger, Jill, Danny, and about a dozen polemen from the late, great poleboat *Misery* to an exposed sandbar in the middle of the river.

Nat Bundlestraw was among them, which gave William hope. Taylor said he had known her dad, so maybe they could count on him if things went wrong—even though it was too late for him to double-talk them out of the current mess.

William nervously tapped his fingers against Cora's banjo case as it leaned against his leg.

Osaa (once more in tie snake form), Taylor's grandfather, and the ugliest fae he'd ever seen came out in a much more ornate barge that reminded William of something from ancient Egypt. It had a black canopy amidships, under which was a mass of tie snakes serving as Osaa's throne as well as a couple of black wicker chairs for Cornstack and his ugly attendant.

A few dozen tie snakes swam in the river or crawled onto the sandbar for a better view. There were also a few other creatures there: the ogre Danny had described and a couple of shorter fish-looking humanoids with chalky white skin.

On the banks of the river, others had gathered. To his horror, he recognized some of them: the monstrous cafeteria ladies from school were there, looking as cheerfully pleasant as always. Olga from the lunchroom stood next to the World's Greatest Mom from the park. Looking at them together, William wondered if they could be sisters. He shuddered to think of what growing up in that household would be like.

Among the corporeal beings, William made out the flitting shapes of ghosts. They were partially transparent and seemed to glide across the ground like the two Civil War veterans that had passed through the *Misery*'s camp.

William hoped nobody would be joining the ghostly ranks today.

It was nearly sunset. William wasn't sure exactly how he knew that—the sky was as dim as it had been the whole time they'd travelled through Osaa's territory. Then he figured it out: a handful of stars had become visible overhead, pinpricks of light against the gloom.

The ogre and the two fish-men marked out a circle thirty feet in diameter with torches on poles, which they then drove into the soft earth with their bare hands.

William watched his breathing. He knew what was likely to happen when he announced the contest he had chosen. He'd need all the magic he could muster, and he'd need it fast.

Tobias stepped into the circle and glared at William. Despite the cold, he was barefooted, and his shirt was open nearly to his navel.

The percht stalked back and forth in a crouching stance. His supporters—including most of the surviving crew of the *Misery*—crowded close to the edge of the circle. They watched their crewmate with fierce anticipation, like sharks waiting for the whiff of blood.

The wind picked up, but William was too busy sweating to be cold. He flexed his fingers. His eyes flitted toward Osaa on his barge. He was coiled on his platform with his horned head swaying in a kind of savage ecstasy.

Taylor put a hand on William's shoulder. He took a breath and looked into her icy blue eyes.

"You still sure about this?" he whispered.

She nodded and picked up Cora. "It's a good plan. It'll work."

William still wasn't sure. In the best case scenario, Osaa would go along with it, and William would mop up the floor with Tobias. He hoped his challenge would at least be a distraction to give Taylor and the others time to work.

Of course, in the worst case scenario, Tobias would just blast William then and there. He'd wake up the next day a permanent resident of Osaa's underwater fun park.

Behind Taylor, Jill and Danny stood frozen in place. Jill looked like she was about to throw up. Her backpack rested on the ground between her feet.

Danny's eyes blazed fiery yellow. He bit his lip, but managed to flash William a hopeful smile.

"I will have satisfaction!" Tobias roared. He stepped to the center of the circle. Even the torches seemed to flinch at the sound of his voice.

At Danny's nudging, William stepped into the circle. He kept his hands in front of him, ready to defend himself.

The percht continued. "I am Tobias Glut," he shouted, "a percht and the son of perchts!"

*Okay*, William thought. *Here we go.* Danny had explained that trash talk is always part of these kinds of contests. He ran through some of the things he planned to say when it was his turn.

"Yet this foolish deathling thinks he can best me!" With that, he pointed at William. His untrimmed fingernails looked like claws. Tie snakes hissed in the water around the sandbar. Roger, who towered over the rest of the polemen, let loose an earth-shaking howl.

"I have attended the White Lady in Feenreich!" Tobias yelled. "Three times I have run with the Wild Hunt! I am the guardian of beasts and the scourge of transgressors!" He rounded on William and strode forward. As he did, his face changed as it had on the riverbank and again during the Hexenkreis match: tall goat horns sprouted from his temples, his hair grew out long and wild, and his nose and mouth contorted into a hideous, wolf-like muzzle. His feet morphed into cloven hooves, and a coat of shaggy gray fur erupted over his entire body.

William took a step backward, which only made Tobias laugh in derision.

"Run away, little boy!" he snarled. "Run back to your girlfriend!" William felt something like pressure building behind him. He had a feeling Taylor was bristling at that "girlfriend" comment, but he didn't dare look back to find out.

"There is no magic I have not mastered!" he continued. He extended his hand, and with a savage growl the shimmering waves of magic that had gathered around it congealed. It took the shape of an elongated rod, and color flowed into it: first dull gray, darkening quickly to brown.

It was a bullwhip.

Tobias had just literally conjured a bullwhip out of thin air.

William swore under his breath.

"You are no match for me, deathling!" Tobias snarled. "You are nothing but a helpless child, weak and foolish. I feel sorry for Osaa being stuck with a worthless waste of skin like you as his slave."

William gritted his teeth.

"My lash will burn you with the fires of perdition!" Tobias said, and he cracked his whip. "My claws will rip you to pieces! I will whip your flesh from your bones, smash your skull, and lap up your blood!" The percht's tongue lolled out of his toothy mouth and nearly tapped his chin before he pulled it back in.

"No one can stand before me, boy! You might as well surrender while you still have breath!"

William braced himself. The jet amulet in his pocket was doing its job. He knew Tobias was sending waves of terror his way, but he only felt a slight twinge of anxiety. He forced it aside and growled, "Call me 'boy' one more time..."

"No one can defeat me!" Tobias continued. "I am as strong as the mountains! I am as dark as the sea! I am as swift as the wind! I am as deadly as poison! I am—"

"Can we get on with it?" William said. Surprise him, Danny had said. Make it look like you're bored, like you're in complete control of the situation.

But William's interruption surprised even him.

As soon as he spoke, the polemen sucked in a collective breath. Tobias's face darkened.

*I am so dead!* William thought. But he had no choice but to press on. "It's just I've got things to do once we're finished here. Do you mind?"

Tobias stalked forward. *Got his attention*, William thought. Now it was his turn to lay down some smack. He took a breath and dove in before he could chicken out.

"You got some nerve calling me a weak child...when all I can see is that hair gone wild.... I didn't ask for this fight, but I'm gonna make you pay for that...uh...stupid little stunt you pulled the other day!" His heart was already pounding, but he took a step forward and gestured with his right hand. It gave off a shimmer of magic.

He bowed slightly to Osaa. "Now Osaa is a player, an O.G. slayer, and if you wreck his stuff, fool, then you better say your prayers. 'Cause William is my name and...uh...I'm here to represent. Don't tell me you're so fresh 'cause my patience is spent!"

Tobias quirked an eyebrow.

William was getting into the swing of it now. He tried to channel his inner gangsta. Unfortunately, his inner gangsta helped little old ladies across the street. But Tobias didn't need to know that.

William pressed on. He tried to put a little swagger in his step as he stalked forward. "Do you honestly think you can pin this rap on me? You're lousy old goat...and you...smell like pee!"

The percht's mouth dropped open. He cast a sidewise glance toward Roger.

"So get ready, son, I'ma take your butt to school. Gonna teach you some manners...so you...won't be such a tool!"

William took a breath.

"What...was that?" Osaa said. A bogeyman attendant shrugged.

William's face started to burn. "I...uh...let my actions speak."

"A wise decision," Osaa said. His tongue flicked as he gazed first at William, then at Tobias.


Taylor kept her emotions buttoned up as William stepped into the ring. She knew her plan was a long shot, but it was the only shot they had. Jill rocked from side to side with her backpack between her feet. While Tobias and William traded insults, Danny circled the ring, pretending to check the height of the torches in the hands of Osaa's men, then swiping his foot through the mud, tracing little arcs, surreptitiously dropping flecks of magic powder along the perimeter.

The fish-people made Taylor nervous. She still had bad memories of the family of okwa naholo she'd run into in the Louisiana bayou, and these guys could be cousins of theirs. Plus, she'd already being dragged underwater by monsters once on this trip.

At last, the tie snake addressed the crowd. "The percht denies responsibility for the loss of my property," he said. "Instead, he accuses the deathling and has challenged him to trial by magic."

William tapped his leg nervously.

"The winner shall go free," Osaa said. "The loser shall be bound to me until such time as I am satisfied my losses have been recouped. This is not, then, to be a contest to the death. Am I clear?"

Tobias and William both nodded, though Tobias growled a bit.

Taylor took a fleeting look toward Jill. She nodded, but she didn't look happy. It seemed the more magic she used in the Wonder, the more it threatened to overcome her. At this point, though, they didn't have a choice.

Taylor meditated on her true name, rolling it over and over in her mind as she gathered magic.

"As the one being challenged, it is left to the deathling to name the contest. So what shall it be—William, is it? Conjuration? Transmutation?"

"Pick what you will, deathling," Tobias said. "I will face any challenge your feeble talents can handle."

William's steely gaze met Tobias. He glanced over his shoulder. Taylor subtly urged him on.

*Just keep them occupied*, Taylor thought. *And don't try anything stupid.*

"Well?" Osaa said.

"I choose...," he began. He nervously twisted the gold ring on his finger.

There was a decent chance Tobias would charge him as soon as he said it. Either way, this was bound to be the shortest contest ever. But the longer William could draw it out, the greater their chances.

"He's too scared to choose!" Tobias taunted. "Lord Osaa, surely that in itself is an admission he forfeits the match!"

Danny completed his lazy circuit of the dueling ring. Jill started to whisper an incantation. Thankfully, everyone was too focused on William and Tobias to notice.

"I'm not forfeiting anything!" William said, and his voice squeaked a little. He turned toward Osaa. "I'm ready to face Tobias, and I choose to test my skill against his with..."

He took a breath. "With algebra!"

Silence descended upon the sandbar.

Taylor watched as confused expressions spread across the crowd, starting with Tobias.

"Never heard of it!" Tobias said. "What sort of wizardry is algebra?"

"It's simple," William said, and sauntered forward. "If you've got half a brain."

Tobias scowled at that. Some of the polemen chuckled—until Tobias snarled at them with his game face.

Osaa flicked his tongue. His eyes darted from William to Tobias and back.

Crom Cornstack watched the unfolding conflict impassively. Only he wasn't focused on the ring; his icy blue eyes were squarely on Taylor. If anybody were to guess she'd try something, of course it would be him!

"Algebra," William began, spreading his arms, "is the manipulation and transformation of symbols. It is the art of translating the world around us into numbers and equations..."

"He can't be serious," Osaa said.

"Deathlings do have an odd sense of humor," Crom said. "But I don't believe he's joking."

"I'm not," William said. "You can do all kinds of things with algebra. Of course, if Tobias is scared..."

"Scared of you?" Tobias scoffed.

*Good*, Taylor thought. *The plan is working.*

He pulled his grandmother's blasting rod from inside his jacket and used it to draw two squares in the sand.

"Let's say I've got two fields," he said. "Together, they take up 1,800 square yards, okay?"

Tobias started to interrupt, but William pressed on.

"The first one yields two-thirds of a gallon of grain per square yard, but the second yields only half a gallon."

"Are you trying to buy your freedom with grain?" Tobias scoffed.

"No!" William said. " Look, you're missing the point. It's just an example, okay? Two fields, right? Now, if the first field gives 500 gallons more than the second, how big is each field?"

Tobias scowled. "So...it's some kind of riddle?"

"It's nothing like a riddle. What if I told you I could write symbols on the ground and find the answer to any question like that?"

"I would likely die of boredom."

"The percht is right," Osaa said. "This doesn't sound like an interesting contest."

"Let the deathling have his way, Osaa," Crom said. "He'll be your slave soon at any rate."

228

William clenched his fists but refused to lose control. Jill growled under her breath; she didn't like the sound of that word, either. But he kept his head down, his eyes on the equation he was tracing in the sand.

Crom noticed William's offended expression. He said, "If only everyone knew how to contain themselves—eh, Miss Smart?" His eyes never left Taylor. She felt a shiver from the soles of her feet to the top of her head. She kept repeating her true name to herself.

William kept writing, walking Tobias through basic algebraic concepts.

But Taylor's mind was trained on her grandfather. "Take your father, for instance," he said, shaking his white-blond mane. "Absolutely no self-control." He leaned toward Osaa. "Of course, what do you expect from the spawn of Anya Redmane?"

Taylor's fingertips tingled with magic.

"I never met the woman," Osaa said. "Or her son."

"You're fortunate," Crom continued matter-of-factly. "He was a danger to everyone—not to mention himself." He turned back to Taylor and bored into her with his eyes. "He had to be put down."

Danny placed a gentle hand on Taylor's shoulder. She jerked herself free.

William finished his equation.

"Had he been a worthy opponent, I'd have kept his head for my trophy room."

Taylor gasped.

Frost began to form at her feet as shock gave way to waves of cold fury.

She knew Crom was trying to get to her, but that didn't mean it wasn't working. There he sat, smug and comfortable, discussing how he had killed her father.

"Of course, the decision was out of my hands. Once I'd finished with him, there wasn't enough of his skull left to save."

*That's it!*

Taylor stretched forth her hands. The nearest tie snakes backed away, covered in a fine coating of frost.

Danny's jaw dropped and his eyes glowed yellow. "That ain't the signal!"

"Just go with it!" Jill said, reaching into her bag.

Tobias rounded on William, re-conjuring his bullwhip.

William jabbed his blasting rod toward Tobias's chest and shouted, "*Bazagra!*" The percht stumbled backward, sapped of magical strength.

Danny made an expansive gesture with both hands, and the ring itself erupted in a flurry of thunder, smoke, and flashing lights. Everyone around the ring flew backward.

Jill unzipped her backpack and scooped up half a dozen tiny wax figurines in the shape of life-size bees and flung them into the air. She completed her incantation by hissing, "*Hax pax max!*" The figurines shimmered and glowed. Flitting silvery pinpricks of light emerged from them, two and three at a time. The effigies fell to the ground, but soon a swarm of ghostly ecto-plasmic bees buzzed across the sandbar. Osaa's people ran for cover.


It wasn't how they'd planned it, but it seemed to be working—so far. Jill kept her eyes on the swarm of bees she had conjured. Taylor spun around to addle the fae raftsman who had conducted them to the dueling ground.

The sandbar was in chaos, and the river itself churned with disoriented tie snakes, okwa naholo, floundering ogres, and discombobulated polemen.

The World's Greatest Mom splashed into the water, heading straight toward Taylor.

"Olga! This way!" she called.

Olga bellowed and started after her sister.

Danny's stun distraction was winding down, and the tie snakes were regrouping. Two of them had already begun slithering toward her.

"Time to go!" Taylor shouted. With one arm wrapped around Cora's banjo case, she met their slit eyes with her own icy glare and willed them to become addled. They hissed—and then attacked each other.

Meanwhile, Danny had taken on his dog form. He bounded through the chaos, nipping and barking. A couple of polemen slammed into each other as the pooka raced between them, then he made a sharp turn and headed for the raft at full speed.

Taylor was halfway to the raft when she heard William groan. Tobias didn't have his game face anymore, but he had charged her friend with fists swinging. William grasped the percht's forearm, twisted his own body for leverage, and landed him hard in the sand. He leaped to one side, to where one of the torch poles was fixed in the ground. He uprooted it and swung it in a wide arc, holding at bay the tie snakes and ogres that were advancing toward him. He backed toward the raft.

Danny yipped as a tie snake wrapped the end of its tail around a hind leg. With effortless strength, the tie snake whipped him around like a rag doll and threw him into the river.

Jill kept driving her bee swarm through the confusion. Her face was a mask of raw fury, and her outstretched arms, straight and stiff, crackled with magical energy. She unleashed an animalistic howl, and Taylor realized she was still conjuring. At first there were only about a dozen bees; now there were at least a hundred—and more were coming.

"Jill!" Taylor called. She set Cora on the deck of the raft and took a step toward her friend.

Jill didn't answer. She just swayed back and forth, directing her swarm against anyone who dared make a move in her direction.

"It's time to go!" Taylor shouted.

Tobias fell, howling in pain beneath a thousand wispy, ghostly bees.

"Now!" Taylor yelled, and yanked her toward the waiting raft. William had already put his shoulder to one of its two poles. Taylor grabbed the other and shoved it into the water.

Danny dog-paddled toward them with half a dozen tie snakes quickly gaining on him, rippling over the face of the water. Taylor gauged the distance between the tie snakes and the raft. Danny swam like mad between the two.

"Danny, hurry!" Taylor shouted. She gathered magic. On the raft, surrounded by freezing water, it was like straining to lift a sofa. But she didn't give up.

*I am Neunhirri,* she thought. *I am Laughter in Winter.*

"Jill, get ready to pull Danny up! Jill!" She wasn't responding. She sat at the center of the raft with her eyes glazed over.

Danny was almost there.

"Jill! Help Danny!"

"I'm on it," William said. He set down his pole and crouched at the edge of the raft.

*Come on, Danny.*

The closest tie snake lunged at him but missed. She wanted to blast it, but she held herself back. She didn't have to stop one tie snake; she had to stop all of them.

The tie snake skimmed the surface of the water, baring its fangs.

Danny thrust his front paws onto the raft. William grabbed them and pulled him aboard.

As soon as he did, Taylor let loose all the magic she had. The wave of cold started only a few feet away, at the head of the nearest tie snake. It fanned backward in a broad, icy swath that reached all the way back to the sandbar.

At first, it was only a layer of brittle ice on the surface of the river that stunned the approaching tie snakes and forced them to pull up short. In a matter of seconds, though, the river was frozen beneath at least five feet of solid ice.

Taylor grinned in spite of herself. *By oak, ash, and thorn!* she thought. *It actually worked!*

Danny shook himself dry, splashing ice-cold water in every direction.

"Let's get moving," Taylor said. She couldn't take her eyes off the frozen river.

She couldn't believe her plan actually worked. She had accidentally frozen things before, but never so much—and never so solidly. But this deep in the Wonder, who could say what might be possible?

Then she glanced beyond the river, beyond the sandbar, to where Crom Cornstack sat in perfect calm aboard Osaa's barge. They made eye contact for just a second, and the mosaic of tattoos that graced Crom's face amplified his expression: a wry, knowing smile.

As soon as she saw him, a wave of cold passed over Taylor worse than anything on the river.

She cursed under her breath.

It was the only answer—the only possible reason Taylor's ice attack had so much power.

It wasn't her.

Crom had helped her escape.

## Chapter 23

# Meanwhile...

"Are you sure you I can't bring you something to drink?" Julie said.

Sophie Matthews just shook her head. She hadn't had any appetite since William disappeared on Saturday. But Julie and Fred Smart needed to know what was going on: Jill and that strange Danny person had gone off looking for William and Taylor.

She and her husband, Charles, sat on the couch in the Smarts' living room. Fred sat on the edge of his easy chair to their right. Julie couldn't seem to sit still. She had brought a wooden chair in from the dining room, but kept finding reasons to get up and walk around.

"Sit down, Julie," Charles said. "We're fine. We just wanted to tell you what we knew."

"Thank you," Fred said. He looked like he was about to leap out of his seat—for what purpose, who could say? Julie finally took her seat next to him. "For what it's worth...Taylor speaks very highly of Danny."

Sophie's only comment was an emphatic sigh.

Charles laid a hand on her knee and shot her a glance: *Don't start.* He looked past her to Fred. "This is all...new, I guess."

"It's not 'new,'" Sophie said through gritted teeth. It was all she could do not to lash out—at Charles, at the Smarts, at the world in general. "It's wrong." Her body trembled. Something churned in the pit of her stomach, an emptiness like she hadn't eaten in weeks. "All of this is wrong. Magic spells? *Faeries?*"

"It's hard," Julie agreed. "When Taylor first told Fred and me about...you know...we didn't know what to think."

"And you're okay with it?" Sophie didn't mean for her words to sound like an accusation. They just came out that way.

Fred hung his head. "I don't know."

Sophie shut her eyes. She imagined furtive movement all around her, taunting voices, Donna Summer singing for some reason. But when she opened her eyes, she was alone with Charles and the Smarts. It was all in her head. At least, she hoped it was. The emptiness in her gut echoed all the way up to her brain. It seemed to have a mind of its own, something dark and empty and covered with cobwebs. It had been gnawing at her soul for days, and she couldn't keep it down any more.

"We want to be there for Taylor," Julie said, "just like you want to be there for William and Jill. Even if we don't always—"

There was a rap at the front door. Fred sprang out of his chair. He peeked out the window and then opened the door.

On the porch was a tall man in a black suit that barely contained his broad shoulders. His nose might have been broken in the past—more than once—and he wore his hair in a blond buzz cut. Despite his rough appearance, he bowed slightly at the waist and said, "Mr. Smart? May I come in?" His expression suggested he didn't really want to be there.

"Uh..."

"It's about your daughter." The man looked over his shoulder. Was someone following him?

"What's that?" Julie said. "Something about Taylor?"

Fred shot his wife a nervous glance. Charles tensed his muscles.

"And who are you?" Fred said.

"A friend," the man on the doorstep said, scowling.

"D-do I know you?"

"No. May I come in?" Before Fred could answer, the stranger opened the storm door and stepped inside. As soon as he crossed the threshold, his appearance changed. He shrunk to the size of a five-year-old. His suit dissolved, replaced by an overlarge dress shirt yellowed with age and a pair of woolen trousers held up by suspenders. His ruddy skin darkened to the color of ash, and his buzz cut thinned to a few wild and lonely wisps of gray. His ears grew out to twice the size they should have been and tapered to distinct points at the tops.

"Oh, my word!" Sophie started to swoon. She grasped Charles's arm like a life preserver. The emptiness inside her screamed in revulsion.

"Sorry about that," the man said. "The glamour was meant for the neighbors, not you folks."

Sophie took a deep breath and willed the room to stop spinning.

"And anyways," the stranger continued, "crossing your threshold pretty much sucked the magic out of me. I hope you'll take that as a sign of good faith." He strode to the center of the room. Fred forgot to even try to stop him. "I don't mean to cause you no harm."

He bowed to Julie. "Mrs. Smart," he said gruffly. Then he faced Sophie and Charles. "You must be Jill's parents. My pleasure." He didn't look pleased about anything, but he bowed again anyway.

All of his movements were *off*. He wasn't clumsy. To the contrary, he seemed quick and agile, but there was something about the way he crossed the living room floor that reminded Sophie of a spider's jerky movements. The toenails on his bare feet were long and untrimmed, giving the impression of claws. His bulging, watery eyes and leathery skin didn't help Sophie's impression that their visitor was not of this earth.

Sophie fought back tears—and with them, the churning in her gut. After the initial shock, she wasn't scared of the tiny gray-skinned man. He was loathsome to her for reasons she couldn't put into words, but he didn't frighten her.

All she could think about was getting her children back, and this creature—whatever it was—said he knew something.

"Bludgitt's the name," he said. He turned back to Fred. "I heard Taylor was in trouble and thought I'd come by, see how you all were holding up. You too, of course, Mr. Matthews, Mrs. Matthews. I don't know much about your son, but Jill's a great girl. Lots of spunk. If William is anything like his sister—"

"Where are they?" Julie blurted. "Are they okay?"

Mr. Bludgitt held up his hands. "I don't know much more than you do," he said. "I asked around in Ichisi. The nunnehi think they've found them. But there are...other folks involved, and they're not in a mood to talk. They're trying to negotiate."

"Time out," Charles said. "Speak English. Ichisi? Nunnehi?"

"That's the faery town near here, and the folks that live there," Mr. Bludgitt explained. "The point is, they've been up in arms ever since the attack. They're doing everything they can." The little man scowled. "Apparently, it's not much at this point."

Sophie sucked in a breath. She studied Mr. Bludgitt carefully. Was he telling them the truth?

"These...nahunies," Julie began.

"Nunnehi," Mr. Bludgitt corrected.

"Nunnehies," Julie said. "Can they...help get our children back?"

Mr. Bludgitt's scowl darkened from general discomfort to frustration. "Eventually."

"But how about you?" Fred said. "You're a friend of Taylor. Can't you do anything?"

"I got nowhere to start." He threw open his arms in defeat. "And I don't have the resources." Then he took a step forward. "But I can tell you this," Mr. Bludgitt said, "Taylor made it clear whose side she's on."

"Whose...side?" Julie said.

Mr. Bludgitt sighed. "I don't know how much Taylor has told you about her, uh, other family," he said. "Long story short: they aren't all friendly, and some of them would love to be calling the shots in these parts."

"Some kind of power grab?" Fred said. "And you think Taylor is..."

"No," Mr. Bludgitt said. "That's my point. Some folks had their doubts...but the way Taylor took on those miscreants on Saturday? That settled a lot of people's minds."

"So my daughter isn't somebody's evil minion," Fred said. "I guess that's got to count for something."

"Wait, Fred," Sophie said. The emptiness was back under control, but her anger and frustration were returning. "Are we supposed to take this...man's...word for it?"

Charles gave her that "cool it" look, but she was tired of cooling it.

"Mrs. Matthews—" Mr. Bludgitt started.

"Now you listen here!" she said. "It's bad enough my son and daughter have gotten themselves mixed up with all this... heathenry. Did you really have to come by just to tell us there's nothing you can do?"

"I came to offer support!" Mr. Bludgitt growled.

Sophie scoffed. "I don't even know who you are! I don't even know *what* you are!"

"Sophie," Charles said.

"You've got all this magic, don't you? Why can't you bring my babies back?"

"It just doesn't work that way, Mrs. Matthews." Mr. Bludgitt rocked on the balls of his bare feet.

"Then what good is it?" she blurted.

Mr. Bludgitt took a step backward.

"I'm serious," Sophie said. "I want to know!" Her whole body was trembling, but the floodgates had burst open. There were things she needed to say, and Mr. Bludgitt was going to hear them.

"As far as I can tell, the only thing magic has done is thrown my family into chaos. My babies are out there God knows where, doing God knows what, because they supposedly inherited some blasted 'gift' they never asked for!"

She only then noticed the looks of concern on Fred's and Julie's faces, but it was too late to back down.

"So if you can show me one thing—one single thing—that all this talk about magic and faeries and God knows what has done for my family, then I'd certainly like to see it!"

An oppressive silence hung in the air as Sophie stopped to catch her breath. The emptiness still roiled within her, but her outburst kept it at bay. She started to let loose again, but Mr. Bludgitt cut her off.

"What do you want me to say?" he said. His voice was firm, full of fire, yet barely above a whisper. "Where I come from... Where your kids are...magic is a tool: nothing more, nothing less. It's only as good as the person that uses it."

He took a step toward her. "I get it. You want to talk about magic messing with people's lives? I could tell you stories that would turn your stomach."

"So you admit all this is evil!"

"I admit that people are people," Mr. Bludgitt spat. "It doesn't matter what side of the mushroom ring you live on. Are you telling me no Topsider has ever used a tool to get what they wanted? A gun? A handsome face? A checkbook?"

"Now, just wait a minute," Sophie said. This discussion was about his people—not hers!

"I'm here out of the stinking goodness of my heart," Mr. Bludgitt continued, his volume rising and his face reddening. "I'm here because that's what *good* people try to do, no matter who they are: 'Rejoice with them that do rejoice, and weep with them that weep.'"

Sophie's eyes widened. Never in a million years did she expect... It took her a second to process it.

"D-did you just quote the Bible?"

"Romans. Chapter twelve," Mr. Bludgitt said. "You know what comes a few verses later? 'Be not wise in your own conceits. Recompense to no man evil for evil. Provide things honest in the sight of all men. If it be possible, as much as lieth in you, live peaceably with all men.'"

The words stabbed at Sophie's heart. Hot tears trickled down her cheeks. Her stomach rumbled, but the emptiness remained subdued.

"All I'm trying to do is live peaceably with you folks," Mr. Bludgitt said. "I know you got a raw deal. Taylor and Jill are... I just felt I ought to do something, okay? Drop by. See what's what. So either accept what I have to offer or don't. It's all the same to me."

All eyes were glued to the tiny stranger.

"What?" he said. "You hang around a church long enough, you learn stuff."

He took the moment of silence to address Julie. "You're probably worried sick—all of you—not knowing anything, not able to do anything. And that just sucks. And you can't really tell anybody else, and that makes it even worse. So here's what's going to happen: I called in some favors. Starting tomorrow, some people are going to come around with supper."

"You're...bringing us supper?" Fred said.

"Do you folks like casseroles? Maybe some barbecue?" Mr. Bludgitt said. "All-mortal ingredients, I promise. None of the funny stuff. For you, too, if you want it, Mrs. Matthews. Just say the word."

He turned back to Julie. "And do you need somebody to come in and clean? I know some brownies who could use the work."

Sophie took a breath. Magic and faeries were one thing, but faeries that quote Scripture, bring casserole, and help with the housework? The emptiness inside her settled down a bit—for now.

All Julie could say was, "Uh...."

Fred said, "Thank you."

Mr. Bludgitt backed up so he could speak to all four humans at once. "The brownies'll want to work at night while you're asleep. Just leave some milk and cookies on the back porch. That'll tell them they're allowed to come in. Homemade is best, if it's not too much of an imposition. "

"That's...fine," Julie said.

"I better be going," Mr. Bludgitt said. "I can't leave my dogs too long. They get antsy."

"Right," Fred said. "Thanks again for...supper...tomorrow."

"Yes," Sophie found herself saying. "It's...very kind."

Mr. Bludgitt looked around the room, nodded to everyone, and started for the door. Fred jumped up to walk with him. He opened the door, and the tiny stranger shook his hand.

"Pleasure to meet you folks," he said. He stepped outside and immediately turned back into a six-foot skinhead in a too-small suit.

## Chapter 24

# A Secret Ally?

Taylor reeled and sat down fast before she fell down. Why was her grandfather helping them escape? Or maybe she had just imagined seeing him smiling back at her as he watched from Osaa's barge.

It was too much to take in.

As soon as Danny assumed his two-legged form, he joined William in poling the raft downriver. For a second, Taylor had forgotten that they hadn't technically escaped *yet*. But the tie snakes seemed to be stuck fast in the ice.

She kept her eyes open for signs of anyone—or anything—following them either on the river or through the woods. So far, nothing.

Jill groaned, and Taylor scrambled back from the edge of the raft to kneel at her side.

"Jill? Can you hear me?"

She groaned again. Her eyes were heavy, but now at least there was recognition when Taylor set her hands on either side of her friend's face and spoke to her.

Jill nodded. "I'm okay," she said. She didn't sound okay. But maybe she was getting there. Rushing water sapped Taylor's magic, but it grounded out Jill's and William's completely. Normally, that was probably a real pain in the neck, but for Jill it must have acted like an emergency cut-off switch.

Taylor allowed herself to breathe. "Is everybody all right?" she asked.

"I got a bee sting," William said, rubbing the side of his neck. "It hurts like fire, but I'll wait and give Jill grief about it later. I'm fine."

"Danny?"

The pooka was shivering. "Just a little shaken up is all. It could have been worse...for all of us."

She cast a glance at the confused scene shrinking into the distance. "I know." She smiled at William. "You did it."

He put his shoulder to the pole. "You told me to stall for time. I stalled for time." He offered her his fist to bump. Instead, she grasped his arm and pulled herself up.

"Thank God you're okay," she said. Swinging up onto her feet, it seemed natural for her to wrap her arms around him and give him a squeeze.

"It was your idea," William said. He tentatively hugged her back.

Taylor's face grew warm. This didn't feel like a brotherly-sisterly kind of hug, but she wasn't sure why. She pushed herself away.

Jill had fallen asleep. Taylor stooped to check her breathing and decided to let her get some rest.

"Is she okay?" William said.

"Probably worn out," Danny said. "That was some kind of conjuring she did back there!" A mischievous grin crossed his face, and his amber eyes sparked.

"I've never seen her do anything like that," William said, wide-eyed. "I mean, never."

"This deep in the Wonder, you don't know what might happen," Danny said. "Like Taylor freezing the river like that."

Taylor bit her lip. People were in such a good mood—relatively speaking—that she didn't want to spoil it by sharing her fears about Crom.

"Just remember," Danny continued. "We may be stronger in the Depths, but so is everybody else."

"You just had to say it, didn't you?" Taylor said.

"Did anybody see what happened to Nat?" William asked.

"The pisgy?" Danny said. "Last I saw, he was waving his hands, trying to settle down the crowd."

"I hope he made it," Taylor said.

"Pisgies are pretty tricky," Danny said. "I mean, not as tricky as pookas...but if there's a way for him to come out on top, he'll find it."

It was a clear night. The sky was filled with thousands upon thousands of stars. They seemed closer and brighter than Taylor could ever remember.

As William and Danny poled the raft downriver, Taylor sat and watched Jill sleep. She wouldn't have minded a little shuteye herself.

"Are you sure she's okay?" Danny asked.

Taylor put her hand to Jill's forehead. No fever. "She's just exhausted," she said. She hoped that was all it was. Jill hadn't set foot in the Wonder since two summers ago. To be in this deep couldn't be good for her.

"She'll be fine," William said. "If she isn't, I bet I can whip up a healing potion. Jill's bound to have all the ingredients in her backpack."

"Lucky for us, that Dingle guy didn't take 'em," Danny said.

"That was pretty sloppy for one of Cornstack's men," William said. "From what you told me, he's not the type to leave any loose ends."

Taylor suddenly had a bitter taste in her mouth. "Well, whatever the reason, I'll take it." She spied the horizon. "How long do you figure we still have to go before sunrise?"

No one answered.

The night sky was almost bright enough to read by, especially with the starlight reflecting off the river. It was beautiful out here—but it could turn deadly at any moment. Nat had told her the River of Night was crawling with monsters, and she'd seen some of them herself.

"Whatever happened to Jackalberry?" she asked.

William shrugged, then threw his weight into poling. "I never saw him after the *Misery* went down. I'm...pretty sure he didn't make it."

"You don't mean..."

"It happens," Danny said. He didn't look happy about it, more like something he had learned to accept.

Taylor's eyes drifted down to William. She looked at Jill, at Danny. They didn't have to come after her, and now they were in danger, too. If anything happened to them....

"Not today it doesn't," she muttered.

"What's that?" Danny said.

"I'm just trying to come up with a plan," Taylor said. "What happens if we run into more tie snakes. Or anything else?"

"I'm not sure what Jill and I could do," William said. "With all this running water...we're kind of limited."

"Me and Taylor, too," Danny said. "Maybe not as much, but we feel it just the same."

Taylor nodded agreement.

"If Jill's got some goodies in her bag, they should work just fine," Danny continued. "You all might not be able to draw magic on the river, I mean personally, but that shouldn't keep a magical trinket of some kind from working."

"If Jill doesn't wake up soon," William said, "I'll dig around in her bag and see what she brought. We've at least got Maymay's blasting rod. I wouldn't be surprised if she packed some other stuff as well. Banishing spells, protective charms..." William was suddenly energized, pondering the possibilities. "Maymay left pretty much her whole stock with us when she went back to New Orleans."

"Perfect," Danny said.

"But wait," Taylor said. "Dingle let you have that back?" She shook her head in disbelief.

"Don't knock it," William said.

But Taylor's mind had shifted into high gear. "It's almost like he wanted to help us," she said.

"No way!" Danny said. "This is Dingle we're talking about!"

"Have you got a better explanation?" Taylor said.

Danny knit his brow. "But...that's impossible!"

About as impossible as Crom Cornstack himself helping them escape! But this seemed different somehow. Something wasn't adding up. Her mind raced back to the last time she'd had dealings with the spriggan.

"He came by my house a few days ago," Taylor said. "He said something about the Winter Court being curious about where I stood."

"You mean like what Wasko and those others guys said? Whether they might convince you to come over to their side?" William said.

"I don't know," Taylor confessed. "Probably. And then he said that I was poison. That I should be careful who I touch. When he said it, I thought it was a threat, but what if he was trying to give me a message?"

"Taylor, you're not making no sense," Danny said. "We've had run-ins with Dingle before. He ain't what you'd call an accommodating individual."

Taylor closed her eyes and tried to think. "The last time I saw him—I mean, before a week ago—was in Louisiana, at my cousin Évastre's mansion. Now that I think about it, he seemed... I don't know. Torn. Conflicted. Like he didn't appreciate what Mara was putting us through."

"A spriggan with a conscience?" Danny frowned and strained at his pole.

"I know," Taylor said. "But maybe that's part of it. What if Dingle's had enough?" Pieces started to fall into place. "What if... What if he's trying to help us?"

"He'd have to walk softly," Danny said. "I hate to think what Cornstack would do if he found out."

"So he acts all tough and blustery," Taylor continued, "but he's really trying to help—even though his hands are mostly tied." Something else clicked, and Taylor slapped her thigh. "The jinni at the dance!"

"Jinni? What jinni?" William asked.

"I forgot. There was one more time I saw Dingle. There was... kind of a firefight at school on the night of the dance," Taylor said.

"What?" William said. "Why don't I know anything about this?"

"Because I tried to keep you and Jill out of it," Taylor said. "Dingle was there. He was chasing another fae: a jinni. He ran right into me. Come to think of it, he attacked me—twice! What if Dingle... No, I can't even say it."

"What?" Danny said.

"What if Dingle fought him off...to protect me?"

That thought was so strange that nobody could speak for a good thirty seconds.

"And then he tips me off to the Winters' plan," Taylor said at last. "He lets Jill keep her bag and all her magical tools."

"Tobarty!" Danny gasped.

"Who?" William said.

"Not who. Where. It's on the border. The Winters used to run it, but they handed it over to the Summer Court after Dubessa Fairchild became Chief Matron. It's been giving the Summers fits ever since."

"Wasko and the boys said something about that," Taylor said. "What do you mean, 'fits'?"

"They've been through five Teyrnuses," Danny said. "They all go off in the head about as fast as Belas Wakefire can install them. As I think of it, Dingle said something about that."

Taylor began to shiver—not with cold, but with growing realization. "Well?" she said.

"He said...Mr. Cornstack had an agent on the inside. A strategically placed friend, he called him."

"That can't be right," Taylor said. "The Summer Court isn't going to let anybody from Winter stay on there."

"Are you sure that's what he said?" William asked.

"That's exactly what he said," Danny insisted. "He said there was somebody working right under the Teyrnus's nose."

"Right under his nose," Taylor repeated. She was too agitated to stay seated, so she got to her feet. The raft bobbed a little as she steadied herself. "Right under his nose..."

She imagined her dad's office: his file cabinets, his bookshelf, his computer...

"Cora!" Taylor exclaimed.

"What?" the banjo answered. She sounded like she'd been jolted out of a peaceful sleep.

Taylor bent down, loosened the latches on her case, and flung it open.

"Have you been listening?"

"Honey, I can't hardly hear a thing inside my case," Cora said.

"Please don't take this personally," Taylor said, "but...have you always been a banjo?"

"Born and bred," she answered with obvious pride.

"Then...how do you...?"

"Have such a sparkling personality?"

"Well...yes."

"It's pretty simple, really. I'm quickened. Have been for going on a hundred years now."

"Of course," Danny explained. "People have played her and cared for her so long, she eventually came to life. We call folks like her quickened artifacts."

"I knew I liked you, young man," Cora said.

"It happens sometimes," Danny added. "You've got it in your own Topsider stories. You know: magic harps, singing swords, that sort of thing."

"Precisely," Cora said.

Danny's eyes widened. "You don't suppose—?"

"What if Crom's ally isn't a person—no offense, Cora—but an object, an artifact. Something in the Teyrnus's office, something that's still loyal to the Winter Court?"

"Like a bugging device?" William said. "Some kind of magical spy gadget?"

"Maybe more than that," Taylor said. She turned to the banjo. "Cora, can a quickened artifact do any magic? I mean, other than talking?"

"Honey, what would you like me to do?"

"Nothing. That answers my question."

"But wait a minute," Danny said. "Claudia says the Summers got rid of all the old stuff in the Teyrnus's office. It was pretty depressing, to hear her tell it."

"There's got to be something," Taylor said.

"The desk!" Danny said. His eyes glowed with golden fire. "There's this big mahogany desk. The other week, Aemeron Wakefire was having a fit, shuffling through the drawers. He said somebody had been messing with him, rearranging his stuff. I bet that's it!"

"If every Teyrnus of Tobarty sat behind that desk...," Taylor said.

"And if the desk didn't like them...," William added.

"Or was under orders to throw a little glamour," Danny said. "Put suspicions in his mind, make him hear things, even feel things, that weren't real...."

"What happens if Summer keeps sending Tobarty new Teyrnuses, and each one fails?" Taylor said.

"You ought to be able to figure that out for yourself," Danny said. "It sets everybody on edge. It makes Summer look weak, incompetent. It might even make the nunnehi think about attacking—that whole region used to be nunnehi territory, after all. But one thing's for sure: it makes the Primus look like a dang fool."

"He loses respect in front of his people," Taylor said. "He loses honor."

"By oak, ash, and thorn," Danny said, "sooner or later, the Court's gonna move to replace him."

"Can they do that?" Taylor said.

"It'll be messy," Danny said. "But yeah. If they can bring a strong enough case, they could probably force a vote of no confidence."

"The Court is bound to be divided," Taylor said. "Just look at what happened last year when they tried to add a new member to the Triad. Replacing the Primus will be a hundred times worse."

"And the Winter Court is there to pick up the pieces," Danny said. "Oh, this is real bad."

"All right," Taylor said. She looked at Danny. "As soon as we get out of here, you've got to find Claudia. Let her know what we've found out."

"You got it," Danny said.

"But first we've got to get to the mouth of the river," William said. "That's the way home."

"Through the Narrows," Taylor said. The river did seem narrower than the stretch they'd already covered. They would soon be past the border of Osaa's territory. But she was exhausted. There was just too much to process.

"So we just keep going forward," Danny said. "Right?"

"And hope for an uneventful trip downriver," William said.

"Yeah," Taylor said. "'Cause that's definitely going to happen." She lay down next to Jill, exhausted. She was asleep almost as soon as she closed her eyes.

Chapter 25

# The Narrows

The deep bass voice shook Taylor to consciousness.

"It seems we meet again."

Will-o'-the-wisps, little more than pinpricks of harsh silver light, flitted through the dark, illuminating a large stone-walled room. A fire blazed in a fireplace. Unlit lanterns hung in fixtures on the walls alongside displays of swords, shields, and hunting trophies: a couple of deer, a black bear...and three human heads.

Taylor scanned the room until her eyes landed on Crom Cornstack. The two were sitting across from each other at a great mahogany desk. On the desk were a candle in a brass candle-stick and yet another human head. Up close, Taylor could see it was browned and weathered, maybe covered with some kind of shellac. The ears were subtly tapered. So not human, after all. Some kind of fae. The eyes were thankfully shut, and the black hair was pulled back into a ponytail that looped around into what Taylor hoped was not a handle.

She sucked in a breath and gripped the edge of her wooden chair. She wanted to push it back, to leap to her feet and try to get away, but she couldn't. Her chair was fixed to the floor, and her backside was fixed to the chair. All she could do was rock nervously from side to side.

What was she doing there? And where was she in the first place?

The last thing she remembered, she had nearly dozed off from exhaustion. She must have been dreaming.

But that was even worse. It meant Crom had gotten inside her head.

She cursed under her breath. The fae could fare forth into animals, get inside their skin. But they could do the same trick with humans and, apparently, other fae. Silas Bludgitt had explained once that that trick was at least borderline illegal, but she doubted that technicality would matter to her grandfather.

What really scared her was how much of her mind might be open to him.

She tried to shut down any random thoughts. She concentrated on Crom and Crom alone. Nothing else mattered, nothing else existed, but this dream-world where the two of them were sitting.

She tried to sound bored. "Oh, it's you."

The tattoos on Crom's face accentuated his subtle smirk. He chose to overlook Taylor's comment.

"You and your friends are making good time through the Narrows," he said. "So far."

Taylor folded one hand over the other. *Why do I get the impression you're about to fix that?*

"Unfortunately, your luck cannot last."

Taylor's temples throbbed. "If you do anything to my friends—"

"I hardly need to do anything," Crom said. "It's simply a matter of time, with all the ghosts, water masters, wakomos..."

"I get the point," Taylor interrupted.

"Naked bears, dragons, longnecks, ogres, water cannibals..."

"Look, you don't have to—"

"Kolowas, deer people..."

"*I got it, okay?*"

"I don't believe you do." Crom leaned back in his chair. "The River of Night isn't just a geographical feature. It's part of the geography of the Wonder itself. It has existed from the beginning: in Egypt, Mesopotamia, Greece."

"And now it's in America?" Taylor scoffed. "Sorry, but that plot has already been done."

Crom paid her no attention. "The River of Night tests heroes, Selena. That's simply what it does."

"I'm no hero."

"Then you will soon be dead. Your friends as well."

Taylor bit her lip. She forced herself not to think about William, about Jill and Danny. The only thing that mattered was her and her grandfather.

He sat with his elbows on the desk, steepling his fingers.

"You realize the good guys never steeple their fingers like that, don't you? I mean, you never see somebody planning ways to feed the hungry or clean up the environment do that." She steepled her own fingers, affected a stock evil-mastermind voice, and said, "Soon my plans will succeed and all the hungry children will have enough to eat!" She reverted to her normal voice. "See what I mean?"

"Are you quite through?"

"Are you?"

Crom casually stroked the top of the trophy head. "You've passed beyond Osaa's territory," he said, "but you'll have miles to go to reach the mouth of the river. And then, suppose you miss the sunrise, when the boundary with the Topside world is thin. What then? Can your deathling friends survive another day in the Wonder?"

Taylor clenched her jaw. The image of William gulping down the last of Jill's sandwiches flitted across her consciousness, but she shut it down—hard. She furrowed her brow and glared at her grandfather.

"Or...," he said. He gestured to her as if offering a gift. "I could open a portal and send all of you home."

Her heart pounded. A portal home! William would be safe, along with Jill and Danny. Anya's prophecy would come to nothing.

Then she stopped herself. This was Crom Cornstack talking.

"I suppose you'd want something in return."

Now he didn't merely smirk; he smiled so widely his beard and mustache couldn't conceal it. His tattoos seemed to morph and twist across his face.

"Join me. Pledge allegiance to the Winter Court. Say the word, Selena, and all of this can be over."

Then it hit her: Crom was calling her Selena, not Taylor or Miss Smart. He had never called her that name. She didn't know what that meant, but it couldn't be good.

"Are you kidding me?" she said. She tried to keep her voice even. "Haven't you figured out yet that I'll never be on your side?"

Crom only chuckled. "In fact, you have made it abundantly clear to *everyone* that you will not."

"That's right."

"And for that, I thank you."

That wasn't the response Taylor expected. It left her throat dry and her pulse quickened. She kept her mouth shut and concentrated on Crom alone.

"It turns out the nunnehi have completely exonerated you after the little escapade that brought you here. As we speak, they're trying to get Osaa to admit he knows where you are." He folded his arms. "You know some of them still harbored doubts about your loyalties, don't you?"

Taylor struggled to make sense of what Crom was telling her.

"Not anymore, I'm happy to report. They are completely satisfied that you have been a helpless victim of the big, bad Winter Court." There was that smirk again. "I do believe they feel sorry for you—all you've been through, and at the hands of your own family...."

The whole thing was a set-up. Taylor had known that almost from the start, of course. Now, parts of it were at least starting to make sense. The Winter Court wasn't really trying to win her over. They were *making a show* of trying to win her over. They were giving her every chance to prove that she wanted nothing to do with the Winter Court.

But why?

"We need not belabor this, Selena. If you don't want my help, I shan't force you to accept it. I am, if nothing else, a gentleman."

In a pig's eye!

Crom leaned forward and rested his elbows on the table. "And yet, I imagine it will be...distressing...for you to watch your friends stripped away from you one by one as each of them dies alone and afraid in that swamp."

It was all Taylor could do to keep from lashing out at him, but she knew it wouldn't do any good. All of this was happening inside her head. There was no "Crom" to fight—at least, with any weapon she knew.

"I shouldn't keep you," Crom said. "You've made your decision. Now I believe you have some consequences to live with."


"Taylor!" Danny called.

She shook herself awake as the pooka helped her to her feet. She started to ask what was wrong, but the answer was obvious: the raft was being strafed by wakomos. A flock of the crazed Holstein-patterned cowbirds was rocketing toward them from downriver.

"Finally! I've been hollering at you forever!"

Jill handed off her raft pole to Danny—despite the circumstances, it was good to see her up and moving. Danny swung wildly into the single file line of attackers as it advanced.

The raft bobbed erratically. William was trying to keep it steady with his own pole, but without much success.

A wakomo dived straight for Taylor's face. She flung her arm in the air just in time to avoid having her nose bitten off, but the force of the impact sent her reeling. Jill grabbed her just as she was losing her balance and kept her from falling into the water.

"You've got to be kidding me!" Taylor screamed.

Danny and William poled forward. The river was narrow and crooked. She could only imagine how hard the others had been working to keep the raft afloat while she slept.

She kept her eyes on the flock as it sped upriver, then began to circle back in a wide arc.

"They're coming back," she said. She started to gather magic, but it just wasn't working. Too much time on the river, probably. She knew there wasn't much William or Jill could do, either.

"Hard to port!" William shouted.

"Which way's port?" Danny yelled back.

"That way!" William pointed to the left. Danny stepped forward and dug his pole into the river bottom.

Taylor looked back. The wakomos were still coming. It was only a matter of seconds. She hit the deck as a dozen huge birds dive-bombed the raft.

Danny cursed and unleashed a stunning spell. The flash of light and the thunderous report drove the creatures away...a second time. They sped off to starboard without breaking their single-file flight pattern.

"They're coming again!" William shouted.

"Do we really look that tasty?" Taylor said. She shook her fist at them. "The buffet is closed!"

Jill began to chant her wind spell. A breeze picked up, but only a little, then just as quickly died back down.

"We'll just have to beat them back!" William said. He lifted his pole from the water. Danny did the same.

The raft rocked back and forth. Taylor crouched down and held her arms out for balance.

This time, Danny and William both swatted at the wakomos at the same time. William's pole landed across the beak of the line-leader with harsh, meaty thunk. As it fell into the water, the rest of the flock changed course and veered away. Danny took a swipe at a bird middle of the line.

But then Taylor realized they had another problem.

"We're running aground!"

The raft was heading into another sharp turn to the right. With no one steering, they were heading straight for the left bank of the river. The water churned and sloshed as Danny and William both scrambled to the other side of the raft.

William's pole was the first one down, but by now the raft was going too fast. No sooner had he braced himself, the pole snapped in two. William fell forward with a growl of frustration.

Danny planted his pole, but it was too little, too late. Rather than stopping, the raft whipped around and kept on going. Only now, it was going even faster and at a steeper angle to the riverbank.

"Stupid laws of motion," William muttered.

"Brace yourselves!" Taylor shouted.

Jill shrieked.

Danny hit the deck.

Taylor swore.

The raft slammed into the bank amid sounds of cracking lumber.

And the wakomos were still coming.

"Head for the trees!" Danny yelled.

Taylor bolted for the tree line with wakomos shrieking over her head. Once she hit the shore, she felt her magic returning. As soon as she made it to the trees, she flung a blast over her shoulder into the strafing monster birds.

She might have taken one out; she didn't turn around to see. She just put her head down and bolted down a narrow path into the woods, her heart pounding, her temples throbbing.

"Jill!" she called.

Danny answered, "They took the other path!"

There was more than one path?

"Just go!" Danny hollered. "We'll look for them once we get rid of these birds!"

There was no telling how long she kept running. Ten seconds? A full minute? Everything was a blur. Everything was a complete disaster.

Taylor fell to her knees and sucked in rasping gulps of air. Tears pooled in her eyes and trickled, hot and bitter, down her cheeks.

They were stranded, just like Crom had predicted. The raft was damaged. They had no way to get down the river—by today's sunrise or any other. William and Jill were out there, separated from her and maybe from each other. They'd be easy pickings for practically anything in this swamp, and there wasn't a blasted thing Taylor could do about it.

Just like Crom had said.

"My God...," Taylor whispered.

Danny knelt beside her.

"I've...I've killed them both."

"Ain't nobody dead yet," Danny said. "I know it looks bad and all, but—"

"But I could have gotten us all home!" Taylor blurted. "Now we're stranded here. Didn't you hear the lumber cracking? That raft isn't going to get us anywhere. We've got no transportation, no Topside food...no nothing!"

Danny knelt beside her in silence.

"What am I supposed to do now?" she wailed.

"Taylor, you can't blame yourself," Danny said. "It was that attercop Crom Cornstack that set this whole thing up."

"No," Taylor said. "He offered... He said he'd send us home. If only..."

"He said...? Did I miss that?"

Taylor tapped her temple. "He sort of visited my dreams while I was out. He said he'd help us—but I told him no, and now everything's going to be a hundred times harder. We might not make it."

"Now, don't be thinking like that!" Danny said. He stood up straight. "I don't know what kind of deal Cornstack tried to strike with you, Taylor, but I guarantee you're better off without his help."

Taylor slumped forward and wrapped her hands around her grass-stained knees.

"But he gave me the choice," she groaned. She wiped the tears from her face. Suddenly, words spoken two and a half years ago by a one-eyed dwarf flashed through her consciousness. *You have the power of life and death on your tongue,* he had said. *You have to but say the word, and bring either life or death to others.*

Taylor fell onto her belly and pounded the grass with her fist and remembered what her grandfather had said.

*Say the word, Selena, and all of this can be over.*

She lay on the cold ground, barking out raw, hopeless sobs of grief and fury.

Danny let her get it all out before he spoke.

"Taylor?"

She shivered and moaned, and Danny waited a little longer. "Taylor?" he said again.

She rolled over. Her face must have been a pink, splotchy mess, but she didn't care.

Her body deflated as she expelled a breath. "Let's see if we can find the others." Now that she was through freaking out, her brain was getting back in gear. They were all on foot, and nobody could run too fast through thick woods. Surely Jill and William were close. It was just a matter of retracing their steps.

And Danny literally had a nose like a bloodhound.

Taylor sprang up to a sitting position, then offered the pooka her arm to help her the rest of the way to her feet.

"All right," she said. "We can figure out how to get home later. First, we've got to find my friends."

## Chapter 26

# Something Shiny
# Catches William's Attention

Standing on the shore, William grabbed the banjo and swung it at the wakomos like a baseball bat.

"Put me down!" the banjo hollered.

In shock, William complied. "Sorry! Forgot!" Sentient musical instruments were still a new concept for him.

He and Jill hit the dirt and waited as the rest of the wakomos passed overhead.

"Are they circling back again?" Jill said.

"I don't know," William said.

As he got to his feet, Cora began to vibrate. She shimmered with magic. Her wooden body expanded, sprouted dark, spindly arms and legs like twigs of varnished cherry wood. From out of nowhere appeared a lacy pink dress under a threadbare dressing gown the color of old ivory.

In a second, the banjo was nearly six feet tall, if you counted the long neck that jutted upward like a ridiculous beehive hairdo. Her actual face was on the square head of the instrument, about four and a half feet off the ground. Her wooden feet were clad in dingy gray house shoes.

The shrieks of wakomos were getting louder again.

"Well, don't just stand there," the banjo yelled. "Run for your lives!" And then she bolted down the shoreline with three murderous Holstein-spotted cowbirds in hot pursuit.

The rest of the flock were diving straight for William. He grabbed Jill's arm and took off. There were two paths into the woods. Taylor and Danny had already disappeared down one of them, but he didn't know which. He chose the path to the right and barreled on.

The deeper into the woods he and Jill ran, the more the screeches of the monster birds faded.

It wasn't long, though, before the rough path ended. William remembered his Pawpaw's ring still on his finger. He brought his ringed fist to his lips and whispered the incantation. "Give me the light, upon thy life, I charge thee." The ring began to glow.

"We better get back to the raft," Jill said.

"You mean that pile of firewood by the river?" William said. Then he suddenly held up a hand. "I hear something." He perked his ears as he looked around. "Could that be Taylor shouting?"

"Maybe," Jill said. "Those birds must have followed them instead of us."

"It's coming from over there," William said, pointing.

"We better help them." She looked distracted. Off the river, it looked like the rush of wild magic was getting to her again. Going back to the raft was probably the smarter choice. Jill could settle down, maybe meditate inside a circle of power for a while, or even wade in the river.

But Taylor was out there. She'd tried so hard to keep William safe. Now it was his turn to return the favor.

He extended his fist and willed the light to shine brighter. He studied the ground, looking for the clearest path through the brush. At the same time, Jill pulled a silver cross from inside her shirt. She used the same incantation as her brother, kindling a brighter, colder light.

"This way," Jill said. She crashed through the brush with William on her heels.

There were no further sounds of struggle. William told himself that could mean anything—or nothing. Maybe Taylor and Danny were laying low, waiting for the birds to give up on them.

Even so, he picked up the pace. Jill had the same idea, and it was all William could do to keep up with her.

William noted another sound. At first, it sounded like the rustle of branches, but the further they went, the more it took on the rhythms of whispered conversation.

A shadow moved in the distance.

"Taylor?" Jill called.

The whispers continued, grew louder. There was something hypnotic about them.

Another shadow flitted behind them. William wheeled around and aimed his light at something moving amid the trees.

He could see it now: a young woman dressed in a long, mud-stained dress, with her hair done up in a kerchief.

"Jill," he whispered. He reached out to tap his sister's shoulder, but she wasn't there.

He turned back to the woman. "What have you done with my sister?"

The woman lifted a perturbed eyebrow at William. She raised a finger to her lips and shushed him, then glided out of sight. Her shoulder passed straight through a tree.

A ghost.

"Jill?" he called again. Concentrating took effort for some reason. He turned in the direction she had been heading, but instead of Jill, he saw a translucent Native American warrior with an arrow sticking out of his chest.

William started, but the apparition didn't make a move. Strangely enough, ghosts were shaping up to be the least dangerous thing on the River of Night. He tried to communicate. "I'm looking for my sister."

The ghost said something in a language William didn't understand. He pointed off to the right. William looked that way and saw nothing but trees. When he looked back, the ghost was gone.

He called out his sister's name one more time, but there was no answer.

Then something else caught his attention, a flicker of light over his shoulder. His heart pounded as he spun around, extending both hands. The last thing he needed was to be ambushed from behind by yet another monster.

Nothing was there, but William couldn't shake the feeling he was being watched.

The light had come from the direction the second ghost had pointed. Could he have been saying, "She went that way"?

The whispers subsided. Sounds had a weird way of echoing through the trees. He couldn't say for sure that anything else was out there with him...but there were rustles of leaves that might have been more than the wind, rumbles that were almost certainly not thunder on that cloudless night.

There it was again: another flicker of light. It was brighter this time, and it was definitely coming from somewhere up ahead. He stopped to listen.

More than that, he needed to get ready if something else attacked. He was still breathing hard from running away from those stupid birds. He needed to settle himself. Now that he was off the river, he needed to draw in all the magic he could.

He still didn't dare try Second Sight, but it was easy enough to sense the swirls and eddies of magical energy. They wrapped around him and coursed through him. It made him a little lightheaded.

*You're still deep in the Wonder,* he told himself. *Easy does it.*

He turned toward the light. If something was stalking them, planning to have them for a late-night snack, he needed to know. What was out there? He dimmed the light of his ring and took tentative steps off the path and into the brush.

*It's got to be close.*

Even under the starry sky, it was hard to see. But his eyes soon adjusted to the darkness. After no more than thirty seconds, he inched forward.

Then William heard a deep wheezing sound, like wind blowing through a tunnel. It startled him so much he tripped over a tree root. He shifted his weight to steady himself, but then he lost his balance completely. He stumbled three steps forward, fighting to stay on his feet. On the fourth step, he tripped again and fell face-first into an open patch of ground beside a creek bed.

He planted his hands to brace himself and stand up. But his left hand found something cold and hard in the dark: a leg bone that might have once belonged to a human. William threw it down with a shudder.

He lit his ring light once more and gasped at what he saw. The ground was littered with all kinds of debris: bones, scraps of leather and wood, and even a spear and a couple of flint knives.

He scrambled to his feet, but before he was all the way up, he saw the mysterious light flash once more. Only this time, he saw where it was coming from.

He wished he hadn't.

A snake slithered toward him.

Scratch that. A *humongous* snake slithered toward him. It was impossibly large: nearly fifty feet long and as large around as a tree trunk. Its leathery hide was iridescent gray with darker spots down its back. Its head sported a pair of short pronged horns that gave the impression of a crown. From its forehead jutted a glowing crystal as clear as glass—the source of the flashes of light.

The snake reared six feet into the air to look down upon the crouching William. It opened its mouth, and William realized the whooshing sound he heard earlier was breath from the creature's cavernous lungs.

It kept perfectly still, but the diamond crest on its forehead flashed white light. When it did, the beast's hide glittered and flashed as if sparks of fire were dancing up and down its body.

William should have been terrified but he wasn't. Instead, an eerie calm descended upon him. It was like he had stepped outside his body, a disinterested observer watching to see what would happen next.

He felt the creature's magical aura—stronger than any he'd encountered before. Not even Tobias commanded that much raw power. He filed that detail away like a random note jotted on one of his index cards.

The creature hissed and reared even higher, seven or eight feet.

William's heard pounded. In the back of his mind, he realized he should be running away. Fast. Probably screaming his head off. But he couldn't. He was frozen in place—and something about that gleaming light in the middle of the creature's forehead held him enthralled.

All he could do was stare at it, bask in its hypnotic gleam. *Is that...a dracontia?* Maymay's notes on dragons were pretty sparse, mostly the uses of their blood, fat, bones, and such. The most powerful part of a dragon was its dracontia, a magical crystal that grew in its skull. It never occurred to William that it would poke out from the creature's skin.

Then it hit him.

That wasn't just a big snake. He was crouching in front of a dragon—or at least a close cousin of one. Nat had mentioned one. The great horned serpent?

Faeries and little people were one thing. Magic talking snakes freaked him out a little—too many Sunday school lessons for that one to sit easily in his mind. But *dragons*?

William's body start to shake. He took a long breath and struggled to stay calm.

The creature seemed more curious than belligerent. It looked William up and down. William got the impression the creature was sizing him up—and not just for his nutritional value.

It tilted its head to one side, then drew its mouth open just enough to show a pair of fangs as long as steak knives. The creature might have been smiling.

The creature gazed at the bones and weapons strewn around its lair, then back at William. It let out a deep, throaty rattle.

William imagined it asking if he was nuts or something. *Look at these bones. Do you think you can do any better than the last guy... or the one before him?*

"I'm just passing through," William whispered. He somehow kept his voice calm and steady. "I don't want any trouble."

The creature dipped its head. It was probably thinking, *Smart move.*

The dragon whipped its head around, and its whole body undulated like a cracking whip.

William took a step back.

Jill emerged from the woods ahead to William's right. She was following the creek bed curving back toward the river. She was over the creature's shoulder—if it had shoulders, that is. William hoped it didn't see her.

Barely a second later, Taylor and Danny, in the form of a dog, appeared from a different path flanking William on the left. They stopped, wide-eyed and open-mouthed.

The dragon definitely saw them. It turned toward them and hissed.

Taylor cursed. Danny crouched low, ready to spring. His eyes glowed yellow, and he nervously wagged his tail.

Jill shot William a "What the heck is going on?" look. She crept toward her brother.

William held up his hand, palm-down. *Take it easy. No sudden moves.*

The dracontia flashed white light, and sparks once again rippled up and down the creature's body.

Danny barked and jumped to one side.

The dragon reared back and spat at him. Danny yelped and dodged. Where he was just standing, the ground smoked and sizzled where a gob of sickly green acid splattered against it.

Jill shrieked. The creature slithered backward, putting William, Taylor, Jill, and Danny all in clear sight.

"Just settle down, big guy," William whispered, his hand still extended.

The dragon hissed again and swept its tail in Taylor's direction. She dove for cover. Danny bounded forward, barking. Jill came up beside William.

William advanced. "It's okay!" he said.

But the dragon was through listening. It expelled another spray in William and Jill's direction. Jill hit the ground and rolled toward Taylor. William raised his arms to protect his face. The acid splashed against the sleeves of his denim jacket with a foul stench—but he didn't feel any burning.

*Those charms actually worked!* he thought.

Danny leaped clear and tried to circle around. William guessed he was trying to draw the creature away, to protect the rest of them. The pooka didn't realize he was just making things worse.

"Danny! Just cool it!" William yelled.

The dragon writhed around, lashing his tail at William. He hit the ground just as he heard Danny howl in pain. The pooka disappeared into the woods, a smoking wound on his left hind leg.

Taylor ducked out from behind a tree, braced herself, and glared at the creature. The air suddenly turned cold. The dragon sniffed. Swirls of condensed breath blew from its nostrils. It shook its head and slithered in Taylor's direction.

Jill and Taylor braced for what was bound to come next.

William's heart pounded. Things were happening too fast. There were too many people to protect—including himself! He rose to one knee.

"Hey!" he called. The creature whipped back around.

William froze. *Okay, now what?*

He looked around. If only he still had his staff! But he couldn't think about that. He had to draw the creature away from his sister and Taylor however he could.

By his foot was a flint-tipped spear. It would probably just make the creature mad, but he had to do something. He grasped the weapon and sprung to his feet.

"William, don't!" Jill called.

William waved the spear in the dragon' face. "Stay away from my sister!" he called. "And my—"

The dragon opened its mouth wide. William whimpered as he jabbed the beast with the spear. The weapon's tip slid off the monster's throat. It bellowed, more angry than hurt.

William leaped away.

Then a flash of grayish dust exploded against the dragon's back. It spun around toward Jill as she shouted, *Hexiphore!*"

The dragon reared up and bellowed at her. Jill's banishing spell had no effect at all.

"No!" William yelled.

The creature dropped its head low above the ground and darted toward Jill.

William was in motion before he could think about what he was doing. He jumped on the dragon's back and plunged the spear into one of its spots. It twisted its body, curling its head backward to snap at William. He fell to the ground, rolled, and came up into a crouch.

The spear was still stuck in the dragon's hide.

William was unarmed, exhausted, and apparently magic had no effect on the creature.

It bellowed once more as it closed in on William. He extended his fist and called up the light of his golden ring. He put every ounce of magic he could into the beam and aimed it straight at the dragon's eyes.

The creature reared up, startled and hopefully blinded—at least for a second. Blood trickled from its wound and gushed from its mouth in a frothy spray with every breath. The spot on its back must have been a weak point. The beast thrashed its tail, sending bones and discarded weapons in every direction. The dracontia flashed. Ripples of light coursed up and down its body.

William stood his ground while Taylor and Jill screamed his name.

Jill's backpack was only a few yards away. Does a blasting rod work against dragon magic?

He eyed the bag and shuffled slowly toward it, never taking his eyes of the creature.

It thrashed about the clearing, spraying blood in every direction.

William's hand wrapped around the strap of the backpack. He swung it up and plunged his other hand inside, fumbling for the blasting rod.

That's when the dragon lunged straight at him, roaring like a wounded elephant.

William shrieked.

The dragon missed William by a hair's breadth—apparently it had been blinded for a second. But as it fell, a great gobbet of blood landed in the middle of William's face. He felt blisters erupting on his cheeks, his lips, his tongue.

The iron taste of dragon's blood filled his mouth, along with the caustic taste of sulfur and bile and cayenne pepper. He gagged as a foul odor filled his nose, his sinuses, and his lungs. Before he could process what was happening, he was on his knees. In another second, he had fallen onto his side.

No matter how much he spit, he couldn't get the burning in his mouth to stop. He thought he might throw up. He only wished he could!

The last thing he heard was Jill screaming his name.


"NO!" Taylor yelled. William was on the ground, probably unconscious, twitching like he was having a seizure. Danny had disappeared into the woods, wounded...or worse.

Anya Redmane must have been somewhere, laughing at her.

She grabbed Jill by the shoulders. "Take care of William," she said.

Jill was just as much in shock as Taylor was. Her eyes widened as she ducked another blind sweep of the creature's tail.

"Jill! Focus! You've got to take care of William!"

"How...?"

*"Just take care of your brother! And Danny if you can find him! Nobody is allowed to die, do you hear me?"* With that, Taylor stalked forward.

The dragon bent its horned head in her direction. Its every breath sounded like a blacksmith's bellows or a rolling thunder.

Taylor summoned blue-white balls of faery fire into each hand.

The creature roared. Taylor flinched, but only for a second. She waved her hands, creating an arc of light over her head. It gave the creature—which must have been the horned serpent Nat had told her about—a target to aim at, but Taylor wasn't planning on staying in one place.

She darted along the creek bed. The creature howled and shrieked and slithered after her.

It didn't matter. There was no way William or Jill or Danny were going to die tonight. She'd rather—

"Yaah!" She hit the dirt as a gobbet of acid sizzled against the trunk of the tree she was passing.

*Acid venom. Poison blood. That flashy thing on its forehead deflected my magic.*

She sighed. *This sucks.*

She threw herself forward, ignoring the stinging pain in the heels of her now-muddy hands. She dodged into the woods, darting back and forth among the trees.

Every few seconds, she turned back around and shouted a curse at the horned serpent. She never got far enough ahead that the creature might lose interest. Her only goal was to lead it as far from her wounded friends as possible.

She didn't dare cross the stream. It didn't look very deep, and she could have probably cleared it with no trouble, but she couldn't take the chance of losing even a fraction of her magic. She needed all she had if she was to survive the night.

At that moment, her chances didn't look good.

## Chapter 27

# The Great Horned Serpent

Jill fell to her knees in front of William. Her hands trembled as she rolled him onto his side. He made a gurgling sound, and Jill hoped he would throw up. Dragon's blood was bad news—she knew that much. She held her brother steady on his side as he seized up in pain. When it didn't look like anything was going to come up, she lowered him onto his back.

"Stay with me," she said. She pulled her backpack off her shoulder and started to rummage through it.

William's eyes had rolled back into his head. He was shaking all over.

"Can you hear me?" she said, her voice breaking. "Do you need to say the pain spell?" She didn't know if William heard a word she was saying, but she led him to recite the incantation Maymay had taught them against pain. "*Argidam, margidam, sturgidam.* Remember?"

She repeated the spell as she dug through her bag. She'd packed a couple of plain white handkerchiefs. They could be useful for making cachets of magical herbs, but right now she needed them more to wipe the dragon's blood from her brother's blistering skin. She splashed a little water from a plastic bottle on William's face and wiped the blood off as best she could with her hands. Contact with the blood made her own fingers itch and burn, but she could worry about that later.

Jill dug around in her bag some more. Thankfully, she'd packed some of Maymay's favorite healing salve: an orangey paste of ginger, bloodroot, and a bunch of other things she couldn't remember. She scooped out a finger's worth and smeared it around William's mouth. Then she slathered it on his chin and, finally, she put the last of her supply on his throat.

William kept twitching and spasming. His skin was still red and puffy where the blood had splashed him, but maybe the blisters were shrinking a little. At least Jill hoped so. But it was clear the healing salve wasn't enough.

She was going to have to try a healing spell. Suddenly, it felt like all those bees she had conjured before were throwing a party in her stomach. The thought of casting spells in the Wonder terrified her. The last time, it was like she'd stepped into rushing water—like her soul was being swept away in the current.

But she didn't have a choice. "All right, bro," she said, as gently as she could, "from here on I'm going to have to improvise, so don't give me any lip if I don't do it the same way you would. D'you hear?"

Jill took several slow, shallow breaths. It was hard to calm down with her brother in the shape he was in, but she forced herself to do everything the way Maymay had taught her. Settle the mind. Draw the magic in. Find a focus.

She dared to open her Second Sight. As soon as she did, she felt dizzy, overwhelmed by a flood of sensations. The whole clearing was alive with magic, and all of it swirled before her eyes.

She looked at William, and her stomach wrenched. A ghostly green-gray snake was entwined around his neck, with its head buried in his chest, gnawing away at his insides. From the hole it had opened flowed undulating waves of something like gray sludge.

*It's only symbolic*, she told herself. That was little comfort. She squeezed her eyes shut and counted to three before opening them again.

The ghostly snake vision was still there.

The gritted her teeth and tried again. This time, her normal vision returned. The snake was gone, and there was no gaping wound in William's chest.

"That thing is still fighting you," Jill said, barely louder than a whisper. "Dragon's blood is poisonous, you know. And it looks like you swallowed some. So I'm gonna have to...draw it out...before—" She stopped herself from finishing the sentence.

She went back to her bag. What she wouldn't give for some alicorn powder!

"I wish you could talk me through this...."

There was a rustle in the trees. Danny appeared, limping and in two-legged form. Jill breathed a silent prayer of thanks that the pooka was all right.

He saw William and his eyes flashed amber fire. "What happened? Where's Taylor?"

"Trying to buy me some time." She turned back to her brother. Her hands were shaking.

"What can I do?" Danny dropped to his knees beside Jill.

"Draw me a conjuring circle while I get set up."

"You bet." Danny pulled a bronze knife from his belt and crept about, digging a little trench, groaning with every movement. Jill could see a charred hole on his pant leg where the dragon's venom had landed. He didn't complain, though, as he traced a ten-foot diameter ring around himself, Jill, and William.

While Danny drew the circle, Jill got to work. She set up a little copper incense burner and laid out everything she thought she'd need: matches, a tiny cone of frankincense resin, a sprig of rue.

Danny finished the circle and tumbled outside of it. He winced and clasped his right leg.

"Are you okay?" Jill asked.

"I'll be fine," Danny said through gritted teeth. "Shape-shifting helps the healing...but it takes a lot out of you." He groaned, then threw himself onto his back. "Take care of your brother."

"I'm working on a healing spell," Jill said. "You wouldn't know anything about those, would you?"

When she looked back, Danny had become a very distressed-looking rabbit. She watched with momentary fascination as he returned to his everyday shape.

"Sorry," he said. His voice slurred. His face looked awfully pale. "Maybe rue leaves boiled in molasses?"

Jill looked at her sprig of rue, then shook her head. "No time. And where the heck am I supposed to get molasses?"

"How about adder's tongue? With some sunbeams and just a pinch of salt—"

"Sunbeams?" Jill snapped. "I'm working on a budget here! I don't have any stupid sunbeams!" She turned back to William. His chest rose and fell with obvious effort.

"Sorry. That's all I really know."

Jill hung her head. "I can't do this! I need William!" She brushed tears from her cheeks.

"Just...try to focus, okay?"

"But—"

"No, listen," the pooka said. "You've got this. I'll help however I can."

Jill sniffled. She tried to draw in a slow, measured breath.

"You can do it," Danny said.

"I don't know how! This is ceremonial magic. All I can do is...see stuff!"

"You can do more than that," Danny said. He clutched his wounded leg, but kept his voice steady. "You'll do fine. You got plenty of power."

"It's not about power! What I need to do takes planning. Preparation. Even if I could pull it off, there isn't enough time!"

"Jill, listen to me," Danny said. He grimaced as he sat up. The fire in his eyes was nearly spent. "William needs you to do this...and I think you can. So show me what you've got."

She rummaged through her bag and came upon a vial of dark red liquid. She unscrewed the top and gave it a sniff. It was bitter and piney. "Myrrh?"

"Okay, myrrh's good," Danny said groggily. "Maybe mix it with the rue..."

Jill was already on it. She found her water bottle. It was about half full. She took a swig, then tossed in the rue and the whole vial of myrrh. She passed the mixture to Danny. "Shake this up!"

As Danny shook the bottle, Jill set the frankincense in her burner. She struck the match, but it broke in two in her hands. She cursed out loud and grabbed the sulfur match tip that had fallen on the ground.

This was taking too long!

Worse than that, Jill had a feeling she wasn't alone. She looked up. There was a young woman at the edge of the clearing, dressed in a muddy ankle-length dress. She peered at the ground where William lay.

"Get outta here!" Danny yelled. Then, turning to Jill, he explained, "It's just a ghost. Don't pay her no mind."

"A g-ghost?" That was all she needed: an undead spectator while she was trying to concentrate.

It took three more tries before the stubby match tip sparked to life. She touched the brilliant blue flame to the frankincense, then dropped the match in the burner before it could scorch her fingertips. The sweet, woody aroma ought to have made her feel better, but she had too much on her mind.

One more thing. She slipped her Pawpaw's ring off William's finger and grasped it tight.

"Over here," she called, stretching out her hand. Danny tossed her back the bottle with another gasp of pain.

"Are you sure you're all right?" Jill said.

"I'm great—aargh!" Danny clutched his stomach. "Okay, that might have been an exaggeration." He gestured for Jill to continue. "Don't worry about me." He lurched outside the circle, careful not to disfigure it. Then he fell face-first on the ground.

Two more ghosts had joined the first. An old white man in a 1920s zoot suit and a bare-chested Native American with an arrow sticking out of his chest.

"Is he gonna make it?" the muddy woman whispered to the newcomers. The white guy shrugged.

"He's gonna be fine!" Jill yelled.

She took a deep breath. She had to concentrate, ghosts or no ghosts. If they were some kind of otherworldly welcoming committee for her brother…

No. Jill couldn't think that way. She closed her eyes again, summoning magic. After a few seconds, she reached out to touch the circle Danny had drawn and whispered the word "*Eulamo.*" She felt a pop as the magic circle snapped shut. With an effort of will, she directed the swirling magical currents inside the circle toward the tools she had gathered. Now all she had to do was call forth the magical properties of all her ingredients—and hope they were enough.

"Okay, here goes." She passed the gold ring over the water bottle as she began to intone the incantation.

On the second time through, she stopped. Something was wrong.

"William?" she said. Then more frantically: "WILLIAM!"

"What's wrong?" Danny called.

"He's not breathing!"


The dragon roared, but Taylor didn't turn around to look at it. She just hurried forward, down the creek bed toward the river.

She wasn't trying to lose the creature, just to lead it away, to make herself look like a more interesting target than William and Jill and Danny. Several times, she ducked into the woods long enough to catch her breath, but if she thought the creature was losing interest, she burst into view with gobs of faery fire blazing.

The dragon spat blood. Thankfully, it didn't come anywhere near Taylor.

The spear shaft had snapped in two. Part of it still jutted in the creature's flank. The monster was wounded: that was Taylor's only hope.

If only she could keep up the chase. She didn't have to kill the thing, just stay alive until it was too exhausted to fight. She let magical energies swirl around her, ready to use at a moment's notice.

Suddenly, a spray of caustic venom splashed a tree trunk to her left. It sizzled as it burned into the wood.

Taylor cursed and darted once more into the trees. Twigs snapped along the riverbank as the dragon slithered after her.

*Come on!* she thought. *Come on, you overgrown garter snake! This way.*

"I've about had it with you!" she yelled. She swung around and let loose a faery blast. There was no way she missed, but the crystal on the dragon's forehead flashed again, dissipating the magic.

At the same time, it dropped its head and expelled another spray of venom. Taylor flung out a shield spell and retreated— but not quickly enough. The deadly spray glanced off her half-formed shield and hit her as she twisted away. Most of it got the lower leg of her jeans, where it steamed and hissed. But a single drop landed on the top of her right foot, which suddenly felt like it was on fire.

She screamed as she stumbled away. Bolts of pain shot up her leg. Her eyes started to water, but she had to keep moving— the dragon was close and getting closer.

Taylor weaved through the trees.

Her thoughts turned to William, lying on the ground, fighting for his life. She had to draw the dragon away, to give Jill time to work.

But now she was hurt. Her bad foot would slow her down, and it was already all she could do to keep the dragon at a healthy distance. She wouldn't last much longer at this pace.

*Okay, time out.*

She needed a few seconds of invisibility to catch her breath. Ducking behind a tree, she pulled magical mist around her. Taylor gingerly touched the top of her foot. The venom had slipped under the tongue of her tennis shoe and soaked into her sock. It hadn't gotten into her bloodstream, but it still burned like perdition.

Taylor heard rustling leaves and snapping twigs as the creature rumbled on. Hiding behind her tree, she held her breath and prayed her glamour would hold up.

Was it just wishful thinking, or was the creature slowing down?

She wondered how good a dragon's sense of smell might be.

Her foot was really throbbing now, but she didn't dare stay where she was. She looked around for another option.

Straight ahead was a tree with a trunk that forked only three feet off the ground. Three long strides got her there, and she scrambled upward as fast as she could.

She hissed every time she had to bring her weight down on her burning foot, but hopefully it wasn't enough to catch the dragon's attention. Once she reached a safe height, she could harry it with blasts and other magic from relative safety.

Taylor gripped the next branch and pulled herself up, swinging her left leg up and over. She glanced over her shoulder. The dragon hadn't moved, but its cavernous lungs still heaved, and its massive body rose and fell with every breath.

Its back and sides were plastered with blood where William had stabbed it, but the blood around the flopping spear tip had congealed. The wound had already begun to heal.

At about twelve feet off the ground, she sat and waited. Above her, the branches looked smaller and thinner. Maybe they would hold her weight and maybe they wouldn't.

The dragon coughed up another gobbet of blood. Taylor took that as a good sign: the wound might be closing up, but there were still internal injuries.

*If you'd just hurry up and die, I could get out of here!* she thought.

She took stock of her surroundings. She'd nearly made it to where the creek bed emptied into the River of Night. Starlight reflected off the wide ribbon of water barely twenty yards from her tree. It was as if the river was made of stars. It might have been pretty to look at if she weren't busy not dying.

The dragon swept its horned head from right to left. The crystal in its forehead flashed. Ripples of white sparks danced across its back.

Taylor sighed. It wasn't dead yet.

She wondered if her magic could put the dragon to sleep. It couldn't be much different from addlement, could it? All she'd have to do was plant a suggestion in the beast's head that it was tired, that it needed to take a nap. Injured like it was, that shouldn't be too hard. Maybe something subtle like that could get through its magical defenses.

She let magic gather all around her, coursing up and down her spine, wafting out from her shoulder blades like butterfly wings and wrapping her in its embrace.

*Sleep*, she thought. She forced the magic out from her body, down from the trees, into the creature's skull. *Sleeeeeep.*

Its eyelids began to droop.

*Hmm*, she thought. *Dragons have eyelids.*

She kept it up. Any second now....

Then the crystal flashed again. The creature grumbled as its head shot up and it sniffed the air.

Taylor cursed under her breath.

It had detected Taylor's magic. Worse than that: it had detected her. With another angry bellow, it lurched toward where she was perched in her tree.

"Just give up already!" she shouted.

She had no choice but to climb higher. She had barely gotten to her feet when the dragon slammed into the tree trunk, and she nearly lost her balance. Gritting her teeth, she stretched toward a branch on the other side of the trunk that she hoped could bear her weight.

Taylor grasped a handhold and started to pull herself farther up, but now the tree itself was shaking. She dared to glance downward but wished she hadn't: the dragon had wrapped itself around the base of the trunk and was stretching itself up toward her.

*Rats rats rats rats rats!*

The dragon roared again. Weaker than before—which was good news. But as its weight slumped against the trunk, the whole tree staggered off-center. Taylor heard the noise of snapping wood as she held on with her arms wrapped around the next branch and her legs hanging free.

The creature tried to roar, but instead made a labored choking sound. Flecks of blood erupted from its mouth.

The crystal dimmed.

"Come on," she muttered. "Any time now."

The dragon collapsed. It was still wrapped around the tree, but Taylor couldn't see any movement. Its crystal had gone out completely.

"Finally!"

That's when her branch started to snap.

It began near the base. She hugged the branch tight and fixed her eyes on the widening stripe of pale, naked wood where the bark was splitting. She felt with her feet for any lower branches. No such luck.

She held on tight. The branch cracked, the gap in its base growing wider.

Taylor dangled twenty feet off the ground. The hard, cold, skull-splitting ground.

*Okay, think!* she told herself. She looked around, hoping she'd see a branch below her she had somehow missed before. She checked the skies above. Any giant eagles in the vicinity were apparently off rescuing other hapless adventurers.

*Then again...*

Taylor closed her eyes and took a deep breath. She willed her magic to surge and whip around her.

Her heart pounded against her ribs. She had an idea—a desperate idea, but the only one with even a chance of success.

The branch cracked again. She refused to let it distract her. She had some powerful magic to work, and she didn't have any time left!

Another deep breath. She began to form a picture in her mind, as perfect and detailed as she could manage. She shut her eyes, saw the image right in front of her, meditated on her true name....

Another crack. The whole branch was hanging on by a thin sliver of wood now. It wouldn't last more than a few—

The branch snapped.

Taylor fell.

*Now or never!* she thought.

She imagined herself falling—but not to the ground. Rather, she imagined herself falling straight into the image she had created as if it were a bowl she held in front of her.

And then it happened, just like Danny said it would. But Danny's descriptions could never do it justice.

Taylor felt her body shriveling up, like some bizarre giant had stuck a straw in her navel and sucked out her insides. Her legs shrank to the size of twigs. Her whole body curled in on itself while at the same time it burned with fever. She watched as her hands and fingers dwindled while dark iridescent feathers sprouted all along her arms.

She was flapping her wings instinctively before she realized she even had them.

Taylor had become a blackbird.

She was woozy and disoriented—another thing Danny hadn't warned her about—but she managed to pull up inches from the ground. She let out a triumphant *chup-chup-chupatupateeeee!* as she soared into the air. The pain in her foot (or claw) eased back a couple of notches. It was still irritating, but much more manageable.

*This. Is. Awesome!*

Her tiny heart raced as she circled over the trees, figuring out by trial and error how to control the direction of her flight, remembering how she'd done it while merely faring forth in a blackbird's borrowed body. She soared over the lifeless carcass of the dragon, studying the spear tip buried in its back, the blood stains on its sides and mouth.

There was one thing she didn't see, and that gave her courage in a way she wouldn't have imagined. There were no signs of her clothes strewn on the ground where she presumably would have shrunk out of them.

Apparently she still had them...somewhere...despite Danny's warnings that doing so would take more practice. It was kind of the Wonder to preserve her dignity like that.

But Taylor had things to do. She got her bearings, swooped over the river, and backtracked up the creek bed to where she had left William and Jill.

When she came down through the trees, Jill was bent over William. Danny was there, too.

A small gathering of spectral forms had congregated near the edge of the clearing. They were partly translucent, like the Civil War casualties that breezed through the *Misery*'s camp on Monday night. They didn't seem to be hurting anything, though they gave Taylor the creeps.

Jill and Danny weren't even paying attention to them—or to the nondescript bird that had just landed at the edge of the clearing. Instead, they both looked intently at William.

Taylor's little heart pounded even faster.

*Why hasn't Jill healed him yet?*

She hopped toward them, then she realized she was still a bird. She stopped and concentrated, pulling magic from all around her.

Taylor suddenly felt bloated as the mass she'd thrown off as a blackbird once more infused her body. It took a couple of seconds to resume her normal form—fully dressed, though her jeans felt like they'd shrunk a size.

As soon as she felt steady on her feet, she hurried forward. "Jill?"

Jill didn't look up. She was kneeling over William, pressing down on his chest.

"William!" Taylor called. She bounded forward, but Danny jumped up and held her back.

"Don't cross the circle!" he said, his golden eyes watering.

## Chapter 28

# The Light

The fog made it impossible for William to see more than three feet in front of him.

He wasn't hot. He wasn't cold. There was no breeze, no sound of any kind.

The foul taste of dragon's blood was gone from his mouth—finally! It would be a long time before he tried the hot mustard sauce at the Asian Buffet.

He brushed his fingers across his chin. He didn't feel any blisters. There was no scar tissue.

He looked down at his feet. They both seemed to be attached to his body, but what he was standing on didn't register at all. It was like a solidified block of the same fog he was wrapped in. It was firm as concrete, but it made no sound whatsoever when he tapped his toes against it.

Then he noticed the sleeve of his jacket. His clothes had been bleached to the same gray-white of everything else in his surroundings.

This was getting weird.

Actually, it had been weird for a while now, but this was too much.

"Hello?" he said. His voice didn't echo.

No one answered.

There was a light in the distance, diffused by the fog but still apparent. William took a step toward it.

Even his footsteps were perfectly silent.

For the first time, he realized he didn't have any of his tools. No blasting rod, no staff, no bag, no golden ring. He searched his pockets: even his jet amulet was gone.

"Am I supposed to...like...walk toward the light or something?"

"You tell me," someone said.

William stopped in his tracks. Beneath the light, a dark smudge began to form in the fog. He braced himself to meet it.

"Who are you?" William asked. Possibilities roiled in his mind: God, St. Peter, an angel...

The smudge came closer. And the closer it got, the more defined it became: elongated, powerful, and graceful. It was almost liquid in its movements.

The dragon came into focus. William gasped and backed away, holding his hands out defensively.

"There's no need for that," the creature said. "I've already done everything to you that I'm going to."

"You... You can talk?"

The creature scrunched its head down in what could only be called a shrug. "This is your hallucination, not mine."

It slithered around William, encircling him faster than should have been possible. Six feet of serpent reared up to look William in the eye, another twenty feet formed a knee-high ring around him. That left nearly half the creature trailing off into the fog.

The creature's dracontia gleamed with a pure, white, steady light.

"You said hallucination. So... I'm not dead?"

"Not yet. We'll see."

"What's that supposed to mean?"

"How do you feel?"

William patted his chest. He took a deep breath. Everything seemed to be working fine. "Okay I guess."

"Oh," the dragon said. His fanged mouth dropped into a slithery representation of a frown. "See, that's not a good sign. It means you're coming to terms with it."

William wanted to back up, but he couldn't without tripping over the horned serpent's body.

"Coming to terms...with what?"

His heart should have been pounding like crazy. He should have been sweating buckets. But he wasn't. To tell the truth, he felt perfectly calm. His brain told him that in itself was reason to be worried, but somehow he wasn't.

"Come on, son. Isn't it obvious?"

"I don't understand. What kind of hallucination is this?"

"What do you want? Sunset on the beach? Girls in bikinis?"

"I could live with that," William muttered.

The dragon scoffed. "Look, in case you haven't figured it out, you're dying, okay?"

William gulped. But even then, no butterflies fluttered in his stomach. His pulse—or what he imagined to be his pulse—was steady. The fact that he wasn't freaking out was starting to freak him out.

The dragon continued. "Seriously. What's the last thing you remember?"

"I...stabbed you," he said. "With a spear. But I didn't want to. I was just protecting my friends. I was afraid—"

"No need for apologies, kid. Water under the bridge. What else?"

William searched his memories. "Last thing I knew, I was...uh...covered in your blood."

"Bingo. And you know about dragon's blood, right?"

"It's very magical. And very poisonous," he said. He gulped again. From his demeanor and his tone of voice, he might as well have been discussing the weather. He should have been out of his mind with panic, but he wasn't. And that was seriously messing with his head! "You've got to take precautions or...." He looked at his surroundings. "Yeah."

"I figure you swallowed about two, maybe three teaspoons full. And undiluted! That's some hardcore stuff right there." The creature clicked its tongue and shook its monstrous head back and forth. At the same time, it pulled the edges of its mouth back into a fang-filled smile.

*Huh*, William thought. *Dragons have lips.*

The two stared at each other for the longest time.

"And there's nothing...nothing I can do?"

"You're unconscious. Your airway is shutting down. You're running a fever from my blood you ingested. Do you have any idea how deadly that stuff is?" The dragon tilted its head. "Yeah, I guess you do."

"But..."

"Hey, for what it's worth, you had guts. I admire that. I've got a pretty good eye for talent, if I say so myself. You've got potential, kid.... Well, you did."

"Th-thanks?"

"Don't mention it." The creature started uncurling itself from around William. "I guess I should be going. Your heart's about to give out. So just...follow the light. Or the harp music. Whatever."

"Wait!" William called. "What about my sister? What about Taylor?"

"Well, they'd still be where you left them, right?"

"Are they in danger?"

"How am I supposed to know? I only exist in your head. Remember?"

Now William's heart started pounding. He couldn't leave Jill and Taylor stuck in the Wonder with an angry dragon prowling around.

"What are you going to do to them?"

"Me?" the dragon said. Its affable smile twisted into a sinister sneer. "Or the real dragon? the one in the woods?"

"I can't walk out on them!" William said.

"Not my call. If they make it, they make it."

The creature slithered back into the fog.

"NO!" he shouted. "I want to go back!"

"There's no way back," the creature said. "Do you know how hard it is to fight off the effects of dragon's blood? Your metabolism would have to go into overdrive."

"Let me try!"

The creature gave William another weird snaky shrug. "Like I said, it's not my call. I can't be reasoned with; I'm just a force of nature." It began to slither away. "You ask me, it'd be easier just to move on."

William gritted his teeth. "I beat you once," he said. There was fire in his eyes. "I'll beat you again."

"Suit yourself," the creature said. A second later, it had vanished.

William sat cross-legged on the...whatever it was. He closed his eyes, drew in a slow, shallow breath, and began to meditate.


Taylor had never felt so helpless. Locked in a dungeon and compelled to choose whether to let her mom be executed or to die in her place? Forced to watch as her best friend had magic ripped out of her? Assaulted by someone she had hoped was an ally? None of that compared to watching Jill fighting back the tears as she tried to keep her brother alive.

"What's happening?" she whispered.

"Jill's trying to neutralize the poison," Danny said.

"But she can do that, right?"

"It's pretty tricky." The pooka frowned. "Dragon's blood... I don't know. But I'll tell you this: I wouldn't bet against Jill."

They knelt side by side in silence. Danny gritted his teeth and blew out a labored breath.

Taylor's foot throbbed and itched.

Jill continued to work her magic.

William gasped, a raw, painful gulp of labored breath that sent a shudder through Taylor's whole body. She sat up straight and gazed at Jill as Jill turned William on his side. He coughed... with effort.

Taylor squealed with surprise and squeezed Danny's arm to keep from bouncing up and down.

Jill paid no attention. She laid William back and passed an incense burner over his face, coaxing curls of sweet smoke toward his nostrils, all the while chanting under her breath. It took Taylor a second to recognize the incantation as the chorus from Beyoncé's "Halo."

Even behind the circle of power, Taylor could sense the powerful pulse of Jill's magic.

William started to choke. Jill stopped chanting and heaved him onto his side again. This time, he coughed blood onto the grass.

"That ain't his," Danny whispered. "At least, I don't think it is. Just a little of what he swallowed coming back up."

"That's good, right?"

"It ain't bad," the pooka said. "But it might not be enough."

After checking his airway, Jill let William fall gently onto his back and resumed her healing spell. She waved her hand over William's face, his throat, his chest. Taylor could have read by the light given off by the gold ring on Jill's finger.

Taylor watched the almost imperceptible rise and fall of William's chest. He was doing better. She let out a long, shaky breath and, with it, a prayer of thanksgiving.

She had known him since fourth grade: her best friend's dorky brother with his comic books and his video games. The kid her dad hired to mow the lawn every summer. Honest. Kind. Noble, even. She thought about how he'd spent the last few days trying to protect her even though, deep in the Wonder, he was in more danger than she was.

Taylor had worried for the past couple of years that William might be crushing on her. For half a second, she wondered if she'd missed something by not returning the sentiment.

"I never got to tell him..." Taylor sniffled. "I never got to thank him...for..."

Danny shushed her. "Jill knows what she's doing," he said, and he folded his arms around Taylor. The two of them hugged each other tight.

*Fight, William. Fight.*

He let out another hoarse, rasping breath. This time, he followed it with a moan.

Taylor pulled herself away from Danny and leaned forward to get a better view. Jill kept waving her golden ring over him.

"Can you hear me?" Taylor whispered.

William grunted. Then he expelled a breath, slow and easy. His whole body relaxed.

The ghosts looked awkwardly at each other. The young muddy woman frowned. Then all of them turned their backs at the same moment and slowly drifted away.

Taylor smiled. "He's going to make it!" she said. It was all she could to do keep from giggling.

"He's stable," Jill said, her voice shaky. "I wish I could be sure of more, but..." She wiped tears and sweat from her face, leaving muddy streaks in their place.

"So what do we do now?" Taylor asked.

Jill looked up at her friends. "We need to get him out of here."

"Let's get him back to the raft," Danny said.

"The raft got smashed, remember?" Taylor said.

Danny frowned. "A couple of timbers cracked is all. I bet we can fix it."

"It's the best chance we've got," Jill said, though she didn't look optimistic.

With Jill and Taylor's help, Danny got William onto his back. Then he turned into a horse to carry him. The girls kept William steady as he straddled Danny, with Taylor holding him by his right arm and Jill by his left. Taylor brushed the back of his hand. His skin was hot and slick with sweat. Danny slowly trotted out of the clearing, down the creek bed, and to the riverbank. They had to stop twice when William seized up in a coughing fit. Jill and Taylor held him steady and waited for him to settle back down before they let Danny move on.

The carcass of the horned serpent wasn't visible from the shore, but Taylor could guess the direction that would take her right to it.

Danny transformed again as the girls gently lowered William to the ground.

Jill stooped over William and placed a hand to his forehead.

Danny looked at Taylor and bit his lip. He seemed distracted or maybe embarrassed.

"What's the matter?" Taylor asked. The raft was still maybe half a mile upstream.

"Before we go any further," Danny said, "there was something I guess I ought to ask."

"Yes?"

"That horned serpent. I figure it was rightly William that killed it, wasn't it? You didn't off it with magic or anything?"

"It's not like I didn't try," Taylor said. "No, I didn't kill it. William speared the thing. It just took a while for it to die."

"In that case... Do you figure he would want the adderstone?"

"The what?"

"The adderstone. All dragons have these crystals in their heads, you see? Well, you seen it, didn't you—?"

"Danny. Point?"

The pooka backed up and started again. "See, that's where their magic comes from. And if you can ever kill a dragon, you get to keep the adderstone."

Taylor looked over to where Jill was tending to William. He still looked overheated. His face contorted in agony. It was a blessing he was unconscious. "I don't know if he would want a souvenir of this trip."

"It ain't no souvenir," Danny said. "An adderstone's a pretty useful tool in the hands of somebody that knows what he's doing."

"Can it make William better?" Taylor asked, hopefully.

Danny shook his head. "William's the only person who could use it."

Taylor sighed. "The thing died over that way. Go get it if you think it's worth it." Her eyes drifted back to William. "I'm staying here."

Taylor knelt next to Jill as Danny wandered into the woods. She didn't say anything, just watched as Jill passed her hand over William's face and body like she'd done before, chanting and swaying.

William's expression relaxed. He was resting, gathering strength.

"Can I help?" she asked.

Jill leaned back, sitting on her heels. "Just...stay with me. Stay with *us*."

"Always."

Taylor studied the sky. How long until sunrise, she wondered. Probably too long. They'd never reach the river's mouth in time. They'd be out here at least another day while they repaired the raft. And, of course, they'd have to fend off whatever creature decided to attack them next.

Taylor heard movement: light footsteps and labored huffing and puffing. She peered upriver.

A flustered and bewildered banjo approached on wobbly stick-like legs.

"My word!" Cora said. "I am getting too darned old for this kind of thing!"

She plopped in front of Jill and Taylor without further comment and immediately transformed back into an ordinary musical instrument.

Soon after, Danny returned with the dragon's crystal resting on a dingy handkerchief. Seeing it detached from the dragon, resting in Danny's hand, it wasn't any bigger than a gumball. Taylor studied its irregular, multifaceted surface.

He wrapped it in the cloth and handed it to Taylor. "Maybe you can keep this until..." He gazed over to where William lay, moaning in his sleep.

"He'll make it," Taylor said. "The worst has passed. I think he just needs rest."

"Then let's get moving," the pooka said. "I'll go look for the right kind of lumber if you girls will—"

Danny perked up his tapered ears. He gazed upriver and squinted into the darkness. "Do you hear that?"

"What's the matter?" Jill said.

Now that Danny mentioned it, Taylor heard it, too. "I'm not sure," she said. "Something's coming. I hear...shouting?"

"Maybe we should vanish," Danny said. Taylor nodded. She and Danny drew magic mist around all four of them.

They kept absolutely still, listening in the dark.

Soon, the voice became more distinct. Someone called out Taylor's name and then William's.

"What the...?"

It wasn't long before Taylor spied the source: a poleboat was coming downriver with a bright orange ball of faery fire hovering over the bow. Taylor felt herself grinning as she glimpsed the redheaded man at the bow, the one who had been calling out.

"Taylor!" he shouted again. "William!"

It was Nat. Taylor called to him while letting her part of the mist dissipate. She summoned an orb of blue-white fire and waved it over her head.

Nat barked a command for the boat to make for shore. Immediately, the crew positioned their poles to slow their forward momentum and angle toward the bank.

"Taylor!" he called again. He took in the scene. As the poleboat kissed the bank of the river, his eyes swept down to William, and his face darkened. "What happened?"

"Horned serpent," Danny said. Nat's eyes grew wide and he spat out a curse.

"We could use a lift," Taylor said. "We need to get downriver before sunrise."

Nat turned to the crew. "Mr. Pugmire, Mr. Peaseblossom, we got a wounded man here! Get him to the cabin house, if you please."

Two burly fae leaped ashore and grabbed William, one by the feet and the other at the shoulders. Other polemen lowered the gangplank. The two fae Nat had sent carried William aboard a second after. This boat was laid out the same as the *Misery*, with an enclosed cabin house near the stern. That's where they carried William, Jill following close behind. Taylor picked up Cora.

As soon as Danny and Taylor came aboard, the polemen withdrew the gangplank. Nat called for the boat to get underway. He bowed to Taylor and said, "Welcome aboard the *Slippery Sylph*."

"Nat," Taylor said. She could barely contain her surprise. She threw her arms around him and asked, "Where the heck did you get a poleboat?"

Nat shrugged. "The *Sylph* pulled in at Osaa's place not long after you left," he said. "I convinced them to give me a lift."

"Just like that?" Taylor said, grinning.

"Getting a ride was the easy part." The pisgy shrugged. Then he turned to Taylor with a devilish grin. "Talking them into electing me captain took a little more effort." He sighed with contentment. "I kind of like having my own boat." He waved over one of the polemen. "Mr. Peaseblossom! Bring me that staff!"

The grizzled fae drew a three-foot length of wood from a stack of cargo.

Taylor studied the geometric designs carved at each end. "William's staff?" She slapped her hand over her mouth to keep from giggling.

"The boys say they found it floating in the river. Soon as I saw it, I thought it looked familiar."

A lump formed in Taylor's throat. "Thanks, Nat. He's really proud of that staff."

"Well, he can have it back with my compliments."

With the gangplank retracted, they pushed off and were soon back underway. Jill stepped out of the cabin, and Taylor and Danny crowded around her.

"He's sleeping," she said. Her face showed obvious relief.

Taylor exhaled. She turned to Nat. "You said there's a portal downriver that opens at sunrise. How far do we have to go?" she asked.

"I'd guess about three hours," he said.

"And when's sunrise?"

"About three hours. Maybe a smidge less."

"Nat, we need to make it in time. We can't spend another day in the Wonder, understand?" She glanced at the cabin. "William has to get home."

"You got it," Nat said with a smile. As he returned to the bow, he called out to the crew, "Come on, boys! We've got to make Dead Man's Point by sunrise! Look alive!"

Taylor slumped against a barrel and slid to the deck. Danny reached for her, then saw she was okay and let her sit. "You better get some shuteye," he said.

Jill said, "We all should." So they found corners and gaps amid the *Slippery Sylph*'s cargo to curl up and try to rest.

The constant splash of the river, the footfalls of the polemen, and the melody of their work song soon became a comforting rhythm that lulled Taylor to sleep. When she awoke, with William's staff still in her hand, the eastern sky was just turning purple, and there weren't nearly as many stars.

Sunrise wouldn't be much longer. She got up, stretched, and cast another glance toward the cabin. Danny and Jill were still sleeping curled up alongside the barrels and crates of the *Slippery Sylph*'s cargo. Taylor stumbled toward the stern and gently pushed open the cabin door.

She leaned William's staff against the wall.

William was resting on a ramshackle cot that might have been Revolutionary War army surplus. For nearly a minute, she watched his chest rise and fall by the light of an oil lamp.

He was breathing easily. She let that sink in: he really was going to make it.

*Take* that, *Grandma!*

William was alive, and they were going home. She stood at the door, watching him. It seemed like forever since their first night in the Wonder, when William nearly fell into the clutches of that deer woman. He seemed so clueless then. Was this really William? Half the Wonder had been out to get them, but somehow he'd managed to come out on top.

When she couldn't stand it anymore, she whispered, "William? Can you hear me?"

He opened his eyes.

His voice was croaky, but stronger than Taylor expected. "Did I hear Jill say we got the dragon?" he said. "Or was I dreaming."

"*You* got it," Taylor corrected. She came and knelt beside him. "You're the only one who even laid a hand on it." She reached into the pocket of her leather jacket. "And we got you a souvenir. Danny calls it an adderstone." She showed him the crystal, and he took it from her hand.

"The dracontia?" His mouth fell open.

"Do you know how to use it?"

William shook his head. "I bet Maymay does." He closed his eyes and smiled. "Pretty stupid, though. Trying to fight a dragon."

She let out a labored gasp somewhere between a sob and a laugh. "Knights in shining armor are *so* fourteenth century." Taylor said.

"Yeah, you said something like that before." William chuckled then clutched his side. A flash of pain crossed his face. "Don't make me laugh."

Taylor flashed a wry grin. "I'll never try to amuse you again."

"Well, good." William took a deep breath and slowly expelled it. His eyes moved past Taylor to the wall behind her. Bewildered, he asked, "Is that my staff?"

"It sure is," Taylor said. "I guess that spell of yours worked after all, wizard man."

He closed his eyes and smiled. He really had a great smile.

Even wounded and exhausted, he seemed somehow at ease. Confident. Was this the same guy she'd known a week ago?

"I'm sorry," she said.

"What for?"

"I guess you were always just Jill's brother to me. I never really thought about you as your own person." She rested her hand on top of his.

William quirked an eyebrow.

"That was a mistake," she continued. She looked away, focusing on her hand wrapped around his. "...because you're a pretty awesome person." She felt her face grow warm, and her heart started to pound with nerves. "And...maybe..."

William set his hand on her arm and pulled her closer—up onto the cot so she was resting against his chest. Taylor was surprised he had that much strength, but she didn't mind. She stretched toward him, and before she knew what was happening, his lips brushed against hers.

## Chapter 29

# Yonder Come Day

The kiss only lasted a second or two before Taylor pulled away. She sat on the edge of the cot with her hands folded in her lap, collecting herself.

William's mind raced as fast as his heartbeat. A jumble of thoughts and feelings surged to the surface of his consciousness all at once. He was ecstatic and terrified and embarrassed and contented and generally confused.

What in the world was he thinking, kissing Taylor? Something had just come over him, and he decided to go for it. As soon as he did it, he had second thoughts.

*Way to jump the gun, you idiot!* he told himself. He feared what Taylor might think of him now. If this messed up their friendship, the part of his brain that told him to kiss her was going to get a stern talking-to.

"Uh...," William said, and his head swam.

"Yeah," Taylor said.

He propped himself up. Taylor just looked at the floor, avoiding eye contact. But she wasn't running away, or hitting him, or turning him into anything. That was a good sign. "That was..." He grasped for the right adjective.

"Weird."

"Definitely weird," William agreed. He shivered. "Like kissing my sister or something." He wondered if that was how Luke Skywalker felt that one time.

"Uh huh," Taylor said with a sigh. She hurried to add, "Not that it was a bad kiss. I mean, not too much pressure..."

"You too," William interrupted. "No complaints here. Just… uh…"

"I think—"

"Listen, Taylor," William said. Given the circumstances, he figured he might as well be honest. He took a deep breath and pressed on. "For the longest time, I thought…that…was something I wanted."

Taylor was definitely blushing.

"But…it just didn't feel right, you know?" he continued. "You really are like another sister to me."

"The stubborn, rebellious sister you never had." Taylor smiled at him.

"Jill's plenty stubborn," William said. "But I'll give you the rebellious part."

"Listen, William," Taylor said. "What I said earlier? About you being awesome? About me not seeing it?"

"Yeah?"

"All that's still true."

William smiled.

"But *gosh*, kissing you felt weird!"

"What can I say? It seemed like a good idea at the time."

"To me, too," Taylor said, and her face turned an even deeper shade of red.

William smiled again. "Friends?"

"Friends." She patted William's hand.

"Are we going to tell Jill about any of this?"

"Don't you think one brush with death is enough for a night?"

William laughed a shallow laugh, this time without straining himself. "Yeah, we better hold off on that for a while."

"Good plan." Taylor stood up. Just then, something outside captured her attention. The polemen had started singing a new song. It seemed happier, more bouncy than the last one. "Do you hear that?"

William nodded. He propped himself up and threw his legs over the side of the cot. "Maybe we're close. Give me a hand?"

Taylor took William's hand and helped him up. He staggered a little, but his legs remembered how to work. With a hand on Taylor's shoulder, the two walked out onto the deck.

The polemen had indeed struck up a new work song:

Oh day, yonder come day.
Oh day, yonder come day.
Oh day, yonder come day.
Day done broke into my soul.

Yonder come day, Oh come on day.
Yonder come day, Oh come on day.
Yonder come day, Oh come on day.
Yonder come day,
Day done broke into my soul.

The sky was pink in the east. Danny and Jill were stretching themselves awake. At the bow, Nat was gesturing, calling to life a shimmering wall of magic straight ahead.

Jill gave William a sidewise hug. "You should be in bed."

"I'm good," he said. "You patched me up pretty well. Thanks." Given everything he'd been through, William was surprised he felt as good as he did.

The *Slippery Sylph* passed through a vortex of gold and silver sparkles. The boat itself shimmered as magical mist wrapped around it. William watched as an image superimposed itself over the deck like the hologram of a modern pleasure boat. The stacks of cargo and the aft cabin seemed to become the bulkheads. At the bow, Nat took on the form of an ordinary human boater in an orange life jacket and a skipper's hat like on *Gilligan's Island.*

Out on the river, things looked mostly the same. There was some kind of park on the bank to starboard. It had a small pier and a couple of covered pavilions as well as some other buildings farther inland, but no activity this early in the morning.

"My phone is shot," William said, forlorn. "It got soaked when Osaa's tie snakes got us."

"Mine, too," Taylor said. She slumped over the table and closed her eyes.

"Then it's a good thing I planned ahead!" Jill said, grinning wide. She reached into her bag and pulled out her own cell phone safely sealed in a zip-top plastic bag. She turned it on, waited for it to power up, and then frowned. "No signal."

The sun peered over the tops of the trees.

"We must still be pretty deep in the woods," William said.

"Yeah, I'll try later."

The polemen kept singing.

Yonder come day, It's a brand new day.
Yonder come day, It's a brand new day.
Yonder come day, It's a brand new day.
Yonder come day,
Day done broke into my soul.

"We'll be coming up on a Topsider town in about two and a half hours," Nat called to Taylor. "Plenty of time to get some more rest and make yourselves presentable."

William looked down at his tattered clothing, dirty with mud and blood. Taylor, Jill, and Danny didn't look much better.

"I don't suppose you could lend us some clean clothes?"

"There's a couple of footlockers in the cabin house," Nat said. "Take anything you can use."

By the time the *Slippery Sylph* reached the town, everyone was dressed in clean and mostly unremarkable clothes. William found a pair of well-worn blue jeans and a cotton trade shirt that didn't look too odd underneath his denim jacket. Danny and the others dressed similarly. They'd never win a fashion contest, but at least they weren't likely to cause too much of a stir walking down the street in the mortal world.

Nat ran the poleboat up to the bank underneath a highway bridge. He only stopped long enough to let off his passengers. Taylor couldn't stop thanking him for his help.

"I owed this to Aulberic," he said. "I should thank you for letting me pay my debt—at least in part."

She extended her hand, then ended up giving Nat a hug. Then she hitched up her too-big work pants, pulled her leather jacket close around her, and let Danny lead her down the gangplank.

They walked into town, trying to look like they belonged. A historical marker told them they were at the Fort King George Historic Site in Darien, Georgia.

Apparently, in the 1700s, it was the southernmost outpost of the British Empire in North America. Now it was a quaint little town with lots and lots of character—and not a fast-food joint in site. William was famished, and he couldn't imagine the others being any better off than he was.

They had barely cleared the bridge when William spied a gas station and convenience store a couple of blocks ahead. They pooled their money and found they had enough for three modest breakfasts.

"Don't worry about me," Danny said. "I need to get going anyway. Claudia needs to know what we figured out about Tobarty—and the sooner, the better."

"Be safe," Taylor said, hugging him.

William stretched his hand toward the pooka. "Thanks for helping my sister," he said.

"Don't worry about it," Danny said. "I figure as long as I hang out with you folks, my life ain't never going to be boring." He smiled mischievously as he turned into a dog and trotted away.

With their supply of breakfast burritos, honey buns, and hot chocolate, they stepped outside to a metal table and chairs along the side of the building. It was a fairly cool morning, but not so bad they couldn't sit outside. Plus, they needed a place to sit and talk without worrying about eavesdroppers.

Jill pulled her phone back out. "First order of business is to call home," she said. "Then Taylor can call her folks."

"That's the best plan I've heard in a long time," William said, smiling.


William leaned back in his metal chair, then seemed to freeze, mid-smile. Taylor glanced at Jill, who sat motionless with her thumb hovering over the screen of her phone. Taylor's pulse began to race. Something was definitely wrong.

Taylor whipped her head left and right.

"Good morning," a woman's voice called from behind her.

Taylor jumped out of her chair. It fell backward with a clang as she spun around. She knew whom she would see. This wasn't the first time Mara Hellebore's voice had filled her with dread.

The Chief Matron of the Winter Court stood tall and proud, ridiculously out of place in the parking lot of a Topside convenience store. Her midnight-blue sleeveless gown fluttered in the breeze, but she seemed not the least bit uncomfortable in the nippy air. She no longer wore the dark sunglasses she'd had on a year ago when she had last interrupted Taylor's life. The damage from the face full of iron filings Taylor had flung at her two summers ago was mostly healed, although Taylor saw traces of splotchy redness around her grandmother's eyes.

By her side was a fae woman Taylor didn't know: about Taylor's height, with brown hair and deep, dark eyes, wearing Topside clothes including a black leather jacket a lot like Taylor's.

"What do you want?" Taylor barked, frantically gathering magic.

"Three guesses." Mara crossed her arms, and her mouth twisted into a mirthless grin. The tattooed highlights around her left eye seemed to dance.

Taylor said nothing. She thought about a blast, but knew it wouldn't do any good. Mara Hellebore was as powerful a fae as Taylor had ever had the misfortune of meeting.

"I've said it before," Mara said, "but I truly don't think you're as bright as people say you are."

Taylor clenched her fists. No matter how powerful Mara was, she was about to get blasted!

Quick as lightning, the other woman slashed at Taylor with her fingernails. They dug deep into her cheek, drawing blood. Taylor backed away, throwing up a shield spell a second too late.

Her heart fluttered with panic.

"It's time," Mara announced. "I've come to claim the favor you owe me."

"No!" Taylor gasped.

"Yes," Mara said. She turned to the dark-haired fae. "Layla?"

"Child's play, Chief Matron," Layla said. She licked Taylor's blood from her fingers, giggling and swaying as if the taste made her tipsy. She gazed at Taylor with eyes like deep, black pools. With a shiver, she began to transform. Those black eyes lightened to icy blue. Her hair lightened until it was the color of honey.

And as quick as that, she looked just like Taylor herself.

Taylor took a step toward William and reached out her hand.

"Step away, child," Mara said. "This was your bargain, remember? There is no escaping it."

"But—"

"Layla will do your friends no harm...provided they behave themselves."

Taylor's blood ran ice-cold. "They're never going to believe she's me. They can see through glamour, remember?"

Layla giggled.

"Oh, this is no simple glamour," Mara said, smirking. "Layla is quite the accomplished face-shifter. For all intents and purpose, she *is* you—for the next few days, at any rate." The Chief Matron studied Taylor's face on the imposter's body. "A little taller," she said. "And the eyes are a bit too close together."

Layla's face and body transformed, and Taylor realized that, before, Layla had only mostly looked like her. Now the deception was perfect.

Taylor braced herself. The world began to spin.

She jabbed a finger at her grandmother. "If anything happens to Jill or William—"

"It won't," Mara said. "Provided, of course, that you don't try anything foolish while you are in my service."

Layla pushed Taylor out of the way, set her chair aright, and sat down.

This was all happening too fast. Taylor searched her mind for a plan, a way out. She found none. In frustration, she hurled a faery blast at Mara. As she expected, the Chief Matron deflected it with ease.

"That was your first and only infraction," Mara said. "I will not tolerate a second. It wouldn't be pleasant for your deathling friends if you were to cross me, Selena."

Taylor breathed hard and fast. Sweat trickled down the sides of her face.

"Are we clear?"

Her head swam. This couldn't be happening!

"Selena?"

Taylor bit her lip. Seething with rage, she nodded.

"Then let's be going, shall we?" Mara gestured, and a razor-thin portal materialized at her side. She extended her hand to Taylor.

Taylor gritted her teeth and took it. They both stepped into the rift and vanished.

William fazed out for a second. It was like he passed through a fog, disorienting him, making him lose track of time. The excitement of the last couple of days must have finally gotten to him. Or maybe he needed a fresh dose of Jill's healing spell.

He shook himself awake. Jill was dialing her phone. They would all be home soon. It was over, thank God!

He listened intently as Jill explained the situation to her mom. When she finished the call, she slid the phone across the table to Taylor.

"How's Mom doing?" he asked, afraid of what the answer might be.

"Better than I expected," Jill said. Her eyes widened. "She's baking cookies."

"Maybe that's a good sign,"

"She says if Taylor can get us home with magic faster than she and Dad can drive here, then that's okay with her." She sighed and shook her head. "As much as I hate ring travel..."

"I just want to get home," William said. "I can deal with a little motion sickness." He watched as Taylor popped her last bite of honey bun into her mouth.

"Absolutely," she said. Grinning, she added, "The quicker we get home, the better."

"Then I guess you need to find us a ring portal," Jill said. She frowned. "I assume you know how to do that?"

Taylor nodded. "It shouldn't be too hard to find a cemetery or an old Indian mound or something around here." She gazed at William, and her icy blue eyes flashed with excitement. "What do you say? Are we ready to move?"

"Lead the way," he said. He cast a glance at his sister and grinned.

Taylor smiled. "Then follow me."

www.ingramcontent.com/pod-product-compliance
Lightning Source LLC
Chambersburg PA
CBHW070650180626
46817CB00006B/2308